NEW STORIES
FROM THE SOUTH

The Year's Best, 2005

The editor wishes to thank Kathy Pories, Brunson Hoole, Chris and Dana Stamey, and Anne Winslow, colleagues whose talent, skill, patience, and tact are essential to this anthology.

She is also most grateful to the many journals and magazines that, year after year, provide the anthology with complimentary subscriptions.

PUBLISHER'S NOTE
The stories reprinted in *New Stories from the South: The Year's Best, 2005* were selected from American short stories published in magazines issued between January and December 2004. Shannon Ravenel annually consults a list of about one hundred nationally distributed American periodicals and makes her choices for this anthology based on criteria that include original publication first-serially in magazine form and publication as short stories. Direct submissions are not considered.

Edited by
Shannon Ravenel

with a preface by Jill McCorkle

NEW STORIES
FROM THE SOUTH

The Year's Best, 2005

Algonquin Books of Chapel Hill

Published by
ALGONQUIN BOOKS OF CHAPEL HILL
Post Office Box 2225
Chapel Hill, North Carolina 27515-2225

a division of
WORKMAN PUBLISHING
708 Broadway
New York, New York 10003

ISSN 0897-9073
ISBN 1-56512-469-3

CONTENTS

Jill McCorkle

PREFACE:
A BIG STACK OF
TRANSPARENCIES

I am often referred to as a Southern writer. A woman writer. A Southern woman writer. All adjectives accepted. When I show up and open my mouth, that is exactly who I am. My native home and my gender have indeed led me to be the person and the writer I am. The artist Edward Hopper said: "The man's the work. Something doesn't come out of nothing." And when given credit for American scene painting and expressing the loneliness and stagnation of town life, he said: "I don't think I ever tried to paint the American scene; I'm trying to paint myself."

Now that I have lived in New England for over ten years, I am aware more than ever of which traits and details are purely Southern and which are open to a broader arena of people. The foliage that I miss is Southern, and I am horrified each year at the holiday season by what I must pay for big, waxy magnolia leaves and pinecones. Pimento cheese? Grits? (You *can* sometimes find instant.) Country ham? Calabash-style seafood? Goody's Headache Powders? Strictly Southern. Statues in the center of town to commemorate the Confederate dead? Iced tea? My first winter here — still not used to darkness at four in the afternoon — I ordered this beverage in a restaurant only to be told that it was "out of season."

I said, "What, do you have to go shoot it?" I laughed. The waiter did not. Get on an elevator and say "Mash nine" and see where that will get you other than people looking at you like you just stepped from a spaceship. "Mash"? "Might could"? "Sum bitch"?

Southerners have a strong attachment to certain foods and foliage. And an innate awareness of "the war" even when you are liberal minded and very relieved about how it all turned out. This awareness is often set in place in early childhood, when people make you attend C of C (that would be Children of the Confederacy—grandbabes of the Daughters of the Confederacy) meetings, and you are enamored of Scarlett and her vow to never be hungry again. And of course there is a great sense of nostalgia (which has kept "the war" going all these years). The writer Barry Hannah talks about how Southern children are nostalgic by the age of nine or ten, and it is absolutely true. They are already mourning losses—their own, their parents, the South's. It's like that joke: how many Southerners does it take to change a light bulb? Three and preferably more—one to change it and at least two to talk about what a good old bulb it was.

I often tell people that I do not come from a long line of literary people but I do come from a long line of creative ones. The difference is that their creations were either immediately devoured or worn until threadbare or simply given over to the air while sitting out on a porch or under a big shade tree. The form is pretty constant—it's even gotten to be a standing joke—and goes something like this:

"Let me tell you what happened to poor Emily Baker (the hook) but first now I have to remind you about how Emily's daddy used to own the hardware store that was where the Winn-Dixie is now. Remember his store burned all the way to the ground—took the fire trucks from two towns over to help, what's called a five alarm—the same summer we were having a drought so awful that there was a ban on watering and all the azaleas looked terrible and nobody new got asked into the garden club as a result. Well anyway, people always suspected that he might could've burned the building down himself what with the fact that he had not been right in the head since his wife — not Emily's Mama, she died of cancer of the pancreas many years before — but the second wife, when she ran off with the pharmaceutical salesman she met while visiting her sick Uncle Ben at the VA Hospital over in Fayetteville. . . ."

If you are patient, you will probably learn that what happened to Emily was something like she got a flat tire out on the interstate while heading to the outlet mall and had to call Triple A to come help her.

In her wonderful book, *One Writer's Beginning,* Eudora Welty talked about how as a child she learned early to listen "for" the story. I know exactly what she meant. Somewhere woven into the history and detail, the asides that often carry us far into left field, there is a plotline — something actually happened — but there are other stories as well, slipping like bright threads in all directions. You follow first this one and then that one, but if you listen long enough, they begin to come clear. There is indeed a pattern and a texture. And then when they are repeated to you for the fourth or fifth time — in true Southern style — you know them by heart.

My grandmother never could have written the stories she told. Her self-described "chicken scratch" was engaged only for grocery lists and recipes, the occasional letter I received in college (with a dollar and a stick of Juicy Fruit tucked in) that said: "Dear Jill, Please come home soon." And yet her words — her stories — as well as those of other older relatives and my parents, painted a picture of our town for me that went back two generations such that even now my vision of Lumberton, North Carolina, appears in my mind like a series of transparencies. The rural small farms — dusty tobacco fields — the dirt roads and horse and buggies of my grandmother's childhood. The downtown area and the way it looked when my parents were teenagers and walked to the movies and the local drugstore, places I frequented in my own childhood even as I-95 was barreling through town and bringing with it motels and fast food. We were still allowed to stay out until the streetlights came on. We rode our bikes behind the mosquito truck, lost in clouds of poison; we put pennies on the railroad tracks and waited for the train to come by and flatten them. But even within that nostalgic safety, there was grief and loss. A dying grandparent. Hometown boys killed in Vietnam. A brilliant Green Beret officer accused of murdering his young family.

My hometown, so firmly etched in my mind by those stories, serves as backdrop to my fictional world again and again. It is home. Interestingly, the first time I ever felt at home in Boston was on the way to the Franklin Park Zoo when I found myself in Roxbury surrounded by Baptist churches and collards being sold by the roadside. I felt myself relax completely, though I realized the people with me were anything but relaxed. Turns out I was in a rough part of town populated mostly by African-Americans. All I had noticed was that it looked like home, smelled like home, made me feel at home. And yes, I know that the theater in my town once had a sign that said "colored" and designated the balcony seats accordingly. It's a memory I wish I didn't have to have. I also know that by the time I was in the sixth grade, our schools were integrated and it was not an unusual sight to find people of all shapes, sizes, and colors wherever you went.

This leads me to the whole topic of the Southern stereotype — one I might add that seems still an acceptable prejudice, perhaps the *only* remaining prejudice in which people who consider themselves PC indulge and laugh about. I have had people assume from my accent or from my raising in the Baptist church that I might be racist, speak in tongues, have an IQ the same as my shoe size. I am told jokes about incest and hookworm. I once heard a highly intelligent person (a non-Southerner visiting the South) say that PBS in the South meant reruns of the Dukes of Hazard — with me listening! It made me want to tell him to git his lard ass outside before I fetched my gun. I wanted to slap his hand and ask: Where are your manners?

And manners! That's a big one. Once when my parents came to visit me, I noticed that my poor dad stood each and every time a woman or older gentleman got on the subway car. I was nine months pregnant at the time and the only person who had ever offered me a seat was a woman so old we fought over who needed to sit the most.

There is often the assumption that the South is nothing more than Bible Belt politics and those still waiting for the news that we lost "the war." Misconceptions as ridiculous as any other racist and belittling stereotype. And this is where I begin to see the overlap of Southern culture with other groups. This is where I see our body of literature — as richly defined and devoured as any out there — join others thematically. The attention to food and drink, a brand of humor that speaks to hardship and pain, a language that is clearly heard and unique in its own right, and reams of memories and histories that are told again and again. Irish writers? Jewish? African-American? I believe that any group of people that has been set aside or deprived by poverty or illiteracy or prejudice has an even greater need to preserve the past and tell its stories. Its historians and entertainers find what is comic in the midst of tragic so as to keep moving forward, keep breathing, laughing. It is survival. Twain said laughter is the human race's only really effective weapon, and George Bernard Shaw said that his way of joking was to tell the truth. Lenny Bruce said "People should be taught what *is,* not what should be." He said all his humor was based on destruction and despair.

Pain, sorrow, grief — isn't that what we really want to see, to experience and to learn from? Who wants to read a story where everything is perfect and nothing whatsoever happens? It would be like an endless pile of those holiday brag letters where no one tells of the year's misfortune and losses but only of brilliance and success and good times. Who wants to read such? Give me something that will break my heart. Make me ache. Make me laugh and weep simultaneously. Make me feel and care. That is what a story should do, and oftentimes a story is as much about what has come before as the situation at hand. There is history and nostalgia. There are regrets and losses. There are joys that in hindsight take on a different level of pain. Read a story that really works and you will find that dark taproot.

The South will always exist as a big stack of transparencies, one laid on top of another, tracking the history from the war to a present-day population as varied in beliefs and cultures as any, and yet securely bound by the climate and the landscape and the accent and the food and the camellias blooming in some Southern yard at this very minute as I sit here with snow and ice outside my window and a vaseful of magnolia leaves that cost the same as dinner. There is a longing for home and there always will be. Even when I am there, I am still longing. Always longing. For me that's what literature is all about.

Born and raised in Lumberton, North Carolina, Jill McCorkle has taught creative writing at the University of North Carolina, Bennington College, Tufts University, and Harvard. Five of her eight books of fiction—five novels and three collections of short stories—have been named *New York Times* Notables. Winner of the New England Book Award, the John Dos Passos Prize for Excellence in Literature, and the North Carolina Award for Literature, she lives near Boston with her two children.

NEW STORIES
FROM THE SOUTH

The Year's Best, 2005

Michael Parker

HIDDEN MEANINGS: TREATMENT OF TIME, SUPREME IRONY, AND LIFE EXPERIENCES IN THE SONG "AIN'T GONNA BUMP NO MORE NO BIG FAT WOMAN"

(from *The Oxford American*)

In the song "Ain't Gonna Bump No More No Big Fat Woman" by Joe Tex, the speaker or the narrator of this song, a man previously injured before the song's opening chords by a large, aggressive-type woman in a disco-type bar, refuses to bump with the "big fat woman" of the title. In doing so he is merely exercising his right to an injury-free existence thus insuring him the ability to work and provide for him and his family if he has one, I don't know it doesn't ever say. In this paper I will prove there is a hidden meaning that everybody doesn't get in this popular Song, Saying, or Incident from Public Life. I will attempt to make it clear that we as people when we hear this song we automatically think "novelty" or we link it up together with other songs we perceive in our mind's eye to be just kind of one-hit wonders or comical lacking a serious point. It could put one in the mind of, to mention some songs from this same era, "Convoy" or "Disco Duck." What I will lay out for my audience is that taking this song in such a way as to focus only on it's comical side, which it is really funny nevertheless that is a serious error which ultimately will result in damage to the artist in this case Joe Tex also to the listener, that is you or whoever.

"About three nights ago/I was at a disco." (Tex, line 1.) Thus begins the song "Ain't Gonna Bump No More No Big Fat Woman" by the artist Joe Tex. The speaker has had some time in particular three full days to think about what has occurred to him in the incident in the disco-type establishment. One thing and this is my first big point is that time makes you wiser. Whenever Jeremy and I first broke up I was so ignorant of the situation that had led to us breaking up but then a whole lot of days past and little by little I got a handle on it. The Speaker in "Ain't Gonna Bump No More No Big Fat Woman" has had some time now to go over in his mind's eye the events that occurred roughly three days prior to the song being sung. Would you not agree that he sees his life more clear? A lot of the Tellers in the stories you have made us read this semester they wait a while <u>then</u> tell their story thus knowing it by heart and being able to tell it better though with an "I" narrator you are always talking about some kind of "discrepancy" or "pocket of awareness" where the "I" acts like they know themselves but what the reader is supposed to get is they really don't. Well see I don't think you can basically say that about the narrator of "Ain't Gonna Bump No More . . ." because when our story begins he comes across as very clear-headed and in possession of the "facts" of this "case" so to speak on account of time having passed thus allowing him wisdom. So the first thing I'd like to point out is Treatment of Time.

There is a hidden meaning that everybody doesn't get in this particular Song, Saying or Incident from Public Life. What everybody thinks whenever they hear this song is that this dude is being real ugly toward this woman because she is sort of a big woman. You are always talking about how the author or in this case the writer of the song is a construction of the culture. Say if he's of the white race or the male gender when he's writing he's putting in all these attitudes about say minority people or women without even knowing it, in particular ideals of femininity. Did I fully understand you to say that all white men author's basically want to sleep with the female characters they create? Well that just might be one area where you and me actually agree because it has been my experience based upon my previous relationships especially my last one with Jeremy that men are mostly just wanting to sleep with any woman that will let them. In the song "Ain't Gonna Bump No More No Big Fat Woman," let's say if you were to bring it in and play it in class and we were to then discuss it I am willing to bet that the first question you would ask, based on my perfect attendance is, What Attitudes Toward Women are Implied or Explicitly Expressed by the Speaker or Narrator of this Song? I can see it right now up on the board. That Lindsay girl who sits up under you practically, the one who talks more than you almost would jump right in with, "He doesn't like this woman because she is not the slender submissive ideal woman" on and on. One thing and I'll say this again come Evaluation time is you ought to get better at cutting people like Lindsay off. Why we have to listen to her go off on every man in every story we read or rap song you bring in (which, okay, we know you're "down" with Lauryn Hill or whoever but it seems like sometimes I could just sit out in the parking lot and listen to 102 JAMZ and not have to climb three flights of stairs and get the same thing) is beyond me seeing as how I work two jobs to pay for this course and I didn't see her name up under the instructor line in the course offerings plus why should I listen to her on the subject of men when it's clear she hates every last one of them? All I'm saying is she acts like she's taking up for the oppressed people when she goes around oppressing right and left and you just stand up there letting her go on. I'm about sick of her mouth. Somebody left the toilet running, I say to the girl who sits behind me when-ever Lindsay gets cranked up on the subject of how awful men are.

Okay at this point you're wondering why I'm taking up for the speaker or narrator of "Ain't Gonna Bump No More" instead of the big fat woman seeing as how I'm 5'1" and weigh 149. That is if you even know who I am which I have my doubts based on the look on your face when you call the roll and the fact that you get me, Melanie Sudduth and Amanda Wheeler mixed up probably because we're A: always here, which you don't really seem to respect all that much. I mean it seems like you like somebody better if they show up late or half the time like that boy Sean, B: real quiet and C: kind of on the heavy side. To me that is what you call a supreme irony the fact that you and that Lindsay girl spend half the class talking about Ideals of Beauty and all and how shallow men are but then you tend to favor all the dudes and chicks in the class which could be considered "hot" or as they used to say in the seventies which is my favorite decade which is why I chose to analyze a song from that era, "so fine." So, supreme irony is employed.

As to why I'm going to go ahead and go on record taking up for the Speaker and not the Big Fat Woman. Well to me see he was just minding his own business and this woman would not leave him be. You can tell in the lines about how she was rarin' to go (Tex, line 4) that he has got some respect for her and he admires her skill on the dance floor. It's just that she throws her weight around, literally! To me it is her that is in the wrong. The fact that she is overweight or as the speaker says "Fat" don't have anything to do with it. She keeps at him and he tells her to go on and leave him alone, he's not getting down, "You done hurt my hip once." (Tex, lines 25–27.) She would not leave him alone. What she ought to of done whenever he said no was just go off with somebody else. I learned this the hard way after the Passage of Time following Jeremy and my's breakup. See I sort of chased after him calling him all the time and he was seeing somebody else and my calling him up and letting him come over to my apartment and cooking him supper and sometimes even letting him stay the night. Well if I only knew then what I know now. Which is this was the worse thing I could of done. Big Fat Woman would not leave the Speaker in the song which might or might not be the Artist Joe Tex alone. Also who is to blame for her getting so big? Did somebody put a gun to her head and force her to eat milkshakes from CookOut? Jeremy whenever he left made a comment about the fact that I had

definitely fell prey to the Freshman Fifteen or whatever. In high
school whenever we started dating I was on the girl's softball team
I weighed 110 pounds. We as people nowadays don't seem to want
to take responsibility for our actions if you ask me which I guess
you did by assigning this paper on the topic of Analyze a Hidden
Meaning in a Song, Saying, or Incident from Public Life which
that particular topic seems kind of broad to me. I didn't have any
trouble deciding what to write on though because I am crazy about
the song "Ain't Gonna Bump No More" and it is true as my paper
has set out to prove that people take it the wrong way and don't
get its real meaning also it employs Treatment of Time and
Supreme Irony.

One thing I would like to say about the assignment though is
okay, you say you want to hear what we think and for us to put
ourselves in our papers but then on my last paper you wrote all
over it and said in your Ending Comments that my paper lacked
clarity and focus and was sprawling and not cohesive or well organized. Well okay I had just worked a shift at the Coach House
Restaurant and then right after that a shift at the Evergreen Nursing Home which this is my second job and I was up all night writing that paper on the "Tell-Tale Heart" which who's fault is that
I can hear you saying right now. Your right. I ought to of gotten
to it earlier but all that aside what I want to ask you is okay have
you ever considered that clarity and focus is just like your way of
seeing the world? Like to you A leads to B leads to C but I might
like want to put F before B because I've had some Life Experiences different than yours one being having to work two jobs and
go to school full time which maybe you yourself had to do but
something tells me I doubt it. So all I'm saying is maybe you
ought to reconsider when you start going off on clarity and logic
and stuff that there are let's call them issues behind the way I write
which on the one hand when we're analyzing say "Lady with
the Tiny Dog" you are all over discussing the issues which led to
the story being written in the way it is and on the other if it's me
doing the writing you don't want to even acknowledge that stuff

is influencing my Narrative Rhythm too. I mean I don't see the difference really. So that is my point about Life Experiences and Narrative Rhythm, etc.

The speaker in the song "Ain't Gonna Bump No More No Big Fat Woman" says no to the Big Fat Woman in part because the one time he did get up and bump with her she did a dip and nearly broke his hip. (Tex, line 5.) Dancing with this particular woman on account of her size and her aggressive behavior would clearly be considered Risky or even Hazardous to the speaker or narrator's health. Should he have gone ahead and done what you and Lindsay wanted him to do and got up there and danced with her because she was beautiful on the inside and he was wanting to thwart the trajectory of typical male response or whatever he could have ended up missing work, not being able to provide for his family if he has one it never really says, falling behind on his car payment, etc. All I'm saying is what is more important for him to act right and get up and dance with the Big Fat Woman even though she has prior to that moment almost broke his hip? Or should he ought to stay seated and be able to get up the next morning and go to work? I say the ladder one of these choices is the best one partially because my daddy has worked at Rencoe Mills for twenty-two years and has not missed a single day which to me that is saying something. I myself have not missed class one time and I can tell even though you put all that in the syllabus about showing up you basically think I'm sort of sad I bet. For doing what's right! You'd rather Sean come in all late and sweaty and plop down in front of you and roll his shirt up so you can gawk at his barbed wire tat which his daddy probably paid for and say back the same things you say only translated into his particular language which I don't hardly know what he's even talking about using those big words it's clear he don't even know what they mean. I mean, between him and Lindsay, my God. I loved it whenever he said, "It's like the ulcerous filament of her soul is being masticated from the inside out," talking about that crazy lady in the "Yellow Wallpaper" (which if you ask me her problem was she needed a shift emptying bedpans at the nursing home same as that selfish bitch what's her name, that little boy's mother in the "Rocking Horse Winner.") You'd rather Sean or Lindsay disrespect all your so-called rules and hand their mess in late so long as everything they say is something you already sort of said. What you want is for everybody to A: Look hot and B: agree with you. A good thing for you to think about is, let's say you were in a disco-type establishment and approached by a big fat man. Let's say this dude was getting down. Okay, you get up and dance with him once and he nearly breaks your hip, he bumps you on the floor. Would you get up there and dance with him again? My daddy would get home from work and sit in this one chair with this reading lamp switched on and shining in his lap even though I never saw him read a word but "The Trader" which was all advertisements for used boats and trucks and camper tops and tools. He went to work at six, got off at three, ate supper at five thirty. The rest of the night he sat in that chair drinking coffee with that lamplight in his lap. He would slap me and my sister Connie whenever he thought we were lying about something. If we didn't say anything how could we be lying so we stopped talking. He hardly ever said a word to me my whole life except, "Y'all mind your mama." Whenever I first met Jeremy in high school he'd call me up at night, we used to talk for hours on the phone. I never knew really how to talk to anyone like that. Everything that happened to me, it was interesting to Jeremy or at least he acted like it was. He would say, "What's up, girl?" and I would say, "nothing" or sometimes "nothing much" and I would hate myself for saying nothing and being nothing. But then he'd say, "Well what did you have for supper?" and I'd burst into tears because some boy asked me what did I have for supper. I would cry and cry. Then there'd be that awful thing you know when you're crying and the boy's like what is it what did I say and you don't know how to tell him he didn't do nothing wrong you just love his heart to bits and pieces just for calling you up on the telephone. Or you don't want to NOT let him know that nobody ever asked you such a silly thing as what did you eat for supper and neither can you come out and just straight tell him, I never got asked that before. Sometimes my life is like this song comes on the radio and I've forgot the words but then the chorus comes along and I only know the first like two words of every line. I'll come in midway, say around about "No More No Big Fat Woman." I only know half of what I know I guess. I went out in the sun and got burned bad and then the skin peeled off and can you blame me for not wanting to go outside anymore? She ought to go find her a big fat man. The only time my daddy'd get out of his chair nights was when a storm blew up out of the woods which he liked to watch from the screen porch. The rain smelled rusty like the screen. He'd let us come out there if we'd be quiet and let him enjoy his storm blowing up but if we said anything he'd yell at us. I could hate Jeremy for saying I'm just not attracted to you anymore but hating him's not going to bring me any of what you call clarity. Even when the stuff I was telling him was so boring, like, then I went by the QuikMart and got seven dollars worth of premium and a Diet Cheerwine he'd make like it was important. Sometimes though he wouldn't say anything and I'd be going on and on like you or Lindsay and I'd get nervous and say, "Hello?" and he'd say, "I'm here I'm just listening." My daddy would let us stay right through the thunder and even some lightning striking the trees in the woods back of the house. We couldn't speak or he'd make us go inside. I know, I know, maybe Jeremy got quiet because he was watching "South Park" or something. Still I never had anyone before or since say to me, I'm here I'm just listening.

I'm going to get another C minus over a D plus. You're going to write in your Ending Comments that this paper sprawls lacks cohesion is not well organized. Well that's alright because we both know that what you call clarity means a whole lot less than whether or not I think the speaker in the song "Ain't Gonna Bump No More No Big Fat Woman" ought to get up and dance with the woman who "done hurt my hip, she done knocked me down." (Tex, line 39.) I say, No he shouldn't. You say, Yes he should. In this Popular Song, Saying, or Incident from Public Life there is a

Hidden Meaning that everybody doesn't get. Well, I get it and all I'm saying is you don't and even though I've spent however many pages explaining it to you you're never going to get it. If you get to feel sorry for me because I come to class every time and write down all the stupid stuff that Sean says and also for being a little on the heavy side I guess I get to feel sorry for you for acting like you truly understand a song like "Ain't Gone Bump No More No Big Fat Woman" by the artist Joe Tex.

In my conclusion the speaker or the narrator of the song "Ain't Gone Bump No More No Big Fat Woman," a man previously injured before the song's opening chords by a large aggressive type woman in a disco type bar refuses to bump with the fat woman of the title. In doing so he is merely exercising his right to an injury free existence. Treatment of Time, Supreme Irony and Life Experiences are delved into in my paper. There is a hidden meaning in this Song Saying or Incident from Public Life. Looking only at the comical side is a error which will result in damage to the artist and also to the listener which is you or whoever.

Michael Parker is the author of four works of fiction, including the novels *Hello Down There* and *Virginia Lovers*. His stories have appeared in the *Oxford American, Five Points, Shenandoah,* and many other magazines and in the Pushcart, *New Stories from the South,* and O. Henry Award anthologies. In 2004 he received fellowships in fiction from the North Carolina Arts Council and the NEA. He teaches in the MFA writing program at the University of North Carolina–Greensboro. His new novel, *If You Want Me to Stay,* will be published in fall 2005.

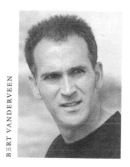

BERT VANDERVEEN

*S*ince I've been a teacher for fifteen years and was a college student, I'm ashamed to admit, for nearly half as long as that, it would be easy to surmise that this story came out of my extended time in classrooms, but I've never been inspired to write stories about academia, and I can't imagine I ever will be. "Hidden Meanings . . ." comes more from my uneasy acknowledgment of the ways most of us take people for granted, underestimate them, judge them for all sorts of ignorant reasons. I suspect such ignorance leads us to miss out on many wondrous stories.

I also wanted to find a way to pay homage to the song in the title. For back in the seventies, it sometimes happened, by chance or simple misadventure, that I would end up at the discotheque (usually disguised as a Moose lodge or VFW hut), wherein the opening bass line of "Ain't Gonna Bump No More No Big Fat Woman," followed by Joe Tex's smoky near-holler, would almost make the experience sufferable.

Stephanie Soileau

THE BOUCHERIE

(from *StoryQuarterly*)

Of course it would be exaggerating to say that Slug had so estranged himself from the neighborhood that a phone call from him was as astonishing to Della as, say, a rainfall of fish, or blood, or manna, and as baffling in portent. Still, as Della stood, phone in hand, about to wake her husband, Alvin, who was sleeping through the six o'clock news in his recliner, she sensed with a sort of holy clearness of heart that what was happening on the television—two cows dropping down through the trees and onto somebody's picnic in the park—was tied, figuratively if not causally, to the call from Slug. "*Mais,* the cows done flew," she thought.

The anchorwoman for the Baton Rouge news announced that a livestock trailer carrying over a hundred head of cattle on their way to processing had plunged over the entrance ramp's railing at the Interstate 10 and Hwy 110 junction that morning. The driver had been speeding, possibly drunk, though definitely decapitated. More than a dozen cattle were crushed outright. Several others survived the wreck only to climb over the edge of I-110 and drop to their deaths in the park below, while the remaining seventy-or-so, dazed and frightened, fled down the interstate or into the leafy shelter of the surrounding neighborhoods, followed by a band of cowboys called in for the impromptu roundup.

Fifty-three of the seventy cows had been recovered already, and all carcasses promptly removed from the roadway in time for the evening rush. Calls were still coming in, however: from kids who had a cow tied with cable to a signpost on their street; from riverboat gamblers who saw a small herd grazing on the levee downtown; from a state representative who stepped in a sizeable patty on the lawn of the Capitol. The search would continue into the night.

It was not the first time an eighteen-wheeler had gone over that railing, Della remembered. Back in the late '70s, absurd but true, some poor woman driving northbound on I-110 was killed when 40,000 pounds of frozen catfish dropped on her Volkswagen. Della thought then, as she did now, that it was certainly a shame to lose all that meat, with so many people starving in this world.

When Alvin finally snorted himself awake, he first tried to make sense of the man on horseback in a cowboy costume, waving a lasso at a red shorthorn under the statue of Huey Long—another advertising bid for Texas gamblers?—before he noticed his wife in the doorway, waving the phone and hissing, "*Ç'est* Slug! *Ç'est* Slug!" Alvin yanked the lever on his recliner, sending the footrest down with an echoing concussion that catapulted him up and out. "*Ç'est* Slug?" he said. The name dropped out of his mouth in the Cajun-French way, with a drawn out *uuhh*. "Let me talk to him."

Della held the telephone out, covering the mouthpiece with her palm. "Poor thing, you can't hardly understand what he says." She rushed to a notepad on the coffee table and scribbled Slug's name under the names of her four children and five grandchildren, all scattered to the ends of the earth. Next to Slug's she wrote: *Face. Visit, cook, clean?* Tomorrow, in a quiet moment, the list of names on the notepad would be passed to Pearl, then from Pearl to Estelle, from Estelle to Barbara, and on down the telephone prayer line.

Alvin squinted at her and leaned into the phone. "*Quoi?*" he said quietly. "*Ain?*" he said gently. "*Ain? . . . Ain? . . . Quoi t'as dit?*"

Della thought of how foolish Slug's wife Camille had been. A doctor had told Camille she needed to watch her cholesterol, so she cut all meat but chicken from their diet, and would not at all countenance an egg. They stopped visiting their neighbors, terrified of the gumbos and *etouffees* that threatened their blood at every house. At church each Sunday for two years, the neighborhood watched Camille grow thin and papery, painted with watercolor bruises, and when finally she died of pneumonia, no one wondered why. Many now attributed Slug's present condition to the two years he'd been deprived of meat's vital nourishment. Why else would the removal of a tiny melanoma turn into an infection that, having started at such a small place by Slug's ear, crept fast over his face like mold on bread? It was so simple. Why couldn't the doctors see?

"Ain?" Alvin said. *"Une vache?"*

Alvin wasn't much of a carpenter; measurements bored him, and he didn't have the tools or the fascination with things intricately wooden. While a gibbet did not have to be intricate, only sturdy and built to fit inside his fourteen-by-twenty-foot garage, Alvin could not even vouch for that. But Claude, down the block, could do amazing things with wood. He made reclining porch swings out of cypress, which never rotted. He whittled his own fishing lures. Many years ago Claude had helped Alvin right a fallen chicken coop in exchange for a dinner of the last pullet left alive.

Because Alvin could not build, he butchered, and he was not so sure, despite what his wife said, that the stink of guts and mess of feathers, or the old ways of village barter, were at all worse than the mad relay at the Winn Dixie on senior discount days: he and Della in separate lines, each with the limit—two nine-cent-a-pound turkeys—then the dash for the car, turkeys into the trunk, and right back for two more each at different registers before some faster senior citizen in one of those go-carts snatched them all up. These cheap and plentiful turkeys provoked his wife's instinct to hoard. In three deep-freezers, Della had turkeys for the next five years' holidays, and they were not to be traded, these hard-earned birds. At the same time, she fussed, she threatened: no more live chickens, no more rabbits, no more pigeons, doves, or squirrels in traps. She griped that she would never live to see the end of this meat.

Around the neighborhood though, Alvin's garage butchery was held in the highest esteem, so for Alvin's promise of a fresh brisket and sweetbreads, Claude traded woodworking consultation, even at this late hour. He took one look at Alvin's paper-towel blueprint and smeared on a few changes with a leaky pen. "That's how they do for deer," he explained. "But deers aren't near as heavy."

"Us, we used to do it from a tree," Alvin said.

Claude said, "Us too. We from the same place, you know. Or you forgot that?"

Claude traced over Alvin's lines until the paper towel split into a fuzzy stencil of an A-frame, and he deliberated aloud over weight limits and angles. Then he sketched his own design on the back of a receipt from his wallet. To the basic frame, he added a crossbar with two hooks. He attached the crossbar to a block and tackle that could be tied to a truck, in case the bare strength of all the neighborhood's aging men wasn't enough. He even drew the truck.

"You got him tied in your yard right now?" Claude said.

"Aw, no, man," said Alvin. "He went in those Indians' yard. Slug says we better come get him quick before that little lady gets scared and calls the cops."

"He's a peculiar fella, Slug."

"Aw, yeah, he is."

A moment of silent contemplation passed in observance of Slug's peculiarities. It had been a long, long time since anyone had seen Slug up close. It had been a long, long time since Slug had participated in the give and take.

The Indians were actually from Sudan, and had been living in the house next to Slug's for three years now. Through the mail carrier, Della stayed informed about them and their funny ways. There was a mother named Fatima, a little girl, another littler girl, and the oldest, a boy. Their last name was Nasraddin. They sometimes got packages of meat, frozen over dry ice and labeled PERISHABLE, from HALAL MEATS WHOLESALE, through overnight mail. There had been no sign of a father, but they had twice received official-looking letters from Sudan. Wasn't Sudan, Della guessed, a part of India? She never thought to look it up.

When the Sudanese first moved in—the woman and the three children on their own—the neighborhood watched from windows and porches. After hauling each heavy piece of furniture from truck to house, the mother and son, both small and narrow, stood panting in the driveway while the little girls picked at acorns on the ground. The neighborhood watched them survey the remaining pieces for the next lightest, putting off the inevitable six-foot hideaway sofa, bulky and impossible as a bull. The bright flowered shawl wrapped around the woman's head was wet with sweat and kept sliding off. When Alvin and a few other men offered to help, the woman waved them away. She and her children climbed into the truck and surrounded the sofa. They pushed. "Not heavy," she said. The sofa shifted slightly toward the loading ramp. Her shawl slipped off again, but this time she untied it and draped it over her shoulders, like an athlete drapes a towel. The woman said, "Thank you." The men, so ox-like and unsmiling, might have seemed presumptuous, a little crude, even threatening perhaps, advancing uninvited onto her lawn, but still Alvin thought it was a shame she didn't have someone to help her get along in a strange place, tiny as she was, with three kids.

For months, the neighborhood watched as the woman came and went at odd hours in the familiar uniforms of food service and checkout counters, with her long hair pulled tight into a bun at the back of her neck. When they sometimes found her at the end of a line, bagging their turkeys and toilet paper or wrapping their hamburgers, the people of the neighborhood wanted to say something to her, if not *welcome*, then *hello*, maybe, or *what do you need*; but she would thank them and look away before they had decided; and then, they would doubt that it was her at all, but perhaps one of the many other dark people whose faces under fleeting scrutiny looked, quite frankly, alike.

The neighborhood watched when, a year later, the mother and son stood again on the lawn, this time with a garden hose and scrub-brushes, washing splattered eggs off their windows and bricks. Much to the neighborhood's surprise, Slug emerged from his hermitage next door to cut down the deer skin that was strung like a lynching from the low branches of the Nasraddin's oak tree. News of a bombing in a government building had goaded the restless college and high school boys, who for love of country and trouble patrolled these neighborhoods in their pickups, rattling windows with speakers bigger than their engines, and shouting: "U! S! A!" and "Arabs, go home!" Fatima's boy for days afterward lurked on the front porch with a baseball bat or lingered at the gate. He silently dared the white faces in every passing car, and when no one took his dare, he battered the knobby, exposed roots of the oak tree instead.

By the end of the second year, the neighborhood had accepted the Sudanese in that they had lost interest in the family altogether. From time to time, Della still sent a prayer around for the woman Fatima and her three children. She knew the name Fatima only as the holy site of Virginal apparitions somewhere off in Europe, Italy or France maybe. To Della, that a brown woman could be so named was another sign that all the world's people more or less worshiped the same god. When she called Claude's wife Pearl to deliver the prayer list, Della said, "They just like us, them Indians. They love Mary and Jesus, same as us." Pearl said, "I don't think they're the same."

Last year when Alvin slaughtered the last of his rabbits, Della put in a busy morning of head smashing and fur scraping, and sent him around the neighborhood, a gut-reeking summer Santa with a bag full of carcasses and orders to visit the Indians. Alvin knocked at Slug's door first, encouraged by the blue television light flashing on the curtains. He saw a shadow, movement across the room, and knocked again. He waited, knocked, prepared himself for the shock of Slug's disfigured face should the door finally open; but it did not open.

When he rang the bell at the Nasraddin house, all at once he heard many bare feet running on linoleum. A dense uneasiness pressed on the door from the inside, but here too the door stayed shut. Alvin thought maybe he could just leave a rabbit on the front steps, and as he was fishing in the bag for a nice big one, the chain clattered, the door opened. Fatima, swathed in a purple cloth that dragged the floor, said, "You are bleeding?"

There were spatters of blood on Alvin's coveralls and, though he'd washed his hands, red on his elbows. "No, ma'am. I'm Alvin Guilbeau. I brought you a rabbit."

Fatima shook her head. She smiled and waved him inside her house. The shy little girls, eyes wide and wet, peeked around her purple cloth.

"I raise rabbits. Me and my wife, we can't use them all, so I give them away."

Behind his mother, the boy, about thirteen by then, leaned against the wall dressed in tight yellow sweatpants and a red T-shirt. He had grown since Alvin first saw him out on the lawn shoving hopelessly at furniture. His shoulders were wide, his chest thick. He was almost as tall as any man. "Mama," he said, "he brought us a rabbit. *Arneb.*" His voice was still a boy's voice, but it had an oscillating croak. He grinned a wicked grin at Alvin, then said to his little sisters, "Do you want a bunny?"

Fatima said, "No, no," and shook her head so vigorously that long fuzzy hair exploded out of its bun. She blurted Arabic at her son. "No," she said to Alvin.

"It's cleaned and skinned. Fresh," Alvin said. Alvin reached into his bag again, yearning to prove they were pretty rabbits, but Fatima swung her purple cloth around and scurried to the kitchen. The two big-eyed girls were marooned; they drew closer together. Over her shoulder, Fatima communicated something to the boy in what sounded to Alvin like angry coughs and gurgles.

"She says we cannot eat that meat. That's what she said." The boy's English bubbled and flowed, smoother and more proper than Alvin's.

"It's clean," Alvin said. "Y'all don't eat meat, maybe?"

"We eat meat." His eyes took in and then avoided the blood on Alvin's coveralls. "That's what she said to tell you."

Alvin was deciding whether or not he should be offended when Fatima returned, her purple cloth pinched into a sack in front of her. "Thank you," she said. She jutted her chin at Alvin's bag. "Open," she said. He did. She stood over it and let the cloth drop, dumping several pounds of candy over rabbit meat. "Thank you," she said.

"Thank you," Alvin said.

"Sorry. We cannot eat this meat," she said. "Stay for tea?"

"No, no, thank you," Alvin said, backing toward the door. "I got to go give these rabbits away."

"Come for tea."

"Thank you."

"Tell your wife," Fatima said, smiling, thanking, waving, closing the door.

Alvin stopped on the sidewalk and dug a caramel out of the bag. He unwrapped it thoughtfully, popped it into his mouth and continued down the block, wondering what in the world people eat if not meat.

All the way to Slug's, flashlights in hand, Alvin and Claude scoped a route to Alvin's garage that would avoid attention. They met no one on their two-block trek. One or the other of them knew almost every resident within a four-block radius, many of whom would be invited to share in this lucky blessing from the Lord, but it was the passers-through, like the students from the college, who might make trouble, or the policeman, a neighbor's grandson, who rolled down the block every now and then to check on the old folks.

Claude and Alvin turned the flashlights off near the Nasraddin house and paused at the chain-link gate to look and listen. Light from Fatima's windows overflowed the curtains and pooled in a narrow moat around the brick walls. Alvin clicked on his flashlight and made a quick sweep of the yard, but the beam only fell upon a droopy fig tree and a rusted barbecue pit.

The sound of an opening door sent Claude and Alvin ducking to the ground. "Y'all signaling planes out here?"

Alvin shined the beam on Slug's porch where Slug stood, one hand holding him up against a column and the other lingering self-consciously near his chin. Only one eye, the left, reflected back under one silvered, bristling eyebrow. Half of Slug's head, from brow down to chin and back over an ear, was taped up in brown-ish bandages, and Alvin thought of the cartoons he'd watched with his grandchildren: the sweating, pink pig who dabbed with a hand-kerchief and wiped his face right off, then thrashed around, grabbed blindly, a bewildered pink blank until the cartoonist leaned in with a giant pencil and gave the pig back to the world. "You looking good, Slug. You feel good?"

"Jesus," Claude said.

Slug pulled down one corner of his mouth to straighten it. "I feel alright. Can't do nothing 'bout it anyway." The words melted, dribbled down the steep slope of his mouth and drained out.

Slug's front room was tidy, tidier than Alvin expected considering how long the man had been hiding out with no company except his son, who drove two hours every other weekend from Alexandria to haul his father to specialists in New Orleans, another hour away. But the house did not feel clean. Dust coated the furniture, evidence of a life in stasis, like gangrene in an occluded limb. Slug's house had al-ways been neat, thanks to his fastidious wife, but a fishing maga-zine might be left here, or an empty glass there. Alvin saw nothing to indicate that Slug did more than mope from room to room, or sit contemplatively, brooding or resentful in his armchair. The only thing not coated in dust was the TV remote control. There was a sour-and-bitter odor hanging around Slug, of clothes left too long in the washing machine then scorched in the dryer. Alvin noticed wetness on the bulge of bandages over his ear. He tried to focus on Slug's speckled blue eye, yolk-yellow all around like a crushed robin's egg. "You doing everything them doctors tell you to?"

"*Ça connaisse pas rien,* those fool doctors." Slug dared Alvin or Claude to say otherwise.

"Okay," Alvin said.

"Y'all want that cow or not? She's in those Indians' backyard," Slug slurred. "The boy didn't see her and he shut the gate."

On the way to the back door, Slug tied a lasso out of a rope that was waiting on the kitchen table. When Claude turned on his flashlight, Slug swatted at it, nearly knocked it out of his hand. "You gonna scare that little lady," he said.

The men crossed Slug's dark, tangled lawn with their flashlights off. Something wild and quick jetted back to its den in the hedgerow at the rear end of Slug's property, and in answer, from beyond Fatima's chain link fence, came a snort. Alvin felt the heavy presence of the animal all of a sudden. It was startling and near—all the more real for being unseen. He remembered: cows have horns, hooves, heads, tails, and they are so damned big. Ever so slowly, a very large and pale silhouette developed against the darkness like a photo negative. Grabbing up a wad of grass, Slug clucked and cooed, and the silhouette trudged closer. The big white head swung up and took the grass from Slug's open hand. He rubbed the wide space between her eyes, pinpointed one spot with his thumb, just right of center. The cow shook her head and puffed out a wet breath.

Each holding a handful of grass, the three men edged down the fence toward the gate, and the cow followed. The lights in the Nasraddin house were still on, and shadows moved against the curtains, the two little girls jumping on the sofa. Once the men were nearer the gate, Slug widened the lasso and slipped it around the cow's neck. Alvin lifted the gate latch, but the gate hung badly on its hinges and as Alvin dragged it open, it scraped against the driveway. The cow stomped her feet. Slug bent his knees and held on to the end of the slack rope as the cow backed away. Alvin could only see the blank side of Slug's face, impassive as the moon. The rope tightened. "Grab it!" Claude yelled. The cow swung her head from side to side. Pulling against them, she let out a loud and awful *moo.*

The little girls in the house stopped jumping and poked their heads between the curtains. The men dropped the rope. The cow retreated to the backyard.

With her boy behind her, Fatima stepped out of her front door waving a baseball bat. "Who's that?" she said.

Alvin turned a flashlight on his own face. "It's Alvin Guilbeau." He presented himself to her in the light of the open door. "You got a surprise in your backyard."

She let the bat drop to her side and said something in her language to the boy, who then disappeared into the house. Tonight, instead of a long sheet, she wore a maroon fast-food uniform with yellow stripes on the sleeves. There was a turquoise shawl wrapped around her shoulders. Her feet were bare. In the air, Alvin smelled spices he couldn't name and remembered, for the first time in many years, the Indian markets he'd seen during the war, the cyclone of dark people in bright colors.

"*Chere*, you seen the news report tonight? You got one of them cows in your backyard," Alvin said. Fatima shook her head slightly. "A cow," Alvin said. He gestured at the backyard. There was, to Alvin, a shroud about the faces of people who spoke languages other than his. Even when silent, they wore a vagueness about the eyes; their body language spoke in impossible accents. "Cow," Alvin said again. "Cow. Cow." Fatima readjusted her shawl, and seemed to teeter between frustration and understanding.

Then Slug and Claude rounded the corner, tempting the animal with grass and leading it by the rope. All at once, the vagueness lifted from Fatima. With the baseball bat hanging like a billy club to one side of her hips, she swaggered down her front steps. The little girls watched from the window.

"I saw on the television!" she said.

"That's right."

"Khalid!

The boy appeared again, his arms crossed over his chest, trying very hard to fill his doorway, to be the man of his doorway. "She wants you to have some tea." His voice had changed entirely. Alvin and Fatima both pointed at once, and the boy gasped.

"We should call the police?" Fatima walked boldly up to the animal and motioned for her boy to do the same. Alvin watched the mother and son as they patted the cow's haunches. While the boy whispered to the creature, Alvin wondered if the Nasraddins could be trusted.

"Come inside, use the phone," Fatima said.

"You don't want to call the cops," Claude said. He sounded, Alvin thought, absurdly menacing. The boy pushed between his mother and Claude, and his smooth, brown face radiated outrage as clearly as any man's. Fatima only looked from Claude to her son, and she made pensive birdish noises between her lips, unable to decode the language of a threat, or maybe just not threatened.

"I don't think we should call the police," Alvin said, "tonight."

Slug said, "Let's wait and see."

"What should we wait to see?" the boy said. He glared at Claude. "We will call the police."

"Khalid!" Fatima wrapped an arm around her boy's waist and drew him close to her. She spoke to him in their language, and Alvin saw a mother like any he had known, who could calm her son, and entreat, and explain, and who was confident in her own wisdom. "We will not call tonight," she said to the men.

"So she'll call tomorrow?" Claude said. "The cow can't stay here."

"It can stay in the yard. We can close the gate," Fatima said, "until tomorrow."

"No, ma'am," said Alvin. "We need to take it to my garage."

"Why take it? I don't mind."

Slug emerged from the shadows. He tugged at his mouth. "Ma'am," he said, "Ma'am. We don't want to call the cops at all." He spoke very slowly, took care to make each word clear. "Miss Fatima, one cow is a lot of meat."

Khalid yelped. "You're going to eat this cow!"

"Y'all welcome to some of it," said Slug.

The boy bubbled over with Arabic. He flung his hands around, pressing closer and closer to his mother, and trailed off into English. "They're crazy!" he said to her. "They want to eat it!"

The woman said, "If you want to share, my son must kill her with a knife." Even her laughter rippled with foreignness; the men could not translate it. By way of explanation, she only said, "Khalid is a big boy," and laughed again. The boy seemed both astonished and very embarrassed. She patted his arm.

In the humans' confused silence, the cow tore at grass and swished her tail.

Fatima poked the bandage around Slug's ear, not so gently, with three fingers. "You need to change this."

"Maybe so, yeah."

"You are not listening to the doctor." Next, she addressed Alvin: "Will you come tomorrow for tea? Will you bring your wife?"

Before he meant to, Alvin said, "Yes, ma'am." Fatima turned back to her house. Khalid started to follow, but Fatima threw out the baseball bat to stop him. "Help them, Khalid," she said. She gave him the bat and went in to her little girls.

The boy walked along the animal's right shoulder and stroked her swaying neck. Her hooves thudded on the grass, clopped on the pavement as they passed through yards, across driveways, and behind houses. On the cow's left side, Slug and Claude each sulked in his own way, for his own reasons. Alvin walked ahead, leading the cow by the rope and listening for cars.

Claude said, "You got your daddy over there in India?"

The boy didn't answer.

"Ain't none of your business," Slug said.

In one backyard, the cow took control of the men. She dragged them over to a garden of mustard greens and devoured half of a row before haunch-swatting and rope-tugging finally coaxed her on. The boy dropped far behind. He took swings with the bat at dirt, trees, and telephone poles.

"I got to see India," Alvin said. "During the war. They let the cows roam the streets."

"I seen on TV," Claude said, "how they make the women walk behind the men."

"I don't know about that, but I seen the cows for myself." Alvin looked around for the boy. "I guess his momma's used to having cows all over the place."

"I'm telling you, they don't even let them show their faces, those women."

"We aren't from India," Khalid shouted from the darkness behind them. "We're from Sudan!"

By the time they came to Alvin's house, the boy had disappeared. They led the cow into the garage and tied her to one of the beams overhead. She lifted her tail and dumped a heap onto the concrete floor. With a shovel that he took down from the rafters where it balanced along with rakes and fishing poles, Alvin shoveled the crap into a paper bag so that he could use it later to fertilize the muscadine vines that crawled up a lattice at the back of the garage and covered the only windows.

"She's crazy," Claude said. "We ain't gonna let a boy kill that cow."

"Aw, she was pulling our leg. Don't get all worked up," Alvin said.

"You don't know what she's joking about or not. I wouldn't be surprised if she was dialing 911 right now."

"*Bouche ta gueule!* She won't call no cops!" Slug stood at the garage door, his one eye peeping through a crack for any sight of the boy. "You know that little lady," he whispered, "she went to school for law in her country."

"Is that right," said Alvin.

"And her husband. He was some kind of politician. They didn't like what he had to say over there. They shot him dead."

"Aw, no," Alvin said.

"So don't you ask that boy about his daddy no more."

Slug slipped out of the garage into the darkness and crept homeward like a possum, along walls and fences and hedges.

Della, in bed and asleep by eight o'clock, long before Alvin came in, and awake again at dawn long before Alvin awoke, had no idea, when she went out to the deep-freezers in her housedress and slippers for a package of *boudin* to boil for breakfast, that she would find a cow in her garage. When she saw it there, smelling like a circus and totally composed, she turned immediately back toward the house, and just as she opened her mouth to yell, Alvin rounded the corner, still in his pajamas. He started at her in French before she could argue. He told her about Slug and the Sudanese, and he made her see that it would be just like at Pepere's farm on autumn Saturdays when their children were still babies. God knew what He was doing, sending that trailer-truck flying in November instead of July. The flies had slacked off. The air was light and thin, perfect weather for slaughter. The neighbors would come and ask for this or that part, the brisket, the ribs, the sweetbreads, or the brains, and there would be no fights about it, only merry hacking and sawing and yanking at skin. She would stuff her red sausages. Pearl would make liver gravy. Inside, their house would be close, wet with the boiling of sausages and the heat of a crowd sweating from homemade wine. "Besides," he said, "if we don't slaughter it ourselves, they just going to haul it off, cut it up, and send it right back to us at three dollars a pound. That cow came to us. She's ours." He made it sound like a good idea.

By noon, thanks to Della and the Catholic sisters of the prayer line, word got around that God had delivered unto the neighborhood a fat, unblemished cow, and they planned, sure enough, to eat it. Although some of the ladies had concerns, they had to admit the price of beef had gone up, and their little bit of social security certainly did not allow for steak and brisket every night of the week, and furthermore, if so-and-so down the block was in for a piece of the cow, then they should be, too. Della passed along all her prayers for Slug, for her children and her grandchildren who never called or wrote or prayed for themselves, and for Fatima, her little ones, and that angry young man of hers. "And pray," she said finally. "Pray tonight we don't get caught."

It took little for Alvin to convince Della to visit Fatima with him in the very early afternoon. Della did her hair and powdered her face, Alvin tucked in his shirt. They found a jar of fig preserves in the back of a cabinet, dusted it off, and wondered if the Nasraddins would say they could not eat figs.

The boy answered the door, slouching in his jeans and sweatshirt.

He said nothing, only stepped aside to let them in. The little girls played dominoes on the carpet. The littler one said, "Hi." She looked like she wanted to say more, but the bigger one shushed her and started to pick up the dominoes. The boy led them into a tiny green kitchen, where Fatima stood before the stove stirring milk in a saucepan.

"You are Mrs. Guilbeau?" Fatima smiled. Della and Alvin smiled back. "Sit down," Fatima said, and gestured to the kitchen table. Della and Alvin sat.

"Your house is very nice," Della said. She searched the walls and countertops for anything unique to a Sudanese woman's kitchen but saw only the usual things: clock, potholder, sugar bowl, flyswatter. Della wondered what strange foods had been cooked on that stove and stored in that refrigerator. She wondered especially what might be in the freezer.

"Do y'all like figs?"

"What is *figs*?"

Della held up the jar for Fatima to see.

"Yes," she said. "Thank you." She said something to the boy in her language, and he went to the pantry and took out some bread. Meanwhile, an itch grew in Della to talk about the cow, cows, any cow; it seemed frivolous to talk about anything else.

Alvin said, "We weren't sure if y'all could eat figs."

"Just meat sometimes we can't eat," the boy said.

"You can eat beef?" Della asked.

"Sometimes." The boy started to leave the kitchen, but his mother spoke again, and he sat down at the table across from Della and Alvin. Fatima set four cups and saucers on the counter. To Della's surprise, five ordinary little tea-flags dangled by strings from the lip of the saucepan from which Fatima poured.

Fatima served the tea then sat down next to her son.

She smiled at her guests and sipped from her cup. They smiled back and sipped from theirs. The boy kept adding sugar to his. He frowned and sighed.

"My father had cattle in Sudan," Fatima said.

"Is that right," said Alvin. "For milk?"

"Some for milk, some for eating. We always had food."

"You were blessed," Della said. "All those people starving." She did not know for sure if there were people starving in Sudan, but she thought it was a good guess. "When I was a little girl, we didn't have nothing for a long time. No cows. No chickens. Nothing. That was the Depression."

Alvin said, "No, ma'am, we didn't have much."

Della held the cup close to her mouth and blew at the surface of the tea, wrinkling the milk skin, which she then dabbed with a forefinger, lifted out of the cup, and deposited on her saucer. Fatima graciously handed her a napkin.

"We wish you and your children would join us tonight," Alvin said. "There's going to be plenty." He sounded to Della like the door-to-door peddlers of peculiar religions who would show up every spring to invite them to revivals.

Fatima looked to her son, who had not drunk his tea, but was staring down into it. "You see?" she said.

"I thought you were joking."

"Khalid does not know where meat comes from."

"I do!"

"He's a good boy," she said, "but he does not remember Sudan."

The boy pushed his chair away from the table and left. A moment later, a door slammed somewhere in the house.

As best she could, Fatima explained about meat, what Muslims could and could not eat, and also about something she called *ummah*. She kept using that word to describe the people among whom she now lived, and this word sounded more lovely, and because of its newness to their ears, more important than the words they might have used to describe themselves and their gentle loyalty to each other. Behind her halting English was a persuasive warmth and insistence, a tenor that made every word seem lawful and good. She had been a lawyer, Della could see, and what a shame, she thought, that in this great country such a gifted woman had to wrap hamburgers.

● ● ●

In the *World Book Encyclopedia,* copyright 1965, that they'd bought for the children, volume by volume per ten-dollar purchase from the grocery store, Alvin read that Sudan is the largest of all African countries. Its capital, a town called Khartoum, sits on the banks of the Nile like Baton Rouge sits on the Mississippi. There is a North and there is a South. The North has cities and deserts. The South has swamps and mosquitoes, and months of nothing but rain. These people are poor. Poor, poor. Some parts of the year, they starve, even though certain tribes hoard millions of cattle, sheep, goats, and camels for social prestige, and because there just aren't enough trucks to haul them anywhere.

The name "Sudan" comes from the Arabic expression *bilad as-Sudan,* Land of the Blacks, which seemed to Alvin to mean that the Sudanese are as likely to look like your run-of-the-mill African American down at the Wal-Mart as they are to look Indian, that is, from India Indian. They are Muslim. There are some Christians, in the South, who have been Christians longer than the French have been Christians, longer than the French have been French. How about that. There are some who believe in spirits—water spirits, tree spirits. The Muslims are moving in on them. When boys become men in Sudan, Alvin read, when they kill an enemy, their backs and arms and faces are cut in stripes of scars. A picture showed a young man in a white gown and turban with three dark hatch-marks across his cheeks. *Cicatrization,* it was called. *Ci-ca-tri-za-tion.*

Alvin's eyes gave out just before the section on the History of Ancient Nubia. He closed the encyclopedia, closed his eyes, and saw Fatima propped up by a walking stick and her little girls with distended naked bellies. Sand spun around them like sleet. Or maybe there was no sand. Maybe their bare feet were sinking into an island of mud and swamp grass. Mosquitoes and deerflies swirled around them like slow sand. They were part of a circle of many people: Arabs and Africans and some lean-looking and dusty white people. In the center of the circle, a black man, shriveled, desiccated—by sand or by mosquitoes—held Fatima's boy by the shoulders. The boy, Khalid, faced his mother and sisters. Alvin saw Khalid's wide back bisected by the skinny and dark line of the old black man. The man withdrew a straight-bladed knife from the toolbelt-thong that hung cockeyed on his hips. One smooth stroke across Khalid's shoulders, and blood swelled and overflowed. While the circle of men and women and children hooted and raised fists over heads, Khalid stood perfectly still. Alvin wished he could see the boy's face. He seemed so very young.

Alvin went to the garage and opened the long, flat, wooden case where he kept his butchering tackle. He surveyed the contents: fillet knife, boning knife, a cleaver as heavy as a hatchet, a carver, a simple and gently curved butcher knife. None of these would slice through a cow's thick neck, not neatly, not painlessly. The cut would have to be smooth, straight, decisive. The boy's hand would have to be steady. Not one of them could handle a thrashing cow.

Then he thought of the thirty-inch blade from his riding lawn-mower and spent the rest of the afternoon sharpening it, in the backyard so as not to upset the cow. Round and round, on one side and then the other, Alvin honed the blade against the whetstone. There could be no nicks or dull spots. He knew from cutting his own hands so many times that the dull knives hurt, while he never felt the nick of a sharp one at all. So he sharpened and sharpened, took a break for a glass of wine, and sharpened some more.

The boy came early in the afternoon. "Mama sent this," he said. He had an armful of old newspapers and a nearly empty roll of butcher paper. Before sending him home, Alvin took him out to the garage. With the garage light on, they both looked smaller— the boy and the cow—big but not quite fully grown. Maybe they could handle her. Maybe the boy could handle her. He had thick arms, and she really seemed to be a placid cow.

The cow pissed, loud as a rainstorm on the concrete floor, and Khalid jumped back from her. "She almost splashed me," he said. Then he said, "Gross," and the word sounded silly and even more American dressed up in the boy's lilting accent. Alvin had heard his grandchildren say it hundreds of times, about *ponce,* and chicken livers, and the orange-yellow fat of crawfish tails, among other things. It was a silly word, in any case. "That's gross, yeah," Alvin said. "I'll hose it off tomorrow. Come here, boy."

He handed Khalid the lawnmower blade to make him understand. He said, "You think you can do that, what your mamma wants? You think you can, boy?"

Khalid balanced the blade on his flattened palms with his fingers stretched back, away from the edge. He looked incredulously at Alvin. "You know she was joking," the boy said. "They don't do this in Sudan."

At eight in the evening, the neighborhood began to gather in Della's kitchen where she sat steadfast on a stool by the stove, stirring hot praline goo with one hand and doling out wine with the other. Claude and Pearl came first, with a loaded shotgun and the A-frame gibbet, which the men quickly installed in the garage. When Alvin saw the shotgun, he motioned for Claude to follow him to the backyard. He pointed to the long, sharp blade lying across an old sycamore stump. Claude said, "For them Indians, you'd do that?"

"They're from Sudan," Alvin said. "She'll call the cops if we don't let the boy do it." This was a lie, of course, and Alvin hated to tell it, but he knew that no diplomatic somersaults in French or English, no Arabic invocation of community could justify such a strange decision to Claude. Claude picked up the blade and strummed it with his thumb. "Be careful," said Alvin. "It's sharp, sharp."

"It better be sharp," Claude said.

There was a small crowd gathered in the driveway when the neighborhood policeman pulled over to the curb and rolled down his window. "How y'all?" he called, and cracked good-natured jokes about drunken old Cajuns until his own grandmother came out of the house and pressed a bottle of homemade wine and a tin of pralines, still warm, into his hands. "Go bring that to your wife," she said, and then, "Y'all still looking for them cows?"

"They still can't find some of 'em," her grandson said.

"They done got ate, I bet you."

The policeman drove away and his grandmother came back to the group laughing from her rolling belly. "Us coonasses been stealing cows since the dawn of time," she said. "That's part of our culture, that." Most of them laughed, but some, Claude especially, speculated in French that Fatima had called that cop after all, that he was reconnoitering and most certainly would be back.

By nine o' clock, Alvin and Della's house was teeming, the table crowded with food. Many had brought the Saturday paper, which featured on the front page a photograph of yesterday's accident: a dead steer, roped by the neck, dangling from an overpass. They would use this page, they decided with glee, to wrap up their takings this evening.

From time to time, Alvin checked on the cow. She had been quiet all day, but now, with so much commotion, she huffed and stomped her feet. Alvin, who could not stand to see an animal suffer, cooed at her in French and patted her flaring nose. He had not given her anything to eat or drink—she would clean easier that way—and wondered how thirsty she was. When he held a mixing-bowl full of wine under her nose, she sniffed it, tested it with her tongue, then drank up every drop and flipped the bowl looking for more. Alvin gave her more.

At ten o'clock, the crowd, pressed elbow to elbow in the steamy kitchen, quieted down. The ominous booming from the students' passing cars shook the windows and pulsed like tribal drums in the chests of the old people. There had been no word from Slug or the Sudanese. Della called Slug's house but got no answer, and none of them could spell Nasraddin to find it in the phone book.

Had they been in their own homes, rather than here in Della's kitchen, those who lived across the street from the Nasraddins might have looked into Fatima's brightly lit living room and seen her winding bold cloths around her daughters, combing out and braiding their long hair, before she finally took up a roll of bandages and, with blunt efficiency— as though grooming her children, packing groceries, slaughtering cows and disinfecting old men's lesions were all the selfsame gesture— ministered to the ruined face of her neighbor as he sat on her couch and hid behind his hands to spare the little girls. The spies then might have pulled shut their drapes quickly, embarrassed when they saw Fatima glance out of her own window, searching the shadows for her son, who had not returned from Mr. Guilbeau's that afternoon.

And had the people all over this neighborhood been watching from their windows, as they were accustomed to do after nightfall, flipping on their porch lights and peering out at their street, hands cupped around eyes, they would have seen a figure moving in and out of the orange light of streetlamps and trespassing fearlessly into one yard after another. What a shock they'd have had when the face drew close to their windows, as close as they had ever imagined ominous faces in the night, and gazed at them; no, not at them— beyond them, into their homes, at their plain and barely valuable things. And the old couple who lived in the gray brick house on the corner— what would they have done, what would they have thought, when the expression on that face changed suddenly from curiosity to anger, when the young man at their window reared back the baseball bat he carried and swung it with a grown man's strength into the glass?

Under the light of a single bald light bulb dangling from a rafter, the neighborhood gathered into Alvin's garage and formed a circle around the cow. They watched Alvin offer her another bowlful of wine. They watched Claude cross to the center of the circle, shotgun in hand.

It had gotten around, what the brown woman wanted. Everyone knew and agreed to allow it. There was beef in this world before there were guns, they reasoned; people must have killed cows somehow. As the night grew later, though, they began to believe that they had been fooled, not through spitefulness on Fatima's part, but rather through their own provincial ignorance of foreign places and customs; they hadn't gotten her joke. They had been propelled by momentum into this circle and this ritual that was at once familiar and very strange, but now as they saw Claude aiming the shotgun after all, their momentum flagged. Claude set the shotgun aside. He said to Alvin, "Somebody will hear it. If that cop comes by . . . . What do you want to do?"

Alvin took the lawnmower blade from where it lay on top of a deep freezer. "If you hold her head up, I'll do it. She won't feel a thing." One of the men suggested his teenage son hold the gun aimed at the cow, just in case, and this seemed like a reasonable compromise.

Claude held her gently but firmly by the jaws. Turning the blade this way and that, switching it from hand to hand, Alvin walked around to one side of the cow and then the other. He draped one arm over the cow's neck and poised the blade under her throat, but he could find no leverage. He stood back and considered, as Claude hummed and massaged her broad buttery jowls. The teenager stood poised with the shotgun on his shoulder. They all prayed he would not shoot Claude by mistake.

"Hit her in the head with something," the teenager said. From the dark perimeter of the circle, his father said, "Hush boy."

"I can't watch, me," Della said. She cringed back with all her body.

Alvin stood further back. "Somebody look for that cop." Della rushed to the door and opened it just a crack. "Oh!" she squeaked. Hearts pounded and fluttered all around the circle. "Oh! Oh, *chere!* I didn't know you at first. Come in!"

When they saw Slug, most of them for the first time in several years, the people of the neighborhood were less surprised by the bandages and deformity of Slug's face than by the young man who came in right behind him, hanging onto Slug's sagging belt.

It was Slug who had gone looking and heard the shattering glass, who had found Khalid in a dark house picking up and examining all the small, un-incriminating remnants of desk drawers and bookshelves. Somewhere in the circle now, the boy realized, were the old couple whose check stubs and prayer lists he had handled, whose refrigerator he had opened and closed, who would immediately believe it was the work of those college boys, drunk on a Saturday night, when they later found their window broken and things upset. Khalid let go of Slug's belt and stood up straight, seeing no one and nothing but the cow and the blade cocked under her throat.

Fatima followed, with her two little girls, all three draped in bright fabrics. A silk veil covered Fatima's head and black hair. To the neighborhood, which had seen her only in uniforms—tired, bagging groceries—Fatima seemed in these foreign clothes strangely like the Virgin Mother.

Slug's one eye winked at all of them as he looked around the circle. When his eye landed on them, they wondered, each in turn, why they had not knocked louder at his door or longer, why no one had insisted on driving him to doctors, or cleaning his house, or helping him change his bandages.

Like an altar boy presenting the Bible, Alvin held the blade out to Khalid. "Take it," Slug said, and Khalid picked up the blade.

Alvin lunged for a mop bucket near the door, and positioned it on the ground under the cow's head. They all knew it would never contain the blood. Alvin took the shotgun from the teenager, who stepped back into the circle, pressed close to his father. Alvin aimed, just in case.

Claude cupped his hands around the cow's jaws again. He pulled her head up so the skin on her neck stretched flat, taut. Slug and the boy stood by her side, on the right. The boy was losing his color. He held the blade feebly. It trembled in his hands.

The neighborhood watched the boy move his lips, but no words came out. The mother said, "Khalid—*Bismillah ArRahman*." The boy tried again. His face blanched.

Slug laid his hand over the boy's. He hugged the boy against his chest, pressed him tightly to stop his quaking. The cow snorted. She stepped back and nearly broke free of Claude's hold. They all heard the shuffle and click when Alvin set the shotgun.

Slug and the boy cocked the blade at the cow's neck. She pounded one hoof and took a deep breath that swelled her. As she started to moo, Slug and the boy leaned forward together. Slug said, "Y'all say a prayer."

The blade wrenched across the tight white line of throat, like a bow on a silent fiddle. Claude stroked her cheeks while blood gushed from her neck, saturated his jeans, and pooled in the bucket at his feet. The bucket filled and spilled over, and the pool spread fast, outward and outward to Slug and the boy who had fainted in his arms, to Alvin, to Della, to the woman Fatima and her wide-eyed girls, to the circle's perimeter, to the feet of the people who watched and remembered the country farms, the spoken French, the good of home-stuffed sausage. The blood spread out toward the garage doors, and under the doors, out to the driveway, into the street. Enough blood, they all thought, to flood the neighborhood.

Stephanie Soileau grew up in Lake Charles, Louisiana. Her stories have appeared in *StoryQuarterly* and *Gulf Coast,* and she is a recent graduate of the Iowa Writers' Workshop. She lives in Chicago.

Several years ago, a livestock trailer did in fact tumble off the interstate into downtown Baton Rouge, and there was speculation that the missing members of the herd ended up in stewpots and freezers. Around that time, I'd been trying to get my grandmother to say into a cassette recorder everything she remembered about growing up as a Cajun sharecropper in the 1930s. On one of her tapes, she describes the boucheries that happened every week or so through the fall and winter to keep the country families in meat; one family would donate a cow, and after a festive slaughter, everyone would go home with a chunk of beef. When my grandmother made the tape for me, she and my grandfather had been living in the city of Lake Charles for fifty years—in

the same neighborhood all that time—but they and their friends had brought these communal country rituals with them. There were no cows killed in the garage (chickens, maybe, and squirrels, absolutely), but there was the same devotion to good neighboring, and that struck me as a rare and extraordinary thing. Is it? I hope not, but I wanted to write about it in any case, and a stray herd of cows seemed like the perfect opportunity.

Fatima is based on several women I knew in Iowa City, where I worked at a community center that served a large population of Sudanese refugees. One of those women was the daughter of a significant Muslim political leader who had spoken for peaceful coexistence among ethnicities and equality for women; he was ultimately hanged for sedition and apostasy. When I knew her, his daughter was herding four-year-olds at a preschool for a little more than minimum wage. She did make very good tea.

Dennis Lehane

UNTIL GWEN

(from *The Atlantic Monthly*)

Your father picks you up from prison in a stolen Dodge Neon, with an 8-ball of coke in the glove compartment and a hooker named Mandy in the back seat. Two minutes into the ride, the prison still hanging tilted in the rearview, Mandy tells you that she only hooks part-time. The rest of the time she does light secretarial for an independent video chain and tends bar, two Sundays a month, at the local VFW. But she feels her calling—her true calling in life—is to write.

You go, "Books?"

"Books." She snorts, half out of amusement, half to shoot a line off your fist and up her left nostril. "Screenplays!" She shouts it at the dome light for some reason. "You know—movies."

'Tell him the one about the psycho saint guy." Your father winks at you in the rearview, like he's driving the two of you to the prom. "Go ahead. Tell him."

"Okay, okay." She turns on the seat to face you, and your knees touch, and you think of Gwen, a look she gave you once, nothing special, just looking back at you as she stood at the front door, asking if you'd seen her keys. A forgettable moment if ever there was one, but you spent four years in prison remembering it.

". . . so at his canonization," Mandy is saying, "something, like, happens? And his spirit comes *back* and goes into the body of this

37

priest. But, like, the priest? He has a brain tumor. He doesn't know it or nothing, but *he* does, and it's fucking up his, um—"

"Brain?" you try.

"Thoughts," Mandy says. "So he gets this saint in him and that *does it,* because, like, even though the guy was a saint, his spirit has become evil, because his soul is gone. So this priest? He spends the rest of the movie trying to kill the Pope."

"Why?"

"Just listen," your father says. "It gets good."

You look out the window. A car sits empty along the shoulder. It's beige, and someone has painted gold wings on the sides, fanning out from the front bumper and across the doors. A sign is affixed to the roof with some words on it, but you've passed it by the time you think to wonder what it says.

"See, there's this secret group that works for the Vatican? They're like a, like a . . ."

"A hit squad," your father says.

"Exactly," Mandy says, and presses her finger to your nose. "And the lead guy, the, like, head agent? He's the hero. He lost his wife and daughter in a terrorist attack on the Vatican a few years back, so he's a little fucked up, but—"

You say, "Terrorists attacked the Vatican?"

"Huh?"

You look at her, waiting. She has a small face, eyes too close to her nose.

"In the *movie,*" Mandy says. "Not in real life."

"Oh. I just—you know, four years inside, you assume you missed a couple of headlines, but . . ."

"Right." Her face is dark and squally now. "Can I finish?"

"I'm just saying," you say and snort another line off your fist, "even the guys on death row would have heard about that one."

"Just go with it," your father says. "It's not, like, real life."

You look out the window, see a guy in a chicken suit carrying a can of gas in the breakdown lane, think how real life isn't like real life. Probably more like this poor dumb bastard running out of gas in a car with wings painted on it. Wondering how the hell he ever got here. Wondering who he'd pissed off in that previous real life.

Your father has rented two rooms at an Econo Lodge so that you and Mandy can have some privacy, but you send Mandy home after she twice interrupts the sex to pontificate on the merits of Michael Bay films.

You sit in the blue-wash flicker of ESPN and eat peanuts from a plastic bag you got out of a vending machine and drink plastic cupfuls of Jim Beam from a bottle your father presented when you reached the motel parking lot. You think of the time you've lost, and how nice it is to sit alone on a double bed and watch TV, and you think of Gwen, can taste her tongue for just a moment, and you think about the road that's led you here to this motel room on this night after forty-seven months in prison, and how a lot of people would say it was a twisted road, a weird one, filled with curves, but you just think of it as a road like any other. You drive down it on faith, or because you have no other choice, and you find out what it's like by the driving of it, find out what the end looks like only by reaching it.

Late the next morning your father wakes you, tells you he drove Mandy home and you've got things to do, people to see.

Here's what you know about your father above all else: people have a way of vanishing in his company.

He's a professional thief, a consummate con man, an expert in his field—and yet something far beyond professionalism is at his core, something unreasonably arbitrary. Something he keeps within himself like a story he heard once, laughed at maybe, yet swore never to repeat.

"She was with you last night?" you say.

"You didn't want her. Somebody had to prop her ego back up. Poor girl like that."

"But you drove her home," you say.

"I'm speaking Czech?"

You hold his eyes for a bit. They're big and bland, with the heart-less innocence of a newborn's. Nothing moves in them, nothing breathes, and after a while you say, "Let me take a shower."

"Fuck the shower," he says. "Throw on a baseball cap and let's get."

You take the shower anyway, just to feel it, another of those things you would have realized you'd miss if you'd given it any thought ahead of time—standing under the spray, no one near you, all the hot water you want for as long as you want it, sham-poo that doesn't smell like factory smoke.

Drying your hair and brushing your teeth, you can hear the old man flicking through channels, never pausing on one for more than thirty seconds: Home Shopping Network—zap. Springer—zap. Oprah—zap. Soap-opera voices, soap-opera music—zap. Monster-truck show—pause. Commercial—zap, zap, zap.

You come back into the room, steam trailing you, pick your jeans up off the bed, and put them on.

The old man says, "Afraid you'd drowned. Worried I'd have to take a plunger to the drain, suck you back up."

You say, "Where we going?"

"Take a drive." Your father shrugs, flicking past a cartoon.

"Last time you said that, I got shot twice."

Your father looks back over his shoulder at you, eyes big and soft. "Wasn't the car that shot you, was it?"

You go out to Gwen's place, but she isn't there anymore. A cou-ple of black kids are playing in the front yard, black mother com-ing out on the porch to look at the strange car idling in front of her house.

"You didn't leave it here?" your father says.

"Not that I recall."

"Think."

"I'm thinking."

"So you didn't?"

"I told you—not that I recall."

"So you're sure."

"Pretty much."

"You had a bullet in your head."

"Two."

"I thought one glanced off."

You say, "Two bullets hit your fucking head, old man, you don't get hung up on the particulars."

"That how it works?" Your father pulls away from the curb as the woman comes down the steps.

The first shot came through the back window, and Gentleman Pete flinched. He jammed the wheel to the right and drove the car straight into the highway exit barrier, air bags exploding, water barrels exploding, something in the back of your head exploding, glass pebbles filling your shirt, Gwen going, "What happened? Jesus. What happened?"

You pulled her with you out the back door—Gwen, your Gwen—and you crossed the exit ramp and ran into the woods and the second shot hit you there but you kept going, not sure how, not sure why, the blood pouring down your face, your head on fire, burning so bright and so hard that not even the rain could cool it off.

"And you don't remember nothing else?" your father says. You've driven all over town, every street, every dirt road, every hollow you can stumble across in Sumner, West Virginia.

"Not till she dropped me off at the hospital."

"Dumb goddamn move if ever there was one."

"I seem to remember I was puking blood by that point, talking all funny."

"Oh, you remember that. Sure."

"You're telling me in all this time you never talked to Gwen?"

"Like I told you three years back, that girl got gone."

You know Gwen. You love Gwen. This part of it is hard to take.

You remember Gwen in your car and Gwen in the cornstalks and Gwen in her mother's bed in the hour just before noon, naked and soft. You watched a drop of sweat appear from her hairline and slide down the side of her neck as she snored against your shoulder blade, and the arch of her foot was pressed over the top of yours, and you watched her sleep, and you were so awake.

"So it's with her," you say.

"No," the old man says, a bit of anger creeping into his puppy-fur voice. "You called me. That night."

"I did?"

"Shit, boy. You called me from the pay phone outside the hospital."

"What'd I say?"

"You said, 'I hid it. It's safe. No one knows where but me.'"

"Wow," you say. "I said all that? Then what'd I say?"

The old man shakes his head. "Cops were pulling up by then, calling you 'motherfucker,' telling you to drop the phone. You hung up."

The old man pulls up outside a low red-brick building behind a tire dealership on Oak Street. He kills the engine and gets out of the car, and you follow. The building is two stories. Facing the street are the office of a bail bondsman, a hardware store, a Chinese takeout place with greasy walls the color of an old dog's teeth, and a hair salon called Girlfriend Hooked Me Up that's filled with black women. Around the back, past the whitewashed windows of what was once a dry cleaner, is a small black door with the words TRUE-LINE EFFICIENCY EXPERTS CORP. stenciled on the frosted glass.

The old man unlocks the door and leads you into a ten-by-ten room that smells of roast chicken and varnish. He pulls the string of a bare light bulb, and you look around at a floor strewn with envelopes and paper, the only piece of furniture a broken-down desk probably left behind by the previous tenant.

Your father crab-walks across the floor, picking up envelopes that have come through the mail slot, kicking his way through the paper. You pick up one of the pieces of paper and read it.

Dear Sirs,

Please find enclosed my check for $50. I look forward to receiving the information packet we discussed as well as the sample test. I have enclosed a SASE to help facilitate this process. I hope to see you someday at the airport!

Sincerely,

Jackson A. Willis

You let it drop to the floor and pick up another one.

To Whom It May Concern:

Two months ago, I sent a money order in the amount of fifty dollars to your company in order that I may receive an information packet and sample test so that I could take the US government test and become a security handler and fulfill my patriotic duty against the al Qadas. I have not received my information packet as yet and no one answers when I call your phone. Please send me that information packet so I can get that job.

Yours truly,

Edwin Voeguarde

12 Hinckley Street

Youngstown, OH 44502

You drop this one to the floor too, and watch your father sit on the corner of the desk and open his fresh pile of envelopes with a penknife. He reads some, pauses only long enough with others to shake the checks free and drop the rest to the floor.

You let yourself out, go to the Chinese place and buy a cup of Coke, go into the hardware store and buy a knife and a couple of tubes of Krazy Glue, stop at the car for a minute, and then go back into your father's office.

"What're you selling this time?" you say.

"Airport security jobs," he says, still opening envelopes. "It's a booming market. Everyone wants in. Stop them bad guys before they get on the plane, make the papers, serve your country, and maybe be lucky enough to get posted near one of them Starbucks kiosks. Hell."

"How much you made?"

Your father shrugs, though you're certain he knows the figure right down to the last penny.

"I've done all right. Hell else am I going to do, back in this shit town for three months, waiting on you? 'Bout time to shut this down, though." He holds up a stack of about sixty checks. "Deposit these and cash out the account. First two months, though? I was getting a thousand, fifteen hundred checks a week. Thank the good Lord for being selective with the brain tissue, you know?"

"Why?" you say.

"Why what?"

"Why you been hanging around for three months?"

Your father looks up from the stack of checks, squints. "To prepare a proper welcome for you."

"A bottle of whiskey and a hooker who gives lousy head? That took you three months?"

Your father squints a little more, and you see a shaft of gray between the two of you, not quite what you'd call light, just a shaft of air or atmosphere or something, swimming with motes, your father on the other side of it looking at you like he can't quite believe you're related.

After a minute or so your father says, "Yeah."

Your father told you once you'd been born in New Jersey. Another time he said New Mexico. Then Idaho. Drunk as a skunk a few months before you got shot, he said, "No, no. I'll tell you the truth. You were born in Las Vegas. That's in Nevada."

You went on the Internet to look yourself up but never did find anything.

Your mother died when you were seven. You've sat up at night occasionally and tried to picture her face. Some nights you can't see her at all. Some nights you'll get a quick glimpse of her eyes or her jawline, see her standing by the foot of her bed, rolling her stockings on, and suddenly she'll appear whole cloth, whole human, and you can smell her.

Most times, though, it's somewhere in between. You see a smile she gave you, and then she'll vanish. See a spatula she held turning pancakes, her eyes burning for some reason, her mouth an O, and then her face is gone and all you can see is the wallpaper. And the spatula.

You asked your father once why he had no pictures of her. Why hadn't he taken a picture of her? Just one lousy picture?

He said, "You think it'd bring her back? No, I mean, do you? Wow," he said, and rubbed his chin. "Wouldn't that be cool."

You said, "Forget it."

"Maybe if we had a whole album of pictures?" your father said. "She'd, like, pop out from time to time, make us breakfast."

Now that you've been in prison, you've been documented, but even they'd had to make it up, take your name as much on faith as you. You have no Social Security number or birth certificate, no passport. You've never held a job.

Gwen said to you once, "You don't have anyone to tell you who you are, so you don't *need* anyone to tell you. You just are who you are. You're beautiful."

And with Gwen that was usually enough. You didn't need to be defined—by your father, your mother, a place of birth, a name on a credit card or a driver's license or the upper left corner of a check. As long as her definition of you was something she could live with, then you could too.

You find yourself standing in a Nebraska wheat field. You're seventeen years old. You learned to drive five years earlier. You were in school once, for two months when you were eight, but you read well and you can multiply three-digit numbers in your head faster than a calculator, and you've seen the country with the old man. You've learned people aren't that smart. You've learned how to pull lottery-ticket scams and asphalt-paving scams and get free meals with a slight upturn of your brown eyes. You've learned that if you hold ten dollars in front of a stranger, he'll pay twenty to get his hands on it if you play him right. You've learned that every good lie is threaded with truth and every accepted truth leaks lies.

You're seventeen years old in that wheat field. The night breeze smells of wood smoke and feels like dry fingers as it lifts your bangs off your forehead. You remember everything about that night because it is the night you met Gwen. You are two years away from prison, and you feel like someone has finally given you permission to live.

This is what few people know about Sumner, West Virginia: every now and then someone finds a diamond. Some dealers were in a plane that went down in a storm in '51, already blown well off course, flying a crate of Israeli stones down the Eastern Seaboard toward Miami. Plane went down near an open mineshaft, took some swing-shift miners with it. The government showed up, along with members of an international gem consortium, got the bodies out of there, and went to work looking for the diamonds. Found most of them, or so they claimed, but for decades afterward rumors persisted, occasionally given credence by the sight of a miner, still grimed brown by the shafts, tooling around town in an Audi.

You'd been in Sumner peddling hurricane insurance in trailer parks when word got around that someone had found a diamond as big as a casino chip. Miner by the name of George Brunda, suddenly buying drinks, talking to his travel agent. You and Gwen shot pool with him one night, and you could see his dread in the bulges under his eyes, the way his laughter exploded too high and too fast.

He didn't have much time, old George, and he knew it, but he had a mother in a rest home, and he was making the arrangements to get her transferred. George was a fleshy guy, triple-chinned, and dreams he'd probably forgotten he'd ever had were rediscovered and weighted in his face, jangling and pulling the flesh.

"Probably hasn't been laid in twenty years," Gwen said when

George went to the bathroom. "It's sad. Poor sad George. Never knew love."

Her pool stick pressed against your chest as she kissed you, and you could taste the tequila, the salt, and the lime on her tongue.

"Never knew love," she whispered in your ear, an ache in the whisper.

"What about the fairground?" your father says as you leave the office of True-Line Efficiency Experts Corp. "Maybe you hid it there. You always had a fondness for that place."

You feel a small hitch. In your leg, let's say. Just a tiny clutching sensation in the back of your right calf. But you walk through it, and it goes away.

You say to your father as you reach the car, "You really drive her home this morning?"

"Who?"

"Mandy?"

"Who's . . . ?" Your father opens his door, looks at you over it. "Oh, the whore?"

"Yeah."

"Did I drive her home?"

"Yeah."

Your father pats the top of the door, the cuff of his denim jacket flapping around his wrist, his eyes on you. You feel, as you always have, reflected in them, even when you aren't, couldn't be, wouldn't be.

"Did I drive her home?" A smile bounces in the rubber of your father's face.

"Did you drive her home?" you say.

That smile's all over the place now—the eyebrows, too. "Define home."

You say, "I wouldn't know, would I?"

"You're still pissed at me because I killed Fat Boy."

"George."

"What?"

"His name was George."

"He would have ratted."

"To who? It wasn't like he could file a claim. Wasn't a fucking lottery ticket."

Your father shrugs, looks off down the street.

"I just want to know if you drove her home."

"I drove her home," your father says.

"Yeah?"

"Oh, sure."

"Where'd she live?"

"Home," he says, and gets behind the wheel, starts the ignition.

You never figured George Brunda for smart, and only after a full day in his house, going through everything down to the point of removing the drywall and putting it back, resealing it, touching up the paint, did Gwen say, "Where's the mother stay again?"

That took uniforms, Gwen as a nurse, you as an orderly. Gentleman Pete out in the car while your father kept watch on George's mine entrance and monitored police activity over a scanner.

The old lady said, "You're new here, and quite pretty," as Gwen shot her up with phenobarbital and Valium and you went to work on the room.

This was the glitch: You'd watched George drive to work, watched him enter the mine. No one saw him come back out again, because no one was looking on the other side of the hill, at the exit of a completely different shaft. So while your father watched the front, George took off out the back, drove over to check on his investment, walked into the room just as you pulled the rock from the back of the mother's radio, George looking politely surprised, as if he'd stepped into the wrong room.

He smiled at you and Gwen, held up a hand in apology, and backed out of the room.

Gwen looked at the door, looked at you.

You looked at Gwen, looked at the window, looked at the rock filling the center of your palm, the entire center of your palm. Looked at the door.

Gwen said, "Maybe we—"

And George came through the door again, nothing polite in his face, a gun in his hand. And not any regular gun—a motherfucking six-shooter, like they carried in westerns, long, thin barrel, a family heirloom maybe, passed down from a great-great-great-grandfather, not even a trigger guard, just the trigger, and crazy fat George the lonely unloved pulling back on it and squeezing off two rounds, the first of which went out the window, the second of which hit metal somewhere in the room and then bounced off that. The old lady went *"Ooof,"* even though she was doped up and passed out, and it sounded to you like she'd eaten something that didn't agree with her. You could picture her sitting in a restaurant, halfway through coffee, placing a hand to her belly, saying it: *"Ooof."* And George would come around to her chair and say, "Is everything okay, Mama?"

But he wasn't doing that now, because the old lady went ass-end-up out of the bed and hit the floor, and George dropped the gun and stared at her and said, "You shot my mother."

And you said, *"You* shot your mother," your entire body jetting sweat through the pores all at once.

"No, you did. No, you did."

You said, "Who was holding the fucking gun?"

But George didn't hear you. George jogged three steps and dropped to his knees. The old lady was on her side, and you could see blood staining the back of her white johnny.

George cradled her face, looked into it, and said, "Mother. Oh, Mother, oh, Mother, oh, Mother."

And you and Gwen ran right the fuck out of that room.

In the car Gwen said, "You saw it, right? He shot his own mother."

"He did?"

"He did," she said. "Baby, she's not going to die from that."

"Maybe. She's old."

"She's old, yeah. The fall from the bed was worse."

"We shot an old lady."

"We didn't shoot her."

"In the ass."

"We didn't shoot anyone. He had the gun."

"That's how it'll play, though. You know that. An old lady. Christ."

Gwen's eyes were the size of that diamond as she looked at you, and then she said, *"Ooof."*

"Don't start," you said.

"I can't help it, Bobby. Jesus."

She said your name. That's your name—Bobby. You loved hearing her say it.

Sirens were coming up the road behind you now, and you were looking at her and thinking. This isn't funny, it isn't, it's fucking sad, that poor old lady, and thinking, Okay, it's sad, but God, Gwen, I will never, ever live without you. I just can't imagine it anymore. I want to . . . What?

Wind was pouring into the car, and the sirens were growing louder, an army of them, and Gwen's face was an inch from yours, her hair falling from behind her ear and whipping across her mouth, and she was looking at you, she was seeing you—really *seeing* you. Nobody'd ever done that, nobody. She was tuned to you like a radio tower out on the edge of the unbroken fields of wheat, blinking red under a dark-blue sky, and that night breeze lifting your bangs was her, for Christ's sake, her, and she was laughing, her hair in her teeth, laughing because the old lady had fallen out of the bed and it wasn't funny, it wasn't, and you said the first part in your head, the "I want to" part, but you said the second part aloud: "Dissolve into you."

And Gentleman Pete, up there at the wheel, on this dark country road, said, "What?"

But Gwen said, "I know, baby. I know." And her voice broke around the words, broke in the middle of her laughter and her fear and her guilt, and she took your face in her hands as Pete drove up on the interstate, and you saw all those siren lights washing across the back window like Fourth of July ice cream. Then the window came down like yanked netting and chucked glass pebbles into your shirt, and you felt something in your head go all shifty and loose and hot as a cigarette coal.

The fairground is empty, and you and your father walk around for a bit. The tarps over some of the booths have come undone at the corners, and they rustle and flap, caught between the wind and the wood, and your father watches you, waiting for you to re-member, and you say, "It's coming back to me. A little."

Your father says, "Yeah?"

You hold up your hand, tip it from side to side.

Out behind the cages where, in summer, they set up the dunk-ing machine and the bearded lady's chair and the fast-pitch ma-chines, you see a fresh square of dirt, recently tilled, and you stand over it until your old man stops beside you, and you say, "Mandy?"

The old man chuckles softly, scuffs at the dirt with his shoe, looks off at the horizon.

"I held it in my hand, you know," you say.

"I'd figure," the old man says.

It's quiet, the land flat and metal-blue and empty for miles in every direction, and you can hear the rustle of the tarps and noth-ing else, and you know that the old man has brought you here to kill you. Picked you up from prison to kill you. Brought you into the world, probably, so eventually he could kill you.

"Covered the center of my palm."

"Big, huh?"

"Big enough."

"Running out of patience, boy," your father says.

You nod. "I'd guess you would be."

"Never my strong suit."

"No."

"This has been nice," your father says, and sniffs the air. "Like old times, reconnecting and all that."

"I told her that night to just go, just put as much country as she could between you and her until I got out. I told her to trust no one. I told her you'd stay hot on her trail even when all logic said you'd quit. I told her even if I told you I had it, you'd have to cover your bets—you'd have to come looking for her."

Your father looks at his watch, looks off at the sky again.

"I told her if you ever caught up to her, to take you to the fairground."

"Who's this we're talking about?"

"Gwen." Saying her name to the air, to the flapping tarps, to the cold.

"You don't say." Your father's gun comes out now. He taps it against his outer knee.

"Told her to tell you that's all she knew. I'd hid it here. Somewhere here."

"Lotta ground."

You nod.

Your father turns so you are facing, his hands crossed over his groin, the gun there, waiting.

"The kinda money that stone'll bring," your father says, "a man could retire."

"To what?" you say.

"Mexico."

"To what, though?" you say. "Mean old man like you? What else you got, you ain't stealing something, killing somebody, making sure no one alive has a good fucking day?"

The old man shrugs, and you watch his brain go to work, something bugging him finally, something he hasn't considered until now.

"It just come to me," he says.

"What's that?"

"You've known for, what, three years now that Gwen is no more?"

"Dead."

"If you like," your father says. "Dead."

"Yeah."

"Three years," your father says. "Lotta time to think."

You nod.

"Plan."

You give him another nod.

Your father looks down at the gun in his hand. "This going to fire?"

You shake your head.

Your father says, "It's loaded. I can feel the mag weight."

"Jack the slide," you say.

He gives it a few seconds and then tries. He yanks back hard, bending over a bit, but the slide is stone.

"Krazy Glue" you say. "Filled the barrel, too."

You pull your hand from your pocket, open up the knife. You're very talented with a knife. Your father knows this. He's seen you win money this way, throwing knives at targets, dancing blades between your fingers in a blur.

You say, "Wherever you buried her, you're digging her out."

The old man nods. "I got a shovel in the trunk."

You shake your head. "With your hands."

Dawn is coming up, the sky bronzed with it along the lower reaches, when you let the old man use the shovel. His nails are gone, blood crusted black all over the older cuts, red seeping out of the newer ones. The old man broke down crying once. Another time he got mean, told you you weren't his anyway, some whore's kid he found in a barrel, decided might come in useful on a missing-baby scam they were running back then.

You say, "Was this in Las Vegas? Or Idaho?"

When the shovel hits bone, you say, "Toss it back up here," and step back as the old man throws the shovel out of the grave.

The sun is up now, and you watch the old man claw away the dirt for a while, and then there she is, all black and rotted, bones exposed in some places, her rib cage reminding you of the scales of a large fish you saw dead on a beach once in Oregon.

The old man says, "Now what?" and tears flee his eyes and drip off his chin.

"What'd you do with her clothes?"

"Burned 'em."

"I mean, why'd you take 'em off in the first place?"

The old man looks back at the bones, says nothing.

"Look closer," you say. "Where her stomach used to be."

The old man squats, peering, and you pick up the shovel.

Until Gwen, you had no idea who you were. None. During Gwen, you knew. After Gwen, you're back to wondering.

You wait. The old man keeps cocking and re-cocking his head to get a better angle, and finally, finally, he sees it.

"Well," he says, "I'll be damned."

You hit him in the head with the shovel, and the old man says, "Now, hold on," and you hit him again, seeing her face, the mole on her left breast, her laughing once with a mouth full of popcorn. The third swing makes the old man's head tilt funny on his neck, and you swing once more to be sure and then sit down, feet dangling into the grave.

You look at the blackened, shriveled thing lying below your father, and you see her face with the wind coming through the car and her hair in her teeth and her eyes seeing you and taking you into her like food, like blood, like what she needed to breathe, and you say, "I wish . . ." and sit there for a long time with the sun beginning to warm the ground and warm your back and the breeze returning to make those tarps flutter again, desperate and soft.

"I wish I'd taken your picture," you say finally. "Just once."

And you sit there until it's almost noon and weep for not protecting her and weep for not being able to know her ever again, and weep for not knowing what your real name is, because whatever it is or could have been is buried with her, beneath your father, beneath the dirt you begin throwing back in.

Dennis Lehane is the author of seven novels, including *Mystic River* and *Shutter Island*. He is currently working on a novel set in 1919 during the Boston Police Strike. He lives in Boston.

SIGRID ESTRADA

*U*ntil Gwen" *was originally commissioned by the novelist John Harvey for an anthology of stories entitled* Men from Boys. *The only requirement was that the story have something to do with fathers and sons. At the time, I'd been teaching a lot and trying to get my students to understand that a character is defined most adroitly by his actions. I eventually decided to practice what I preached, and "Until Gwen" became a story in which the main character reveals himself entirely by what he does, as opposed to by what he thinks or says. I'd also had the first line in my head for several years, so it was nice to finally attach a whole story to it and stop obsessing over it.*

Judy Budnitz

THE KINDEST CUT

(from *The Oxford American*)

The journal begins with his arrival at the makeshift hospital. "A church pressed into service, men laid out on the narrow pews, most of them strapped down to prevent their rolling off," he writes. The stained-glass windows shed colored light on faces, hands, bedclothes, the viscous oily surface of the puddles on the floor. I'm paraphrasing here. The nurse who greets him has a crimson cheek and a green one, and a yellow stripe across her mouth. Voices bound and rebound in the empty space above their heads in rhythmic waves. The sound, he writes, is "that of an enormous barrel filled with children rolling down an endless flight of stairs." He is not particularly gifted with metaphor.

The nurse's lips form a question. He shouts that he would like to wash his hands. She leads him between rows of benches. Hands reach out at her from all sides, sleeve-tugging, skirt-clutching. She brushes them away with brisk swipes, then swivels and holds a bucket out to him. He dunks his hands in the soapy solution and looks around for a towel. She offers the front of her uniform. Her whole body is hard, like a clenched fist. "Even her breasts," he writes, "feel angry."

He understands her fury soon enough. "It is like trying to move an ocean a teaspoonful at a time," he writes. Every day more men

are brought in on wagons and stretchers. They wait in the cemetery behind the church, lying on the ground, leaning against the
stones, until their turn comes to be sorted and seated in a pew. Not
enough anesthesia, not enough instruments, not enough bandages, not enough hands. "I have never in my life been made to
feel so impotent," he writes. Perhaps he is wiggling his eyebrows
suggestively as he writes this, perhaps not. Men in our family consider themselves wits but are not known for their sense of humor.

Not enough water to go around. The well has run dry. The
stream behind the church is a dusty crease in the ground. They are
hoping it will snow soon. "Cold," he writes, "equals numbness.
Poor man's anesthesia." Not enough light, not enough air.

The journal has been passed down in my family for generations,
hand to hand, usually from mothers to daughters-in-law, accompanied by oral footnotes: gossip, speculation, stories worn down
to singsong by repetition. The women of my family seem to be the
ones concerned with lineage; the men are at most ghostly pres-
ences. We have a tendency to disappear or fade away while our
women cling tenaciously. My wife sometimes eyes me specula-
tively, sadly, as if wondering when I will follow family tradition.
Sometimes in the night, when she thinks I'm asleep, she takes up
my hand and holds it tightly, tightly. I sell real estate, although I
haven't actually made a sale for some time. A bit of a lull; nothing
to worry about, nothing worth mentioning. The journal's cover
is cracked leather, the pages crumbling. The handwriting lies in precise rows on the unlined paper, with no breaks or blots. He is a
man who today would do a crossword puzzle in ink. Only near the
end do you see a change in the script. It softens. As if someone is
tugging at a loose thread somewhere and all the knotted words
begin to unravel. The last words trail off the page.

The writer is Solomon, Sol, an immigrant, the first of my family to come to this country, and who has newly completed his studies as a doctor. He has been trained in the most demanding of
surgeries, binding the body's most sensitive tissues. He comes
from generations of tailors who all turned blind before the age of

forty, but continued to stitch away their remaining years by touch alone, calling for their wives or daughters to choose colors and patterns. In his new home he has already gained a reputation, in spite of his youth and his foreignness, for his gift for weaving torn flesh together, for sewing up a wound with curlicues and rosettes.

It is this reputation that has landed him here, in the midst of a civil war he only vaguely understands. He doesn't notice if the uniforms are blue or gray. Certainly he believes that slavery is wrong, that all human beings should be allowed to live freely. But by that logic, should not the rebellious states be allowed to do as they please, if they desire it so badly? It seems hypocritical to him. Apparently he keeps these thoughts to himself. He arrives at the military hospital with his careful hands and his case of clamps and sutures and curved needles no bigger than an eyelash. He is handed a surgical saw and told to begin his new work: separating gangrenous limbs from their owners.

"I have heard that such work has a deleterious effect on a man's mind," he writes, "so I am keeping this journal to make a record of the descent." He dissects his own behavior as dispassionately as he would a cadaver. "First day vomited three times. Dizziness, and weakness in the legs. Clearly due to physical exertion rather than circumstances. Second day vomited once. Man screaming uncontrollably. Watched the blue patch of light on his tongue until he fell unconscious. Third day: no physical effects. Man says he would rather die than lose his leg. They all say this. I would like to tell him that he will most likely die anyway, but I do not. Am learning tact. When there is a pause in the screaming one can hear artillery booming in the distance. Everyone pretends not to hear it. This place is a charm school. Fourth day: all clear. Ate a sandwich at the operating table. All the others do it. Benita holds it for me and catches the crumbs in her cupped palm."

He reports that he has successfully made what he calls in his mind "the divide," so that he can perform his work in a detached way, without thinking of the life lying vulnerable in his hands. He teaches himself a kind of tunnel vision, so that in the operating room he sees mere objects in need of repair. Only afterward, in the recovery wards, does he allow himself to think of them as people.

The legs and arms pile up at his feet. He ignores them (or he reports that he ignores them: a contradiction here). Even the screaming ceases to bother him. "The acoustics of the room round out the tones," he writes, "so that it all becomes a dull roar." He believes he is doing good work, even improving these people by trimming away their excesses, these messy fringes, these frayed ends. The stained-glass light creates a carnival air. It is necessary, on days of heavy fighting, to wear wading boots and raincoats. I assume the drainage in the church is not good.

One day he records a lovely sight. He turns and sees that the sun has struck the stained-glass windows at such an angle that a blue-gold-white angel is perfectly projected on the white sheet of a bed. He points it out to the patient beneath the sheet, who looks and begins to scream, tries frantically to brush the image away, thinking it is a heavenly portent.

His sense of humor surfaces now as he grows more comfortable in his surroundings. He writes, "A man today was screaming that if I took his leg, he'd be half a man. I disagreed, but said that I could certainly take care of that if he would like, and I gestured with the saw. No one laughs, they are all prigs here. But I think I saw Benita smile."

He writes, "When I am off duty I go to the recovery hall, to remind myself of whom I am saving. These are men, with names and families and histories. They seem whole and healthy when they are lying in their beds with blankets up to their chins. I love them dearly. I give them affectionate nicknames. Shorty, Stumpy. Hoppy, Skippy, and Jumpy. Their eyes light up when they see me. I call them a band of pegleg pirates, and one of them gets in the spirit of things by trying to put my eye out. It does me good to see such feistiness."

The sign above the church door reads, GOD WELCOMES HIS CHILDREN HOME. And Sol, too, thinks of them as his boys, his children. He likes to see them bobbing on crutches or dragging themselves along by their arms. "Like toddlers learning to walk for the first time. Oopsy-daisy." He has his favorites, how could he not? "There's a soldier with black hair and a red raw face who says, 'Doctor, give me something for my ankle. It hurts, so bad.' 'Soldier, you can see for yourself there's nothing there.' 'But I can feel it exactly.' 'Phantom limb. A common effect. The nerve damage. There's nothing to be done. Patience.' 'Doc, my phantom leg is kicking you so hard in the teeth right now, if you only knew . . .'" He likes this spirit, and returns several times, but the boy always feigns sleep, a stained-glass Noah's rainbow tinting his face. He has tunneled an empty ridge under the blanket where his leg should be. Sol smooths out the blanket each time. There is no need to foster fantasies. At a certain point he knows from the smell that the boy will die soon. Soon enough, the boy is gone and a truculent one-armer has taken his place.

"Must do something about all the screaming," he writes. "My boys need their sleep. Open the windows and let it out? Hang flypaper from the ceiling to trap it?"

Benita appears in the journal more and more. She of the stubborn chin and unflinching front. He has never heard her voice. He had assumed, that first meeting, that the cacophony drowned her out, but no. Even during their brief walks in the stunted wood behind the church, he has to read her lips. He wonders if she is mute. Her tongue, he reports, "seems functional, the sublingual thread intact." Her eyebrows and arms are so declarative that there is never any doubt as to her meaning. She swabs, stitches, cauterizes. He likes the way her tiny nostrils twitch. He likes to watch her move. She shoots off sparks, exclamation marks. "Her legs," he writes, "are well-formed and exceptionally fine. Except that sometimes, when she is running quickly, her legs are almost a blur; there somehow almost seem to be too many of them."

I can see her clearly, this Benita. His descriptions are meager but I can extrapolate, color inside the lines. I know the way he thinks.

He writes of the other nurses as a herd. "They adore me from afar. They stand amazed, like chickens in a solar eclipse. I keep them at arm's length, though I could have any I choose." The narrative has been scrupulously honest throughout, so I have no reason to doubt him here. I might, however, take into consideration the fact that, as one of the few whole men among hundreds of splintered bodies, Sol would have seemed much more attractive than he otherwise might. In fact, to judge by his descendants, including myself, he must have had very little to recommend him. And as he himself writes of our family, "We are a breed impressive in neither length nor breadth, with hair inclining to the greasy, eyes tending to goggle, features unpleasing in symmetry but betraying intelligence."

Come to bed, my wife says at night when our children are asleep. Soon, I say, batting her hands away. Her fingers will soil the pages. I have not shown a house in weeks, but I still dress carefully each morning before driving away. This town does not lack for quiet places where a man can read and re-read in peace.

When my wife frowns the flesh creases and bunches between her brows. I would like to pinch it off like clay, that bit of flesh. I remember when her brow was as smooth and pure as a young girl's.

There is a soldier who grabs Sol by the jacket after an amputation and says he wants his leg back. "I can't put it back on," Sol says.

"Get it," the soldier says, "I want to be buried whole." The voice is rising, booming through the sanctuary, the fingers are digging into Sol's skin. Benita's eyebrows signal to him from across the table: Do something, they say, or all the others will start demanding theirs back too. So Sol tells the man, "Yes, yes, you'll have your leg," and the fingers loosen their grip. Sol's already thinking logistics: how to contain, conceal, preserve. How long need the leg last? How long will this one live? A day or a week at most, he thinks.

But when he looks below the table for the leg, it's already been cleared away with the others. He spots the orderly with the cart. "I want, I need," he calls but his voice is lost in the hubbub. He chases the cart outside, follows the trail of flies past the stunted wood and over a ridge and sees the pit where the orderly is dumping his cargo.

"Wait," he says, but the cart is already tipped, its cargo falling. He peers over the lip and sees the tangled mass of hundreds of arms, legs, unidentifiable bits. Each has lost its individuality and become part of a texture, a many-limbed slumbering creature. The smell is nastily familiar. Now the orderly is sprinkling lime.

"I need," Sol says, "a leg."

"Take your pick," says the orderly, mouth and nose muffled in a handkerchief. If only there was a distinguishing mark, Sol thinks. Would he recognize his own leg if it were taken from him? He looks down. Probably not. He knows others' bodies much more thoroughly than his own. I doubt he gets many chances to mirror-gaze.

"Tell you what we'll do," the orderly says, pulling him back from the edge. "I've got a lot of shoes." They bind together a stick of wood, a soldiers boot, some scraps of uniform, a bundle of rags to approximate muscle. This will never work, Sol says, but the orderly assures him it will. "I've done this before," he says, "At least I think I have. I can remember fifty years ago clear as day. But yesterday, the day before? Gone. Its a blessing, really."

And sure enough, when Sol gives the soldier the rag doll of a leg, the man is strangely comforted, hugs it like a baby.

The jealous men around him fight over it, toss it from hand to hand. The rightful owner weeps until it is back in his arms.

After several bites, instances of tripping-by-crutch, and jabs with forks, Sol is learning not to pat them on their heads.

Another time he hears a belligerent voice crying, "But I have to do it myself! I have to write my girl!" He turns to see the familiar legs (trapezoidal birthmark on the back of the right calf) of Benita bending over a boy. She's holding pen and paper, ordering him to dictate to her. The boy refuses, butting her away with his head. Sol sees that the boy has no arms. He writes, "I remember trimming this one myself. He must have been holding something that exploded in his hands, leaving shredded wings."

"They have to be my words!" the boy keeps screaming, red and writhing. "How can I send her a letter written by another woman?"

Benita is firm, insisting, shouting at him with her whole face. Just when Sol expects her to slap him, she instead steps behind the boy, props his body against hers, and threads her arms through the empty sleeves of his bathrobe. She places her chin on his shoulder, lifts pen and paper, and waits. The boy arches away from her in surprise, then looks at the perfect white hands emerging from his sleeves, poised and obedient as marionette hands. He relaxes into her embrace. He raises his knees to provide a writing surface, and puts his lips to her ear.

Sol announces in his journal that he has learned to distinguish the exact point at which the life flows out of a half-severed limb. "There is a moment, independent of the cutting of nerves or the drainage of blood, in which the life force flares before going out. It can be felt on the skin, an electrical charge. The little hairs stand up; there may be a subtle twitch."

He writes that everyone looks eagerly ahead to the snow and cold, for winter will dampen the fighting, lighten the flow of wounded, deaden the smells. But the weather refuses to oblige them. It is the most brilliant autumn he has ever seen, the leaves and the light outdoors make even the stained-glass glow inside the church seem muted. The sky is such a color, he writes, "that it makes the heart hurt."

He writes that Benita is the most exquisite woman he has ever seen.

There is a sketch of her in the margin, analytical, anatomical, unsparing in its scrutiny, neatly labeled. But not lacking in feeling.

My wife suggests that I sell the journal, or donate it to a museum. She tells me it should be locked away, kept safe. She says I am destroying it by constant handling, by the exposure to air. She says it is probably worth a lot of money, that there are collectors who would kill for this sort of artifact. "You know, the nuts, the ones who live completely in the past, the war buffs who go around reenacting the major battles with their historically accurate guns and boots and long underwear and what-have-you." She talks about the car payments, my daughter's gum surgery, and my son's college applications, but I can see in her eyes that she doesn't care about the money; all she wants is to get the book out of my hands. She thinks it is giving me ideas.

Sol writes more and more of the pleasures of pruning, of reducing bodies to their intended, essential shapes. "I am excising tumors," he writes. "I am sanding away rough spots, I am creating more perfect beings." He is shaving away corners and protuberances, revealing sleek curves. He does not understand this intense need to clutch at things, to gather all the bits of oneself together and let none escape. "Why hold together that which would rather be separate?" he writes. "Scientifically, politically, philosophically, it goes against logic. Cut off the excess, let it rot. Expose the innermost core. The natural inclination of matter is toward dispersal, chaos, not unity. I am merely helping it along. Trimming hair and fingernails is only the beginning." My illustrious forebear seems unaware that his anti-unity philosophy goes against that of the blue-uniformed army he serves. He is more concerned with the lack of gratitude among his patients.

He walks through the recovery hall now and the men pelt him with bedpans full and empty, wet socks, single shoes. They call him "The Butcher" and ask what's the special today? Chops? Flank steaks? Mincemeat? Pinches and punches land on his thighs. Kicks, both real and phantom, are frequent. "My children, my wayward children," he writes. "They don't appreciate what I've done for them." He looks into their scowling faces and is nevertheless pleased. They will come around.

Were I in his shoes, I doubt I would be so oblivious.

"I want Benita to share it," he writes. "I want to feel it together." He's referring to the electric spark, the life going out of a marooned limb. He tries to arrange the event without her knowing; when she's assisting him, he maneuvers her hand into the right spot, next to his, at just the right moment. The first attempts fail amid the confusion of the operating room—she is needed elsewhere, someone shouts, she moves her hand at the crucial moment to cauterize a spurting vessel. Time and again a limb is hanging by a thread, she turns away, and he absorbs the delicious shock alone. There comes a time when he thinks he has orchestrated everything to perfection, she is here beside him, the bough breaks, he feels "a charge so strong my fingers vibrate against hers." He checks her reaction; she is blank, but her mouth is gaping. He is certain she felt it too. "It was by my estimate ten times stronger than usual. Two receptors must increase the flow."

He's anxious to try again, and cannot resist telling her of his exciting findings. He writes that "her face immediatcly shut up like a suitcase and I could not guess her thoughts." He deduces that she did indeed feel the life force beneath her fingertips, but rejects it due to her "dour Puritan all-work-and-no-play attitude. She sees this as taking pleasure in another's pain."

She stops speaking to him completely. Though she's never said a word aloud, this new silence is a weight upon him. "She's an imbecile," he writes. "How could I not see it before. Deaf as a door, dumb as a post. I have nothing more to say to her."

Despite the break in communication, however, their relationship appears to continue. His sketches become more explicit. He details cross-sections of her limbs, trunk, nasal cavity. He draws her fingerprints, line by line. I imagine him holding her hand an inch from his measuring, tailor's eyes, studying the whorls, memorizing every ridge. Would he pause to kiss her palm, or is he too focused on the work?

I picture them as I drive to meet a potential seller. The shades are drawn. No one answers the bell. I go back to the car and wait for an hour. How do they do it? How do they find the time to be together? Sol reports working double, triple shifts without a break. They must give up precious minutes of sleep. His beard bristles must raise a rash on her neck. Her lips are chapped and dry. If only he would stop drawing long enough to kiss them. Rain patters on the roof like shot. I look at the numbers on the mailbox, at my notebook: I'm at the wrong address.

He seldom washes his body. He doesn't have the time. He is covered day after day in the sticky crust of young men's blood. One chilly evening an insistent Benita sends him down to the sluggish, rejuvenated stream in the woods with a bar of her carefully hoarded soap and a clean shirt. He writes that he is horrified by what lies beneath his clothes. "My legs, wriggling and antic, gave me the impression of beetles, centipedes, overturned, millions of legs waving madly in the air. I had the urge to stamp them out." He writes that entering the water made the situation worse. "The reflections. Everything doubled. Four arms. Horrid."

He does not report whether he completes the bath. And does not mention bathing again for several weeks. I imagine Benita's beloved nostrils cringing.

"I feel like a frog who hasn't managed to shed his tadpole tail," he writes. "A shameful aberration. Sometimes nature stalls and requires a bit of a nudge, does it not?"

Now there are sketches in the journal of streamlined bodies without fingers or toes. Fish-like, neckless stumps with fin-like appendages.

"Benita will no longer assist me at surgery," he writes. "But her heart, her heart is mine." Followed by a detailed and labeled drawing of same. The four chambers, the arching aorta. I imagine him lying with his head on her belly, his hand on her chest. His eyes are closed. He is feeling, measuring the quivering thing beneath the ribs in the same way that his blind father and grandfather and great-grandfather measured ladies for their dresses and never made a mistake.

He writes of his disgust for his body, how big and ungainly it is, how flabby and awkward. The flakes of skin, the bits of hair.

He writes that he has been warned about this feeling of his. It is not unique. The other doctors have warned him of amputation envy, an urge born out of guilt or curiosity to experience what his patients so ungratefully endure. Today it is a disease recognized by the medical community, known as Barnesfeltner's Syndrome; the men in my family have a genetic predisposition towards it. In most cases, if caught in time, it can be held in check with therapy and antipsychotic drugs.

In his time, however, it is considered sacrilege, or a weakness of character.

He does not look down when he walks. He cannot bear to watch his hands at work.

I have not told my wife about the affliction that runs in my family, but she has nevertheless intuited something. From my face, perhaps. Who knows, she may have noticed a twitch, a spasm of the lips, something that looks like disgust. In recent years she has dieted compulsively, so that she seems to be in a gradual state of disembodiment. It is as if she has removed pieces of herself and hidden them away in some safe, invisible place. She swaddles her body from my sight; she seems to feel most comfortable, most secure, in an enormous woolen poncho that hides her arms. What is it, what have I done? I ask her. Nothing, she says, smiling, laughing; nothing, she says as she takes a step back.

The weather turns colder, the days shorten, the sunlight grows pale and milky. The stained-glass windows turn dull and matte, and their projections grow faint. Gone is the magic-lantern show against the bed sheets, which has been the only entertainment for the bedridden men. They had liked to watch the colors shift, place bets on where the pictures would fall. As the sun moved, the lucky ones would get a naked golden Eve spread out across their laps, or a welter of Noah's animals sprinkled over their faces. The unlucky ones got a dying Christ's morose face on their chests. Now the show is over. Now they have nothing to contemplate but their own stumps, which nudge and wave to each other and burrow into the pillow with minds of their own.

A wave of fever invades the church, drifting from bed to bed. Bodies are carted out daily. They are buried in a field not far from the resting place of marooned limbs. Local children make temporary crosses of sticks and twine. These will be replaced by real markers soon, everyone says, but no one knows when.

A patient drags himself from his bed and hangs himself in the night. Others follow his example.

Sol is devastated. How could they destroy his work so selfishly?

Sol recalls a scene from childhood. A long table set behind a low, stone house in a golden field. Distant hills, narrow trails of white smoke from other farms chalked against the vibrant blue sky. Benches around the table, each bench crowded with sunburned men in baggy trousers, bearded elders, old women in kerchiefs, young women in kerchiefs with fat babies in their arms. Sol has been sent to stay with his great-aunt and -uncle for the summer, to keep him out of the cramped tailor shop and the deadly summer fevers sweeping through the city.

It's a celebration of some kind. Uncles, aunts, cousins, hired field workers. His great-aunt brings platters of food, jugs of wine. The other children run about the field or crawl under the table bumping people's knees, but Sol stands at his great-uncle's right hand. He holds his great-uncle's wine cup and in return his great-uncle gives him the best bits from his own plate, offered on the tip of his knife. Sol doesn't know why he is given this place of honor. Perhaps he is the favorite, for some reason. Perhaps he is simply the oldest of the small children, least likely to spill the wine.

He is watching his great-uncle carefully, ready to offer the cup before he is asked, when he sees his great-uncle's face tense up, as if he is about to sneeze. He follows his great-uncle's eyes and sees a dark figure on the hills, a rider on a spotted horse. He sees a second rider cross the hills, then a third.

His great-uncle says nothing and calmly finishes his meal. The other men do the same, lingering over the last of the wine. A silence falls over the table. The women get up and slowly begin to gather the dishes. By now there are ten, twenty figures converging on the edges of the field, and still more crossing the hills in the distance. They bring the sound of hoofbeats; the smell of torches. Slowly, slowly his great-uncle rises from his bench.

Looking back, Sol doesn't know what to make of it— the calmness, the lingering. Was it pride, or stupidity? Did the men know there was no escape, did they know they were going to die, and did they choose to face it this way, with their dignity intact, no scattering, no screaming? Sol fled, he doesn't remember where, but crammed in some tight hiding place with his fingers plugging his ears he managed to escape the devastation that followed.

Even now, even after all he has seen, he cannot say. What is better, to face death willingly and proudly, to go easily into the dark; or to fiercely cling to life, to go down fighting, enduring the messiest of indignities for the sake of a few more breaths?

The fever claims more and more of the soldiers, two of the doctors. Benita drags Sol down to the stream and forces him to wash, rubs snow into his hair. She is strong, this woman. Smothers him in her arms, shows her teeth. She could chew through the bark of a tree. I can feel how her fingers dig into flesh. He continues to write of his disgust for his body, how cumbersome and feeble it seems, shaking in the cold.

The wounded keep arriving in a ceaseless flow. The unseen war is, in his mind, nothing more than a mechanical process, and he is the final step. He continues to work, but stops visiting the recovery hall. All his favorites are gone. The armless letter-writer, the cradler of false legs. Buried, most of them. All the men he sees now are faceless; their voices are the same. "If I have to listen to one more of them cry about this person, this 'mother' they all seem to miss so much," he writes. He slices, saws, sops, and moves on.

One day Benita stops his hand. He pushes her away angrily, then sees: he has cut into the wrong leg, a healthy leg. He stares at the leg. The leg stares back, innocent, vulnerable, the red gash a seeping mouth. The bumps and tucks of flesh over the knee have a facial aspect. Why have you done this to me? it seems to say. After this, he begins to pay closer attention to his work, to the limbs he is removing. To his surprise, he sees astonishing variety and character. The arms with their branching veins ending in the fascinating mechanism of the hand. The legs with their lumps, bulges, their noble weight-bearing sturdiness. Each unique and eloquent. How could he have not noticed before? He realizes that it is the patients who sicken and die; their limbs are merely bystanders, abused beasts of burden. They do not deserve such irresponsible keepers.

"Where were you today?" the voice on the phone hisses through a storm of static. A client, a colleague, my wife?

"I was there," I say.

"No," says the voice, "you weren't."

The journal is now filled with page after page of arms, legs, feet, fingers. He feels the need to record each day's "harvest." They are arranged in neat rows, drawn in the moments before stiffness has set in, while there is still some life to them. Benita appears, jarringly, on one of these pages. It is unclear whether the limb specimens were drawn after her, or whether she was drawn on top of them. In contrast to the meticulous detail of the limb drawings, she is a hasty scratch, the lines hairy and jagged. "She has lost that buoyancy, that angry firmness," he writes. "Now her body has a sadness to it, a slackness and sag. It frowns." In the drawing, she is bent over, perhaps washing something, her hair falling down, her back a melancholy curve. He rather cruelly emphasizes the knobby bumps of her spine, the fleshy ripples on her thighs and arms. The other arms and legs seem to be raining down on her, engulfing her.

My wife has not read the journal. I should let her read it, as my mother intended. It is her right. Such has been the prescribed route of the book: from mothers to daughters-in-law, through the generations. The journal, accompanied by whispered gossip and conjecture, serves as both explanation and warning to the women marrying into this family: This is what you're letting yourself in for. I should let her read it. I will let her read it. But not yet.

Now Sol murmurs comforting words to the limbs as he removes them from their uncaring owners. He cuddles them in his arms, briefly, surreptitiously, before handing them over to the old man with his cart. Benita watches him from across the room.

She still comes to him at night, and they find private corners and hallways to lie nestled together. She tries to tell him, with her body, that she will stand firm, that she plans to survive this war, pick up the pieces, pass on the story. He is not listening.

She comes to him night after night all through the winter until the night she wakes to find his hand on her leg and his surgical saw poised four inches above her right knee. On her skin she sees the faintest of ashy lines, where he has already made the first practice stroke. His expression is stern and tender, the face of the kindly family doctor with a spoonful of cod-liver oil in his hand and a peppermint waiting in his pocket. This will only hurt a minute, his face says, you know it's good for you.

Later, remembering, she can never be entirely sure where his nurturing gaze was directed — at her face or her shin. She will later ask herself which side of the blade was to him the superfluous part, the part that needed to be pared away.

He is sorry, no, he is glad, when she runs away, the beloved birthmark on her calf dancing inside his eyelids for a long time.

Come to bed, my wife says again.

I would like to, but how can I? I have too much to do. I might miss something.

Sol discovers he cannot sleep without her. He lies awake at night clenched and staring at nothing with the wide-open, painted-on eyes of a wooden toy.

He discovers he does not really need sleep.

He draws her, inside and out. He draws her in layers, the skin peeled back. There is one mistake in his drawing, something omitted: a pear shaped swelling cradled within the flaring iliac petals, with a ripening pear-seed inside. She has not told him about it yet.

Now he focuses entirely on his work. His cataloging becomes increasingly intricate. "When a man is brought in," he writes, "I want to harvest it all, every piece. It requires all of my self-control to restrict myself to only the damaged part." At the end of his shifts, he refuses to rest, instead watching enviously as the other surgeons hack and hew.

One particularly restless day, he approaches the orderly and offers to man the refuse cart for the afternoon. The orderly eyes him with curiosity, but agrees. "I felt such ecstasy, I could feel the potency emanating from the cart, I couldn't escape quickly enough with my precious cargo." Once away from the church, he pauses to admire his booty. He confesses to chatting with his passengers, tweaking toes, though he does not record any affectionate nicknames.

He cannot bear to dispose of them in the pit with the others, so he pushes his cart into a neighboring field where the earth has been broken up and furrowed and left to rest until the following spring. After months of inhaling human emanations, the smell of soil seems utterly new. Breathe it in. He kneels, digs a shallow hole, cradles a sinewy and freckled arm for a moment, and then sticks the severed end in the ground.

He plants another. And another. The arms are mottled and stiff, raised beseechingly to the sky.

After all, he says to himself, they are not so different, are they? Armlets, leglings, seedlings. The vascular systems . . .

He plants them all. And then, like a child exhausted after play, he falls asleep. He sleeps deeply and dreamlessly. The first time he has been able to sleep without Benita's arms around him.

He wakes at dawn to a gentle shushing sound, like the ocean. He is five years old, lying on a warm beach, scent of brine and grasses in his nostrils, and a hand like his mother's hand stroking his cheek. He opens his eyes to a field of undulating arms, the palms turned toward the sunrise and nodding like sunflowers.

He returns to the hospital barely able to contain himself. He works his shift, again requests the cart, and returns to the field. The arms reach out to him in welcome.

He plants, he sleeps, he wakes to gentle fingers tickling his face.

The third day the orderly is suspicious and clings to his cart. It's heartbreaking to watch the load being trundled off to a mass grave. But it doesn't matter—we return to the field to find that the arms have multiplied and spread on their own. They are growing strong and tall. The hands begin to clap and snap as we approach. The legs kick up their heels. Sol walks through the field, caressed by hands, they tug at his pant cuffs, they wave for his attention. Clapping, wringing themselves, clutching at one another for comfort. The sound they make as the wind blows through them is like a deep and cleansing sigh, a contented murmur. As an experiment, he uproots an arm. It immediately goes limp in his hands. He feels a vicious pinch on his backside. He won't do that again.

We visit the crop every day. Soon the small patch overtakes the whole field. The arms grow tall and healthy, they are burnished brown from the winter sun, grown muscular from fighting the wind. When Sol walks through the field they reach up past his waist. We spend many nights here, warmly nestled among the arms.

We do repair work in the field occasionally: stitching, pruning. Scrapes, blisters, calluses, insect bites. Nothing serious. Nails that need trimming. Sunburn.

Come back to bed, where are you, a voice calls from far away.

All this time, Benita watches him in the operating room. He speaks to no one. He has always been an outsider, tolerated for his skill. Now he gazes into space and lets warm blood flow through his fingers. But times are desperate, doctors are scarce. He cannot be spared. Not enough hands. Benita has news to tell him but wants to wait for the right time. He will be pleased, she thinks. But is not sure.

The day he packs up his instruments and slips his journal into a pocket, she follows him.

She hears the humming roar first, and then she tops a rise and sees it: the field of golden arms waving. The boiling motion makes her think of scattering flocks of birds with a stone. She does not understand what she is seeing, at first; she thinks it is a mass of soldiers. She is accustomed to seeing masses of soldiers, perhaps they are involved in some sort of complicated exercise. Then she sees her lover striding through the field waist-deep in swaying arms, and she sees. He brushes his hands lightly over the surface as he walks, a bobbing skin of fingertips. He combs his fingers through them like hair. He grasps a wrist here and there; he falls and allows himself to be caught.

Now he has reached the far end of the field, and she thinks she will go out to meet him when he returns, and tell him her news.

She waits. She sees his head dip down and it does not rise again. She begins to run around the perimeter of the field. Barbed wire she has not noticed keeps the arms from spreading further. He is lying down. She sees his hat. One of the hands has seized it, now it is being tossed up in the air. Don't lie down, she thinks and wants to shout it. Don't lie down. She thinks of the drowsiness of drowning.

Sol rears up and sees her. He wants to wave to her, but he's got a pen in one hand, the open journal in the other, and we must finish this entry before doing anything else.

She shreds her hands on barbed wire.

By the time she reaches him most of his body has already sunk softly into the ground. She sees a patch of his brown hair merge with the soil; a scrap of his white shirt, the moist glimmer of an eye, and then there is nothing to be seen but bare earth and his hands, which she would recognize anywhere as his even if they were not adding a few final looping words to the journal before shutting it. She snatches up the journal and stuffs it inside her uniform, then reaches toward his hands, to press her cheek to one palm or both, one last time, to whisper her secret into the earth, but she is borne away almost immediately on a sea of other hands. She gets one last glimpse of his fingers, waving, penitent, raised in benediction or curse, and then his hands are swallowed by others and she is swept away. They wipe her tears, tickle her, tug at her clothes. She is passed from hand to hand, caressed, tossed, squeezed, spun. She finds her tongue and lets out a caw. She does not know, in these buoyant minutes, whether she will be raised up to the sky or torn limb from limb.

Judy Budnitz grew up in Atlanta. She is the author of one novel, *If I Told You Once,* and two story collections, *Flying Leap* and *Nice Big American Baby*. Her stories have appeared in the *New Yorker, Harper's Magazine, McSweeney's,* the *Paris Review,* The *Oxford American, Prize Stories 2000: The O'Henry Awards, The Best American Nonrequired Reading 2003,* and elsewhere. She has taught creative writing at Columbia University and Brown University.

JEFF LINNELL

I wrote this story after reading some firsthand accounts of the Civil War. Before that, I'd had only a simplified, high-school-history-class understanding of the war, so I was absolutely astonished by the carnage— fields covered with corpses, severed limbs piled up to the rafters, rivers literally running red with blood. These things sound like some sort of horrible fairy tale, but they really happened. Right here. Not so long ago. With this story, I wanted to try to use the Civil War setting to explore what war does to people—both the participants and those left behind by war, the widows and children and future generations, who must pick up the pieces when it's all over and try to make sense of it all.

James Lee Burke

THE BURNING OF THE FLAG

(from *Confrontation*)

When bombs fell on the ships at Pearl Harbor, we lived on a quiet, dead-end street, in a city not far from salt water, where palm trees, palmettos and live oaks grew side by side in meadows that stayed green through the winter months. It was a wonderful street, lined with brick houses, each with a roofed porch, closed off at the end with a cul-de-sac and a dense cane-brake, on the other side of which horses grazed in a pasture. On a rainy day, on the far side of the pasture, you could see the lighted tower of a movie theater glowing against the evening sky.

My best friend was Nick Hauser. If it was a time of privation, we did not think of it as such, primarily because no one in our neighborhood had money and most considered themselves fortunate to have survived the Depression years with their families intact. Wake Island and Corregidor fell and we heard terrible stories about the decapitation of American prisoners. But on our block, and that is all we ever called the place we lived, "our block," the era was marked not so much by a distant war as it was by the presence of radios in people's windows and on their front porches, the visits to the block of the bookmobile and the Popsicle man, and games of street ball and hide-and-seek on summer evenings that smelled of flowers and water sprayed from garden hoses.

One night a week during the summer of 1942 the entire city was blacked out for an air-raid drill. My father sat on the front porch, smoking a cigarette, a white volunteer Civil Defense helmet cocked on his head, sometimes reading the newspaper with a flashlight. Once the drill was over, the theater tower in the distance rippled with neon, and the voices of Fred Allen and Senator Claghorn or Fibber McGee and Molly could be heard all over the neighborhood. I believed no evil would ever enter the quiet world in which we lived.

But if you crossed Westheimer Street, the soft aesthetic blend of the rural South and pre-war urban America ended dramatically. On our side of Westheimer was a watermelon stand among giant live oaks, and on the other side of the street a neighborhood of boxlike, utilitarian houses and unkept yards where bitterness and penury were a way of life, and personal failure the fault of black people, Yankees, and foreigners.

The kids on the opposite side of Westheimer gave no quarter in a fight and asked for none in return. Some of them carried switchblades and went "nigger-knocking" with B.B. guns and firecrackers. Their cruelty was seldom done in heat but instead visited upon the victim dispassionately, as though the perpetrator were simply passing on an instruction about the way the world worked.

The five Dunlop brothers were legendary in the city's school system. Each of them was a living testimony to the power of the fist or the hobnailed boot over the written word. The youngest and meanest of them was Vernon—two years older than Nick Hauser and me, bull-necked, his limegreen eyes wide-set, his arms always pumped, his body as hard as a man's at age fourteen. He threw an afternoon paper route and set pins side by side with blacks at the bowling alley and as a consequence had more money to spend than we did. But that fact did not make us safe from Vernon Dunlop.

In July and August Nick Hauser and I picked blackberries and sold them in fat quart jars door-to-door for two bits apiece. Vernon would wait for us on his bicycle behind the watermelon stand, where he knew we would come in the evening, then pelt us with clods of dried clay, never saying a word, sometimes slapping us to the ground, kneeling on one of our chests, frogging our arms and shoulders black and blue. There was neither apparent purpose nor motivation in his attacks. It was just Vernon doing what he did best—making people miserable.

Then one evening he got serious. His lip was puffed and one eye swollen, his forearms streaked with red welts, his T-shirt pulled out of shape at the neck. While Nick stood by helplessly, Vernon hit me until I cried, twisting his knuckles with each blow, driving the pain deep into the bone. Then I committed one of those cowardly acts that seem to remain inside you forever, like you give up on being you and admit your worthlessness before the world. "I'll give you half my money. The blackberries are for everybody, anyway. We should have included you in, Vernon," I said.

"Yeah? That's good of you. Let's see it," he said.

He was still straddled on my chest, but he lifted one knee so I could reach into my trouser pocket. I pressed three quarters into his palm, my eyes locked on his. I felt his weight shift on me, his buttocks and thighs clench me tighter.

He cupped his palm to his mouth, spit a long string of saliva on the coins, and stuffed them inside my shirt, pressing the cloth down on them so they stuck to my skin.

"I just thought of names for you guys," he said. "Nick, you're Snarf. That's a guy who gets his rocks sniffing girl's bicycle seats. Charlie, you're Frump. Don't know what a frump is? A guy who farts in the bathtub and bites the bubbles. Snarf and Frump. Perfect."

He wiped his hand on my shirt as he got off my chest. I wanted to kill Vernon Dunlop. Instead, I ran home crying, the wet coins still inside my clothes, sure in some perverse fashion that Nick had betrayed me because he had not been Vernon's victim, too.

That evening I sat by myself at the picnic table in the back yard, throwing a screwdriver end over end into the St. Augustine grass. Our lawn was uncut, the mower propped at an odd angle in the dirt alleyway. I threw the screwdriver hard into the grass, so it embedded almost to the handle in the sod. The kitchen light was on, the window open, and I could hear my parents arguing. The argument was about money or the amount of time my father spent with his friends at the icehouse and beer garden on Alabama Boulevard. I went through the side door into my bedroom, and stuffed my soiled shirt and trousers into the clothes hamper. I bathed and put on my pajamas, and did not tell my parents of what Vernon had done to me. I told my mother I was sick and couldn't eat. Through my screen window I could hear the other kids playing ball in the twilight.

When I woke the next morning, I felt dirty all over, my skin scalded in the places Vernon's salvia had touched it. I was convinced I was a weakling and a moral failure. The song of mockingbirds and the sunlight filtering through the mulberry tree that shaded our driveway seemed created for someone else.

Nick did not come over to play, nor did he come out of his house when the Popsicle man peddled his cart down the block that afternoon. At 5:00 P.M. my mother sent me to the icehouse to tell my father it was time for supper. He was talking with three other men about baseball, at a plank table under a striped canopy that flapped in the wind, a bottle of Jax and a small glass and salt shaker in front of him.

He pulled out his pocket watch and looked at it. He had started his vacation that day and had been at the icehouse since noon. "Is it that time already? Well, I bet we still have time for a root beer, don't we?" he said, and told the waiter to bring me a Hires and my father another Jax.

My father was an antithetically mixed, eccentric man who lost his best friend in the trenches on the last day of World War I. He detested war and particularly the demagogues who championed it but had never participated in one themselves. He flew the flag on our front porch, unfurling it from its staff each morning, putting it away in the hall closet at sunset. He taught me how to fold the flag in a tucked square and told me it should never touch the ground or be left in the rain or flown after it had become sun-faded or frayed by the wind. But he attended no veterans' functions, nor would he discuss the current war in front of me or let me look at the photographs of enemy dead that sometimes appeared in our subscription to *Life* magazine.

My father had wanted to be a journalist, but he had left college without completing his degree and had gone to work for a natural gas pipeline company. After the Crash of '29, any hope of his changing careers was over. He never complained about the work he did, but each day he came home from the job and repeatedly washed his hands, as though he were scrubbing an irremovable stain from fabric.

As we walked home from the icehouse, I asked him if we could go fishing down at Galveston.

"Sure. You want to ask Nick?" he said.

"I don't hang around with Nick anymore," I replied.

"You boys have a fight?"

"No," I replied. Then I felt my mouth flex, waiting for the words to come out that would explain how I let Vernon rub his spit on me and call me Frump, how I gave him half my money just so he would climb off my chest, how I could still feel his scrotum and buttocks pressing against my body.

But I crimped my lips and looked at the cars passing on the street, gas ration stickers glued to their front windows. The light on the trees and lawns and cars seemed to shimmer and break apart.

"You all right, son? You having trouble with the other kids on the block or something?" my father said.

"There's a new kid on the next street from Chicago. He thinks he's better than everybody else. Why doesn't he go back where he came from?" I said.

"Hey, hey," my father said, patting me on the back. "Don't talk about a chum like that. He can't help where he's from. No more of that now, okay?"

"Are we going fishing?"

"We'll see. Your mother has a bunch of things for me to do. Let's take one thing at a time here," my father said.

My parents had a fight that night and my father and I did not go to Galveston in the morning. In fact, I didn't know where my father went. He was gone for two days, then he came home, unpacked his suitcase, read the newspaper on the front porch, and walked down to the icehouse.

I started to have trouble at school that fall. I had thought of myself as a favorite of the nuns, but on my first six-week report card for the term the gold stars I had previously received for "attitude" and "conduct" were replaced by green and red ones. To combat wartime scarcity of paper, Sister Agnes examined the Big Chief notebooks of everyone in class. Those who wasted any paper at all were classified as "Germans." Those who wasted egregiously were classified as "Japs." I was designated a Jap.

Later, that same day, I pushed the boy from Chicago down on the ground and called him a Yankee and a yellow-belly.

In January the weather turned cold, streaked with rain and smoke from trash fires. The kids in the neighborhood constructed forts from discarded Christmas trees in the pasture at the end of the block, stacking them in front of pits they had dug to make mud balls that they launched with elaborate slingshots they had fashioned from bicycle inner tubes.

But I took no part in the fun. I read the Hardy Boys series I checked out from the bookmobile and listened to "Terry and the Pirates," "Captain Midnight," and "Jack Armstrong, the All-American Boy" in the afternoon. Then my mother brought home a box of Wheaties that contained a picture of a Flying Fortress, and a coupon, which, when filled out and returned to the cereal company, would entitle the sender to have his name placed on a scroll inside the fuselage of a United States Air Corps bomber.

My father saw me printing my name on the coupon at the dining room table. "You sending off for another decoder badge?" he asked.

I explained how my name would be inside a plane that was bombing the Nazis and the Japanese off the map.

"Not a good idea, Charlie. Where'd you get that?" he said.

"Mom brought it home."

"I see," he said. He cracked open a beer in the kitchen and sat down at the table. His package of Lucky Strike cigarettes had a green dot on it with a red circle around the dot.

"Innocent people are dying under those bombs, Charlie. It's not a game," he said.

"I didn't say it was," I replied.

He caught the resentment in my tone and looked at me strangely. "Saw the Christmas tree forts you boys were building," he said.

"Nick and the others are doing that."

"What's going on, son?"

"They don't like me."

"I don't believe that. Tell you what. Does Nick have a flag for his fort?"

"Flag?"

My father rubbed the top of my head and winked.

Saturday morning he and I walked down to the end of the block and cut through the canebrake into the pasture. It was a fine morning, crisp and sunny, the live oaks by Westheimer puffing with wind. Kids were hunkered down behind their barricades of stacked Christmas trees, lobbing mud balls at one another, a star-spangled kite that a kid had tied to one fort popping against a cloudless blue sky.

The exchange of mud balls stopped when the kids saw my father. Nick came out from behind his fort and looked at us, his faded clothes daubed with dirt, his face hot from play.

"Got room for one more?" my father asked.

"Sure, Mr. Rourke," Nick replied. His eyes didn't meet my father's, and for the first time I realized Nick had been injured by Vernon Dunlop in ways I had not understood.

"Do you fellows want to fly this over your fort?" my father asked, unfurling our flag from its staff.

"That'd be great," Nick said.

"But you've got to take care of it. Don't let it get stained or dirty. Make sure you take it inside when you're done," my father said.

While my father walked back home, Nick and I raised the flag on our ramparts, loaded our slingshots with hard-packed mud balls, and opened fire on the enemy. For just a moment, out of the corner of my eye, I thought I saw Vernon Dunlop watching us from the grove of oak trees, his muscular thighs forked across the frame of his bicycle.

Nick's father was a decent, religious, blue-collar man, who built a clubhouse for us in one of the live oak trees on Westheimer and sometimes walked us to the Alabama Theater on Friday nights. The family did not own a car and Nick's father rode the city bus to his job as a supervisor at a laundry on the north side of downtown. He had been a Golden Gloves boxer as a teenager in Mobile, and he owned a set of sixteen-ounce boxing gloves that he used to teach Nick and the other kids to box. But he was a strict disciplinarian and admonished his children to never bring home a mark on their bodies that God didn't put there. When he took out his razor strop, Nick's scalp would literally recede on his head, as though it had been exposed to a naked flame.

At the end of the first afternoon we had flown the flag at the fort, Nick rolled the flag on its staff and handed it to me.

"My dad wants you to keep it at your house," I said.

"Is your dad mad at me?" Nick asked. His dark hair was buzz-cut, his skin still brown from summer, his face round, his cheeks pooled with color. There were dirt rings on his neck, and I could smell the heat and dampness in his clothes from playing all day.

"Why would my dad be mad at you?"

"I didn't help you when Vernon rubbed his spit on you."

I felt my eyes film at the image he had used. "I didn't tell my dad anything," I said.

"When I get bigger, I'm gonna break Vernon's nose. He's not so tough with big guys," he said.

But Vernon was tough with big guys. He found that out the

next week when Nick and I started our first afternoon paper route together. The paper corner where the bundles were dropped for the carriers was across Westheimer. Not only was it a block from Vernon's house, it was the same corner where Vernon and his brothers rolled the papers for their route. I couldn't believe our bad luck. We sat on the pavement, our legs splayed, rolling our papers into cylinders, whipping mouth-wet string around them to cinch them tight, while Vernon did the same three feet from us.

A jalopy packed with northside kids, the top cut away with an acetylene torch, ran the stop sign, all of them shooting the bone at everyone on the corner. They parked by the drugstore and went inside, lighting cigarettes, running combs through their ducktails, squeezing their scrotums. Vernon got on his bicycle, one with no tire guards and a wood rack for his canvas saddle bags, and rode down to the drugstore. He calmly parked his bike on its kickstand, flicked opened his switchblade, and sliced off the valve stems on all four of the jalopy's tires.

Ten minutes later, when the jalopy's occupants came out of the drugstore, Vernon was back on the corner, rolling his papers. They stared at their tires, unable to believe what they were seeing. So they would make no mistake about who had done the damage to them, Vernon stood up, shot them the bone with both hands, followed by the Italian salute and the eat-shit horns of the cuckold sign. Then he bent over and mooned them and shot them the bone again, this time between his legs.

He took a tire iron from his saddle bags and clanked it on a fireplug until the northsiders got back in their jalopy and drove it on the rims out of the neighborhood.

For a moment I almost felt Vernon was our ally. He disabused us of that notion by hanging Nick's bicycle on a telephone spike fifteen feet above street.

That spring Nick and I collected old newspapers, coat hangers, tin foil, and discarded rubber tires for the war effort, and hauled them down to the collection center at the fire station. We used bal-

ing wire to attach the staff of our flag to the wooden slats on the
side of Nick's wagon, and we worked our way up and down alleys
throughout the neighborhood, the wagon creaking under the load
of junk stacked inside it, confident that in some fashion we were
fighting the forces of evil that had bombed Pearl Harbor, Warsaw,
and Coventry.

At the outset of the war families in our neighborhood had hung
small service flags in their windows—blue stars on a white field, inside a rectangle of blue and red—indicating the number of men
and women from that home who had gone to war. Now, in the
spring of '43, some of the blue stars had been replaced by gold
ones.

The Sweeney boy from across the street parachuted into Europe
and eventually would be one of the soldiers who captured Hitler's
fortified chalet at Berchtesgaden. My cousin Weldon gave up his
ROTC deferment at Texas A&M and came home with the Silver
Star, three Purple Hearts, and one lung. Nick and I began to collect meat drippings from people's kitchens and take them to the
local butcher, who supposedly shipped them in large barrels to a
munitions factory where they were made into nitroglycerine.
Everyone in the neighborhood knew us by the flag on our wagon.
My father's friends at the icehouse bought us cold drinks. Nick and
I glowed with pride.

"Y'all think your shit don't stink?" Vernon said to us one day on
the paper corner.

Nick and I buried our faces in our work, rolling the top newspapers on the stack, whipping string around them, pitching them
heavily into the saddlebags on our bikes. Vernon grabbed my wrist,
stopping me in mid-roll. "Which one are you—Frump or Snarf?"
he asked.

"I'm Frump," I said.

"Then answer my question, Frump."

"My shit stinks, Vernon," I said.

"You a wise ass?" Vernon said.

"Why don't you leave him alone?" Nick said.

"What'd you say?" Vernon asked.

The only sounds on the corner were the wind in the trees and a milk truck rattling down the street.

"Your brothers went to the pen. That's why they're not in the army. Charlie's cousin won the Silver Star. I heard your sister dosed the yardman," Nick said.

I could hear the words *no, no, no* like a drumbeat in my head.

"Tell me, Snarf, did you know Hauser is a kraut name?" Vernon said.

"My dad says it's a lot better than being white trash," Nick said.

Vernon lit a cigarette and puffed on it thoughtfully, then flicked the hot match into Nick's eye.

After we threw the route, I put my bike away in the garage and walked unexpectedly through the back door of the house, into the kitchen, where my mother and father were fighting. They both looked at me blankly, like people in whose faces a flashbulb had just popped.

"Why y'all got to fight all the time?" I said.

"You mustn't talk like that. We were just having a discussion," my mother said. There was baking flour on her hands and arms and a smudge of it on her cheek.

I went back outside and threw rocks into the canebrake at the end of the street, and did not go home for supper. At sunset Nick and I sat in the treehouse we had built on the edge of Westheimer, and watched the electric lights come on in the oak grove where the watermelon stand was. Vernon's father, with two of his older sons, crossed the street and sat down at one of the tables, a cigar between his fingers, his bald head faintly iridescent, like an alabaster bowling ball. The smoke from his cigar drifted onto another table, causing a family to move. His sons cut in line by pretending they were with a friend, and brought chunks of melon, as red as freshly sliced meat, back to the table. The three of them began eating, spitting their seeds into the grass.

"I hope the Dunlops go to hell," I said.

"Sister Agnes says that's a mortal sin," Nick replied. Then he grinned. The burn on his face looked like a tiny yellow bug under his eye. "Maybe they'll just go to purgatory and never get out."

"You stood up for me and I didn't try to help you," I said.

"It wouldn't have done any good. Vernon can whip both of us."

"You were brave. You're a lot braver than me," I said.

"Who cares about Vernon Dunlop? I got a dime. Let's get a cold drink at the filling station," Nick said.

Through the slats of the treehouse I could see the Dunlops slurping down their watermelon. "I don't feel too good. I don't feel good about anything," I said.

"Don't be like that, Charlie. We'll always be pals," Nick said.

I climbed down the tree trunk and dropped into the tannic smell of leaves that had turned black with the spring rains and that broke with a wet, snapping sound under my feet. Out in the darkness I heard horses blowing and I could see lightning flicker like veins of quicksilver in a bank of stormheads over the Gulf of Mexico. But the nocturnal softness of the season had no influence on my heart and a few minutes later I knew that was the way things would go from there on out. When I got home my father was gone. That night I slept with my pillow crimped down tightly on my head.

Early Saturday morning, Nick knocked on my screen window. He was barefoot and wore short pants, and his face looked unwashed and full of sleep.

"What is it?" I whispered,

"The flag. It's gone," he replied.

"Gone?"

"I left it on the wagon. I forgot to take it in last night," he said.

We stared through the screen into each other's face. "Vernon?" I said.

"Who else?" Nick replied.

I spent the entire day locked inside my own head, my throat constricted with fear at the prospect of confronting Vernon Dunlop. My father had not returned home and I went to the icehouse to see if I could find him. His friends were kindly toward me, and when they sat me down and bought me a cold drink and a hotdog I knew they possessed knowledge about my life that I didn't.

I tried to convince myself that someone other than Vernon had stolen the flag. Maybe it had been one of the colored yardmen who worked in the neighborhood, I told myself, or the Cantonese kids whose parents ran a small grocery up on Westheimer. Maybe I had been unfair to Vernon. Why blame him for every misdeed in the neighborhood?

At dusk I rode my bike down his street, my heart in my throat, as though at any moment he would burst from the quiet confines of his frame house, one that was painted the same shade of yellow as the buildings in the Southern Pacific freight yards. A dead pecan tree stood in the front yard, the rotted gray ropes of a swing with no seat lifting in the breeze. Inside the house someone was listening to "Gang Busters," police sirens and staccato bursts of machine-gun fire erupting behind the announcer's voice. But no American flag flew from the Dunlops' house.

I made a turn at the end of the block and headed back home on a street parallel to Vernon's, temporarily triumphant over my fears. Then, through a space between two dilapidated garages, I saw our flag and staff nailed at a forty-five degree angle to a post on the Dunlops' back porch.

I pedaled straight ahead, my eyes fixed on the intersection, my face stinging as though it had been slapped. I wanted to find Nick or go look for my father again, or to get hit by a car or to do anything that would remove me from what I knew I had to do next. The sun was a molten ball now, buried inside a strip of purple cloud, the sky freckled with birds. I turned my bike around and rode back down the alleyway to the Dunlops' house, through lines of garbage cans, my heart hammering in my ears.

Then a peculiar event happened inside me. Like the stories I had heard on the radio of a soldier going over a parapet into Japanese machine-gun fire or an aviator with no parachute leaping from his burning plane, I surrendered myself to my fate and crossed the

Dunlops' yard to their back porch. With my hands shaking, I pried the flag staff from the wood post, the nail wrenching free as loudly as a rusted hinge, and walked quickly between the Dunlops' garage and the neighbor's to my bicycle, rolling the flag on its staff, confident I had rescued the flag intact.

I stuffed it in one of my saddlebags and kicked my bike stand back into place. Just as I did, I saw Mr. Dunlop shove Vernon from the back door of the house into the yard. Mr. Dunlop wore a strap undershirt and blue serge pants, and he had a dog chain doubled around his fist. He whipped his son with it four times across the back, then threw him to the ground.

"You stole money out of a nigger's house? Don't lie or I'll take the hide off you for real," Mr. Dunlop said.

"Yes, Daddy," Vernon replied, weeping, his face powdered with dust.

I thought his father was going to hit Vernon again, but he didn't. "Folks is gonna say we're so hard up you got to steal from niggers. What we gonna do with you, son?" he said.

Then he sat down on the step and stroked Vernon's head as though he were petting a dog. "What are you looking at?" he said to me.

I crossed Westheimer and pushed my bike through the oak grove by the watermelon stand and followed the path through the canebrake to Nick's house. I knocked on the door, then unfurled the flag as I waited. My heart dropped when I saw the streaks of grease and dirt and pin-like separations across one side of the cloth, printed there, I suspected, by the chain or spokes of Vernon's bicycle. But he had hung it from his porch anyway, like a scalp rather than the symbol of his country.

Nick opened the screen door and stepped outside. "Wow! You got it back. You slam ole Vernon upside the head with a brick or something?" he said.

"It's ruined," I replied.

Nick placed his hand on the bottom side of the cloth. The pinkness of his palm showed through the separations in the thread. "What are we gonna do?" he said.

My father had taught me not only how to care for the flag but also how to dispose of it if it was soiled or damaged. That night Nick and I conducted a private ceremony under our treehouse. We built a fire of grass and decayed oak limbs, and spread our stained flag on top of the flames. We stood at attention like toy soldiers and saluted the thick curds of smoke and black threads of cloth that rose out of the heat, some of them sparking like fireflies among the oaks where people were still eating watermelon. Someone called the fire department, and the owner of the watermelon stand told us he would have our treehouse torn down. Almost simultaneously Mr. Dunlop and his sons showed up, enraged that I had stolen and destroyed *their* flag.

It was a year of Allied naval victories in the Pacific, rationing about which no one complained, and Tommy Dorsey and Glen Miller on the jukebox. It was the year in which a group of good-natured firemen and the Dunlop family and the patrons of a watermelon stand stood in a circle around two small boys, like creatures whose exteriors were made of tallow, warping in the fire-light, exposing for good or bad the child that lives in us all.

It was 1943, the year my father died in a duck hunting accident down at Anahuac and the year Nick Hauser and I beat the world and never told anybody about it.

James Lee Burke was born in 1936 in Houston, Texas, and grew up on the Louisiana-Texas coast. He attended Southwestern Louisiana Institute (now called the University of Louisiana at LaFayette) and later the University of Missouri at Columbia, where he received an AB and an MA in English literature. Over the years he's worked as a pipeliner, land surveyor, social worker, newspaper reporter, and U.S. Forest Service employee. He has also taught at several universities. He

PEARL BURKE

published his first short story in 1956 and wrote his first published novel, *Half of Paradise,* between the ages of twenty and twenty-three. To date, he has published twenty-three novels and one collection of stories. Mr. Burke also managed to go thirteen years—during the middle of his career—without publishing a novel in hardcover. During that period, his novel *The Lost Get-Back Boogie* was rejected by one hundred editors. Finally published by Louisiana State University Press, it was a Pulitzer Prize nominee. His recent crime novels have received two Edgar Awards, and he has been the recipient of a Breadloaf Fellowship, an NEA grant, and a Guggenheim Fellowship. He divides his time between Missoula, Montana, and New Iberia, Louisiana.

The man who was my oldest and best friend died in February of 2004. Since his death, I have written three stories based on our boyhood, in part to commemorate his life, in part to write down my recall of what the country was like when the real Nick Hauser and I were kids.

I think my generation is the last one that will remember in an accurate fashion what we refer to as traditional America. The 1940s was a fine decade to grow up in. It was marked by privation and war, certainly, but also by enormous courage and resilience. My pal "Nick" always represented those values to me. We had wonderful times back then, and we felt good about who we were. I don't think an era like it will come aborning again, at least not in my lifetime. "The Burning of the Flag" is my tribute to it.

MR. SENDER

(from *Image*)

Obituaries, *Fayton Sun,* May 5, 1963
Hamilton Sender, Prominent Insurance Broker

Mr. Hamilton Sender, founder and owner of Sender Insurance of Fayton, died Saturday of a gun accident at his home. He was forty-two. Mr. Sender was born in Fayton and was a lifelong resident of this city. He attended East Atlantic University in Keaneville and served for four years in the navy in the Pacific Theater, reaching the rank of second lieutenant. . . . Survivors include his wife, Mrs. Olive May Sender, née Olive Carter, a daughter, Cheryl Ann . . .

Lily

If you wear a mohair sweater with just about nothing underneath, your daddy will come out on the porch cocking a shotgun. This proves he cares about you. I am eleven years old and I know this for a fact.

Mr. Sender is out there, next door. But Cheryl Ann keeps walking no matter. It's her reputation that concerns him, I am sure. She goes to her fellow, who is leaning on an Impala at the curb, his arms folded. It is December. Mr. Sender says, "Come back here." I hear him from my bedroom. The fellow holds out a cigarette he's already half-smoked. When Cheryl Ann gets to him, she takes it between two fingers and pulls on it hard, like it will take her to heaven. I wonder will it.

They drive away. I feel sorry for Mr. Sender, how Cheryl Ann defied him when he was right.

I tell Pauline about this, and her friend Sidney, who is the Senders' new maid. It's when they come back to work after the holidays. "Cheryl should have worn a blouse," I say. "People can see through the holes in mohair sweaters," I say.

"Men, you mean," Sidney says. "Not people. Well what was she wearing under?"

"A slip," I say. I saw it in the porch light through that loose knit. The color was nude. I know a good girl would never do that.

Pauline who has raised me says I shouldn't say that word *nude*. Even worse than *naked*.

"Maybe she should have worn a blouse," Sidney says. "Washed all her white ones when she came home for winter vacation. Then we wouldn't have had this trouble."

"You probably got that right," Pauline says, but Pauline sounds to me like she doubts it.

Mr. Sender is spending all his time in his tiny den, Sidney tells Pauline. Sidney's not that used to him. She's only been working over there ten months. She says she told him that Cheryl's off at the college, that she's grown. She says he walked right out not touching his eggs in a fury over that.

"I thought you didn't care about them," Pauline says to Sidney.

"I'm just saying," Sidney says. "What's he doing all day in that den? He writes insurance. His secretary covers the work, but he got to go in once and a while. It don't look right." Sidney has worked for doctors, school principals, bankers. She knows their hours, what little work they can get away with. She's always talking about what goes on in white people's houses. She likes to say. *I mean I could tell you a few things, uh-hun.*

I can hardly imagine a white man who stays at home. My daddy owns a drugstore and my mamma keeps the books. I am mostly with Pauline. My daddy doesn't see me even if I am standing right in front of him in the middle of the room. Or if he does see me sometimes when he's riled, I wish he hadn't. Mamma thinks I get away with too much. She is certain I am fat. I am ashamed of weighing ninety-seven. Pauline says it's okay if I eat something she makes, her collards with ham hocks, her shelled peas stuck up inside the refrigerator in jars only we know about. Her late lunch, what she shares with Sidney and with me. I know I shouldn't eat the food, but I can't help it. We all sit around and talk while they are waiting for their ride home. I am big for my age, thick on my thighs, and I am starting to need a training bra, but my mamma won't get it. She says I need to live on hard eggs and boiled chicken. I try, but Pauline tells me the opposite, that men love big thighs and I'm going to have me some hams. She pinches me and tells Sidney don't I have a pretty leg, won't I be something. When she says it I smile and think maybe one day I will go somewhere this is true, that men like big legs. Surely they don't in Fayton. I know this for a fact. Here white men like tiny feet and tiny hands, and the limbs to go with them. The only thing that can be big is bosoms, and girls have to look like Cheryl Ann but not dress like a you-know-what. She used to dress nice, Cheryl Ann. I used to think she was the finest girl there was. I have watched the junior high girls and the high school girls and Cheryl Ann herself grow up. She was so beautiful in high school she wouldn't have anybody. The man she found in college who came in December in the Impala is the first date she's ever had. He is handsome as all get out.

"Thighs are the whole story, you get right down to it," Sidney says, and I say, "Story of what?" Sidney tells Pauline to tell me, but Pauline says she can't.

All this time, this spring, Mr. Sender is inside his den with his rifles for hunting and his pipes and his duck decoys. He never goes out, doesn't shave for a week at a time. Sidney has kept saying, "It's Cheryl. He's pining. He writes out long letters to her he doesn't send."

"He have to let her go," Pauline says.

I have trouble imagining it. A man who loves his daughter and misses her when she is gone.

So Palm Sunday is coming on. Everything is early this year. I am standing in the doorway at the Senders' house with a tray of leftover cupcakes from the sixth grade Easter party. On top of each one is a marshmallow chickadee. I might have eaten them all in a single afternoon in front of the TV, but instead I bring them to Mr. Sender, for he needs some cheering up. I know this is Christian of me.

Sidney stands in the Senders' back hall and tells me I am sweet, but she is under instructions from Mrs. Olive not to let people bother Mr. Sender. But then he comes out of his den. He is smiling a little, and wearing a robe and pants, and he says, "What is it, Sidney?" And he grabs a cake off the tray.

"Delicious, devil's food," he says with his mouth full. It is a big mouth, I notice. So is his Adam's apple, and his neck is long. "You the little Stark girl?"

I think of course he must know about me, since I know so much about him. I live right next door. But I say, "Yes, sir," because you never tell a man what you think. I know this the same way I know about mohair sweaters and reputations, and the shame of showing slips and wearing dark hose before high school. You tell men what they want to hear. You need to learn that if you are going to get one. I know I have to practice.

The next week Sidney comes over to my house with a present. A stuffed animal for me—it says my name, Lily Stark, on the card. It's from Mr. Sender. It's a green duck with small black eyes.

"Looks to me like a duck he might hunt," Pauline says.

I know why Pauline would say that: she doesn't like Mr. Sender. I am thrilled no matter. I go upstairs and put a big lilac bow around its neck. One of my own, for my ponytail. Next day I go over there to thank him. This time Mrs. Sender asks me what I want. When I say, she says, "My husband is indisposed. You know what that is?"

Of course I know what *indisposed* is. I have a good vocabulary.

Mr. Sender comes out then and tells his wife to shut her mouth, and he brings me back into his den. Then he shows me a thing I don't know: what pipe cleaners are for. For going down inside the shaft of a pipe, not just for crafts at school. He shows me about packing the bowl, and puffing on the pipe to get it going.

When I tell Pauline about this time I spent with Mr. Sender, she doesn't see what a nice man he is. She says, "He got guns in there, don't he?"

"He's so lonely," I say. "He misses Cheryl Ann. It is going to be Easter. He gave me a present for Easter. Easter is about loving people and rising from the dead."

"Well why don't you stay over here in the afternoons for now?" Pauline says. "You do that for me?"

I know this isn't Pauline's business. I say to her, "I don't have to listen to you." When I see what comes over Pauline, how her eyes float and fill, I cry. I won't say I'm sorry. I know I don't have to. I am growing up, and I don't have to. I don't even have to mind her. She works for us.

When I run upstairs I hear Sidney going at Pauline for being partial to me. Sidney doesn't believe in taking up for white people, or spoiling their children, at least to hear her talk. Sidney says I am spoiled and I hear her. Spoiled sounds to me like something that's turned like milk, and then you throw it out. I hate that word. There is no coming back from spoiled.

This is the routine on Saturdays since I turned eleven: my parents go to the store at seven-thirty to open up, while I am still in bed. Pauline goes shopping and then comes home in a cab with the groceries. She gets to the house about the time I wake up to watch cartoons, sometimes about an hour later. She makes me breakfast.

This Saturday the phone rings before Pauline gets there. It wakes me up, and Mr. Sender says on the phone, "So, do I have the little Stark?"

I have dreamed of this call. I have hoped all along he was going to call me.

"You want me to show you a trick?" he asks.

I get up and put on my shorts and a sleeveless top—a pretty set, with ruffles—and I run over there in my flip-flops.

The Sender house is all open doors. I find him in his den. He's unshaven. His shirt is old and worn, and his head looks too long and seems too pale, but I know I must overlook all that. He looks right at me like he can see me, all of me. He says, "Did you ever get that duck?"

I think it is odd he's forgotten I'd thanked him, but of course I lie. He is a man, "Oh yes, I never told you. I am so sorry. I gave him a bow."

The door to his den swings closed. I see he has one of his shot-guns on the leather-top desk. It's not too long. Its handle is wooden. Same one he took out on the porch that night.

He says, "Come here."

And I go.

And then he says, "Watch me," and he takes up his pipe. He draws a mound of smoke into his pipe with that mouth of his, and he blows out a ring after a minute. Then he blows out another ring, inside of the first. And the two rings float there as if they are doing a dance. This is magic to me. He hands me the pipe. A pipe, and I have never smoked. Cheryl Ann took her fellow's cigarette, I know. So I take it.

He says I should take my tongue and put it at the top of my mouth. Then when the time comes, I do it, with the smoke hovering there at the roof of my mouth. Just when he says to, I let it go out from the perfect circle I have made with my lips like he told me to do. First try, there it is.

"Beginner's luck," he says.

And he has seen how I can be wonderful, and no one else except Pauline has ever seen that. But I am mad at Pauline. Then he touches my cheek, and he says, "Come here." While I watch the ring, I come there, to him. And I see how the smoke is floating in the air, catching light like dust, for it is dust, dirt, and it makes me cough, but I tell myself it is nothing, and I tell myself to look at it. In this light it is beautiful and bluish. I know sometimes you have to ignore things, just look at the bright side. Ladies do that all the time, I know this. Being a lady is all about ignoring things.

And then when I am in his lap, he puts his hand on my waist, and then he puts his hand down under the elastic, and down, way down there. I know he has made a mistake; his hand has gone down inside my shorts, not outside. So I buck my hips up, because this will make his hand slide out without embarrassing him. I know that's the right thing to do, not embarrass him for his mistake. I think I hear someone outside, someone calling me. I buck up my hips, but when I do this, he puts his hand right back. I squirm over a little, and then I look into his face, because I will have to explain to him. I will have to say it sweetly, in a whisper, I know this, that his hand is in the wrong place. I shouldn't seem mad. And when I am about to look in his face, I think, maybe he will say my name and give me a kiss, when he takes his hand out. But when I look up he hasn't got a kiss, just licking. He should know my name. He calls me the wrong name. He calls me Cheryl.

"Be still," he says. "Don't you know what you came for? What is the matter with you? Don't you know? Don't you know? Don't you know?"

Pauline

Everything happens at once, but you have to look at it one thing at a time. That is being alive and it is a shame sometimes. There are several mysteries in this story, if you go through it from one end to the other, event by event. But there is a place you can reach where the mysteries disappear.

After Christmas that year, it bothers me Lily has gossip. She says Mr. Sender next door was chasing after his daughter Cheryl. Cheryl's eighteen, in college. She can date, but her daddy has never liked it. The child says it was how Cheryl was dressed that he didn't like, and I say, "Uh-hun, I see," like that was it. But that is how you have to raise them so they don't know anything.

My friend Sidney Byrd is at the table listening. She works for the Senders, but she was off Christmas week too, and didn't see this fight. She thinks the Senders are one family don't have enough to say to each other, so she is surprised there was carrying on over there. Husband and wife never speak, never argue. Sidney doesn't know Cheryl Ann, because she's been away at the woman's college. I have seen her grow up. Mrs. Olive don't think much of her daughter. This has been true for years and years, I'd say since the child was ten. Sidney has noticed it the short time she's been there.

Of Lily's gossip, Sidney says, "I think Cheryl seems all right, but some will surprise you. No telling what hell the girl might raise."

"Sidney," I say, to tell her not to say *hell*, for the child, Lily, is just eleven. Her mother don't want her to curse, and I don't believe in it. I have been watching Lily since she was born—took her home from the hospital cause her mamma wanted to sleep off the labor in the quiet.

Sidney tries to fix it. She says to Lily, "I'm not talking about preacher hell."

There, that word again. Sidney Byrd has been getting in trouble for what she says long as I have known her.

I have known her since I was sleeping three to the bed with my sisters in my daddy's house when he was a sharecropper down at the south of the county. We put up tobacco when we were girls and should have been going to the school. She likes to speak her mind, but I love her.

Since she has been working at the Senders', every weekday afternoon I call for her when I am finished with cleaning and supper, and ready to go home. I use a field-hand whoop that slides from low up to high. For town it sounds a little wild and we both know it, but we like it.

I have a late meal with her—piece of pork with greens, maybe corn bread, food I don't make for Lily's parents. We have our time out together, waiting for our ride.

The man I used to be married to, Miller Jones, is our ride. He has a big red Pontiac with a turquoise interior. He has been coming around lately.

The Starks are the only white family I ever worked for. Sidney has been working in town much longer. She has lost more than one job for gossip, some because her bosses are crazy. White people don't know how to act, is what she always says. She has studied it. They are Baptists and they have fine things and ought to know something, but they do not. We have an excuse, she says, we have white people, but white people don't have one. In the houses she has worked in — not trash, the good families — mostly the white women are crazy the way they run from the men. They can't breathe hardly in their girdles, much less make any headway. Like they like to get caught. She's seen rich women be tackled by their husbands and their clothes torn, tumbling like football boys, and smile during it. The men can do anything they want, anything, she says. And sometimes the women. Whichever it is, one day you get caught in the middle.

I say it is not true, for it has never happened to me. I have never been caught in the middle. But it is getting ready to happen.

"You ever notice a white man won't take up with a woman who has any normal idea what is going on?" she asks me that night, after we hear the gossip from Lily. We are riding in Miller's car.

I say, "White women can't think too good, because none of them eat enough. They wouldn't know a meal if you put it right under their chins." I start to laugh, and I turn to Sidney who is in the back. Sidney won't sit up front with me and Miller even though he has the room.

"I mean it, why you cut them slack?" Sidney asks.

I don't answer. I don't know. I was born a peaceful person, want everybody to get along. Which is what makes all this hard to explain, if you look at it as it goes along, not all at once.

We get to her place, a tiny pink house with a porch coming off and trumpet vines all over, not blooming, but full and still green, which seems a miracle this late in the winter. She lives with her mamma since her boyfriend Raoul was shot at the Golden Parrot. He was with another woman at the time. She has not gotten over it. I say good night to her. And all Sidney says to Miller is, "You go in to work after this, don't you?" Not even a thank you for the ride.

Miller mumbles at her. He has a mustache these days, and as always, the big head. He is after me to marry him again, and he knows how Sidney feels. She believes he will run all over me if I let him back into my life. The way he did before.

I tell Sidney he has half an hour before he has to leave for his shift. And she says to me, "You can get into something in half a hour, Pauline. You watch it."

She slams that Pontiac door. I have always let Sidney tell me what to do, some. She has always had more opinions than I have.

I have been with Miller two different times: once when I was sixteen for two years, and again when I was twenty-five, for three and a half. Now we are in our thirties, and he says he has changed. In some ways he has.

The first time I ran off with him to get away from my daddy's house—I was the second oldest girl and my mamma was almost blind. We married quick in South Carolina, where you didn't have to be but sixteen, lived in colored enlisted housing at Fort Bragg down in Fayetteville. The apartment was cinderblock, which was the most solid house I had lived in up to then. We had good times. But Miller made me sick and I didn't know. By the time I saw the army doctor he just went in without asking and took my nature. After that I was nearly too sad to breathe. I wouldn't go when Miller got transferred to California, even after my daddy told me I was his wife and I should follow. I didn't want nothing to do with him, when I learned what he had done, how he got what he gave me. So I left and decided to see my oldest sister, Rose, who lived in Philadelphia on welfare for four daughters and worked besides. She had a huge apartment, nice, warm, with big windows, but there were too many streets in Philadelphia and too many strangers. I worked in a factory sewing life preservers and had to ride a whole lot of busses to work before the sun rose, and I never knew for sure the bus drivers would take me where they said they were taking me. I just didn't trust them, don't know why. Besides my sister Rose had men friends and one of them liked me, and I was done with men then, so I left. Went home and found work with the Starks.

I liked Mrs. Stark at the start. She was dark-haired and from the North, that is, Big Washington, and she said she would teach me what I didn't know about cooking for white people and keeping a house. And she did. Then she got pregnant with Lily and handed the child over—like I was the one knew everything about a baby—because I was colored I would know. So I learned. Lily was a fat one with long arms, a girl with sweet breath. I couldn't stand it almost, how pretty she was when she came out.

About that time I was set up at the Starks, Miller showed in his Pontiac. Drove it home from California. He had money for a house from the Veterans and he said he would be true. So I went and lived with him in a house with shingles and brick. But then he was gambling and drinking and we lost it all, including the furniture I had bought on time with Mr. Stark's name on the notes. I had to divorce him good that time, to leave his debts. Mr. Stark told me. I made Miller go to the courthouse and we both signed the paper.

And now, years have passed, and Miller has sobered up and paid back everybody, including Mr. Stark, and got a good job—shift cook at the hospital—and the Pontiac engine rebuilt, and seats recovered. And he has started showing up every day to give me a ride home from the Starks. And I have been bringing Sidney along so he doesn't try anything. He knows Sidney doesn't like him, but he drives her to keep me happy.

Sidney wants me to hate him. It has always been hard for me to hate people up until this.

February and March, Mr. Sender is Sidney's only subject besides Miller. I wish she wouldn't keep on it, for Lily hears everything. So I say to mock her, "Sounds like you care for him."

"I am just saying," she says. "I don't care. You the one who cares."

I think, it is not a sin to care for a person. Even if they are white. But Sidney is stronger than I am, so I have always believed, and I don't cross her.

"What do the preacher say?" Sidney says, to apologize. "I have been to that well many times, and I know now by heart it is dry."

She means white people will always let you down and down and down no matter how they may seem. I am not ready to believe this about all of them, and she knows it.

"Something wrong with him," she says. "Like he's sick or dying. He don't leave the house. I'm just wondering what it is."

I see Lily wondering about Mr. Sender. Lily has sympathy for people. In this she takes after me.

But Lily is white with brown hair, nothing like me at all. She has glasses, and her mouth is crooked, and she thinks her daddy won't look at her because she is ugly, and her mother says she shouldn't eat so much. Yet I do feed Lily like a human being: I won't starve her. Every way else, I raise her like they want me to. I don't tell her what men do, or what her period is going to be, because her mother don't want me to. Mrs. Stark is a businesslike woman, works all the day long, but she thinks Lily should be spared, should grow up and marry rich, never cry. To do this you have to stay ignorant, she believes.

Palm Sunday coming on, Lily starts going over there to see Mr. Sender. I don't like it. He's not doing well, not going to work.

Right before Easter he sends over a big ugly fluffy stuffed duck with Sidney. I think she is getting pretty old for a stuffed toy, but she thinks it is great, and she runs upstairs and gives it a ribbon of her own for round its neck. So I am alone at the table with Sidney, who has been riding me all afternoon about Miller. I don't like looking at everything the way Sidney does. It makes me distrustful, and agitated.

Then Miller comes.

"Ready to go?" he asks at the back screen door, same as he always asks. He's on time, four-thirty. He's been on time for six months.

And something gets into me. I say to him, "Will you wait till I am done cooking? The corn pudding has not set."

He stands there a minute with his hat in his hand. He is balding some and his eyes are dark and large. He says, "If you say." And he sits on the back stoop and waits for us, like that.

When I have closed the back door on him, Sidney says, "Well, I didn't think I would live to see that."

I say, "See? He's changed, like he says he has." I am more amazed than Sidney. And I don't even feel terrible about it. I feel pretty good. This is the first mystery in this story.

"Just wait," Sidney says.

When I get home that night my sister Rose calls long distance from Philadelphia to tell me she is having another baby and she don't want it and she has prayed on it. She wants to go to a man in Allentown to get rid of it. She might die if she goes to Allentown, but she wants to do it. Her boyfriend doesn't know, and he wants to live with her, and four children is enough. If he lives with her she won't get as big a check, but he is a mason and he has work. So what should she do?

"Well, tell him, and ask him is he a man," I say to her.

She says would I say that. I say maybe, and this seems true, although I never asked it of Miller. I think now I might.

"You, Pauline?" she says. "You?"

A few days later Lily says Mr. Sender had her over to see him again, and I tell her right out she had better not go over there. He has guns in his den and he is out of his head, can't even get washed and dressed and go to work.

And Lily for the first time gets that look other older white people get, and she says, "I don't have to listen to you."

There is no way around what she means.

Then she runs upstairs and she's crying.

Sidney says, "See? She just like the rest. Why you spoil her? See? Look at it Pauline. And why can't she give her own self a ponytail, you still combing out her hair? And why can't she clean her room, or put her clothes in the hamper, or run her own bath?"

It breaks my heart how Lily spoke to me. And then I think, it's not right, the way she can say anything she wants.

A few days after, I am out in the garden hanging wash. I come in the house to see her, but the child doesn't answer. I remember that Sidney has left early for a funeral. I go over to the Senders and stand on the back porch. There is a door split in the middle, and window on top. I can see in—the back hall that goes to his den, unlit. Mrs. Olive's car is not in the driveway. I wonder if Sidney has locked up. I reach for the doorknob, then catch myself. My heart hurts in my chest.

Then I see Lily turn in the drive on her bicycle, so I settle down. She's sweet to me. She's sorry what she said the other day. I don't believe she is a bad child. I still don't believe that. But she is not my child.

That Friday Sidney tells me Mr. Sender is not even coming out to eat anymore. She says she doesn't think he wants to live.

That next Saturday in the A&P, I feel as if I've left the Starks' house with a pot going. I haven't even been to there that day. I go shopping for the Starks before I go to work. I have the manager call for me, and I am waiting outside for one of the four cabs in Fayton what will haul colored people. I have hoped to get Sol Bascomb, who is one of my favorite white men. He has helped me from time to time with my sweet potato pie business at Christmas, delivering.

It is Abel Odom who finally shows. A good old boy, the worst. I ask him can we hurry. He says he will see about that. There is something wrong with the latch on the trunk in his nasty cab, so he puts the Starks' groceries in the back. There is no room on the seat for me when he is through. I am too wide. I hesitate.

"What?" he says.

Sol and the other taxi drivers let me sit in front. I reach for the front door handle.

"What makes you think you can ride there?" he says.

So I get in the back, squeezed against seven brown bags of groceries. He slams the door before I'm all the way in, so my face jams up against the celery stalk poking out of one. The door handle is pressing in my back. He is going slow as he can down Sycamore Street. I am not going to be provoked, I tell myself. I am not, and on an ordinary day, I wouldn't be, but today I can hardly bear it. I am burning. I stare out the opposite window, over the seven standing bags of food. I see the white bungalows with waxy-leaved bushes in the yards, look like they never grow or change. These neighborhoods are hunched under the gray clouds. A house is never a color in this part of town, just brick or ghostly. The whole town of Fayton seems like it is hunkered down. Finally, we pull into the Starks' drive.

Closer I get to the kitchen door, the worse I feel. Inside, I say, "Lily? You up?"

Odom is bringing in the bags because he knows I will tell Mrs. Stark if he doesn't. When he's finished I leave the tip on the table and go into Lily's bedroom. Nobody in the bed, nobody in the yard when I look out her window.

Soon as he's gone I run out of the Starks' house, across the side yard, and through the Senders' back gate.

I get to their back stoop. Dutch door is closed. I take the knob this time. Then I am standing in the back hall calling Lily's name. I see Mr. Sender's den door is closed.

I am strong in my body at this point in my life. I have put up tobacco and slaughtered stock from the time I was eight until I left home with Miller. But this is the second mystery here, how I push in Mr. Sender's door, don't think about it.

He stands and Lily rolls out of his lap. Her shorts down around her little thighs, she tumbles to the floor.

I look at him straight in the face. I have never done this with a white man. This is the third: I see something gleamy-glinting dart behind his eyes, trying one eye and then the other, as if his eyes are lookouts, and if it is quick enough, I won't be able to look in. I am held there in a stare. Lily is struggling with her pants. They are little cotton pique I put in bleach-water and washed the day before. I yell at her to get out, but she can't walk yet. Her legs are bound by the elastic.

That's when Mr. Sender reaches down for his long gun. Old, like the one my daddy borrowed once for close range, not for hunting, to kill a pig who had eaten what they had put in the barn for the rats. He wants to know what I think I'm doing in his house.

You know what he calls me.

He is looking right at me, with that pistol pointing in the air, the butt of it in the crook of his elbow jammed into his side. So I can't look down. Finally Lily crawls to my leg. I reach down one hand and yank up her shorts. I thank the Lord there is no zipper. I tell her to get out again, and she does it. I am still staring at Mr. Sender.

I see it again behind his eyes. It is trying to cram itself down into some lie. I see that.

When Lily is gone, it comes all the way out. And it is going to spit in my face and then beat me good, and say how sorry it is. It is going to grab hold of me and throw me down. I see it swirling around everywhere, not only in this time and in this room, but about Lily and me when we are alone, in the lies I have to tell her, the lies I have to go along with. And around me and Miller when he's been cruel. I see that army doctor took what wasn't his to take. I see Odom when he slammed that car door on me, just ten minutes before.

I see it spread out over the whole of Fayton, and the people having to crawl low down, afraid to pull up for fear of it. It is stealing everyone's sight. It is the same as Mr. Sender's pipe smoke but it don't let up. It is drifting dark, making it hard to see or breathe, or to want to.

Then I see Mr. Sender there. He's in front of these other things I see. Yet I see them all. He is the gate to them. His open mouth is the door. He's calling me things, saying filthy things. There's his gun, but he looks too pitiful to be able to shoot me. It is pointed up, towards himself. I reach for his fingers holding that pistol. My hand covers his hand. I cannot believe what I am about to do.

Later in the day, Sidney says she is so shocked: "I thought some were bad, but I wasn't ready for this white man. I revise my opinion. Mr. Sender takes the prize." Sent in there to clean up the blood, Sidney has read the notes he wrote that say, *I love Cheryl more than my whole life.*

"Been crawling in his daughter's bed since she was nine," Sidney says. "Imagine that. He confessed it on paper. I'd kill myself too if I was a wretch like that. Mrs. Sender don't think I can read? Been mulling over it holed up in that room, brokenhearted over his baby daughter taking a new lover. Call him her *new* lover. Can you imagine?"

And I lie to her and I say I can't.

For I don't say what I have done. Or anything about Lily. After, I have picked up Lily's flip-flops from the yard, and I have told Lily nothing happened, because that is my job and now I despise it. Lily has gone fast fast fast asleep.

By that night I know I must live another life. On that Monday I stop working for the Starks. I have been caught in the middle. I have been party to too much that is false.

Very late in my life, when I am about to die, I tell Miller the truth, because it doesn't seem right to pass on with it, take it with me where I am going. I still doubt myself sometimes. I still wonder then. He says, "You, Pauline? You a saint. You?" He refuses to believe me.

And I still cannot explain how it happened. How I knew. How I went through those two doors without fear. How I faced him, a white man holding a real pistol mouth wide open, gaping gate to all those lies.

And I can't explain what happens right after: it comes to me to boss my sister Rose, that very night, tell her she better have that baby, and in a few months I go to Philadelphia on a bus and am not afraid of the driver. I am there when she is born, and I name her Tamara. I bring her home from Philadelphia and I decide I will not stunt her, I will raise her right. I move in with Miller, and this time he does respect me because I make him. And we have Tamara for our child. He becomes a different man. Even Sidney admits it finally. The best part of my life happens after that day in Mr. Sender's den.

That Saturday, though, I can't know any of what will happen. In fact, I have no thought of the future, for if I do, I will surely run for my life. For the future I have just described cannot be imagined. I am just staring into his ugly eyes watching something I've never seen so clear dart from here and there, trying to hide in some claim he is about to make. It is amazing to behold, brazen, dark. I know more words and more words are going to come out of his big brown pink mouth where the barrel will fit so perfectly, I see. I know what he will say: that the whole world is his, how that will never change. But he only owns one mean little part of the world. It is his lie that the smallest part is the whole, is everything. I must already know there is more that day when I reach up toward his arm and pull down a little and squeeze his hand on the trigger, so the bullet goes through the roof of his mouth and into his brain. I just can't stand to hear him anymore, hear him tell his small mean lies over and over and over as if that would make them true.

Born and raised in Goldsboro, North Carolina, Moira Crone is the author of three books of fiction and the forthcoming *Where What Gets Into People Comes From*, a collection that includes "Mr. Sender." She has taught at Louisiana State University for many years and directed the MFA program in 1992 and from 1997 to 2002. She has received fellowships from the Bunting Institute of Radcliffe College and the NEA. She has also been awarded the Pirate's Alley Faulkner Society Award for short fiction twice. This is her fourth appearance in *New Stories from the South*. She lives in New Orleans.

RODGER KAMENETZ

This story began with an image that no longer exists in the story. When I was driving one day in Baton Rouge, I saw an oyster-shell path in a cemetery. For some reason I remembered that the first funeral I ever went to was one for a man in our neighborhood who had killed himself by putting a shotgun in his mouth. Someone said at the time—I recalled this thirty-five years later—that the man had "loved his daughter too much." On the street in Baton Rouge, something that was not meant by this remark started to form into a story in my mind. It became a broad story, with even another point of view, in which Sidney has the last word—about Pauline and about Lily, and about Mr. Sender. I have gone on to give Sidney her own story, in which she is still, as an old woman, haunted by these events. I have also written a story in which Cheryl Ann is living in Paris. What began with a remembered, misinterpreted remark has begotten a rather extended web of voices that explore how such an evil could have branched out into the world. No other work I've written has been quite as generative as this one, or as difficult to find an end to. Mr. Sender has that name because it's associated with cinders, Hell.

Robert Olen Butler

SEVERANCE

(from *The Cincinnati Review*)

After careful study and due deliberation it is my opinion the head remains conscious for one minute and a half after decapitation.

—Dr. Dassy D'Estaing, 1883

In a heightened state of emotion, we speak at the rate of 160 words per minute.

—Dr. Emily Reasoner, *A Sourcebook of Speech*, 1975

EARL DAGGETT
laid-off Mississippi heavy-equipment operator, beheaded by his lover's husband, 2003

Elmer, that economy-size coon turd who is my friend, points his shotgun straight up over his dang head—and mine, if you please, I'm standing right next to him—and he goes and does this so fast I ain't got time to jump away from sharing his rightly-earned fate, he pulls the trigger fixing to kill a squirrel and instead of bringing buckshot and tree limbs and small-animal guts raining down on our heads, like ought to be the outcome, he plumb misses the whole tree and falls backwards—he's got that bad a damn aim—and likewise his thumbs is always about hammered to pulp whenever it's

time to tarpaper his barn or fix a porch plank or whatever, and he
don't even deserve the love of Maisie who has billowy warm thighs
and Elmer probably can't even manage to get it into her honey pot,
not with both hands on his pecker and a red flag flying between
her legs, so I figure I'm okay as I open one eye and it's only half
past two and he should be at the planing mill and Maisie is still
snoring like a rotary saw beside me and I just jump up and grab my
pants and make one clean leap: here I go right now I am so light
and graceful like a greyhound at the track I am through the window and clean plumb away from his ax

MAISIE HOBBS
Mississippi woman, beheaded by her husband, 2003

night dark as fresh tar on the county road we roll through our
trailer park late from Wednesday church and I rest my chin on our
Chevy's door and one lit window after another goes by Mandy
Lou leaning into Henry him putting his arms around her and shadows going up and down beside the flicker of Lila's TV and I'm
thinking I'm fixing to grow up and take a man inside me and I'm
moving along in another tarry night through the woods out back
of Stanco's Lawn Ornaments and Tombstones and he's got me by
the hand saying sweet things like *you little dual-exhaust you, you little roadrunner let me rev you up,* and I keep on batting at him till
we're on a stump at the quarry pond and this is the good part this
is the part I knew I'd like, the cuddle beforehand, him knowing I'll
say yes and it makes him cuddle good cause I told him already it's
the only way he's going to get inside me and I say I got to have a
great kiss first and then he can go down there to what he wants and
he squares around and puckers and he moves in fast glancing off
my nose and sliding along my cheek and he says *oopsie doops sorry
there Maisie* and I say *that's okay Elmer* he's so cute being clumsy I
know I'll marry him

CHICKEN
Americanas pullet, beheaded in Alabama for Sunday dinner, 1958

little grit things in the straw here and I peck and peck and they're gone and I go over there a wormy thing but it's a leaf stem which I always grab but it never goes mush like an actual worm which I look and look and listen for and the flying ones come down and they walk among us and they cock their heads and hear the slither in the earth and they grab and up one comes but after a rain it's good for me the worms come up and I run here and I run there and I eat and the grit is good too over there I go for grit though the soft slither is even better but it's dry now dry all around and they are vanished, wait, wait, the rest of me is gone and from beyond the wire from past the dog-leap from down the long ruts I can hear a muttery cluckering and it is like when I broke at last from the eggy wall and into the light and a fluff of feathers hovered near and made this same sound but this muckery wuckering is vast, this at last is the hen who fills the sky, and I am rushing now along the path and the clucking is for me and it is very loud and a great wide road is suddenly before me and she is beyond and I cross

---

Robert Olen Butler has published ten novels, four volumes of short stories—one of which, *A Good Scent from a Strange Mountain,* won the 1993 Pulitzer Prize for fiction—and a book of lectures on the creative process, *From Where You Dream.* His latest book of very short stories, *Severance,* debuted with Rivages in France this year (as *Mots de Tête*), to coincide with a ballet based on it and performed in Lyon. His stories have appeared in many publications and have been chosen for inclusion in four volumes of *The Best American Short Stories* and eight volumes of *New Stories from the South.* Among his awards

are a Guggenheim Fellowship in fiction, the Richard and Linda
Rosenthal Foundation Award from the American Academy of Arts and
Letters, and a National Magazine Award for fiction. He teaches creative
writing at Florida State University.

*I*n 1995, I took my soon-to-be wife to Saigon for the Vietnamese New Year.
We visited the War Crimes Museum, and there, among the rusted
American tanks and artillery and the unexploded bombs, was a guillotine
that had gone steadily about its dark business until the French abandoned
Indochina in 1954. I was stunned by its ethos, and I soon learned of the lore
surrounding it: a severed head, it was long believed, had enough blood left in
it to sustain consciousness for a period of time, the exact length of which was
hotly debated. A book of very short stories thus began to shape itself in my
imagination, each story the internal monologue of a recently severed head. At
first I thought they would be strictly Vietnamese heads, produced by this
machine I'd seen. But soon the whole history of decapitation opened itself to
me, and the several dozen heads I have now written range from Medusa to a
truck driver in Iraq. These three Southern heads are among my favorites,
especially because an age-old question is answered in one of them. Not
incidentally, on the basis of the math implied in the two epigraphs, each story
is exactly 240 words long.

Cary Holladay

JANE'S HAT

(from *Five Points*)

Back when stocking caps were in fashion, those long knit caps of bright yarn with tassels on the end, back when my friend Jane had the best stocking cap in school, Mr. Overton Underhill came hiking up behind us and snatched Jane's cap right off her head.

It was February, 1968. Just that afternoon, Mr. Underhill, who was the principal, had lectured our class on earthquakes. "The ground opens up in a sneer," he had said, and thus I had learned the word *sneer*.

And now he had stolen Jane's cap.

"Ha!" he said and pedaled away with it, his face—with its stubbly cheeks and eyebrows like check marks—swivelling back to gloat at us, the cap rippling in his grasp.

Jane and I were on bikes, too, and we gave chase, pumping our legs hard as we could, keeping him in sight, once getting near enough to see that one of his shoes was untied. He was too burly for his bike, but he was so fast. Sweet wind blew through the broomsedge on either side of the road, and the overarching trees were rusty with winter. Yet it was a warm, fine day.

He beat us to the railroad tracks, where a train came by. It was such a long, long train. Jane and I stood straddling our bikes in its smoky breeze, and when it was past, we rolled across the tracks, but he was gone. He wasn't at the grocery store or the post office or on the porch of the old hotel—the public parts of Glen Allen—or if he was, he'd hidden the bike and gone inside. He must have been far down Mountain Road by then, or off on one of the side roads that still felt like country.

"Where's your hat, Jane?" her mother asked when we burst into her house.

"Mr. Underhill's got it," Jane said, but her mother wasn't listening. She was fitting a cowgirl dress on Jane's sister Tammy.

"Where's my boots?" Tammy demanded.

"Mr. Underhill's got 'em," I said, and we all laughed, even Jane's mother with her mouth full of pins. Tammy giggled, but carefully because of her lipstick. In my mind I heard what Mama always said about Tammy: *Five years old and lipstick on, and the way she dances.*

Jane never did get her hat back. From then on, whenever we couldn't find something, we'd say, "Mr. Underhill's got it!"

But hadn't he given us something, too—the beautiful chase with the sweet wind and the trees overhead and only the three of us on that empty road almost too narrow for two cars to pass? The intervening train was only fate, and the world was about to change anyway, so why worry about a hat?

"Have you ever seen a blackbird fly with a dove?" Mr. Underhill asked everybody, in assembly, the day after he stole Jane's stocking cap. "No, and you never will. Still, we must accept the decisions the government makes for us, however misguided."

I thought of the earthquake lecture, how he had interrupted Miss Stancil in the middle of her math lesson to deliver the information about the earth opening up like a sneer. "I must ask you to make them welcome," he said, turning to address the teachers, who sat very straight in the aisle seats of the auditorium as he strode back and forth on the stage, "but I don't ask you to fly with them."

The blackbirds would not come in a flock, just a few at a time, we learned: a trial period. There would be a girl, Dorothy, in the sixth grade, and her brother, Herman, in Miss Stancil's fifth-grade class—Jane's and my class.

Mr. Underhill said, "Any questions?"

How vast the silence was, with a hundred children and six teachers thinking about blackbirds and doves. I stood up and said, "What about Jane's stocking cap?"

But the instant I spoke, the bell rang, just as the train had hurtled between Mr. Underhill and Jane and me on our bikes, twenty-three hours earlier. So nobody heard me. They just got up and shuffled out the double doors at the rear of the auditorium.

Back in the classroom, Miss Stancil announced that she had intended to give us a quiz on earthquakes. "But I forgot to write it up!" she said.

Jane laughed, with Miss Stancil joining in. So did everybody but me. I felt vaguely disappointed, for I loved mimeographs, if not quizzes: purple sheets of paper with that chemical scent. No quiz. And it was time to go home.

But I was marking time by the theft of Jane's hat. I had loved it, the knotty, holly-green expanse of it and the ball of yellow fringe on the end.

It had smelled of Jane's mother's perfume, ancient precious stuff from France with that smell like cider and roses, the perfume that Tammy wore for her Little Miss Virginia pageant rehearsals—where who would preside as chief judge, but Mr. Overton Underhill? Tammy was doused with the fabulous perfume, whereas Jane and I had to steal it, drop by drop.

The day of not-flying-with-blackbirds wasn't over, not even after the assembly and the canceled quiz. As Jane and I set out on our bikes, we encountered Mr. Underhill again, but this time he was on foot, beside the chain-link fence of the playground, on the path we sometimes took through the woods—the alternate way to Jane's house. The previous day, he had addressed us both, or maybe just Jane, with the one word, the syllable, "Ha!"

There on the path, he raised his palm and spoke only to me, as if we'd been talking for a long time. "Laurie," he said, "don't ever let anybody know *how* easy it is for you."

"What's easy for you?" asked Jane, as we hurtled pell-mell

through the woods, leaving him behind. "Math?" she said. "What did he mean?"

My mouth opened, and the answer came out: "Forgiveness."

Jane stopped her bike so fast she fell off it. "What?"

And I said it again.

"I don't remember that," Jane says of the stolen hat, as we eat bistro fare at a restaurant in downtown Richmond, nine miles from Glen Allen, a restaurant that used to be a train station. Its great round clock still hangs on the wall. The ticket counter is a salad bar. Jane wears thin, elegant black clothes. Her fingernails shine; her scarlet lips purse when she smiles. Her rich husband is a bad, bad man, who will gain your trust in a real estate deal and take you down with him. Jane never wants to leave her house. She will talk on the phone, but it's hard to get her to come out to lunch. Unless I go visit her, I rarely see her. She spends her days watching rented shoot-em-up videos and laughing, laughing when the bad guys win. Or the good guys, either one. Just as she laughed when Miss Stancil said, "No quiz!"

Yet isn't there understanding in that laugh, of a kind I haven't got yet?

"Do you remember Dorothy and Herman?" I say.

"Dorothy and Herman who? Hey, leave me some of that goat cheese, Laurie."

They had their parents' eyes. They had known longer than we had about the integration: I read it in their faces.

"Get away from the raisins!" boys yelled from the monkey bars at recess that first day, while Dorothy and Herman held hands in silent counsel on the playground. I watched as a sixth-grader—Andrea was her name, a preacher's daughter—lured Dorothy and Herman to a seesaw. The arch in Andrea's neck should have warned them. Once they were seated on the seesaw, decorously rocking up and down, Andrea reached out and punched Dorothy in the back, fast as a blink.

Dorothy felt it. Of course she did, but she didn't show it. She kept riding the seesaw, slowly, her eyes on her brother's. Herman lowered the seesaw to the ground. Together, he and Dorothy retreated to the edge of the playground, to the spot where Mr. Underhill had spoken to me. Andrea, with her best friend Marge, chased them and chanted, "Blackbirds! Mr. Underhill says you're blackbirds!"

Their mother did cleaning, sometimes, for my mother. Mama had praised her for the way she could iron a shirt. Their father had helped my father tear down a tiny old house in our backyard, and Daddy had let him have some of the lumber.

Jane and I had stood out back, watching the house come down, and I think Herman was out there too, helping his father.

"Who used to live there?" Jane asked my father.

"Oh, servants," Daddy said cheerfully, stacking the weathered green-painted wood, "servants for people long ago, people who had money. Not like us. We're poor folks."

So the old house came down. It was a fire hazard, Daddy said. He called the Negro man "Joe." Joe called him Mr. Spires. But even now, wouldn't that be all right, when one man employs another?

See-saw, Margery Daw. How does the rest of that rhyme go? Was Andrea's friend really named Marge, or am I getting it mixed up with the rhyme?

"Go away," Andrea said after she hit Dorothy, and again after Herman led his sister away from the seesaw. Marge echoed, "Go away!" But Herman and Dorothy had already gone as far as they could, without running away from school. They ignored the taunts from the swingsets and the jungle gym, where children cavorted and hung upside-down.

I was with Jane, of course. I said the dumbest thing: "I bet Dorothy and Herman would like to climb the monkey bars, but nobody'll let them."

"It's too hard, anyway," Jane said in the reasonable way that I loved, "and it's not that much fun."

"Think of something fun," I said, feeling sick as I watched the brother and sister, severely composed, keep up a semblance of conversation with each other, out of earshot of the rest of us.

"I can't," Jane said. She was watching them, too.

"It was fun when Daddy tore down the old house," I ventured.

"No, it wasn't." Jane turned on me, her eyes flashing. "That could have been a great big doll's house for us, if your father had let us have it."

"He was afraid it would fall down on top of us," I said.

"And how would that have felt?" Jane asked accusingly, as if a caved-in house would have been my fault.

Tammy's pageant was the same week as the hat theft and the integration, and at the last minute, she changed her mind about what to wear.

"I want to be a hula dancer," she told her mother, who had lost so much weight in anticipation of the pageant that she looked like the praying mantis on Miss Stancil's desk at school, a dried mantis that a boy had found in a field, its hard, plated face all anxious. "I want a grass skirt and flowers in my hair."

Tammy's mother said, "But you'll have to learn a whole new dance, a hula dance, in just three days."

"I will," said Tammy.

And she did. Jane and I were her audience, while their mother played "Aloha-Oe" on the thumpety piano and Tammy swayed her hips, shook her silvery curls, and minced around barefoot.

"You're really good," I couldn't help but tell her.

"Thank you," Tammy said, but she was accustomed to compliments. She had won beauty prizes before, but they were small-time ones. Little Miss Virginia was major.

"And it can't hurt that we know Mr. Underhill," Tammy's mother said for the thousandth time, with a rippling chord on the piano keys.

"Mr. Underhill," I said, his image lurching into my mind, the green stocking cap a pennant in his hand.

"Don't tell," Jane hissed at me.

"Play it again, Mama!" cried Tammy. "And this time, make it sound more like Hawaii."

She pronounced it "Ha-*wah*-yah."

The pageant was held at the Miller & Rhoads Tearoom. The tearoom had a real runway, where on weekdays, at lunchtime, stylish models showed off the store's latest fashions. Jane, her mother, and I watched in disbelief as Tammy was knocked out in Round One, not even making the semi-finals, despite the presence of Mr. Underhill with his bald head bowed beneath the lights of the runway and the fact of his chief-ness in the whole row of famed, prominent judges.

Afterwards, heading back to the car, Tammy tore loose from her mother's handhold. She shredded the grass skirt so that her green panties flashed to all the other parents and contestants, many of whom sobbed as they raced to the sanctuary of their cars. Tammy's face was a wrecked palette of mascara and rouge.

The judges had unanimously chosen a red-headed juggler from Norfolk who I could swear had breasts, though she was only seven. She looked dumb: her tongue poked out from her teeth. Yet she won.

During the ride home, while a last gardenia blackened in Tammy's hair, a conviction lodged itself in her mother's mind: the belief that Mr. Underhill wanted to kidnap Tammy.

"You stay away from him, you hear?" her mother said.

"I never even see him," said Tammy, who would not start first grade until September.

"I'm afraid he might try to get you," her mother said. "I have good instincts for this sort of thing."

In the back seat of the car, Jane widened her eyes at me. I thought she was incredulous, as I was, at her mother's remark. Instead, she was gazing raptly past me, at an old downtown bridge with stone arches.

She said, "It's beautiful, isn't it?"

"No more pageants, Tammy," their mother declared, "not when the judges are kidnappers and crazies."

"But Mama," Tammy bawled, "I want to be Cleopatra next time."

Jane let her head fall back and stared at the bridge as we drove beneath it. "Beautiful," she whispered.

Jane started finding beauty everywhere: the toilets, for example, in the school restrooms, toilets that were cracked porcelain affairs from the nineteen-teens. Their design was so graceful, Jane said. There was beauty in the amber light of afternoon when we rode our bikes, and she used the word *amber* proudly. Miss Stancil's voice was beautiful, Jane said, when she led the class in the Pledge of Allegiance. "Notice it, Laurie," she said, "such a pretty, clear voice, with the same local accent that you and I have got."

How did Jane at ten know about local accents, our accents, apart from the way other people talked?

And Herman's face. Herman was beautiful, Jane said: "See the way his cheeks are round, but the rest of his face is thin."

"I'm going to tell him you said so," I said.

"I already did," she said. "I love Herman. I told him that, too."

We watched as he tossed a ball to Dorothy, a blue ball they had evidently brought from home, their wrists poking out of their coat sleeves. Dorothy was as tall as a grown woman.

I said, "Does Herman love you back?"

"I'm not telling you," she said. "I know better than that."

Beyond that day, I have no clear memories of Herman, and only one more of Dorothy. She was in my home ec. class in high school. I can see her bent over her sewing machine, feeding bright cloth to the needle, her foot working the electric pedal.

In the restaurant, twenty years after saying she loved Herman, Jane smiles as she says, "Tell me the rest of the story, Laurie, but fast, because I have to get on home."

"I hated Mr. Underhill," I said, "because of Herman and Dorothy. I never spoke to either one of them. That was my fault."

"I just don't remember that," Jane says. "I do remember that pageant, when Tammy didn't win." And she chuckles.

Mr. Underhill did one other extraordinary thing.

This was at Christmastime of my junior year, when Jane and I were going to the big high school that served the whole county. By then, Mr. Underhill and Miss Stancil were far, far behind us. Mr. Underhill never kidnapped Tammy. He quit his job as principal and was teaching geography at a small private school. He lived at the old hotel, which hadn't been a hotel for about fifty years and was instead a rental property for the humble, just a few families in the big drafty building—though Mr. Underhill surely had enough money to live somewhere else had he wanted to. He'd gotten funny over the years, as my mother put it, getting so very quiet, he who had once burst into classrooms and held assemblies.

Back in the glory days of the hotel, so the legend ran, a deer park had surrounded it, and sure enough, the descendants of those deer were still around, shy creatures living in the nearby forest. Walking very quietly in the woods, you might glimpse one. Somehow, Mr. Underhill captured two of them and put them in a home-made wire pen outside the old hotel, a large comfortable pen equipped with hay and a water trough and strung with Christmas lights. A sign said, SANTA'S REINDEER.

I loved the deer. I went every afternoon to visit them, to reach my hand through the pen and pet their noses if they'd let me. They were magical, splendid, and amazingly tame—two small does. They smelled like the woods, and their eyes, when they met mine, were so gentle that I wanted to cry.

Everybody went to look at them, feeding them carrots and apples and sugar cubes and calling them reindeer, even though they didn't have antlers. Their pen was the center of Glen Allen in those days before Christmas.

Every morning when I rode the bus to school past the old hotel, I saw Mr. Underhill out front tending to them. Jane didn't ride the bus. She had a wild boyfriend, Dave Becker, who drove her to school and back. Some days, they didn't make it to school.

Jane and I led busy lives. We had "school spirit." We sang in the glee club and had parts in the class play. We were cheerleaders, even though we thought our orange uniforms were ugly. We brushed our long hair flat and wore thin black ribbons around our necks. And all the boys were after Jane.

Even the young, handsome history teacher, Mr. Wells, seemed to have a crush on Jane. I was madly in love with Mr. Wells. I dreamed of going to the prom with him, of sneaking kisses, of having as many babies as he wanted.

He pointed out that our neck-ribbons were not a new fashion. "During the French Revolution, aristocratic ladies tied red ribbons around their necks to mock the guillotine," he said, stopping Jane and me in the hallway one day, as people rushed around us.

I grinned at him, waiting for Jane to flirt back. She always knew what to say. But she snapped, "Don't *talk* to me about death."

She grabbed my arm and hustled me down the hall with her. "I just can't stand it, is all," she said, pulling the ribbon off her neck and throwing it to the floor.

"What's going on, Jane?" I said.

"It's stupid old Dave," she said. "He said how much fun it would be to shoot those reindeer. He's got a bow and arrow. I broke up with him this morning, but it's all I can think about—that he might do it."

"He better not," I said, my stomach lurching.

"Let's go check on the deer," Jane said, "right now."

"How? We don't have a car."

"We'll get Mr. Wells to drive us," Jane said, as if this were routine.

We found him in his empty classroom, eating lunch from a paper bag. He listened gravely to Jane's story, and then he did drive us, cutting out of school in mid-day to take us back to Glen Allen in his van. Snow was falling, but melting as it hit the windshield. Jane sat up front with him and I sat in the back, thinking, even through my fear for the deer, how fascinating Mr. Wells was, how much he knew. He pointed to a sweet gum tree and said that during the Civil War, with candles in short supply, Southerners soaked the round green seedpods in lard and used them instead, lighting the stems for wicks.

Jane said, "But still, they lost."

"You could have said *we* lost, Jane," said Mr. Wells, "but you didn't. Interesting."

"Oh, it was so long ago," Jane said, "and war is so boring."

"Not really, on either count," he said, pulling up in the yard of the old hotel.

"They're gone!" I cried.

We tumbled out of the van. The pen was empty, its chicken-wire walls and log corner-posts stripped of the Christmas lights and hay. The dirt floor was covered with hoof prints, as if the deer had danced there, or struggled to get away from Dave Becker and his bow and arrow, but there was no blood.

"Where are they?" said Jane.

"I let them go," said a voice behind us. We turned and found Mr. Underhill standing there, burly as ever, his arms crossed over his chest. "They were restless," he said. "It was never my intention to make them unhappy. I took them back to the woods."

Jane burst into tears and hugged him, while his arms dropped to his sides and his check-mark eyebrows rose up and up. How long had it been since anybody hugged him?

"I'm so glad," Jane said. "Thank you."

"I've got to get back to school. We all do," said Mr. Wells. "Laurie, Jane, let's go."

"I'm not going back," I said.

Jane released Mr. Underhill, wiped her eyes, and said, "Laurie, we've got cheerleading practice!"

"You go on," I said, turning away from her. "I'll call you tonight."

"Aren't you glad about the deer?" she said. "What's the matter, Laurie?"

"Of course I'm glad," I said, and I was. A sob of relief hovered in my chest, right by my heart. So what was I mad about? "Go on."

And she and Mr. Wells rolled away in his van.

"I remember now, I do!" Jane's eyes meet mine fully, her mouth an O of surprise. She counts out a big tip for the waitress. "I remember Mr. Wells driving us out there. So what happened next? Did you call me that night?"

"No," I say. "I had too much on my mind. I kept wondering if you and Mr. Wells had pulled over in that van and, you know, taken advantage of it. He was damn good-looking."

"Laurie!" she hoots, swinging her head over her empty plate of cream cake. "He was never my type. Look, I've got to go."

She hugs me and takes off, shrugging a black shawl around her shoulders, shaking back her blonde hair. On the table is the little Styrofoam box that the waitress brought for Jane's leftover sun-dried-tomato ravioli. "Jane, you forgot something," I call after her, but she's gone—fast—just like she and Mr. Wells had left, once they knew the deer were safe.

In retrospect, in make-believe, I confront Mr. Underhill. I say, "Stocking cap," and he grovels. I ask how he caught the deer, and he tells me a secret, that all he had to do was step into the woods and open his arms. I say, "Blackbirds," and his confession is ringing and passionate.

But I was sixteen, and melodrama was too tempting, too everlasting, to resist. The van was far down the road, Jane's waving hand still visible. I knew Mr. Wells was talking to her in his urgent way, and that he would not miss me one bit. My anger fell in on itself like the little torn-down house.

"I'm never going back to school," I told Mr. Underhill. "Sure you will, Laurie," he said, as if we talked about this all the time, "and it'll be grand."

The sun came out as I turned and left him. I headed home, telling myself I was letting him off easy because it was Christmastime, that another day I would punish him as he deserved. Sunlight caught in the trees, and I was the only one on that old, narrow road, so how could I help but be happy?

A native of Virginia, Cary Holladay is the author of a novel, *Mercury,* and two collections of short stories, *The People Down South* and *The Palace of Wasted Footsteps*. Recent stories appeared in the *Hudson Review, Black Warrior Review, Idaho Review, Gulf Coast, New Letters,* and the *Southern Review*. Holladay received the 2002 Paul Bowles Prize for fiction from *Five Points* and an O. Henry Prize in 1999. She teaches in the creative writing program at the University of Memphis.

I hadn't thought of stocking caps in years. Then I saw a child wearing one, and the first event of "Jane's Hat" took shape in my mind: an eccentric principal biking up to steal a girl's hat off her head. The memory of that fleeting fashion brought back recollections of something much more important—the process of integration at the semirural school I attended in the 1960s. Black students were enrolled gradually, a few at a time. It must have been so hard for them, but they were mature, gracious children.

I envisioned this narrator first as an adult, trying to maintain a friendship with a mysterious woman who had been her childhood chum, and then as a child, gradually becoming aware of all the secrets surrounding her. It's fascinating when two people's memories of shared experiences don't match. That divergence of personal histories is where I find a lot of stories.

Lucinda Harrison Coffman

THE DREAM LOVER

(from *West Branch*)

Two weeks after Dr. Congreve's last lover, her absolutely final attempt at romance, a mainland Chinese Ph.D. ABD graduate student in economics with a carload of books and a heavy political agenda, stormed out of her life, shouting over his encumbered shoulder up her apartment stairs, "tie ash beech," she began to dream of his would-be successor, an image of a man so bizarre it could have been dredged up only from the brackish backwater of her childhood. She had been raised in a less than modest concrete block house next door to a shop that retreaded old tires in a Southern town where the exciting thing to do on Saturday night was to walk down to the Electric Freeze Drive-In and sip a milkshake and watch the bugs hit the electric bug zapper. She had escaped the despair of her youth by pursuing an academic career, and now being an educated Southerner and rapidly descending into middle age, she supposed she was obliged, even in dreams, to conceive of life and love in terms of the grotesque.

In the dream her next lover, a redneck with hairy arms and a beer belly the color of a catfish's underside, is coming to pick her up. She has not bidden him to come, or agreed to his coming; there hasn't been as much as a phone call, only a certain and dreadful knowledge in her heart that he will come. She hears the backfire of his muffler, the screech of some disintegrating automotive part against concrete, the groan of the dying behemoth as he cuts off the engine. She parts the curtain to peek out. There it is, the huge old sea-green car, fenders painted in black primer, the door on the driver's side battered and wired shut. Her horror increases. Her revulsion at all that is poor and ignorant— and proud to be so— rises in her throat, but she cannot scream or turn from the window. Empty beer cans clatter to the gutter as her dream lover scoots across the dirty sheepskin-covered seat and kicks open the passenger door. Sometimes his hair is black, sometimes as pale as a baby chicken's; it is always long and greasy. But the unnerving detail, the thing that has nailed her soul to the despised cross of being Southern, and therefore second-rate, whose axis of geography and blood has crucified her ambition to set herself above all this, are the words emblazoned on his T-shirt, IF YOU AIN'T IN DIXIE THEN BUDDY YOU'RE IN HELL.

She woke with the taste of burning rubber in the back of her mouth and the clear conviction that it was only a matter of time until the dream lover would come for her in reality. Who was he, what did it mean? As real as the dream had been she had only an impression of a face, at once deformed, ugly, yet beautiful and generous. The nature of the deformation remained veiled. What was it? A broken nose, a harelip, a geosyncline of upthrust and overturned teeth? But his eyes were a deep, moist brown— and kind— that much was clear.

It went back to her childhood, as everything always did, the exhusbands, the former lovers, the Chinese graduate student, now the dream. Her father had been a welder, and her mother the putupon kind of woman who stands over a perpetual sink of dirty dishes. In her mother's case the sink was under a window that looked out upon the retread shop and a sea of stacked tires. The odor of burning rubber permeated the house, the furniture, their clothing, even their hair.

"Do we have to live here?" the child who would become

Dr. Congreve protested. "Why can't we live in a place that smells good? Why can't we be like other people and live in a nice house in a neighborhood that smells good?"

"Now, Sister, that ain't no proper way to look at life," her father would say jovially. "What a person smells is all in their head. You don't smell nothing, do you Mother?"

Her mother placed a bowl of soup beans and a plate of cornbread on the table. She was a calm woman who never contradicted her husband—or felt the need to. "I don't smell a thing except maybe the onions in these beans. We're very fortunate people because we have beans to eat and the gift of smell. Be thankful for what you got, Sister. Besides, when you grow up and get married and get a place of your own you won't have time to smell anything, so enjoy smelling while you can. I think the smell of onions is lovely, don't you, Daddy?"

She had no siblings. She was called "Sister" because she was Southern and a girl. If she had had a brother he would have been "Buddy" and she was glad he had not been born. Sometimes she closed her eyes and imagined Buddy only to kill him off in a tragic fire or a lingering childhood disease. In spite of herself she believed in her father's principle of imagination. As she matured so did her imagination. Lovers became the lovers she needed. She imagined herself brilliant and convinced scholarship boards of her brilliance. She loved college and her professors. She saw in their eccentricities and affectations that they, too, had imagined themselves brilliant and exceptional. The world was illusion. She pursued an academic career.

In spite of her understanding the dream lover did not go away. Night after night he drove up to her apartment house and kicked open the car door and a cascade of beer cans clattered to the gutter. He smiled up at her behind the parted curtain, and then he winked, knowing and confident. His features remained vague, at the same time grotesque and beautiful. She woke in a flush, feeling as if she had been sleeping on a stove. She grew weary and baggy-eyed and barely alive for her nine o'clock class. Was he not

some subterranean Freudian forerunner of the next real lover to
come? She decided that what she needed was a change of scene, a
new challenge, a final dispensation from the need to imagine love.
She applied for, and accepted, a position at a small college in New
England. Dr. Prunty, the head of the English Department, seemed
as spare and aloof as the school and the town. The schools where
she had been a student, then a teacher, had all been Southern, state
universities known for their athletics. He rose from his desk and
offered her his hand. His eyes were the color of chocolate and quite
lovely. She stifled her imagination before it could fire its engines
of romance and illusion. "Welcome to Laedmore College, Dr.
Congreve. Quite possibly we may tend to be more classically ori-
ented and committed more to developing a sense of individualism
in the student than your vitae indicates you're accustomed to." He
gave her a secretive, smug look. "We're really quite radical here at
Laedmore. You'll probably have to do a bit of adjusting." She felt
relief that Prunty was pompous and perhaps a fool, at least enough
of one that at the height of her powers of imagining dullards into
princes it would have been a tedious job to have done so with
Prunty. Here she would be safe from the perils of imagination and
love. He gave her the address of a fellow member of the department who was going on sabbatical and had a house to rent. "His
cottage is most charming and quite affordable. And you'll find
Froudard a delightful chap"— he cut his brown eyes to the edge
of his desk—"if you can overlook his most apparent failing, which
considering your background, might be difficult."

As promised, the cottage was made to order, a weathered Cape
Cod. A chubby little man in L.L. Bean clothes opened the door.
"So you're the new girl in Remedial."

Dr. Congreve felt herself bridle; it may have been a rhetorical
question, but she felt it needed an answer. "Actually, to be precise,
Rhetoric and Composition."

"A rose by any other name, my dear. Prunty just phoned. Said
you were from the South and were looking for something charming, by which I suppose he means old and out of plumb. These

Midwesterners think anything a hundred years old is old. Prunty is very Midwestern and intolerably decent. I am, thank god, neither. By the by, I'm Froudard, Renaissance. Do come in." He led her to a comfortable living room lined with paintings and books. He poured sherry into glasses that she guessed were antique and probably valuable, not that she knew or cared about such things. "Has Prunty told you the details of my sabbatical? Of course he hasn't. Compassion isn't his forte. Well, you're a Southern gal and should understand familial responsibilities. My son, you see, is dying."

She started to mumble some words of commiseration when a large yellow tabby appeared and jumped into Froudard's lap. "Actually, Jerome is my adopted son. I've promised him a trip to Italy. Prunty can be such a shit. You know what he said when I requested sabbatical leave? 'I don't think the Dean considers taking young men to Disneyland before they die trips significant academic jaunts.' Can you imagine anyone that heartless?"

Dr. Congreve was beginning to wish she had made her own housing arrangements. It wasn't fair to involve her in personal tragedy and interdepartmental squabbles before she had even begun the semester. Her glance went noncommittally about the room from one painting to another, trying to find something nice and neutral to say. They were abstracts, sharp angles of brilliant color. The best thing, she supposed, was that they would stir one out of whatever sort of torpor one might be in. The sole and welcome exception caught her attention; a reproduction of Renoir's *The Boating Party* hung over the mantel. "I see you like Renoir," she said. Even a stupid comment was better than a conversational vacuum; on that score she would never escape being a Southerner.

"Ah, that pitiful thing," Froudard said, "Jerome insisted on hanging it there. I'm afraid his appreciation of art is at best nascent, and now, of course, it will never become more." Froudard sighed, deflating his L.L. Bean togs. She felt sorry for Dr. Froudard. He didn't seem the type to have a wife and child, and as he showed her around she saw no signs of a woman's presence. The house was dusty and books were piled on every available surface. A rag and a can of furniture polish would do wonders, and the rent was right. She took the house for the school year or "until that time," which they both obliquely understood to mean Jerome's passing.

She settled comfortably and safely into Laedmore and Froudard's cottage. She met no man worthy of her imagining him into a lover other, perhaps, than Prunty, who, thank god, was married and a twit. Fortunately, Laedmore was conservative, WASP, and primarily female. And as yet she had not spotted any good-looking exotic foreign types like Deng strolling across the campus.

She had created Deng, as she had all his predecessors, out of her ragbag notions of broadening her view of life and her need to shock herself perhaps as much as others. They had picked each other up in a bar. When he told her he preferred a woman of experience she took it as a compliment to her maturity and status. When he said he was devoted to the development of democracy in his country she pictured him a freedom fighter in Tiananmen Square. His real interest in her turned out to be sex in every conceivable position and place (wouldn't an older woman be more adept at such things) and his radical politics were sadly consumer capitalism: his vision of a new China had more to do with putting Pizza Huts at every crossroad than with human rights. Love, or her imagination of it, died when she realized that Deng was more American than she. But that was past. Blessedly, the dream lover had vanished, except occasionally at the edge of waking to the groan of pipes or the creaking of a board in the middle of the night, a glimpse of a disfigured mouth or eyes that mocked with their lovely deep brown. Sometimes she imagined she smelled burning rubber when she woke, then realized she had forgotten to change the cat box.

The second week into the semester Prunty left a note in her mailbox to please drop by his office. The departmental inner sanctum was guarded by the obligatory bitchy and graying department secretary and a small herd of graduate students. They lifted their heads in unison as she passed through their territory. Prunty rose when she entered. A tall, slender man, he was unexpectedly clumsy, as if he strove against unseen currents. Getting up from his desk he spilled his coffee. She had known men who were capable of exploiting such awkwardness, demonstrating their boyishness. Prunty, she sensed, was beyond the charm of artifice. She sat down stiffly and pulled her skirt down over her knees. She hoped she looked as proper and fortyish as she felt.

"Just received a note from Froudard in Italy. Can't seem to lay his hands on a copy of Bartelomeo's *Renaissance*," Prunty said, accenting the second syllable so that the word sounded negative and horsy. "I've looked 'round his office, but no luck. So, would appreciate if you'd have a look-see at your place."

"Certainly. By the way, did he say how his son is doing?"

Prunty looked startled. She went on quickly, "The boy who's dying. Jerome, I think his name is." She knew she had blundered, but was at a loss as to how.

Prunty got up and closed the door to the outer office, upsetting the wastebasket. "What I say to you, Dr. Congreve, must remain confidential. But I would appreciate your opinion on these matters because you are a Southerner and you people down there seem to understand doom and damnation and still manage to maintain a belief in something." He turned eyes so intense and brown in her direction that she had difficulty in returning his gaze. "Do you believe in plagues, Dr. Congreve?"

"You mean like the bubonic plague? It might be a shock to you, Dr. Prunty, but the germ theory has gained general acceptance south of the Mason-Dixon." That was too flip, of course. But a conversation without a clear destination might carry her into dangerous waters.

"I speak of the plagues of moral retribution, Biblical plagues, plagues of locusts, Sodom and Gomorrah. And don't feel you have to be politically correct with me, Dr. Congreve. My wife, Betty, teaches in the biology department. Whenever I suggest to her that there might be a statistical correlation between moral degeneracy and biological plagues she laughs at me. The question itself isn't

PC, I am not PC." He swiveled his chair to face the window, exposing thin, elegant shoulder blades, a silky nape above a starched collar. "Froudard always refers to his current young man as his 'adopted son.' This one, the one he's taken to Italy, is dying of AIDS." A shudder moved through his thin body; was it possible that Prunty, an educated man, truly believed in evil as a force in the world? During her youth she had sat in church every Sunday morning and tried to analyze the preacher as he threatened the congregation with hell and damnation. Evil had never had a reality for her. If she had been Prunty's wife she, too, would have laughed. "I know what you're thinking, Dr. Congreve, that I am an antediluvian fool. But consider my position. Sometimes I feel as though I am the last living white male of European descent. And do you know who the enemy is? It isn't them. It's the concept of PC. Every sentiment, every action must *appear,* and I emphasize that word *appear,* to meet some standard of falsely benign, all-encompassing compassion for categories of human behavior which by their apparent uniformity must, due to the laws of human nature, be false. You know the Beast that has been slouching toward Bethlehem, Dr. Congreve?"

He was almost shouting. She wondered if he could be heard through the thin walls. "I know the metaphor, yes. However, we don't attempt to teach Yeats in Remedial."

"Well, he is alive and well and has arrived at Laedmore, Dr. Congreve. Look out at the sea of faces in your classes and you'll spot the little beady eye, the sudden wakening from his slothful sleep. And what is it that has roused the heart of the Beast? The poetry of Shakespeare? Milton? Yeats? Oh, no, Dr. Congreve, he is sifting my words for their *political correctness.* In order to keep my job, to be respected as a professor of English Literature I must hold up the mirror to that tiny brainwashed skull and assure him that all the knee-jerk yes-words fed into him by a corrupted, hypocritical, and venal society for its own profit are not only true, but universally just."

She excused herself by saying she had to prepare for her four o'clock class. As she passed the secretary and the graduate students in the outer office she felt their quiet stares, sheep lifting their heads to observe the strange dog passing through their pasture. Surely they had heard Prunty's ranting, they must know he was nutty. Timid sheep, she thought, and sensed that someone was following her.

"Excuse me, Dr. Congreve." She turned to see the beaming face of LaPage Mucilage—that wasn't her name, but close to it, so close that she had privately associated "Glue" with the large, overbearing woman. "How about I buy you a cup of coffee? Anybody who looks as pissed as you do could use a cup of coffee."

Her defenses down, Dr. Congreve let herself be led to a conspicuous table in the faculty grill. Glue—whose name she finally dredged up from a mental image of the departmental roster, one Bethpage Muccilich, Women's Studies—spoke through horsy bites of a jelly doughnut. "What on earth did you do to Prunty to get him so stirred up? There's a lot of us gals who would like to have Prunty get so hot and bothered. He makes me cream in my jeans, I can tell you."

"It wasn't anything like that. It wasn't personal, I can assure you. He's concerned about student apathy." She wondered just how much of the conversation had been overheard.

"Did he tell you about his wife? They say she might have won a Nobel Prize. Did something with African hissing cockroaches. Sex lives or some such thing. We're all just biological soup, subject to what our genes tell us. Can you imagine watching cockroaches screw when you've got a hunk like Prunty in your bed?"

"You speak in the past tense. You mean they're divorced?"

"They don't award the Nobel posthumously. She's dying. Cancer. Ain't that a bitch?"

Dr. Congreve felt heat rise in her chest and move upward to her neck and face. Glue would think she was blushing over Prunty. That wasn't it at all. Why had she mentioned the dying Jerome? Had what she identified as homophobia in Prunty really been grief? Her head throbbed; she felt sorry for Prunty, she felt sorry for herself.

She posted a note on her classroom door that her last section of Remedial English would not meet. She went home and threw herself on Froudard's sofa. The cat climbed on her stomach and began purring furiously. Was there something in her that unleashed whatever madness lay hidden in men's darkest hearts?

Other women worried about how to attract men physically, she worried about how not to draw them to her imagination, a fraudulent and honeyed elixir that could transform the pungent smell of burning rubber into the delicate fragrance of a Victorian garden. It wasn't sex. It had never been sex. Sex was real, a biological fact, and reality was something to be gotten through, to be imagined away. For her no sensation could ever be quite palpable and immediate, a thing in itself to be enjoyed in the moment, but to be evaluated and compared, as she had been taught by her parents to see the obvious nutritional and economic advantages of a bowl of soup beans over a T-bone steak. Oh, if only her parents had been just plain poor and squalid without all their defensive justifications. She was glad that Prunty was plumb crazy. A man could be a little crazy and still be tempting; plumb crazy was an antidote to involvement. The cat's motor hummed at full speed. Her eyelids grew heavy. She felt wrapped in cotton. Through the cotton she heard a knock at the door. She knew without getting up who it was. He had come for her in his ancient green car with its scabrous vinyl top. He had driven far, day and night, over the low hills and the mountains, mounting them via backroads and interstates, the Alleghenies, the Appalachians, the Adirondacks, pushing north and east like his ancestors had pushed south and west two hundred years before, without doubt of right or purpose, but with the full thrust of acquisition. He had approached the outskirts of town, its landscape of deserted mills, shabby factories, beer halls, and discount stores, with the same mixture of disdain and inferiority that she also had felt. She saw his smirk, his wide-eyed stare, his limp greasy hair catching the breeze of the open car window. On the seat was the opened six-pack and hanging from the rear view mirror a pair of fuzzy dice and a garter belt, trophy from a backseat assignation. In his left hand he held "a cool one" just below the view of passing cops. Every inch of bumper space was covered with the righteous slogans of the disinherited and disillusioned: *"If You Know Jesus, Honk," "America—Love It or Leave It," "Stud on Board," "DAMM: Drunks Against Mad Mothers."* By the time he reached the respectable section of town, the decorous eighteenth-century houses and the college, he was clearly a fish out of water, defensive and absurd—shooting the finger to a staring tweedy professor, growling "Hey, sweet thangs" to a group of tittering, mocking coeds, a roar of muffler and a cloud of oily black smoke at the stop light. But his hunter's instinct was as sound and true as his great-great-granddaddy's. The same genes that could nail a squirrel through the eye with a rifle ball at a hundred yards aimed the ancient green car with its wired-shut door down her street and rattled to a stop in front of Froudard's quaint Yankee cottage. He scooted across the fuzzy seatcover and crawled out the passenger side. Empty beer cans clattered to the gutter. At last her dream lover had arrived at Laedmore.

She woke with a start. She was eye to eye with Froudard's purring yellow cat. She was sweating profusely and her head throbbed. For years she had drilled her students that literature should evoke terror and pity. Now she realized that she had never had the faintest idea what Aristotle was talking about. But how ridiculous! To be afraid of a dream. She commanded her body to breathe slowly and deeply. She would be more careful, watch what she ate, abstain from liquor before bedtime, keep away from Glue and, most especially, Prunty. She would think positive thoughts, forget all claims of the past, her dour parents, her ex-husbands, her former lovers, other people's dying lovers, departmental gossip. Her eyes fell on *The Boating Party* above the mantel. It was a cheap reproduction; she could see the impress of fake brushstrokes on the cardboard, but the unpretentiousness of it, the warmth, the palpable joy of the young Parisians in their blooming vivid world was comforting. If only she could go back in time, close her eyes and escape into the painting, live a life of lazy afternoons on placid rivers, engage in easy harmless flirtations.

In November her mother had a stroke and she flew home. There was no one else, her father having long since gone to a reward which, if he had a choice, was both thrifty and imaginative, a paradise painted on carnival backdrops, stuffed parrots and hoochie-coochie girls in fake tiger skins, just a peek at two dollars a ticket, not the real thing. In the hospital her mother lay propped, face distorted and unfocused. When she spoke her voice was faint and foreign. Dr. Congreve bent to hear words that sounded like those her Chinese lover had once whispered in her ear when they were alone on a high-rise elevator going up. She was shocked, then realized that the stroke had scrambled her mother's tongue. She found a nursing home with a view of the back of a supermarket, a compressor, a Dumpster, and catty-cornered across the street the long-deserted Electric Freeze. Was it better, worse, or indifferent compared to her mother's old view of the retread shop? On the flight north she felt guilty. She loved her mother and could have brought her back to Laedmore. But she hadn't and she wouldn't.

Froudard's yellow tabby was waiting at the door of the cottage. The heat had been turned down and the house was musty from being shut up. She fed the cat, and watched him wolf it down. Then she made herself a drink and sat down on Froudard's sofa. The young men and women in *The Boating Party* were laughing and drinking. The cat rubbed his head against her chin; his breath was fishy. At least he was delighted to see her. Old maid with cat and teacup of bourbon, she thought. She got up and picked up the phone and called Glue because there was no one else.

"A drink?" she said suspiciously. Dr. Congreve was about to say perhaps another time when Glue suddenly made up her mind, "Hey, that's a great idea."

They went to a bar Glue suggested, a working-class tavern on the south end of town where, according to her, the hunks from the packing plant across the street hung out. "This is my kind of place," she said, pulling her large hips free from the strictures of Dr. Congreve's front seat. "Great bunch of guys. I've made some real buds here. Joe's the bartender. You gotta hear his stories."

Two men in green work clothes sat at the bar. The bartender lifted a dirty towel in greeting. "Come in, ladies. In case you're not familiar there's booths in the back if you prefer."

"Hey, Joe, it's me," Glue said.

"How you doing," the bartender said noncommittally.

"It's me, Bethpage, Bethpage Muccilich."

"Yeah, it is getting cold out there, ain't it. What'll it be, ladies?"

They sat at the bar. The men in the tavern seemed to Dr. Congreve to be old and tired and shriveled; their work clothes reminded her of her father. The night seemed more like a Monday than a Friday. Then customers began to trickle in. Glue said hello to each as they entered. One man acted as if he might have met her before, but had no interest in pursuing the acquaintance. She told the bartender to give him a drink on her. She winked at Dr. Congreve. "You ought to experience that guy in the hay. Maybe I can work something out for you. Threw me when you called. Didn't strike me as the type." She winked at another man across the bar. He pretended not to see her. After three drinks she became confessional. "I have a secret, you know."

"Oh, really?"

"I'm from Canada. Being from the South you know what that means. But it doesn't matter in your case that you're from an ignorant place, because you're thin. If you're thin enough you can overcome anything in life." Bitterness edged her voice. "If you're fat like me, in the eyes of the world you're nothing but a fat person and that's it. Thin people like you think it's just a matter of food. It's not. I am fat because I was sexually abused when I was a kid, my mother was an alcoholic, and my father kept my mother and me locked in the basement. I escaped when I was fourteen and joined a Satanic cult in southern Indiana. I was rescued by two Mormon missionaries on bicycles who stopped at the farmhouse where the cult was sacrificing cats and goats and human babies. I beat my first husband. I do everything compulsively, and I have been known to wash my hands a hundred and fifty times a day." She started crying. The men raised their heads from their beers and turned their tired, disinterested faces toward her. "You think I'm a liar. Well, I'm that too. I've had offers from the television people. Hell, I could be a whole season for Jerry Springer. Barkeep, another round."

By the time Dr. Congreve could talk Glue into leaving, she had to be helped to the car. "Don't bother to pretend that you understand me or have any sympathy. The stupidest thing about you people from the States is that you think everything that's broken can be fixed. You are a country of wimps and fools. And don't assume, Miss Skinny Ass, that just because you're thin you are worthy of inheriting the Earth."

Dr. Congreve started to object, but she didn't want to get into an argument. They were driving through what seemed to be a rough part of town. She thought of the dream lover driving these deserted-looking streets and imagined what he would say to the drunk woman beside her. He would tell Glue that she was heavy-set, not fat, and that being heavy-set wasn't so bad if a girl had a pretty face, but that she ought to keep her mouth shut about her past if she wanted to catch a man because men had illusions and didn't want damaged goods.

They had reached Glue's apartment. It was a cold night. She got out of the car awkwardly, then turned and stuck her head back in the door. "And for your information, you don't have anybody fooled. Everybody in the department knows you've got the hots for Prunty." She closed the car door too carefully. Dr. Congreve watched the large woman stumble and lurch toward the apartment house. If she passed out on the doorstep she would freeze. There was some advantage in being a Southerner, Dr. Congreve thought, false dignity was better than none. She decided that if the woman fell she would let her lie there and drive off, but the light in the entry hall came on and then went off.

Christmas break came, the students went home and campus was deserted. She went Christmas shopping. Actually, there wasn't anybody to buy for except her mother and the cat. She passed a card store. She went in and bought a card to send Froudard in Italy and, on impulse, one for Glue. It would probably be the only card she would get, but at least she wouldn't be able to whine around the faculty lounge about not receiving anything. Coming out of the card shop she ran into Prunty and his wife.

Betty Prunty offered a surprisingly firm hand. Obviously she had once been a person of great beauty and was now upholding herself through charm and determination. Her deterioration was a winnowing down of soft blonde luxuriance to a bony fineness, and soon she would vanish altogether. "Devon said you were from the South and I can hear it in your voice, Dr. Congreve. Those lovely vowels. We're leaving for Mexico for a few weeks, but when we get back you must come for dinner."

"Yes, come for dinner when we get back," Prunty repeated. His brown eyes crinkled with holiday good cheer; he was almost ebullient. "Betty and I have just been to the travel agency to pick up our tickets. They've got one of those embryo extract therapies down there I want Betty to have a go at."

"Actually, it's a vacation for both of us. I'm much better really, but it's been rough on Devon." Betty Prunty leaned into her husband's elbow in a motion so frail and Victorian that the December wind might have swept her into the gutter.

They wished her a Merry Christmas. Dr. Congreve watched them walk to their car. Prunty held his wife's elbow, a gesture that was not so much supporting a dying wife as accompanying a frail beauty. She turned a radiant smile on him. He was charming; she was genteel. How much was theatre? They moved slowly and elegantly down the street festooned with plastic greenery and electrified Santas. Obviously Betty Prunty was sparing her husband from the pain of her death as she had probably spared him from every other unpleasantness in their life together. Dr. Congreve imagined them on the plane, their conversation animated and filled with vacation plans, never touching on illness or death.

All through January postcards arrived at the department: "Weather wonderful. Betty responding beautifully," "Progress slowed, still much encouraged," "Temporary setbacks, but keeping the faith," "Betty in hospital, slight complications," "More tests scheduled. Betty learning chess." Glue read the latest postcard on the bulletin board out loud to the other teachers drinking coffee in the lounge. "You mean to tell me Betty Prunty is just now learning to play chess? It's his idea, isn't it? Take your mind off death with a rousing game of chess. Do you play chess, Dr. Congreve?"

On a drizzly February evening there was a knock at the door of Froudard's cottage. She had fallen asleep grading papers. At first she was alarmed, then disoriented. A drenched and weathered Froudard greeted her. He seemed to have aged. "Sorry to barge in on you, but it seems I have to reclaim the old manse."

"Oh, I'm so sorry. I hadn't heard the bad news. No one told me of Jerome's . . . passing." She heard herself being Southern, politely evasive, feminine. She hated that it came so naturally to her.

"Oh, no, I'd like to kill him, but Jerome's not dead yet. He's in a hospital in Rome. He had pneumonia and the priests did all their last rites folderol. But he fooled them this time. Jerome is the kind of boy who fools everybody," Froudard said meanly. He looked around the room. "You haven't changed a thing. I thought you'd at least take down that dreadful picture." He indicated the Renoir reproduction above the mantel. "Do you think you can find another place by the first of the month? I'm not well. I've tested positive. I need my house."

"I don't know, I'll see what I can do." She knew she wasn't being assertive enough. They had agreed upon terms, and he was the one who was abrogating them and at the same time acting the injured party. The trouble with being Southern was that good manners required you to immediately absorb all the fault, even when you knew better.

Froudard walked over to the bookshelves in search of something. "There was a photograph album here. Have you seen it?"

"No," she lied. Her manners also required her to lie about nosiness. She had studied the faces in the album with great fascination, Victorian ladies in high collars and skinned-back hair, Edwardian bankers, children in flouncy linens with ponies, on wicker chairs, in nurses' arms, all presumably Froudards and Froudard in-laws, all ugly, and invincibly prosperous, smiling their well-to-do smiles right through the Depression. Then there were the pictures of Froudard as he progressed from babyhood to graduation after graduation, a whole series of mortarboards and gowns. The album had filled her with envy; her family pictures were of farmers holding teams of mules, women in housedresses holding babies or dogs, her parents and herself on vacation in the Great Smokies, pale, heads tilted in apology, unremarkable and poor.

Froudard located the album and settled himself on the sofa. "Family makes all the difference, but I don't need to tell you that, do I? You're a Southerner." The cat wandered in. He sniffed Froudard's pant leg, then walked across the room and jumped up in her lap. "As I've always said to all my boys a family is built on trust. If you can't trust family who can you trust. Ah, here she is, Great Aunt Polly." He pronounced "aunt" beautifully, without making it sound like something to be stepped on. He pulled out a photo circa 1910 of a smug and ugly young woman with a great wad of hair and too many ruffles. "She never married, always had too much fun at home to leave, she said. Great practical joker. She lived with my grandparents. I adored her. Once we made chocolate pudding with Ex-Lax and served it as dessert to the others."

Dr. Congreve wondered what this had to do with trust and was about to suggest that it would be more suitable for her to move in April during spring break when Froudard began to blubber. "You know what I think, I think he was lying from the very first. When I adopted Jerome he seemed so sweet and pure, but now I know he lied to me. When he ran away and came back sick he assured me that he had caught AIDS after he had left me. And fool that I was I trusted him."

Why hadn't he just called or e-mailed to tell her he needed his house? This was an imposition, dragging her in, making her feel sorry for him. She thought of Prunty: would his response be what she was feeling? If so, she wouldn't feel this way, she would never allow herself to be a bigot like Prunty.

"Aunt Polly was wonderful, very eccentric of course, but so

much fun. When I was a very small boy she took me up to her room and set me in this barber's chair where we always played dentist or barber or beautician or anything that called for such a grand chair, and she said, 'Harold, dear, you have been given the greatest gift in the world, you have been born a male Froudard. And male Froudards are very special people. They bestow friendship on only the most deserving, they associate only with the highest and best.'" Froudard was openly weeping. "Before this I have believed all my boys to have been male Froudards—adopted male Froudards."

He stood to leave. "Forgive the emotional outburst. Of course the blessing is that Prunty is out of town. I suppose poor Betty is dying. Poor woman. Can you imagine having to flatter that man's ego all these years, his right-wing piety, his alternate views of reality. You look surprised. You mean you haven't heard that one? I thought he hit all you new girls in Remedial with that one first thing." At the door he paused. He held the photograph of his long-dead great aunt. "Do you believe that when you die someone you loved very much comes for you? Nonsense, don't you think? When you're looking for an apartment be sure and ask them if they allow pets. I've decided to leave you my cat. Ungrateful thing, he seems to like you much better than me."

When Froudard had gone Dr. Congreve clutched the purring yellow cat to her chest. She thought she might be going to cry herself. How dare these ridiculous people involve her in their tragedies, their petty quarrels. She had come to Laedmore to escape all that was trite, maudlin, and inevitable in her life. At this moment her poor stroked-out mother was probably looking out at the Dumpster of rotting produce, the mashed cardboard boxes behind the supermarket, trying to recall if she had a daughter and, if she could remember, puzzled as to what she had done to deserve such desertion. A person who could turn her back on her dying mother could only feel so much pity for the likes of Froudard and the Pruntys. She dropped the cat to the floor. He let out a sharp, surprised objection. She would find him a home, and if she couldn't she would take him to the animal shelter.

She found an apartment across town. It was without charm; that had subconsciously been her main requirement— she had had her fill of charm. They also took pets. Her options were open in case she changed her mind. She wondered if Froudard meant for her to take the cat now or later.

She was packing her last box of books when a car pulled up in front of Froudard's cottage. At first she thought it was a student who had come to help her move, and then she recognized Prunty. He was carrying a small enameled box that made her think of candy.

"Dr. Congreve, I'm glad I caught you. I was just driving by." He looked disheveled, as if he had been up for days. "No, I wasn't. To tell the truth, I just couldn't take Betty home to that lonely house. You know what I mean. There and not there at the same time. Might I have a drink?"

She found a bottle of Froudard's Scotch in the cupboard. Prunty balanced the box on his lap while he drank. His eyes were puffy. "You're moving?"

"Froudard wants his house back." She grabbed the cat, who was sniffing at the enameled box on Prunty's knees.

"Disgusting, isn't it, his showing up like this. You'd have thought Froudard would have had the decency to stay in Italy. Now we'll have to have a regular celebration of his disgusting sexual practices. Departmental fund-raisers, consciousness-raising programs for safe sex, the whole silly rot. Just wait and see, you'll see PC at Laedmore like you've never seen it before. If his kind would just keep their trousers on we wouldn't have this mess, if you'll forgive my plain speaking. Is that Froudard's cat you're hugging so tightly? Cats carry germs."

"Not really," she said, demonstrating her affection for the cat. "Actually, he's mine." She wasn't going to be drawn any further into partisan sentiments.

"Betty always loved this cottage. The outside, that is. She's never been inside before." His brown eyes glistened. "You know the line from Yeats, Dr. Congreve, 'How do we know the dancer from the dance?' How perfectly that captures our perception of reality. Don't worry, Dr. Congreve. I haven't lost my mind. I know that if I go in that house Betty won't really be there, but she's in my perception of the house. She's there for me. Reality is what we make of it, isn't it? Might I have another drink?"

She poured him another drink from Froudard's bottle. He began to speak of Plato's cave. She felt as if she were a student in a freshman lit class. He was putting her to sleep with his crap about reality. She was glad he was a fool, but did he have to be all that much of a fool? She closed her eyes and saw her Chinese lover drinking tea, his arm lifted, rounded, smooth as marble, golden. "How about another?" As Prunty held out his glass he knocked the enameled box to the floor. "Oh, dearest," he cried as if his wife really were in the box. But he made no move to recover it.

"Let me," Dr. Congreve said. The box was surprisingly heavy. It must be lined in metal, she thought. She placed it on the mantel beneath the reproduction of *The Boating Party*. Prunty poured himself a large glass of Scotch. He seemed suddenly to be feeling much better. What had her father always said? "More folks are educated than are doing well." Her father would have spotted Prunty for an educated fool.

Prunty moved swiftly and drunkenly to Descartes. He rambled on, then suddenly stopped. He lifted his glass to the mantel. "I will arise now and go to Innisfree." He sank back into the sofa and his eyes closed. After a few minutes Dr. Congreve removed the glass from his grasp and covered him with a spread. Then she picked up the cat, turned out the lights, and went upstairs. Froudard was coming to reclaim his cottage in the morning; so what if he found Prunty asleep on his sofa. They would, of course, be sweet as pie face to face, full of compassion, consolation, all very academic and PC. She pulled off her clothes and climbed into bed. She heard the cat purr, felt him palpate her thigh, and fell asleep.

They were on the outskirts of Laedmore, headed south, and the dream lover reached out his hand to pat her knee. She could see the dirty nails against her pale skin and feel the rumble of the big engine pulse through her body. Inside the car was like being in a tanker on a sea of great long waves. She looked out the porthole windows at the ugly, deserted factories, the discount houses and their acres of blacktop, the bars, the adult bookstores with their gigantic busts and butts reaching out to the street.

"This ain't for you, Sister," the dream lover said. "Ain't no kind of a place for a woman where a man don't know enough to call a gal 'Sister.'" She knew without being told that his name was Roscoe and that he had a long string of ex-wives and children to whom he owed money and obligations he would never pay, yet she felt safe. He would never ask her to perform sex in any position that a good Baptist wouldn't approve of; she would bear him at least one child which she would name Jason or Jennifer, and her reality would be whatever soap opera she was currently watching on TV. He turned his beautiful brown eyes on her. She saw the harelip, the pink diseased gums, the grotesque tobacco-stained teeth, but nothing mattered except his eyes. The engine started to knock. The car bucked and then died. She woke and sat upright in bed. She heard Prunty on the stairs. Sorrowfully and pitiably caught in reality, he called "Betty . . . Betty . . . Betty."

Lucinda Harrison Coffman, a native Kentuckian, has lived and been educated in both the North and the Deep South. Her short fiction has appeared in the *Southern Review, Kansas Quarterly, 13th Moon: A Feminist Literary Magazine,* the *Iconoclast, Cimarron Review,* and other journals. She lives in Shelby County, Kentucky, on her family farm, Twin Springs, a saddlebred nursery for over a century.

CHRISTINA HILLING

I *have always disliked academic stories because they tend to be predictable:*
smart, sensitive me enters the groves of academe—smart, sensitive me gets
screwed. However, I overcame my natural prejudice and started this story
shortly after I had completed my second "terminal degree" (an apt term), and
I suppose the outrage and amusement just had to go somewhere. The dream
lover, the long-awaited gentleman caller who will rescue the fair damsel from
the tragedy of being female and single, seems a particularly Southern theme
and an outdated comic figure from the patriarchal past—at least I hope he is.

Tom Franklin

NAP TIME

(from *The Georgia Review*)

The baby was finally down, so the parents took a nap, too. But they couldn't sleep.

Her husband said, "Listen how quiet."

They listened. It was late in the evening and the walls of the room were colored red by the sun through the red drapes, drapes she hated but hadn't yet replaced. The landlord had told them they could make any cosmetic changes they wanted. But nothing came off the rent, he'd said.

"How long does it normally last?" her husband asked.

"Two or three months, according to the book. Didn't you read it?"

"Not yet." He rubbed his eyes with the heels of his hands. Except for their socks, both were naked, thinking they might have sex before their nap. Until now, they'd mostly been too tired to try, and when they had, she'd been too sore.

Then she said, "When he's screaming like that and you've been carrying him all night, swinging him till you can't feel your arms, do you ever think about, like, dropping him? Just letting him fall out of your hands?"

Her husband didn't answer, and she thought she'd said the wrong thing.

But he took a breath. "Yeah," he said. "Sometimes I do. Sometimes I think about dropping him on the porch." Which was concrete.

She propped up on an elbow. "Really? God, I'm relieved to hear you say that. I've been thinking I'm the worst mother imaginable."

For a while, neither said anything.

Then, "Sometimes," he said, "I go farther with it."

"Farther? How?"

"I'll be driving, like on the interstate, and he'll be screaming, and I'll think, what if I were to sling him out the window. Car seat and all."

She didn't say anything. She wished it were darker in the room.

He looked at her. "You must think I'm terrible."

She leaned and kissed his shoulder blankly. "No, of course not." She sat up, her elbows orange in the light, Band-Aids on her nipples, and reached for her cigarettes and shook one out of the package. "The other day I thought—" She lit the cigarette.

"Tell me."

"I was carrying him, I'd been lugging him around in that colic hold for two hours and he was crying, crying, crying. Nothing would make him stop, and I was so exhausted. I'd walked around the house so many times I'd started doing it with my eyes closed, counting my steps, and he still kept crying." She drew on her cigarette. "I went through the kitchen for like the thousandth time, and I thought, god, of putting him in the microwave."

He moved his feet under the sheets. "We did that to a hamster when I was a kid."

"Really?"

"Yeah. My brother was at school and I was home sick. I wasn't really sick, I'd pretended to have a stomachache. Me and my little sister took his hamster out of its cage and I held it under the faucet. We wanted to see what it looked like wet. But when we did it, we realized mostly all it was was hair, the little body was only as big around as your finger. We thought, he'll know we did this. So I put the hamster in the microwave." He hesitated.

She could feel him breathing. "What happened?"

"It started steaming, so we took it out. It seemed fine at first. Then, about two weeks later, it grew this huge tumor on its neck. It kept crawling in a circle in the cage until it finally stopped under the little Ferris wheel and lay there breathing hard. In the morning it was dead."

"God," she said. She looked at her cigarette and dropped it in the Diet Coke can on the table beside the baby book. She'd quit smoking when she learned she was pregnant, and except for New Year's Eve and Mardi Gras and two or three other nights she'd been vigilant. With drinking too. But when the baby came she'd had problems breastfeeding, her milk ducts infected, oozing thick green pus, the baby almost malnourished, screaming so loud in the doctor's office the nurses had to yell to hear each other. So she'd been forced to use bottles and thought, Why not smoke? But she didn't enjoy it anymore.

"Did your brother ever find out?" she asked, lying back.

"No. I told my sister if she ever blabbed, I'd put *her* in the microwave. To this day she won't use one." He gave a dry laugh.

She looked over at him for a long time, taste of nicotine in her mouth and nose. Then she said, "Okay. I've got one." She put her arms under the covers, felt his foot brush against hers. "Growing up, I knew this girl who was murdered. Somebody grabbed her off the street while she was walking home from the pharmacy where she worked after school. It was almost dark. They found her body in the woods half a mile from this dirt road she'd never been on in her life. She'd been hit in the forehead with some kind of hammer. She was dead. My best friend's older sister."

"You never told me that," he said. "Did they find out who did it?"

"The Mobile police went crazy looking. They were interviewing everybody they could find. They stopped people on the street and went door to door, but all they ever got was that somebody might've seen a pickup. Then one night, it was a week after the funeral, I had this dream. I dreamed I was her, and I was walking home from the pharmacy. Wearing the same green pastel dress she'd had on. I knew it was me, but I was her, too, somehow. And I knew what was going to happen, but I couldn't stop it. I turned around and this truck had pulled up beside me, a blue pickup truck. The door opened and this guy I sort of knew was driving it. He was our preacher's son's friend, who'd been kicked out of the marines. I knew not to get in the truck with him, but he showed me that he had a joint, and so I got in anyway. We drove without saying anything. His radio was playing Dylan, but I can't remember what song. He turned on a county road and kept driving. I couldn't remember his name but he had cute sideburns and a cute little chin. I liked the way his Adam's apple bobbed and the way he smoked his cigarette. The way it looked in his fingers. Then he turned onto the dirt road."

Her husband had rolled to face her. He put his hand on her stomach, which was softer than before, the skin loose and cool.

"He stopped the truck right where all the police cars and the ambulances would be later," she said. "We got out and he took my hand and led me into the woods. On a path I hadn't even seen. We walked for a long time, holding hands, till you couldn't hear any cars anywhere. You couldn't hear anything. We smoked the joint and he started unbuttoning my dress. I let him. I was buzzing all over. I let him do whatever he wanted—"

"What'd he do?" He was moving his hand on her stomach, going lower. She could feel him getting hard against her leg.

"I let him, you know."

"Did you like it?"

She shifted her hips. "Yes," she said. "I liked it."

He said, "Then what happened," as his hand opened her thighs.

"He took this hammer out of his pocket," she said, "and I shut my eyes, and he hit me right here—" She touched herself at the bridge of her nose. "And I woke up panicked, with this splitting pain in my forehead."

He moved his hand gently into place. "Was it him? Was it the preacher's son's friend?"

"I don't know. Nobody was ever arrested."

He began to rub her with the pad of his thumb, the way she liked. "Did you tell anybody?"

"No," she said, her eyes closed, "I never told anybody . . ."

He whipped the sheet up and in the tented air rolled on top of her. When the sheet had floated back down around them he was already edging in in his familiar way. He went slowly and she stretched her legs so exquisitely her hips popped and when he murmured against her neck did it feel good she could only nod and raise her knees. She was climbing in the truck again and there he was, holding his cigarette in his fingers. He offered it to her across the long bench seat which had a quilt over it, and she took the cigarette and put it to her lips and sucked in the good-tasting hot smoke. Drive, she told him.

But something was wrong. She opened her eyes.

"Listen," she said.

In his room, across the hall, behind the closed door, the baby was silent.

———

Tom Franklin, from Dickinson, Alabama, is the author of *Poachers,* a collection of stories, and *Hell at the Breech,* a novel. Winner of a Guggenheim Fellowship in 2001, he now teaches at Ole Miss and lives in Oxford with his wife and their young daughter.

MAUDE SCHUYLER CLAY

N*ap Time" began as a one-note idea: a tired, bedraggled couple fantasize about hurting their colicky baby, fantasies (I expect) that every parent has had in his or her worst moments. Friends of ours had a colicky baby, and their stories, the details, haunted me. I was lucky, though, in that "Nap Time" took a sharp turn away from that single note of escalating thoughts of violence against the baby when the microwaved hamster turned up. That surprised me. So did the wife's story about her friend's sister.*

Bret Anthony Johnston

ANYTHING THAT FLOATS

(from *The Paris Review*)

M y mother dumped my father for an ostrich farmer," Vince said yesterday. We were in a semi-private room in the heart wing of Spohn Hospital. I lay on the other bed and said, "Did she now?" but just thought the codeine drip was scrambling his memory in lascivious ways. Today he's lucid again, eating and joking about his IV, and when our son, Tyler, starts in about wanting to go swimming, Vince looks at me and tells us to get lost.

So I'm driving to the Sea Ranch Motel; our regular pool at the rec center is closed because the city's in a drought. This is an unseasonably mild afternoon in Corpus Christi because there's a trough of cool air in the Gulf. I try to see that patch of distant coolness as if it were a cloud. Instead there is only the soapy, opaque bay, a few collapsed beach umbrellas in front of the condos, and the trees along the seawall, whose dry, brown palms hang like scraps of parchment. Tyler sits cross-legged in the passenger seat. He's reading a book on boa constrictors, one I believe he stole from the hospital library.

Our house is full of snakes. When we learned Tyler was allergic to pet dander and had to give our collie to a woman with acreage in Orange Grove, he and his father convinced me to let him keep a garter snake in his room. Now, we have two gray rat snakes trying to mate in an aquarium under one of my old curtains, a banded king snake that only eats after dark, a corn snake and an albino bull snake under heat lamps in the garage, and a lazy royal python in a terrarium behind the kitchen table. Each week we buy seven mice (the python gets two) that Tyler drops into the cages. The owner of the pet store is smitten with him, with his unlikely and considerable knowledge; she arranged a job for him lecturing at the museum. On the third Saturday of every month, families and retiree tours pay to hear my eight-year-old son speak on the surprisingly docile temperament of death adders.

"This book is wrong," he says now. "It says retics are the biggest."

Retics are reticulated pythons; we did a book report. They're the second largest snakes in the world, though now I can't recall the name of the longer one—possibly it's a boa. Ahead, the ceramic seahorse perched atop the motel becomes visible. I say, "Maybe they found a longer one."

"Doubtful," he says, never lifting his eyes.

On the awning above the U-shaped driveway, the words *Sea Ranch* are scripted in elegant curlicues, but MOTEL is in block letters. This has always struck me as cheap and sexy, like blue eye shadow. Two cars are parked by Room 17, and the flatbed trailer with the broken window units is still behind the whirlpool gazebo. A sign on the hurricane fence around the pool reads: YE OLDE SWIMMIN' HOLE.

I say, "We're the only ones here. You can practice your dives."

"Where's the diving board?"

In the rearview mirror, my face is that of a woman who spent the night on a hospital cot. I say, "You can practice from the side."

In June, his father brought home the advertisement for the Anything-That-Floats-But-A-Boat event at this year's BayFest, and he told Tyler that if by the end of the summer he could dive without belly-flopping and tread water for three minutes, they would enter. Before two of Vince's ventricles seized shut and his boss from the shipyard called me to meet him at Spohn Hospital, the two of them—Vince and Tyler—spent evenings designing their vessel. The last drawing showed a plastic barrel housed in the middle of a plywood X. The sketches lie on the bedside table in the hospital, but he hasn't picked them up again. BayFest starts in three weeks.

The Sea Ranch will get busy tonight. Room doors are open and laundry carts are out. As always, Christmas lights dress the balcony eaves. Tyler stands on the edge of the deep end, wearing lizard-printed trunks; most everything he wears depicts a reptile. He looks puzzled, concerned. He hasn't swum since Vince was admitted, and he's losing his tan. Still, his skin is almondy like his father's. Once, crossing the border back from a day in Mexico, Vince had to show his driver's license and answer various patriotic questions to prove residency. I was feeding Tyler in the passenger seat, expecting the officers to make my husband sing the "Star-Spangled Banner," when I realized I'd dreamt the ordeal years before.

"Maybe you should practice floating first," I say. "Maybe it's too shallow for good dives."

He nods, defeatedly, but he's relieved to have me to blame. Diving still scares him. He lowers his feet into the water, then drops in completely. While he's under, I glance toward the office, and Gilbert Salazer's already crossing the caliche parking lot. He's chewing a toothpick, watching the ground as he passes through the lattice gate. He scoots a cedar bench under its picnic table and walks the length of the pool to stand at the foot of my plastic lounge chair. Tyler breaches the surface, then ducks under again.

Gilbert says, "Ma'am, may I see your room key?"

Maybe he wants me to give him a thrill by flashing the key to Room 22, but I've not seen it in months. For a while I expected Vince to toss it like an accusation onto the kitchen table, but now I think it fell from my pocket in a Laundromat dryer. I admit the prospect of saying something coquettish *does* excite me — something like, "My husband has it" — but I don't want that hassle. I say, "I know the manager."

The toothpick jumps to the other side of his mouth. A breeze riffles the dried-up crepe myrtle on the fence, and with the clouds dispersing, the sun casts a harsh ivory glow on the bricks around the pool; the water catches the light like a sapphire. Gilbert eyes the book on boas, says, "You like big snakes?"

"My son does." My answer comes so fast he probably thinks I've missed his point. Behind Gilbert, Tyler floats on his back, eyes closed.

"Certainly," Gilbert says. "The little snake king, the giver of speeches."

"If we're disturbing the guests, we can leave. Or I can pay—"

"Today, of all days, is when I wear a guayabera."

I smile, letting my eyes linger on the embroidered shirt, his trunks that are a size too small. This little show is why, of the many motel pools in Corpus, I've brought us here, for a reprieve from the hospital and transplant negotiations. I say, "I wondered what you'd be wearing."

"Do you know what I wonder? I wonder how long since Colleen's visited old Gil."

When I stay quiet, he pivots toward the pool. Tyler is spitting water like a fountain; he's trying to spray a sun-whitened NO LIFE-GUARD sign.

It was short-lived, maybe two months, over a year ago. Gilbert had come into the showroom—I sell pool supplies—because the filter on the deep end was collecting algae. Vince had recently admitted about Annette Maldonado, so I told Gilbert I'd have to see the filter firsthand to diagnose the trouble. *Diagnose* was the word I used, and every time I hear it now, I recall the itchy, seafoam bedspread in Room 22. Whether Vince knows about Gilbert is not something I've discerned. During the bypass surgery, one of my disgusting thoughts was that if he died, at least he'd never learn about Gilbert. There was mercy there, but also a traitorous yearning for relief.

Tyler pushes himself from the pool and comes slapping his feet on the polished aggregate, trailing shallow puddles that immediately evaporate. He pauses beside a rolling barbeque pit to shake water from his ears. I work his towel out from under me. He says, "I dreaded for four minutes, possibly five."

"*Treaded*, honey," I say, blocking the sun from my eyes. "That's your world record."

Just then he notices Gilbert. "Hello," he says. Then, of all things, he extends his little hand: "Tyler Moody."

Gilbert glances at me, expecting a cue, but my heart lifts so swiftly I can only shrug. What manners! Sometimes the same feeling rushes me when I hear Vince dress for work; the three smart taps of his razor on the basin can fill me with almost unbearable reassurance. In my dream, we were not traveling from Mexico, but through Russia, and I was cradling a small javelina, not Tyler.

"Pleased to know you," Gilbert says. "You're the snake man, yes?"

Tyler tips his head to his shoulder, apologetically. A small crucifix—a gift from Vince's father—hangs on the thin chain around his neck. He started wearing it the first night Vince stayed in the ICU. He says, "When my dad gets out of the hospital, we're going to build a boat from a highway barrel. But not really a boat."

Gilbert nods, frowning slightly. "Hospital?"

"He has diabetes, but they just found it. I might have it, too."

"Like father, like son," Gilbert says, but nice. He and Vince are not so different. "I'm sure he'll come out fine, and you'll make your boat that's not a boat."

Tyler's hair is drying. The sun and water have bleached and puckered his skin, brought out his chicken pox scars. Once he sat on the kitchen floor and covered himself—face, pajamas, hair, and feet—in butter. Gilbert says, "Call me Gil. I'm your mother's old friend."

An ostrich farmer. Vince's mother *did* leave his father, but he's not spoken of it for years. She was a dowdy, capricious woman who refused to go to the ER without making up her face. In one of our closets sits a box with her sterling and turquoise jewelry and her last wallet, still holding a lock of hair from Vince's first barber visit. What enters my mind is an old photo, pasted in an album on black construction paper, of Vince tossing seeds to an ostrich. He's tiny, wearing a bonnet that will soon come untied. The picture has always struck me as one from a vacation. Maybe that's where his mother met her lover, in Wyoming or Michigan's Upper Peninsula. I saw the album when we cleaned out her house in Sugarland, outside Houston. Tyler stayed with my parents in Corpus. He was starting to sleep by himself, and most nights I woke thinking to check on him; I worried about gas leaks and kidnappers. Two in the morning, the unfamiliar room lit by a paper-thin moon, Vince wasn't in bed. He sat in the attic, sorting ephemera. He wasn't morose, but anxious, his mind and body fiending for order. He showed me his uncle's Purple Heart, telegrams sent to his mother during the war, a picture of his father—who remarkably resembled his son—standing before Niagara Falls, and the picture of himself feeding the ostrich. He mentioned nothing of his mother's infidelity, and soon I kissed his neck and led him to bed and made love to him so he could sleep.

Tyler has been talking to Gilbert, explaining the rattlesnake races in San Patricio. Hundreds of rattlers are caught on watermelon and pecan farms—though some aficionados raise their own snakes— then men race them against each other in chalked-off lanes. Contestants wear plastic bite guards on their shins and guide the stout-bodied snakes with aluminum poles. There is also a carnival with booths selling diamondback hatbands and paperweights and sandwiches, and clowns who paint cobras on children's faces. Tyler is ten years too young to compete, but he and his father have mounted a campaign to sidestep the restrictions; if we sign extra waivers and if Vince stays in the lane with him, they might let him enter. We're waiting to hear back.

Tyler says, "Saint Patrick led the snakes from Ireland. That's why the races are in San Patricio."

"You are the snake encyclopedia," Gilbert says. "The snake almanac."

An ease has spread between them and they're talking like old chums. Tyler moves from my feet to sit beside Gilbert. He tells him that our python, though this breed won't grow over five feet, is technically outlawed in Corpus city limits. We bought her in Southport and named her Ms. Demeanor.

"Ask your mother to drive you to San Antonio, to the Snake Farm," Gilbert says.

I kick him, hard but playful. He's flirting again—the conversational equivalent of massaging my thigh under a table. The Snake Farm is a brothel. There *are* snakes there, dozens of venomous and constrictor breeds, crammed in tanks too small and cold for them. The rub is that men ask the attendant to break a hundred dollar bill, then get led to a double-wide behind the building, where the girls operate. Gilbert told me all of this. Before managing the Sea Ranch, he drove a Pepsi route in San Antonio.

I'm about to shoot back some spicy, undermining answer when Tyler says, "My dad took me."

In unison, Gilbert and I say, "He did?" Then he slaps his knee and says, "A little father-son time."

"At Dad's training," Tyler says, and I remember. Vince had to attend a seminar and took Tyler for a weekend trip; I spent most of that time sunbathing beside this pool, and in Room 22. I'd not known they visited the Snake Farm and I imagine starting a fight over it later.

"A man got bit by a mamba," he says. "It happened that morning, but it was a dry bite."

Gilbert laughs. "Change for a hundred."

"What's a dry bite?" I ask.

"No venom," he says, as if he's already explained this. Then, brightly, to Gilbert, "Name Texas's four venomous snakes."

"Copperhead, rattlesnake, coral snake . . ." He pauses, stumped.

"Water moccasin," I say. "Cottonmouth water moccasin."

"Mother." Tyler glares at me. "Let Gil say them."

Then he sets in asking more trivia—which is the fastest snake in the world, the most deadly?—and an appalling, placating ordinariness prevails. A cleaning woman shuffles into a room with an armload of towels; maybe she recognizes me, maybe not. Gilbert nods while Tyler explains that a spitting cobra can hit a predator's eyes from four yards away. My palms tingle, the way they do when an airplane lifts off, the way they did when I used to wait for Gilbert on the seafoam bedspread, naked in the television's flickering light. Dry, ragged clouds cover the sky, and a cool, gray wind brings the smell of chlorine. And suddenly I realize it: My husband has died. His heart has stopped during his nap. This hits me with a brutal, leveling clarity. They're trying to revive him right now while the three of us lounge beside the water, but it's too late; the heart monitor's spiking green line has given up. When we return to the hospital, a nurse will intercept us and I'll be ushered into a lamplit room without windows, a Bible and phone on a table between two leather chairs, across from a couch. His cardiologist will enter and my stomach will knot and I'll dash to the ladies' room to dry-heave over the toilet, realizing that Vince had always known about the ostrich farmer, as, of course, he'd known about Gilbert.

Where is Tyler in all of this? With the nurse, in the windowless room with the doctor, now joined by a priest? I simply don't see him. He's removed from me, from the earth, drowned in a motel pool or in the Gulf, or bitten by a rattlesnake or cottonmouth. His absence drains me; it contents me. Contents me because he won't have to lose his father, or me, won't have to stumble through his own mostly good marriage and bear the burden of becoming a parent and in that same instant, a murderer. This is how I feel, like I've failed and wounded all of these men who need me.

"Boa constrictor?" Gilbert offers. I don't know what they're talking about.

Tyler stands on his heels. He hops once, then again, shaking his head. I'm sweating, the backs of my thighs stick to the chair; Gilbert sucks his toothpick.

"Python?"

"You already said that," he says. He's beaming, jumping in place, brimming with excitement. His crucifix glimmers. Does it matter if Vince had the second heart attack? Or what about the image of Tyler slathered in butter, my dream of Russia? Here's what I want to say: Truth is a coiling, slippery thing, and you can receive it any number of ways.

"Tell him, Mom," Tyler says, but then he's running and cannon-balling into the pool. There is no time for me to worry that he'll slip, no chance to warn or reprimand him; his entry hardly disturbs the water. A patch of sunlight has spread over us; I can feel Gilbert growing anxious because we're alone again. I'm about to admit I don't know the answer to my son's question, about to explain the pitiable situation with Vince, but Gilbert says, "Anaconda." He says it quietly, as if he's testing the pronunciation. Then he booms it out in his full voice, "Anaconda! It's an anaconda!" Tyler starts clapping and hollering in the deep end, and suddenly Gilbert barrels toward the pool and jumps in, guayabera and all. His splash is huge and wasteful and some of it comes back on me. The water is warm as rain, and for a moment I imagine the drought has ended.

Bret Anthony Johnston is the author of *Corpus Christi: Stories,* in which "Anything That Floats" appears. He holds an MFA from the Iowa Writers' Workshop. His work has been widely published and has twice before appeared in *New Stories from the South.*

STEPHANIE DIAN

A nything That Floats" owes a lot to Elizabeth Gaffney at the Paris Review, *and I also appreciate the efforts of an unidentified library patron. After I read this story to an audience at a Texas library, this patron asked if I'd named the character of Gilbert after Hurricane Gilbert, a brutal hurricane that hit the area in 1988. He posited that, like the hurricane, the character in the story is a South Texas storm, one that gathers strength near the water, one that leaves families trembling in fear because his existence threatens to tear apart anything and anyone in his path. I thanked the man for his close reading — he said he'd been researching the parallels for a week — and I said that his work had paid off, because I had indeed named the character after the infamous hurricane. Everyone clapped, more for his scholarship than for my writing.*

Of course, I was lying; I'd never conceived, let alone intended, any of the overlap this good soul had found. However, that reality shouldn't contradict anyone's reading of the story. Maybe the mark of successful writing is when readers understand the work differently, or more completely, than the author does; maybe a reader reading a story completes it, makes it more than it was. I certainly hope so.

Ada Long

CLAIRVOYANT

(from *PMS*)

My name is Clarence Day, and my parents were normal. That's what it says on my traveling van right after it says, in perfect red letters, that I'm twenty inches high and weigh thirty-nine pounds, THE WORLD'S SMALLEST MAN. It also says I have a high school education. When that got added to the sign, my income went up 17 percent. My wife did that calculation, she keeps the books. It doesn't say so on the sign, but she's normal too. The loudspeaker tells about her once we've settled in at the fairgrounds and opened up for business. I hear over and over again, maybe eighty times a day, that I have a normal wife and two perfectly normal children. One of them collects the money while the other one hangs around a lot and calls me Dad. We all work together, and we eat well.

You're probably wondering if those two boys are really my children. People want to know that but they never ask. I guess there's just no way to ask that question and feel good about yourself. If someone could figure a nice way to ask, I'd tell the truth. I'm pretty sure they're mine—as sure as any man is. I don't think about it much.

I'm good at my job. The sign says I'm small, and I am. I don't cheat people, even though they think I do. When they see me, I can tell they expected more for their fifty cents. I guess they expect a perfect little man, a tiny mirror of themselves, a little doll. They don't expect the head and trunk of a midget (even though they have to admit I'm a very small midget) with vestigial legs. But that's what they get. I'm not a doll. And nothing is perfect, not even freaks.

To be honest, I don't enjoy my work like I used to. Used to be that I'd hear footsteps on the wooden platform outside my trailer and my stomach would tighten as I waited for the faces to appear at the door—confident, happy faces on their day off, all lit up with the expectation of seeing something they could talk about back home on the front porch with a cool pitcher of lemonade sitting by. That wasn't the part I enjoyed, not that I begrudged it or anything. I liked the next part, the sudden bewilderment when those faces took account that it wasn't just them seeing me but I was seeing them right back again. They hadn't reckoned on that when they paid their fifty cents, and I could see the sweat come up, see the eyes check for escape routes. I had them then—the world belonged to me in those moments they were recalculating, and I could have sent it spinning out of control. They were mine, and for a split second they almost were me, I was that real to them. But I did nothing, of course. I just watched and enjoyed those moments until they got control of themselves again and said hello, clearing their throats of the fear that had got lodged there. We could chat then, with the touching formality of strangers who have survived a crisis together.

The chat hasn't changed. How do? Think there might be rain coming on? Hope not. Left the windows open back t'home. Ain't rained all month—be just my luck to have it coming in the windows the one day me and the family step out some. Ain't that always the way. Same conversations I've been having all my life, in uncertain weather. Rain and sun mean minor adjustments. Some folks don't put high value on that kind of chat, think nothing's getting said. But from where I sit, it seems like more's being said than any creature can take stock of. People come in there to see me and, no matter how disappointed they are, I expect they remember me a good long while. I expect what they remember, what pulls their coats every now and again, is the questions they didn't ask, that I didn't answer. Same thing I remember about them, all of them, and it's a lot to remember from so much chat, so many unanswered questions.

Could be I'm getting weary from so much remembering. Maybe that's where the salt's gone. Could be time for me to move on, do some other work. It's not always that I've worked the fairgrounds here in upstate Alabama, not by a long shot. It was some thirty years ago that we first settled on the outskirts of Gadsden. Had us an old farmhouse in those days, and a yellow Packard, a clear and shiny yellow that nature never thought of, unless you think people are natural. Every time I looked at that Packard I got hungry for sweets. Gained four pounds the year we got it, four delicious pounds that made me sick and happy. In those days we had a makeshift wagon, a box on wheels is what it was, that we'd hook up to the Packard on work days. Thinking back on it, I guess that box was real paltry. We painted it with at least twenty different shades of yellow, but next to the Packard it was nothing but dull and puny. No light inside except what came through the door and the chinks in the wood. When folks came in to see me, they were really thrown off balance. Face to face with a freak in a dark box, nothing else to look at and no place to run. Pretty near all the men and women who walked through that door wished they hadn't, wished they could vanish back out into the sunlight in the blink of an eye. But every single one of them stayed for at least a minute or two. It wasn't the money they'd paid that made them do it, it was their pride. It's human pride that's kept me in business all these years, and I'm mighty thankful for it.

Things are different now. You step in the door it's almost like stepping into somebody's living room. There's carpeting, electric lights, a kitchenette. Even upholstered chairs if people want to sit down. Most prefer standing. Still, that old box on wheels had some magic in it. Maybe magic is the price you pay for comfort.

We gave up the farmhouse, too, for a split-level ranch-style, indoor-outdoor carpet, twenty-nine-inch color tv, furniture from

Ethan Allen. It's more than comfortable. Funny how most folks just assume we live right here in the trailer, all four of us and not a bed in sight. Nice place you got here, they say, meaning nice home. But usually they ask if I come from around these parts—my accent isn't quite right, although I try—and I say, sure do, have a split-level just southeast of Gadsden. That's all they need to hear.

They also like to ask how long I've been married. I say forever, and they laugh. So I laugh too. But I don't let it stop there like I do with the weather. I go on and tell them that she's the finest woman on the face of the earth, and that's a fact. They look over at her—she's always right there—and I can see her in their eyes, see a normal woman flash up on their eyeballs. Then comes the squint, barely perceptible, while they wonder—wonder what it's like between me and her. Behind those eyes there's a quick parade of snapshots—her and me at the dinner table, in the living room, in the bed. Finest woman on earth, I repeat, and the eyes come back to me. That's when I stop. I don't say that when we lie down together I'm tall.

Being the world's smallest man is my job. It's my work, and we all have to work one way or another. I do my job well, but doing it poorly would be just as much work, probably more.

There were some folks walked through my door just last week, young folks just starting to get the feel of being on their own. You have to admire the courage it takes to get the feel of that. Whatever else the young ones do or don't have, they've got courage. It's as common as the sparrow, and no less precious. Well, these kids are larking, and they come busting in the door full of fresh air and junk food and high spirit, till the hush settles on them. Four of them there are, and who's going to speak up first? You know they can't take too much of the hush. The guy that's first through the door stops short two steps in, causing a jam-up at his rear, so they're all stuck there together, a single lump of young humanity with eight big eyes. I never speak first.

Hi.

The sweetest sound you can imagine, and we're all grateful. Hi back to you, I say, with the emphasis on *to*. Come on in if you'd like. They separate out into two girls and two boys. The girl that said hi walks right up to me. Young Mr. First doesn't budge, and the other two shuffle in line between them. Where you folks from? I'm from Birmingham, says Hi, and I see myself in her eyes big as life. Bigger. I look down the line, getting smaller and smaller, and I say you sure did pick a nice day to come to the fair. Mr. First has his eyes on my wife already, wondering, and Hi says yeah, it's real nice out there. She's worried now, doesn't want me to think she meant it isn't nice in here, so she asks if I come from around here. You know what I say, about the split-level outside Gadsden. Oh, she says, you don't sound like you're from Alabama. I say, you wouldn't believe all the places I've been in my life, telling her the truth. How'd you end up here? she asks. (My wife speaks up, says the kids are going out for hamburgers. Do I want one? No, I'm not hungry just yet, thank you.) I don't have to answer the question now, but I do. I say it's a good place to work. She wants to know why but doesn't ask, trying to figure it out for herself. Mr. First down there is thinking, what does this dwarf know about work, sitting around on his tiny can all day, talking shit and collecting money? He's thinking about how hard he works, stashing all the goddamn pork loins and margarine and Kotex into the goddamn bags for a bunch of old hags who don't even give him a goddamn tip. And here he is spending fifty cents to see a dwarf sit on his can.

He's right, of course. He works hard, too hard. It's a crying shame anyone's got to work as hard as he does, and it's a job to figure what makes them do it. It's not the money like he thinks it is. Twenty years from now he'll be rolling in money, eating tenderloin and lying down each night with a woman who doesn't tip the grocery sackers. And he'll still be working too hard. I won't be here then, but when he drives past the fairgrounds I'll be bile in his belly. His eyes will narrow in remembrance of the little fucker who sat on his can for a living.

On down the row, the skinny fellow with curly hair—it's brown in here but outside I know it's been golden—is looking at me in the past tense. I'm a story he's telling one Thursday night at Dugan's, story about a city boy venturing up a forlorn stretch of I-59 to experience the carnival of life among yesterday's people. His friends are enjoying the story, and so am I. He sets it up real good: the sunlight glinting off his Honda Civic in a field of unwashed pick-ups, the arduous journey from the parking lot through rows of pit bulls and coon hounds that are bought and sold by danger-ous characters (he describes them—big bellies, no teeth, huge bi-ceps; oddly cordial, even gracious, but scary as shit, like dams that could burst any minute and ravage everything in their path), the tables piled high with stolen hubcaps and ghetto blasters next to a table with nothing to sell but two rusted kettles and a broken toaster (Westinghouse, 1961). In the midst of it all a preacher, a kid in a J.C. Penney double-knit suit stained with his sweat, yelling about Gawd and Cheesus. Gathered around him are eight slack-jawed farmers in overalls but no shirts, all twice the age of the preacher but awed, respectful, nodding as he tells them—begs them—to bring prayer into their lives and prepare for the coming of the Lorrrr-d—"For I say unto you, my brothers (hunh), that just as you put on your socks in the morning (hunh) before you go to put on your shoes (hunh), you must put on the Lorrrr-d, my brothers (hunh), before you can enter His Kingdom (hunh). The Kingdom awaits you, my brothers (hunh), but you have to dress rightly (hunh). Put on Cheesus every morning, brothers (hunh), and you'll march to Jerusalem (hunh) in Gawd's very own shoes . . ." (A dramatic pause from our young storyteller here, and a giggle.) Suddenly a small projectile rebounds off the sweaty sleeve of the double-knit suit. In the booth next door a man is throwing choco-late Ex-Lax into the passing crowd—chocolate Ex-Lax, for chris-sake—and people are down on their knees scooping the stuff up. You can tell the old farmers are tempted but don't want to be rude to the preacher, who's ignoring the Ex-Lax as best he can. (The crowd at Dugan's is laughing, but the story could be better, still needs work.) Finally, at the edge of the fairgrounds is this big yel-low trailer with a banner on the side that says THE WORLD'S

SMALLEST MAN / CLARENCE DAY / 20" HIGH / 39 LBS / NORMAL PARENTS / HIGH SCHOOL DIPLOMA / ADMISSION 50 CENTS. This voice is squawking on a loudspeaker about this guy's got a normal wife and two perfectly normal kids. I see a blond-headed kid, looks just like my little brother, hanging off the door, asking his dad for lunch money. Vick didn't want to go in, said it was all bullshit hype, but Nancy and I paid our 50 cents and you know Vick, wouldn't be caught missing anything and starts acting like it was his idea in the first place. Pays for both him and Rose and we all go in. (Pause) I don't know what I was expecting, but, man, it was *weird*. (How was it weird? — this story's losing momentum, it isn't going anywhere.) I mean, it's like a normal room in there, little lamps and chairs, curtains on the window. There's a woman standing by the refrigerator, a plain woman, not bad looking, about my height. But right in the middle there's this box-like thing, like a little stage sort of but more like a little barn with one wall missing, and that's where the world's smallest man is, looking right at us, very casual as if . . . as if this was just an ordinary thing. It's kind of hard to describe but, I mean we were supposed to be looking at him but he was looking at us and just kind of like, well, *waiting*. I mean he was a real disappointment in a way. Vick was right, I guess — he was just a regular midget with no legs. With legs he'd have been normal height, for a midget, so it was like cheating. But it was weird. *(How?)* I mean, we had this perfectly normal conversation, very boring really, but it was a strange experience. I can't describe it.

And finally he stops trying. There's something good here, he thinks, something about the South, about human nature and values, something that will make people laugh in just the right way. But he can't quite get it. It needs more work. He orders a rum and coke, feeling distracted and uneasy, but nobody seems to notice.

I like the storyteller. Next time he'll edit me out and be a big success, but he'll keep knowing I'm there, wondering how to tell it right. Right now, looking down at me in the trailer, he's pleased with his story and the day's outing.

The other girl . . . well, she's having a hard time dealing with this and would rather not. It's gotten real hot in here all of a sudden, and there's a musty smell—not a particularly bad smell, but she feels herself breathing it in and doesn't want it inside of her. If she'd known what it was like, she'd have stayed outside. Can't imagine why anyone pays money to be uncomfortable like this. The only right thing to do in here is stare at this poor little man, but out on the street it would be the wrong thing to do. It's impolite to stare at the handicapped, not very pleasant either. She remembers going with her mother to the dimestore when she was a kid. A lady was there at the lunch counter eating a hamburger and she had this huge lump on her neck, like a balloon that got stuck to her face from the cheekbone down to the collar bone and the skin had just grown right over it. Her mom was busy fingering through the cosmetics display, and Rose just stared at that lump, hands clenched at her sides, afraid to feel her own face. As the lady chewed her hamburger, the lump didn't move at all—it was solid and still. The whole world narrowed in on that lump and that hamburger. The smell of the hamburger. Rose threw up all over the floor of the dimestore and didn't feel right again for days. God must have a reason for doing this to people, maybe so the rest of us could count our blessings that He could have done it to us but didn't. Well, she sure does feel blessed, but it's not right to stare at people who aren't.

My wife is checking Rose out pretty close. Every once in a while we have folks getting sick in here—we've even had a few faint on us—and, believe me, it ruins our day as well as theirs. I'm hoping these kids are out of here before Todd gets back with the burgers, when suddenly Nancy asks, what's it like?

You can tell she's surprised she asked it and spooked now that it's out. She glances at Vick and Rose, who are wishing they didn't know her. Daniel lost the drift somewhere and doesn't know what she's asking. Fact is, she isn't sure either. Well, I'm on the spot now. I could say pretty near anything and it would be true, but what's the best truth for her and me right now? Nothing rises up to say itself like her question did. I have to choose an answer, and I want to do a good job. That's it, of course, so I tell her that it's a job. It's what I do, and I try to do it well. Right away I recognize that I haven't gotten through to her, I've just gotten us both off the spot. The weariness comes on me, and I wish it didn't have to be like this. I wish I could open up her head and put the answer inside, put myself inside, and sleep. And sleep. I think I know what it's like to sleep, but I can't say I remember doing it myself. I close my eyes sometimes, but I don't see less clearly. Fact is I see more clearly, not just the upholstered chairs and lamps, the wife and kids, but lawns and battlefields, rug salesmen, princesses, outhouses, astrolabes, Walter the Penniless, Jane Fonda, broken scissors and Fabergé eggs. Some folks say they have trouble remembering things, but the real trouble is forgetting. When those four kids said their good-byes last week and filed on out of the trailer, they marched right into the thick of my memories, and they'll stay there forever, rubbing elbows with people they don't even know about. At least not yet. They're still young now, and they think their lives are their own, but they're wrong about that. They're mine, too, and—like it or not—I'm theirs. That's what they got for their fifty cents. What I got was four new voices.

Ada Long has spent the last twenty-seven years teaching English and directing the honors program at the University of Alabama at Birmingham. Most of her publications have been occasional and academic essays, poetry translations, reviews, and honors-related books; she is coeditor of the *Journal of the National Collegiate Honors Council*. Her finest creation was the UAB Honors Program, which proved that students from all backgrounds, ages, races, interests, politics, and religions could learn, teach, and thrive together. In July of 2004, she retired to an island off the Florida panhandle, which—except for all the water—is just like Alabama.

BRUCE McCOMISKEY

*C*lairvoyant" is the introduction to a collection of five stories, one of which is still unpublished and another, still unwritten. It was the first story I wrote, reflecting and deepening my fraught love affair with the South. Having spent the first half of my life feeling a fine Yankee contempt for the South, I have spent the second half enthralled by it and coping with my consequent bewilderment, infatuation, defensiveness, and amusement. All of my stories locate people I know inside of narratives that evolve beyond my control; "Clairvoyant" is the only one that is taken primarily from an actual experience in upstate Alabama.

Ethan Hauser

THE CHARM OF THE HIGHWAY MEDIAN

(from *The Antioch Review*)

In the morning they were quiet like thieves. Silence filled the bulb of the cul-de-sac, the snores of homeowners and their families squelched by brick and stucco. Tall maples were tinged yellow and orange, and soon the leaves would turn brittle with November's bite. Jackson had come to help Mr. Richardson load up the car. It was just past dawn, the sky fresh with steely light, and Mr. Richardson, framed in one of the second-floor windows, dropped piece after piece of clothing. What Jackson needed to do was concentrate, so he didn't let any more white shirts hit the dewy grass. He'd already missed three, and even from twenty feet he could see the disappointment register on Mr. Richardson's face— a tightened squint, the slightly parted mouth. Mr. Richardson wasn't one for invective, but he could say much through wink and sigh, frown and nod. Don't worry, Jackson wanted to call out, they're not stained, just a little damp.

Mr. Richardson extended his arms out the window, curled his fists around an imaginary barbell and mimed lifting weights. Which meant the next item was heavy. Jackson had learned the code months before, when Mr. Richardson made the same signal and then let fly the *N* volume of an encyclopedia. The book sank instantaneously, with all the deliberateness of a bomb. Jackson had missed it, watching the burgundy leather spine collapse as it slammed into the ground. The crushed pictures of Nixon and NASA, he'd thought. A few seconds after this newest warning, three masking-taped tennis rackets sailed through the air. Jackson managed to catch them, but one slapped him in the chest and he knew immediately he'd have a nasty bruise. After the rackets came five tennis balls. They were the kind with orange fuzz, ones they haven't made for years. Jackson lobbed the last ball back up to Mr. Richardson, but he didn't want to play along and gunned it down.

The station wagon was almost at capacity, a wave of random clothes cresting near the tops of the windows. Any higher and it would be unsafe to drive. From his driver's ed classes, Jackson knew all about blind spots, passing on the left, a yellow light not meaning speed up. It's tempting, the driver's ed teacher was fond of saying. Like a beautiful woman. So play it safe, approach with caution, she'll give you the green light when it's time. The driver's ed teacher, his eyes perpetually veiled with mirrored aviator shades, had a mantra: "Reverse is suicide." A local band had adopted the saying as their name, borrowing the sunglasses look, too. Actually, Jackson knew he could pack the car more efficiently, but he wanted Mr. Richardson to think they were almost done.

Jackson yelled, "Mr. Rich—" but he was silenced by a wagging finger. A few seconds later he scrambled to catch a miniature dime-store Indian, and after that a bonsai tree still rooted to its clay pot. Not the stamps, Jackson hoped, remembering the time he watched helplessly as two hundred square snowflakes rained from Mr. Richardson's hands.

They do this once every month, not counting last March, when Mr. Richardson summoned Jackson three separate times. Jackson doesn't mind so much; he just adds on the hours to the bill he submits for the lawn work. Gathering the clothes is a little like bundling leaves, anyway. And he wants to help Mr. Richardson, because he's afraid not many others do.

Close to eight, Mrs. Richardson would wake up. She would appear at her husband's shoulder, pill bottles in one hand, a glass of water in the other. Usually she came down and told Jackson to go home. He would point to a corner of the porch where he'd neatly piled Mr. Richardson's things. She thanked him and always apologized, too, reminding him to add the hours to his invoice, which Jackson would never have done had she not said to. "One more thing," she said. "Would you mind, maybe, not mentioning this to your parents?" Jackson never has, because it's not anything bad, really.

That day, however, Mr. Richardson just kept dropping more things, many more than any previous time. Jackson retrieved them all and shoved them into the car's rapidly disappearing empty spaces, stashing a *Reader's Digest* condensed book behind the driver's seat, some Spanish coins in the ashtray of the back door. He lassoed the left headrest with strands of purple and yellow Mardi Gras beads. It was hard to imagine Mr. Richardson navigating clogged Bourbon Street.

"Everything fit okay?"

The voice surprised Jackson, for he hadn't realized Mr. Richardson had descended from the second floor and joined him by the car. Jackson nodded, his hands stuffed in the pockets of his varsity jacket.

"And the mower, you gassed it up, right?" Mr. Richardson fingered the bungee cords that anchored the mower to the roof of the car.

Again Jackson nodded, uncertain of why Mr. Richardson was so concerned. Occasionally Jackson forgot to remove the mower after he returned home from a job, and his father drove to work with it still hovering overhead. At dinner, the same joke every time: "My secretary wished me the best of luck in my new profession as a gardener. She said she'd have never predicted it from the way I murder my office plants."

Jackson looked up at the second-floor windows, hoping to catch Mrs. Richardson's shadow. He looked for a light switched on, listened for music drizzling from the bedroom—some signal of impending intervention. But he saw and heard nothing.

"Let's get going, then," said Mr. Richardson.

"Is Mrs. Richardson around?"

Mr. Richardson shook his head. "Don't need her for this. Besides, she's visiting her nephew. Tried to drag me along, too, all the way to Kernersville. I told her if they weren't going to the ball game, forget it."

Jackson wasn't sure he believed that. "Do you mind if I get a drink of water before we go?" he said, picturing waking Mrs. Richardson himself. She would pull on a housecoat and apologize, say she hadn't heard a thing. "Sometimes," she would say, "Albert's as silent as a mouse. I lose track of him if I'm not careful."

Mr. Richardson dug a canteen out of the tote bag he was carrying and tapped its aluminum shell. "Got some right here," he said. "Snacks, too," he added, fishing a bag of orange cheese puffs from the bottom of the tote.

"Well, I need to go to the bathroom," Jackson said.

"You can go when we get there. Don't want to waste any more time."

One problem was that Jackson didn't know where "there" was. All Mr. Richardson had told him was to come to the house that morning, even though he wasn't scheduled to mow the lawn until the next week. As if to cover, Mr. Richardson had said that he'd noticed some patches the boy had missed. "Can't let those weeds get any kind of foothold," he'd explained. "They'll take over if you let them."

As they opened the car doors, Jackson blurted, "Where are we going?"

"Just drive," said Mr. Richardson, dropping the two words like heavy sacks. There was something in his voice, some terrible combination of frailty and confidence, that made Jackson shut up, start the engine, and pull away from the curb. Had he said, "Just wink," Jackson would have winked, "Just tell me," and he would have started babbling about the weather, about a crush he had, about anything, and "Just hold me" would have sent the boy's spindly arms lurching toward an awkward embrace. There were years loaded in that voice, decades, something you can't buy or practice, and Mr. Richardson's bald, age-spotted scalp looked at that moment as round and flawless as a Christmas ornament. His stooped posture had all the dignity and peculiar permanence of crumbling temples. Even his arthritis-choked fingers possessed a kind of beauty, as if it was Jackson and the rest of the world, everyone who could still stand board-straight, still thread an arm through the sleeve of a jacket without its aching, who were the exceptions.

Mr. Richardson directed Jackson onto Route 102, a one-lane highway that snaked through rural hamlets. They drove for nearly an hour, under the interminable rise and fall of power lines, the countryside studded with white farmhouses and uncut forest. They passed gas stations, a hitchhiker, families gathering in their driveways before church. There were boys in suits whose sleeves were already too short, little girls fussing with the lace and ribbons their mothers had spent hours ironing. Soon they'd fidget in the hard pews and pray for the sermon to end, an unflagging Sunday ahead of them.

Jackson and Mr. Richardson drove by a woman hanging laundry who kept disappearing behind striped T-shirts and sheets pregnant with wind. She used clothespins her daughter had painted yellow, to match the sun, on a day too rainy to run around outside. That daughter had spent the night at a friend's house, and they'd watched a movie so frightening they had to sleep in the same bed and block the closet door with a dresser, to keep the serial killers out. They talked until their eyelids were leaden with sleep, until the weight of fatigue smothered their fear.

During the drive Mr. Richardson opened the glove compartment, finding two pieces of paper tucked into the car manual. One was Jackson's learner's permit, stating that he could drive only with an adult over 18 with a valid driver's license. It hadn't occurred to Jackson, until that moment, that Mr. Richardson might not have a license. But the way he was studying the pale green card made Jackson wonder, and he scanned the road for police cars and decelerated to well under the speed limit. An endless tractor trailer sped past. The driver gave Jackson the finger for driving too slow.

"What's this?" Mr. Richardson asked as he looked at the second sheet of paper.

"It's my brother's list." Late at night, Jackson and his brother, Max, would sneak the car out. They had to open the garage door by hand because the electric mechanism would wake their parents. Their domain was a far corner of the Safeway lot, behind the darkened, hulking store, and Jackson piloted the car from one Dumpster to another. Often Max begged for a turn at the wheel. Not now, Jackson said, it's too dangerous and your legs won't reach anyway. When I get my license, he promised. The most recent time, Max had taken the list to the car and read it aloud as they surveilled the sleeping neighbors and dreamed of being legal.

"Things Girls Don't Get," Mr. Richardson read. He brought the sheet of paper close to his eyes. "Things girls don't get," he repeated slowly. "What does that mean?"

Jackson could feel himself blushing, and he wasn't sure why. It wasn't even his list, after all. He hoped Mr. Richardson would forget it and talk about something else.

"'One: Motorhead,'" Mr. Richardson read. "What's that?"

"A band," Jackson said.

"Pop band? Like the Platters?"

"A little more rock and roll."

"Oh . . . like the Beatles."

Jackson nodded.

"What do they sing?"

"They have a lot of records."

"Name one."

"Ace of Spades."

"'Two: Nintendo.' What's that?"

"A video game. You know, like Space Invaders. Max has won tournaments," Jackson said. "Should I still be on 102?"

"Have we passed Lenox yet?" Mr. Richardson asked.

"No."

"Good. Stay on this road."

Just off the shoulder, in front of a weather-beaten shack, a man pounded a stake into the ground. He swung a sledgehammer, planting a hand-painted sign that advertised fresh vegetables and honey, and crates of lettuce and potatoes crowded the bed of his pickup. The narrow snout of a collie poked through the driver's side window, trying to nose the glass down. She couldn't bear the loneliness, no matter how temporary.

"'Three,'" Mr. Richardson continued. "'Professional wrestling.'"

Jackson fiddled with the radio, wondering how he was going to explain this one.

"Used to do some of that myself," Mr. Richardson said. "In high school. Coach Bastone. We called him Coach Bastard."

"It's not really the same thing," Jackson said.

"Why not?"

Jackson shrugged. "Don't know, just isn't. Max is talking about, like, Sergeant Slaughter, George 'the Animal' Steele, Nature Boy Ric Flair. That kind of wrestling."

"They used to call *me* 'Shorty.'"

"Are we close to where you want to be?" Jackson asked.

Mr. Richardson stopped reading the list and gazed out at the land. Getting close, Mr. Richardson wanted to tell the boy, that's not the problem. A sprawling farm drifted by and the rich stench of animals filled the car. Cows mingled in the shade of a generous tree, their tails snapping at the flies alighting on their backs. On one distant hillside the wooden skeleton of a house under construction offered progress, a promise, sign of a future. An elephantine cement truck stood guard over the property. Already there was the index finger of a chimney, a bay window facing west. Soon they'd rough out a pond and stuff the slanted attic walls with insulation. In a year a family would lay claim, embed their fingerprints and whispers, their footsteps.

"A few more miles," Mr. Richardson said.

Jackson recognized the song on the radio and turned it louder. "Is this Motorhead?"

Jackson shook his head. The word sounded funny coming from Mr. Richardson's mouth.

"Who is it?"

"The Stones."

"Don't know them either."

They were silent for the next three and a half minutes. When the song ended, Mr. Richardson switched the radio off. "Okay," he said abruptly. "Here."

Jackson slowed the car and pulled onto the shoulder. A guardrail paralleled them, its surface littered with the vows of teenagers sick with love. They were on some anonymous stretch of highway, far from any town, no homes or stores in sight. Ten thousand feet up, an airplane pierced the sky's lone mournful cloud.

There was no way for Mr. Richardson to explain to the boy where they were going. Because it wasn't an exact destination, a precise address. No inch of map was available to circle, no landmarks to watch out for.

What the doctors have said to him is that his brain no longer works like it used to. Your memory functions, one specialist explained, have gotten sort of miswired. Imagine a clock that refuses to keep the right time. You can set it right over and over again, but you never know how far off it's going to be. There's no predicting whether it'll be slow or fast. It means that sometimes he can't remember the route from the bathroom to the kitchen, and at other times the score of a World Series game from sixty years ago will surface — he wanted desperately to be a batboy and retrieve stray foul balls for the catcher. He wanted to bother the players afterwards for autographs and fielding tips. Some days he fills notepads with the titles of books he read in grade school; other times his own name eludes him, and he is suddenly grateful to the telemarketers everyone else loathes. The condition means that he seizes every memory he has, because its half-life may be only a few seconds. The color and shape of lima beans, the name of the drugstore where he buys the newspaper. He likes to write each memory down, to keep a record, to prove they belong to him.

The day before, while eating breakfast, he remembered driving with an old girlfriend, in a state he can no longer name, and pulling to the side of the road to collect wildflowers. She'd taken a rubber band from her hair and stretched it around a bunch, said she'd keep them even after they wilted; she would dry them, and they would become a memento. It was a moment he wanted to hold onto even then, how the sun lit her hair, how a thorn scraped his wrist, how their palm-sized nation seemed so very perfect. And he knew now, from an article in the newspaper, how the highway department had begun to plant wildflowers along the freeway medians. "A beautification campaign," the governor deemed it, justifying the budget to skeptical taxpayers.

Which is why he'd called the boy and why they'd stopped where they had, in the car, about to cross the road and admire the larkspur, Indian paintbrush, the black-eyed Susans. Why they had had to find a median glowing with goldenrod, ground smeared with the work of angels. Because this girl, the one floating, the one holding jewelweed for him to pop, she may be his wife, but he can't be sure and he wants to be.

The boy was fidgeting, tapping the steering wheel. His knee bobbed, straining already frayed jeans. Mr. Richardson sympathized with his impatience and confusion and said, "Okay, let's cross the road."

"Here?" asked the boy. "Is it safe?"

"We'll run," said Mr. Richardson, almost laughing at the thought of ordering his legs to sprint. The boy would protect him, he knew.

Once they were on the median, the boy still seemed bewildered. Mr. Richardson could explain to him why they were there, but he was afraid of how it might sound, how it couldn't possibly make sense to someone so young and hinged. "Just give me a few minutes," he said, and the boy nodded, the permission like a precious gift.

Mr. Richardson gathered a handful of flowers and looked over the slender median. It wasn't so much the smell as the sight that brought him back, nature's confetti, and within an instant it was decades ago, a patch of city, his life with her. He remembered how they used to wake the neighbors, how they didn't care that their moans bled through the walls of the apartment. He remembered the stares they were sometimes the target of while entering and exiting the building, the flashes of disapproval and desire, curiosity and high-mindedness. And he remembered how it made him feel as though he loved her even more, that they shared something others couldn't stop, others craved. Spent, they held each other, under a blanket unearthed from a thrift store, and he glimpsed rough circles of her flesh through the handiwork of moths. An uncurtained window let the breeze in, along with the pink wash from a neon marquee across the street. In the middle of the night, asleep, they would roll into each other and it was one more invitation, maybe a command. So they would have at it again, without words, slipping into a rhythm that felt almost illegal. They never even bothered to stop to think how indestructible they were.

There were times it rained, late-afternoon eruptions, and the slap of the storm drowned out the hiss and whine of the beleaguered radiators. The leaky unit in the kitchen had stained a corner of the linoleum floor a shape that looked like Africa. She pointed with her toe once and said, "That's where Nigeria is." They drank vodka tonics out of mason jars and ate cereal straight from the box. They must have been working, but he has no idea what their jobs were, and he can't imagine they cared much even then. For hours they sat, entwined, watching the moon rise or listening to the top-20 countdown. Years before, in college, he'd wanted to be a deejay, and when his roommate wasn't around he practiced making his voice deeper, enunciating precisely the titles of songs and the names of sponsors. "This segment brought to you by the folks at Bayer," he announced in front of the mirror. "Let's keep those headaches at bay."

He remembered walking around outside, leaping over the lake of rainwater a dammed-up sewer had spit back. On the street corners vendors hawked umbrellas. He didn't buy one, wanting instead to feel the cool drops, not minding that soon his shirt and jeans would be sopped. Under the pelleting storm, he had the city to himself, its uninhabited streets shimmering with possibility. Huddles of men and women, fearful of getting wet, waited out the rain beneath the monogrammed awnings of doorman buildings. Racing cabs sprayed people who had done nothing wrong. Drenched, pants pasted to their shins, they shouted "Fuck you!" and "Bastard!" A singular goal in his mind: They were out of cigarettes. He managed to avoid the flying puddles, and it was one more sign of the rightness of everything.

And they would waste their nights like that, smoking and listening to music, topping off their cocktails until the world seemed impossibly languorous. A tinny radio, Red Foley songs played over and over again that they were too much in love to grow tired of or even much notice. Beneath one of the windows, a woman hurried down the sidewalk, and the girl said, "She's on her way home. She'll cook something warm and delicious for dinner. She's missed her son, though she's only been at the dentist. You can see it in her walk. The rain reminds her of the second summer she spent at overnight camp, how she loved a boy named Edwin so much she thought she would die in her sleep every night." That was their game. He would point at someone, and she would spin an endless story. About a man in a tan trench coat: "He's just come from meeting his secretary at a hotel. They sleep with each other as if it's the last sex they'll ever have, and every night, lying next to his wife, the guilt almost swallows him whole. It's like a tumor that won't shrink. He's tried to end it, but the sight of her won't let him. It's gotten so that he needs sleeping pills to rest for even an hour."

"And her," he said, pointing to a woman with a brown umbrella.

"She's about to tell her life story. On the bus, to whomever she sits next to. It will be a man, and she'll know, before she even opens her mouth, that she wants to marry this man. She has a fantastic story to tell him, how her father was a Saudi prince, how her mother had so many jewels that she could wear a different bracelet every day of the year. They built an estate in the desert, with spires, servants, a moat. She's had a camel spit on her." He kissed her until the stories dissolved. He opened her sweater and slid her skirt down below her ankles to look at her and hold her in the places only lovers can. Then they figured out heaven.

No matter how many moments resurfaced, he couldn't find her name. He could see the mules she kicked off just inside the door, the candles she insisted on lighting every time they shared dinner, even when it was only sandwiches. He could see a time she cried and how he didn't dare tell her, but she looked stunning with the tears trickling down her cheeks, delicate and temporary. Each detail was like a newly minted penny, its copper bold and glowing. He owned a fortune in change.

The boy, he knew, wanted to leave. His friends were waiting to play football, to waste hours in a diner flirting with girls who could snap their hopes without warning. Life must seem to him endless; its unfurling has just begun. To the boy, the narrow median was just that, a skid of highway, a public works project, with none of the freight and lust of memory, no history. One more minute, he wanted to call to the boy. Just another minute to figure it all out. And he brought the flowers to his nose one last time, inhaling until his lungs ballooned with their essence. He felt like a bee, wild with the scent of pollen. He wondered if they had been planted just for him, one more labyrinthine path, a million little clues. The doctors, he thought, are dead wrong. Memory happens in the heart, not the brain.

Mr. Richardson stepped off the median and onto the road. A harsh horn blast startled him, and Jackson grabbed him to keep him from drifting farther into the street. The guttural sound lingered, echoing in the ravine of a nearby mountain.

"Careful," Jackson said, his hand latched to a bony elbow.

Mr. Richardson nodded, his fist wrapped tight around the flower stalks. The two of them crossed the road and another car honked. Its driver leaned on the horn until the vehicle had disappeared around the highway's bend, the dying off of the sound a coda.

Jackson walked Mr. Richardson to the passenger side of the car and then went to his own door. He offered to put the flowers in the back seat but Mr. Richardson shook his head. Before they got in, they looked at each other over the roof of the car, over the small round engine of the mower. Mr. Richardson wondered if the boy knew. The horn blasts weren't warnings. They were cheers.

Ethan Hauser holds graduate degrees from Hollins University and the University of North Carolina–Greensboro. He has published short stories in *Esquire, Playboy, Ploughshares,* and the *Antioch Review,* and nonfiction in the *New York Times* and the *New York Times Magazine.*

I like to think of myself as at least an honorary Southerner: I spent several years living in Virginia and North Carolina; my record collection is thick with Waylon Jennings and George Jones; I have visited Faulkner's home in Oxford; I make twice yearly sojourns to the Skylight Inn in Ayden, for nothing more than a barbecue sandwich (no slaw). My friends who are true Southerners are kind enough not to remind me constantly that I was born in Massachusetts and that a few years in one's twenties does not a local make. This story was written shortly after I moved away from the South, and it's part of a group of stories I like to think of as my homesickness work. When I lived in North Carolina, it sometimes felt like the whole state was under construction to accommodate the population boom. (See? I wasn't the only one who could appreciate pit-smoked pulled pork.) I started wondering what all those highways would look like when the construction crews left, what could be done so the newly tarred pavement wouldn't look all shiny and fake. Then I came up with the opening scene—an old man throwing random things out a window to a teenage boy. The real challenge was how to wed the two.

Rebecca Soppe

THE PANTYHOSE MAN

(from *Ploughshares*)

The sun goes down, and out they come—the phone perverts—like hairy-pawed werewolves roaming the darkened
landscape of the Arkansas (501) calling area, their collective anxiety
burning through telephone wires from Sweet Home to Sheraton
Park. At the Little Rock Marriott Renaissance Hotel alone, one out
of every eighty-two calls received on the nightshift by the in-house
reservations desk is from a phone pervert, or a "caller using inap-
propriate or sexually graphic language," as the Orientation Manual for New Reservations Agents puts it. The average figure was
determined years before by some undergraduate psychology major
working for the summer, or by an overzealous assistant manager
of sales, or by some part-timer red in the face with the number of
times each week she had to hear about the enormity of some
anonymous caller's manhood. This figure, as all of the office girls
who've been there any length of time know, is somewhat skewed,
since pervert calls, like thefts and the deaths of old men, rise slightly
around Thanksgiving and Christmas. It involves some miscalcula-
tion, because several of their strange callers, like the Sunday-night
woman who laughs maniacally into the receiver and the man who
rings up every few months to say, "Hello, I'm a citizen of the uni-
verse, and I'm gonna open up a can of whoopass on you. You still
at 20 Westport Center Drive? Don't leave. I'm on my way," are

shoved into the pervert category even though their inflictions are of an entirely different nature.

The reservations girls at the Little Rock Marriott Renaissance Hotel also know that their own situation is not unique, that the nocturnal love songs of the phone perverts are offered up to women everywhere—women in the pink-collar professions with toll-free numbers and no Caller ID—from the Blue Cross Blue Shield customer service reps in Chicago, to the *Rock-n-Roll Super Hits of the Seventies* album order-takers in Omaha, to the PBS donation operators in Des Moines. These Little Rock reservations girls, at least the ones who've been at it for more than a month or two, know the system; they've identified the habits, the intimate quirks of these anonymous men. They know that the phone perverts are always polite—not the kind of polite that keeps them from saying things like "I'm over at the Hampton Inn, and my mother's here, and I'm fucking her in the ass," but the kind of polite that admits defeat, that forces them to hang up the phone graciously when one of the girls gives them the obligatory "Get a life, sicko" and "Don't call back." The cleverest of these girls have come to appreciate the art of phone perversion: the suspense involved, the holding and delivering of dirty one-liners, the structured conversations as finely crafted as a sales pitch, or a good joke.

According to the Orientation Manual for New Reservations Agents, these phone perverts should be handled in a certain way, and when their shift supervisor, the tall one named Vince who bites his nails and has yellow nicotine rings around his nostrils, is standing over the reservations girls, they do things by the book. "I'm sorry, sir, but I'll have to terminate this call," they say. "I'd be happy to make a reservation for you if you called back and spoke to me in a less abusive manner. Have a nice day." But when Vince or the general manager or the nosy housekeeping supervisor isn't in the office, the girls who've been around for a while prefer to deal with the pervert calls in their own fashion. Chrissie, a nursing student who always has her anatomy flashcards spread out next to her station and hands out cupcakes with little notes on Snoopy paper for

Valentine's Day, usually squeals and tosses the phone down in its cradle, saying, "Oh, that nasty man," and flushing with embarrassment, or with something else like it. Leslie, who was sent back to reservations from the front desk for accepting too many gifts from the Norfolk Southern railroad men, likes to tease the phone perverts. On her days off, she wears dark indigo jeans so tight she has to lie down on the floor to zip them, and everyone knows this is why her two sons have funny-shaped heads; the baby one, Hunter, has a big dent like someone deflated him just above the left eye, and the three-year-old named Troy has a big bulge on top and a tiny chin, an ill-formed peanut head. Leslie taunts the perverts by making them repeat themselves—"I'm sorry, sir, but what did you say? Come again, I didn't quite catch that"—until the men are so frustrated they hang up, their dirty words made useless by Leslie's hard-of-hearing routine. The others—Claudia, the natural redhead, and Lily, who comes from Mississippi—usually swear at the phone perverts, letting loose the pent-up hatred that comes from forty hours a week of haggling with secretaries and travel agents over the price of a hotel room.

Of all the girls who've worked the late shift at the Marriott reservations desk for any amount of time, only Judy, who is gone now, but not so gone that there isn't talk, not so gone that she's disappeared from the lore of the place, ever had the least bit of empathy for these late-night compulsive cold-callers of strange women, and so when there was a phone pervert on Judy's line, swearing or panting into the receiver, she would let him off easy and quietly hang up.

None of the girls on the four-to-midnight shift at the Marriott reservations desk knew much about Judy. They knew she was widowed, or divorced, or maybe just thrown over by a live-in lover, some small-town someone who stole off in the night with her credit card and her grandmother's silver candlesticks. They knew she came to Little Rock and the reservations desk back when Ted Saunders was still the general manager, during the summer when the hotel's air conditioners went out for three days while they were hosting a convention for special children who didn't have sweat glands, and that she spent her first days of training handing out bottled water and icing down the sobbing things after they passed out in the Meridian Grand Ballroom and up and down the hallways. They knew that when Judy came to Little Rock she rented a one-bedroom apartment on Forest Avenue near the park, and that she spent every morning before work for two weeks scouring the stores for bargain housewares, filling the apartment with brightly colored things until it looked like a kindergarten classroom. "An affinity for bright colors suggests a healthy person with a happy childhood," she had said when some of the girls came to her apartment to pick her up for an all-employee meeting. The girls weren't convinced, since they knew that after those first two weeks when Judy filled her apartment with yellow curtains and blue towels, things around Judy's place began to stagnate, with nothing much more than the single occupant and some junk mail and a few bags of groceries each week moving in and out, and with the orange rugs and green sofa growing dingy and fading into pastels.

Judy was twenty years older than the rest of the girls, and for that reason alone, since she got the lowest reservation bonus every month and never got promoted, they let her boss them around a little. She wasn't all that bossy—she kept to herself most of the time, holed up at her station with the latest issue of *Woman's Day* or *Cosmo*—but she did have her moments, like when Leslie would tease the phone perverts and Judy would march up to her workspace and say, "Jesus, Leslie, just hang up the phone and be nice. Don't you know everyone's got their problems?" while she eyed the five-by-seven picture of baby Hunter on Leslie's desk, the one where baby Hunter is dressed like a pumpkin with a big rotten spot just below the stem. Leslie usually smirked at this, but she obeyed, at least for a week or two, since everyone knew a little about the thing between Judy and the pantyhose man.

The pantyhose man was Judy's favorite phone pervert, the only one of these men who ever got more from her than just the usual silent slipping of the phone into its cradle. He was what the girls called a "pervert-in-denial," the gentlemanly sort of obscene caller who refrains from using the standard coarse language, and who draws pleasure from trying to keep the semblance of a normal conversation with the woman on the end of the line. He was the most reliable of the phone perverts, because he called every week— always on a Wednesday evening between eight and ten, since the first November Judy worked at the reservations desk. Each time he called, the pantyhose man kept to the same routine, claiming he was a representative from No nonsense, or L'eggs, or Victoria's Secret, or whatever brand of women's hosiery was currently hot and heavily marketed, and asking one of the reservations girls for a moment of her time to complete a brief questionnaire. The first time Judy had him on the line, before she knew what he was all about, she answered his questions with clumsy honesty.

"Do you wear pantyhose to work, ma'am?" he asked, and she could hear him shuffling papers in the background.

"Yes. We have to, it's part of the dress code."

"And do you enjoy wearing pantyhose?"

"Not really," she said. "They make your feet stink."

"Okay, then," he said. "Moving on. Is there a particular brand you prefer?"

"I usually just buy the generic kind from Walgreens or wherever. I don't know what they call them."

"And what is your hosiery size, if I may?" he said. There was a moment's hesitation, and then he explained. "You see, ma'am, we're sending out free samples of our new extra-strength, run-free nylons, and I'd like to help you select the product that's right for you."

"Oh. Queen One, mostly, but it depends on the brand." With this the pantyhose man sighed, thanked her, and politely hung up.

At first Judy thought nothing of this call, assumed the pantyhose man was simply one of the telemarketers and survey-takers who occasionally called the reservations desk, and who were usually a welcome diversion on a slow and boring shift. But then the pantyhose man called back, first to Claudia's line, then to Lily's, and after a month or so of Wednesdays, the girls caught on to the pantyhose man's scheme. It was Leslie with her taunting who figured out the script, the right set of answers to complete the pantyhose man's survey and get to the grand prize:

PANTYHOSE MAN: Do you enjoy wearing pantyhose?
OPERATOR: Yes, they feel nice next to my skin.
PANTYHOSE MAN: What size do you wear?
OPERATOR: Extra-tall.
PANTYHOSE MAN: What color?
OPERATOR: White.
PANTYHOSE MAN: Do you wear them with underwear or without?
OPERATOR: Without.
PANTYHOSE MAN: Would you like a free sample of our product?
OPERATOR: Sure, what do I have to do?
PANTYHOSE MAN: Just send a pair of your old pantyhose — a pair you've worn — to the address I'm about to give you.

When the girls heard this, Chrissie squealed, and Claudia swore, and Judy said, "Maybe he didn't mean it like that," and they all had a good chuckle over the pantyhose man. Still, even though the girls had written him off as just another in the string of pervert callers that came with the territory of the reservations desk, there was something about the pantyhose man — something about that voice, which was both a little sexy and a little sad, or maybe something about that sigh he gave Judy. It was a sigh that said this thing he had to do, this endless waiting for everything to turn out the right way, for the woman on the other end to say the right words, was making him tired — maybe *this* was the something that intrigued Judy, that kept her from hanging up like usual on the pantyhose man.

And so Judy was prepared the next time she got his call, and she breezed through the answers, even embellishing a little, adding, "I wear extra-tall, and it's so hard to find stockings that fit right because my legs are *so long*." She scratched down the address he gave her, a PO box in South Bend, Indiana, and she shoved it inside the pocket of her purse. She carried the address with her for two weeks, trying to decide what to do with it. She tried to imagine the panty-hose man: what he looked like, where he worked, what he wore. Sometimes she pictured him short and dark-haired, a tax accountant dressed in elastic-waist pants and a nubby golf sweater, and sometimes as a lanky strawberry-blonde in a one-piece Dickies jumpsuit like an auto mechanic. Sometimes he had a scar snaking from the corner of his upper lip, leftover from a dog bite when he was six, and other times he had a handlebar mustache or webbed toes or a broken arm. The physical variations were endless, but the setting in which Judy imagined him was always the same: a one-bedroom South Bend apartment, two blocks from the park, with faded wall-to-wall carpeting worn threadbare by his lonely late-night pacing with the cordless phone in hand and the wrench of anticipation tightening with the pulse of each digit he dialed.

When Judy decided what to do about the pantyhose man, she went to the Piggly Wiggly and bought flour and eggs, and then she baked two dozen peanut-butter cookies with Hershey Kisses shoved into their middles. She put them into a cookie tin decorated with a replica painting of the 1940s Tesoro Rancho orange-crate girl, a curly-haired gypsy type with huge, gold hoop earrings and plump legs wrapped in black stockings, and she wrote a note that said, *From the tall blonde with the white thigh-highs. These cookies are not poisoned. Please enjoy,* and then she sent the package to him with the Little Rock Marriott Renaissance Hotel as the return address.

And that's when it began—the anonymous courtship, or friendship, or symbiotic acquaintanceship of Judy and the pantyhose man. It became a regular Wednesday-night thing, with the pantyhose man calling week after week, still pretending he'd never heard Judy's voice before, and with Judy offering up an ever-changing account of her hosiery preferences—nude stockings with a red garter belt one week, lace fishnets the next, navy-blue ribbed knee-highs the week after. The gypsy-girl cookie tin, empty except for a few buttery crumbs, came back to the hotel in a box addressed to the evening reservations staff. There was no thank-you card, nothing but the same PO box on the return label to indicate where it was from, but Judy knew he was grateful, and he began asking for her by name—or not by name, exactly, since name-exchanging was not part of the silent agreement between Judy and the pantyhose man, but by requesting *the older woman in reservations* in a different put-on voice every week.

The girls on the late shift at the reservations desk were not fooled. They heard Judy through the walls of her cubicle in bits and snatches, distinguished words like *control top* and *cotton crotch* in the low murmur of Judy's secret exchanges with the pantyhose man. This eavesdropping had started innocently enough, with the switchboard operator's announcement that there was a man on the phone for Judy, and could someone see if she was in the bathroom because it sounded urgent, and then Chrissie found Judy in the supply closet fetching printer paper and everyone put their calls on hold and discreetly tipped their ears towards Judy's workstation, thinking the man on the phone might be the AWOL lover, or a new admirer, or at least a new friend she had met at the Laundromat or the drugstore. When they realized it was the pantyhose man Judy was carrying on with, there was much talk in the break room over french-inhaled Virginia Slims and Diet Cokes, but no one said a word about this to Judy, just like no one said a word to her when Lily caught her hunching under her desk with her shoe off, sniffing it after someone had mentioned an odor in the back office, or when Leslie and Claudia saw one of the banquet servers back into Judy's Ford Escort, leaving a golf-ball-size ding on the corner of the bumper.

And so Judy continued on with the pantyhose man, unaware that their relationship was quickly becoming public knowledge. It was a relationship, like any other mutually agreeable pairing, that had its ups and downs. Judy began spending time in the public library looking for little gifts for the pantyhose man, tidbits from the Internet to spice up their usual exchange, things like: "Did you know that the 'ny' in 'nylons' comes from 'New York,' because the first pair of nylons made their debut at the 1939 New York World's Fair?" or: "Did you know that some shots of the tornado in *The Wizard of Oz* were created by filming a nylon stocking blown by a fan?" The pantyhose man seemed to enjoy these little tidbits, responding to them with a hearty chuckle that had surprised Judy at first, and made her think that maybe, in some way, she had the power to make this strange man happy.

There were bad times as well, like the Wednesday when Judy was in a foul mood because a little boy in the grocery store pointed and screamed at the varicose veins roping across the backs of her calves, and the Wednesday she spilled a Coke on her white uniform blouse in the car. And there was the Wednesday she came into work and found a note from the sales department on her desk asking her to cancel the forty-five rooms for the Future Farmers of America that she was supposed to get commission on, all because the convention was pulling out after the hotel refused to hire four extra security guards to keep two hundred teenagers from humping in the coatrooms. On these difficult Wednesdays, when the pantyhose man called with his usual "Ma'am, if I could have a moment of your time . . . ," Judy would hiss, "I don't *have* any time for you right now," and hang up the phone. But when things like this happened the pantyhose man would still call the next week, steady as ever, and Judy would feel terrible, and she would apologize by throwing in a little something extra for him—spiked heels, perhaps, or schoolgirl knee socks with tassels.

Things carried on like this for months, years even—a little over two years, anyway, as far as anyone could remember. It got so that the reservations girls grew tired of eavesdropping, began to ignore Judy's steamy exchanges with the pantyhose man, grew accustomed to and ignored them like they grew accustomed to other things around the office: the low buzz of the defunct fire exit sign above the door, the crusty soup bowls stacked on a filing cabinet that the morning-shift girls forgot to take back to the kitchen, the habitual tardiness of a night auditor who came in twenty minutes late every shift and stole the loose change from the bottoms of the other girls' purses. They ignored Judy herself, largely, and Judy seemed content with this lack of attention—she sat in her workspace most days, humming and flipping through magazines, polishing her nails, answering her line with a pleasant chirp and the mandatory department greeting: "Thank you for calling the Little Rock Marriott, central Arkansas's premier hotel and conference center, you've reached the reservations department, how may I help you today?"

And then things changed somehow, almost imperceptibly at first, so that only a couple of the girls noticed it at the beginning. Judy started becoming *louder*—louder in her step, which would drag across the floor and pucker the cheap padding under the industrial-length carpet when she walked, and louder in her movements, louder in the wake of stale office air that whooshed behind her when she entered the room. This loudness, this slamming of phone and flicking of pen, lasted for weeks, longer than any temporary foul mood, any spilled Coke in the car or retracted reservation commission, could possibly explain, and then came the day when Judy breezed in ten minutes after her shift began, tossed the sunglasses from her face, and said (in a gruff voice that suggested a lack of proper rest and loud enough for people on the other side of the door in the lobby to hear her) something along the lines of "What a damn lovely day it is, damn it."

It was then that Judy reentered the collective imagination of the reservations girls, and they began tipping their ears once again to the commotion in her cubicle. It took them two weeks to discover that something was missing, that the shuffling and sighing from Judy's end of the room was filling a void left, they realized, by the disappearance of the pantyhose man. They kept on this hunch for a month, and in the end their theory played out, with not a single one of them picking up the familiar call, receiving the usual Wednesday-night request for *the older woman in reservations*.

By the time the girls figured this out, Judy's loudness had subsided, and suddenly she was not growing more raucous, but *smaller* instead. There was nothing now but a low murmur, a simmer, from her cubicle, and then she was boiling down right in front of their eyes. At first it was the ten pounds she clearly lost—the ten pounds a woman sheds after she's lost a lover, or before she goes on a cruise—the ten pounds they commended her for, saying, "Looking good, Judy," and getting nothing in response. And then it was the *space* she occupied that was growing smaller, the cubic mass of Judy and her various extensions: her splayed-out assortment of magazine articles and perfume samples sweeping into a neat stack, and the stack shifting into a desk drawer, and then Judy sitting more or less motionless in her chair, her arms pulled in tight to her sides and her hands in her lap—Judy growing smaller and smaller in the presence of the reservations girls until the day in mid-October when she simply disappeared, missed her Wednesday shift, and then her Thursday, and the girls never saw her again.

What happens now depends on what you think of the pantyhose man, of phone perverts, of obscene and harassing phone callers in general. Who are these men (largely men, although of course there are women, here and there), and what do they want from you? Are they empty-headed, drunken fraternity boys, out for a chuckle, or are they something more serious—sad and frustrated sexual misfits? Are they somewhere far out there, out past the scope of your peripheral vision, or are they right in front of you: your neighbor, your butcher, the boy you befriended in junior high with the stringy hair and the model glue and the flabby breasts, the one whose lonely antics you eventually ignored in order to glide smoothly into your uncomplicated and healthy adult life? Are they your Sunday school teacher, the Santa Claus stand-in at the mall? Are they your father? And how would you know? And what would you do if you found out?

• • •

THE PANTYHOSE MAN 199

Judy is gone now from the Little Rock Marriott Renaissance Hotel. The girls at the reservations desk did what they could. After the first few missed shifts, they left her long concerned-sounding phone messages, which, after days without return, became short angry messages, with swearing involved, that complained of how they were shorthanded, and where was she when she was supposed to be at work? They even looked for her a little, sending Chrissie out to her Parkside apartment, where she knocked repeatedly on the front door until one of the neighbors poked his head out and shot her a nasty glare. She rattled Judy's doorknob and threw pebbles at her window, and then she tried to peer through the crack between the curtains and saw nothing but a sliver of the orderly corner table next to Judy's sofa in the dim light that filtered in through the thin curtain fabric. She tried to jimmy open the locked mailbox with no success, then gave up and reported back to management, who sent out the official-sounding letter explaining Judy's termination, along with her final paycheck, which the accounting staff reports she never cashed.

Still, even though Judy has disappeared from her workspace, has vanished from the payroll, has never been seen again by anyone who works at the Little Rock Marriott Renaissance, she still lingers, with the idea of her passage in and out of the place remaining in the steady flow of gossip and speculation that passes from employee to employee, from year to year. Like the other hotel employees who left or lost their jobs in a flurry of confusion or deception or violence—like the sales rep who talked the Arkansas Corvette Club into writing their $10,000 convention deposit check to her and stole off with the money just after she got into the computer system and erased every reservation made for the following three months out of spite for a lecherous reservations manager who kept trying to stick his hand up her skirt, like the fired sous chef who quietly peed in the pickle bucket on his way out the door, like the maintenance man named Bill, the one they called Little Romeo, who had a wife and an ex-wife and a girlfriend, each one twice as big as he was, each one unsuspecting and privately scheduled to come see him every day at a different time so she wouldn't get wind of the others, each one so enamored of Little Romeo that the other maintenance men might glance down from the hotel roof and see him with his pants down in a car with one of them, and then they might walk into an out-of-order room two hours later to the sight of the white half-moons of Little Romeo's rear end beneath his work shirt as he labored over another, and so on until the wife or the girlfriend or one of these women found something out and hacked Little Romeo to death with the claw end of his favorite hammer in the rollaway storage room on the second floor, making such a mess that the hotel had to order twenty-two new folding beds to replace the ruined ones—like these former employees who hover in the atmosphere of the Little Rock Marriott, the lore surrounding Judy and the pantyhose man remains with the place, to be summoned up on slow nights when there's nothing much on the radio, or in moments of nostalgia when the reservations girls sit around the office like high school friends ten years gone, rehashing the details of their formerly shared and distant pasts, the phrase "Wasn't that just *crazy?*" the accompanying refrain.

And on these nights of blessed phone silence and delightful regurgitation, the girls in the reservations office sit around one desk with plates of beef stroganoff they sweet-talk from the head chef and go over their theories of what may have become of Judy. Everyone thinks the pantyhose man had something to do with it— even Vince, when he weighs in on the matter, and this makes the girls feel even more sure of themselves, because they know that Vince studied law enforcement for a semester at the community college, and that he spends most of his time at work hiding in the furnace room, chain-smoking and reading Agatha Christie novels, and so they figure he has a mind for such things. One by one the reservations girls tell him their takes on the matter, and he nods with approval at each theory.

Chrissie thinks that Judy and the pantyhose man decided to

meet, and that Judy ran away to live with him in some far-flung and peaceful retreat like Alaska or Rhode Island. Claudia disagrees, swears that the pantyhose man just stopped calling, and thinks that the loss was too much, that Judy simply took off in search of a new place, like she did after Mr. Candlesticks and Credit Card broke her heart. Leslie, who turns everything this way, thinks that Judy went dirty on them and became a phone pervert herself, or at least a phone sex operator, and that she's still around somewhere, maybe even in the same Parkside apartment with the curtains drawn, having her groceries home-delivered while she spends sixteen hours a day moaning into the phone. And then there is Lily, who is often quiet and unsettled, and she swears that she has dreams of Judy—dreams that some don't take lightly ever since Lily found a guest's lost diamond pinkie ring by telling the housekeepers she dreamed it was in the sixth-floor laundry room, in the lint trap, fourth dryer from the right—and in these dreams she sees Judy at the edge of a river, silent and unmoving while the river tide laps at her feet, her face purple and bloated in the moonlight by the pair of extra-strength nylons twisted around her neck.

Rebecca Soppe was born in 1976 in Wisconsin and grew up in Belleville, Illinois. She received an MFA from the University of Florida and is now working on a PhD in writing at Florida State. Her stories have appeared in the *Berkeley Fiction Review*, the *Bellingham Review*, and *Ploughshares*. She currently teaches composition, but once worked for five years as a front-desk clerk at a hotel.

KRIS STOKES

I began writing this story while studying with David Leavitt at the University of Florida. At the time, we were reading "hotel novels," a series of books set in European residence hotels during the early part of the twentieth century that feature the polite adventures of an upper class perpetually on holiday—books like Christina Stead's The Little Hotel *and Willem Elsschot's* Villa des Roses. *They were wonderful, often hilarious novels, but the world they presented was so far removed from my own experience of hotel life that I thought it would be fun to write something less polite, something from the perspective of the wary, contemporary hotel clerk. I like to call it my "no-tell motel" story.*

Allan Gurganus

MY HEART IS A SNAKE FARM

(from *The New Yorker*)

I had a snake farm in Florida. Well, Buck really owned it, but I believe I'm still Board Chairlady. Almost overnight, he hand-sculpted a one-stop two-hundred-reptile exhibit right across the road from me here. At first it was very clean. It drew lively crowds from the day it opened: December 24, 1959.

Then President Kennedy went and excited our nation about putting a man on the moon. That sicced the Future on any act just roadside and zoological. Tourists soon shot through our state, bound only for Cape Canaveral. Our Seminoles? Our bathing beauties? Passé at eighty m.p.h.

Buck's proved the last stand of pure unregulated carny spirit: back in '59, anybody with a placard, some Tarzan gimmick, and a big mouth could charge admission. And you'd pay. And later, even if feeling somewhat stretched and peppery, you'd still be glad you paid.

I myself had just retired from life as a grammar-school librarian. I was an unmarried woman of a certain age, imaginative as one could be on a fixed income. I'd felt a growing hatred of Ohio's ice, of shovelling the brick walk I knew would break my hip if I stayed another year. I was and am a virgin, my never-braced teeth too healthy. Toledo's secret nickname for me even as a girl: Little Threshing Machine.

My worst vice? Letting others *see* me gauge their foolishness. So claimed my lifelong housemate, Mother. Even so, fellow-librarians did make me a national officer, thanks to my way with a joke, my memory for names, my basic good sense. And because, at our dressy conventions, everyone looked better than I and they all knew I knew.

An old college friend urged Florida on me. "But, Esther? Be careful where you first settle. Danger is, once you're sprung from these fierce Toledo winters, the first place you find in the Sunshine State you will—like some windblown seed—take fast tropic-type root." She was a prophet. I drove past Tallahassee and, eager to make good time, got only as far as a crumbling pink U.S. 301 motel called Los Parnassus Palms. "Somebody's thinking," I said, hitting the brakes of my blue Dodge. Been here ever since. Rented a room by the night, week, then year, and wound up buying the whole place for less than my Toledo town house cost. I still keep the towels fresh in all twelve suites.

A previous owner had named (then plaqued) each luxury efficiency: "The Monterey," "The Bellagio," etc. True, I never knew what such titles meant. But I accepted them as part of History's welcome by-product, Romance. Some suites I lined with library shelves, others served recreation needs. E.g., 206-B, "The Segovia": *Periodicals, Ping-Pong, Reference.*

I didn't care to chat up strangers nor wash the sheets of hairy men. So I switched off my place's wraparound neon. But a motel cliff-hangs its highway the way waterfront property has lake. Salesmen kept honking, believing that dead signage (plus one cute wink) might mean a discount.

Now, to me, Virginity and Refrigeration have both always seemed blue. Ditto one small steady NO burning before a too pink and ever-blinking VACANCY. So, ten days into ownership, royally sick of explaining myself, I flipped on that NO full time. Redundant, you say? With me age sixty-seven or eight? Well, let's get this part over:

As to sex, I had one chance once with a beautiful boy but I chose not to. Actually, it was the father of a friend but it seemed wrong in their sedan in the countryside, and I thought there would be other takers. There were not. You can wind up with nothing; but, if you claim that and don't apologize and forever tell it straight, it can become, in time, something. It's not for everybody to marry and have kids, or even to be homosexual. Or even to be sexual. But you can still retire and move to the semitropics and wind up on the board of a Serpentarium. You never know—that's the thing. And I say, thank God.

Except for two middling hurricanes, my first year in Florida proved ever quieter. I'd always said I liked my own company; well, now I had twelve cubic suites' worth. In identical bathroom mirrors, I found one tusky similarity saying, "Esther, you again?" True, the most intellectual Baptist ladies hereabouts invited me to join a Serious Issues book club; yes, I re-linoleumed my whole second story; by then it was almost 1960.

The previous October, Mother'd finally ceased ringing her favorite little bedside bell. I had put it there for emergencies, but soon a moth in the room, any passing car, warranted much brass. By the end, I asked the morticians if they would please place Mother's service bell right in the coffin with her. These large, kind men remembered me lording it benign over their grammar-school library. They now said, "How sentimental. So your mama, in case she wants something, can ring for someone else in the next world?" I lowered my eyes. "Exactly," I said, but thought, *And ring, and ring.* I let gents believe whatever version of me they found easiest to take.

Now I'd retired to wearing flats, finally becoming my own silent hobby, imagine my alarm when the two acres right across my highway here blossomed into Carnival overnight. Someone had leased that swampy inlet and its entire adjoining beachfront. He'd claimed my sole view of the ocean. One morning, two black Cadillacs, sharky with finnage, rolled up, pulling silver-bullet Airstream trailers. A pile driver soon pounded what looked like sawed-off telephone poles right into pallid sand dunes.

The man in charge, I saw from my perch, was a big tanned white-haired fellow, all shoulders and department-store safari gear. He supervised via barks and backslaps, using his beer bottle as a pointer. I always resist such showoff males. (They never notice.) I served under three similar swaggering principals, mere boys. Any Ohio man willing to be called "third-grade teacher" for a few years got promoted above capable senior women. Now I watched this particular bull, six-two, fifty-eight if a day. Dentures probably.

Across the poles, he hand-stretched huge canvas placards pulled tight as fitted sheets. Each showed a different Wild Animal of the creeping, crawling, biting variety. The ocean? Already upstaged. (First a showman hides something, then he describes it so you'll shell out the admission.) Braggart images looked wet with all the drippage colors of tattoos. Crocodiles were shown big as green Chevies. Black snakes glistened in figure-eight oil spills that then lashed up the legs of screaming white girls scarcely dressed. The more pictures this hatchet-faced lion tamer rigged aloft, the slower flowed traffic on old U.S. 301. Beasts scaly, beasts spiny, swarthy, twisted, fanged. "Come one, come all." Not wholly uninteresting.

Meantime, I dragged a cushioned bamboo lounger out of "The Santa Anna." Arms crossed, jaw set, I settled in, daring him to get one centimetre tackier.

The salt-white dunes soon swarmed with antlike workers. Into sand, using driftwood, the head honcho drew a large scallop shell, outhouse-size. He pointed where he wanted it built. Bricklayers scratched their heads then shrugged but, laughing, nodded. Many cinder blocks got unloaded. Within hours, the men had formed three steps, each mitred round as a fish gill in *Fantasia*. Atop these stairs arose one little Aztec ruin dropped beside the sea—a ticket booth, glass-fronted, scallop-crowned.

As masons mosaicked, Jungle Jim praised his artistes, fed them grilled sandwiches, tried their trowels while squinting past his cigarette. His big piñata head moved side to side, judging, as he framed all this beauty between his thumbs. He once backed too near traffic.

Three attractive young women, using hand fans, kept their folding chairs aimed wherever he largely stood. By six o'clock, his cinderblock fortress, shaped like some goldfish bowl's hollow castle, had been painted an odd pistachio-meets-swimming-pool green.

All day, hands on hips, making a jolly silhouette, the man laughed and threw his head back sort of thing. He seemed as entertained as I by how his fantasy could rise in hours from sketch to housing. Come ruddy sunset, these circus folk threw tapering shadows that spanned traffic, just hooking their heads and shoulders into my parking lot. The showman (roughly my age, I now decided, though some men carry it better) mixed two clear pitchers of Martinis. He and his workers toasted their structure and everyone watched the sun sink pinky-gold behind it. Then the boss — with a bullfighter's slash — tossed his whole Martini up the stairs, cocktail glass shattering into sand. His women, stirred, saluted him by knocking back their drinks in single gulps. Thus ended their first day here.

If such a white-trash eyesore had sprung up across the street from my Toledo mews town house, I would've swarmed City Hall with two hundred other irate owner/career girls. But here, even seeing my oceanfront eclipsing fast, I squinted from my greenhouse (formerly 202-A) while pretending to read Fiction (206-C), doubting that things could grow more Gypsy-ish.

The level of construction across four lanes of traffic soon became almost too complex for even me to track. Then two huge snakes arrived U.P.S. How could I know the bundle contents from this distance without using Mother's surprisingly helpful mother-of-pearl opera glasses? Hints: serpent-package length, two added suitcase handles, triangular orange Caution stickers, airholes thickly screened, and how the delivery boy, wearing shorts, held these out like barbells, far, far from his plump legs.

The carnival's first six days here, I played hard to get. I deprived management of my company. I did not even wave. They seemed to be coping all too well.

Nothing like this had ever so directly threatened my privacy tropique, my sense of self. Of course, the previous year, our retired librarians' newsletter, *Ex Libris,* had announced, "Guess which colorful national officer just retired to and purchased her own 'compleat' Florida motel? (As yet unlisted, she is 823-887-9275.) Yes, our darn Esther!" Librarians fetched up here so thick I thought of it as filing. I stuck the Altoona crowd in 104-A, "La Sangria." The louder Texans I sent on purpose to the leaking 307-B, "The Santa Anna," as an Alamo pun that only I got. Eventually, I hung sheets over my office door and windows. And, slowly, even those big-time lending librarians greediest to borrow a free sunny room got the hint. Circulation dwindled.

Alone I was again. Mother's bell had been muted by six feet of Ohio loam long since frozen solid. My studying the ocean? Worth maybe three full minutes daily. Now what?

The ringmaster across my highway finished digging a whole lake using his yellow rental bulldozer. From floor two and then from my flat roof, I caught chance peeks at his radical new land use behind the screening placards. Finally, one afternoon as I sat reading, all at once, in the bull's-eye center of the lake he'd scooped, up spouted a wild central jet. It went off like Moby-Dick sighing straight aloft. This secret fountain caught me utterly off guard. I felt surprised, then half scared by such a tacky surge, felt something possibly akin to sheer dumb joy. A column of white foam shot forty feet, then fell heavily aside to make a plash, half violent, half joke. My every suite felt cooled some eight to ten degrees.

I rose. I saw that I had been a snob. These dark, pretty circus folk were new here and living so en masse—and God knows I was none of the above.

At last I understood it'd been Mother, that old eighty-five-pound Denver boot, still holding me back—her scoldings about manners and the standards required of a family fine as ours. She'd never let me play with my favorites, twins, "coarse, grocer's daughters." Having risen, I now slammed shut my third time through Pearl S. Buck's *Good Earth.* Why be trapped in the past as some Chinese peasant girl when I had Maturity's sloppy, festive here-and-now?

Darting downstairs to my office-kitchen, I pulled forth a fresh-baked piping coffee cake, carried it bold across the highway (as soon as the steady stream of Key-bound tourists allowed a gap for a running gal my age). That's how I first met Buck and his wives.

"Well, aren't you the perfect welcome wagon," he himself spoke, deep. "We noticed you seemed to be in every window. Sure you ain't triplets? Does your coming over mean you forgive a guy's menagerie for complicating your property value? But aren't you scared my prize Burmese python will wind up in your"—he squinted at the unlit neon—"Parnassus Palms dresser drawers?"

"That a threat or a promise, sir?"

Well, this cracked him up. "You're a right good sport."

"Looking like this, do I have a choice?" The ladies laughed, he didn't. I am such a patented virgin I can say things only some ancient cross-eyed nun might risk.

"Everybody has a choice." Buck met me head on. "That's what we mean by 'sport.'"

Soon, over a berry-pink Daiquiri in a teak-lined trailer, I asked Mr. Buck how many snakes he owned—did he hire them from some animal-theatre agent or catch his by hand? The man's voice had gathered accents from pretty much everywhere. These were basted in a unifying baritone the hue of Myers's dark rum.

"Some, lady, I did personally snag in Brazil. The gators seem to find me. Mowgli, she swam up a service-station drainage ditch in Kissimmee. I rescued Stumpy after he fell in some bad motel's pool, no offense. My gators start, like seeds, small, but you feed them into becoming attractions. Funny, but they're loyal in their way. The fancier snakes I have been known to order by phone but will probably *say* I caught bare-handed. I *did,* by dialling Princeton, New Jersey, same outfit that pervides mice to your finer cancer labs. Yep, always have been fascinated by the cold-blooded. As a kid, I tanned muskrat and otter pelts, kept corn snakes as pets,

pretty, nonpoisonous. Been on my own since I was nine. Lost
Mom to diphtheria, Dad to a travelling lady preacher. So be it.
A longish adventure. — But enough 'bout me. What's your setup,
Esther? You didn't start in Florida. Naw, you're like me. On the
lam from another buncha lives squandered elsewheres, eh?"

I lowered my eyes, unwilling to seem simple as the word "un-
opened." But then Buck did something unheard of. Awaiting response, he looked right at me. I peeked back up. I stood here and
he stood there, with his ladies slouched on all sides, and he did not
avert his eyes or flinch, not even men's usual once. "Ouch at first
sight," I call it. My teeth are independent; each has its own unique
sense of direction. And my hair, despite backcombing, has grown
somewhat thin on top. All my life, even when I was six, males have
treated me like The Maiden Aunt. A self-fulfilling trend. But this
Buck, he stared straight at (not through) me. Seemed only he was
strong enough to take it.

Buck soon bounded clear across north- and southbound lanes,
inviting me to his show, for free. He'd asked everybody door-to-
door for miles, be they massage parlors or churches. His toylike
bulldozer had by now piled real hills around Buck's spitting lake.
He'd imported full-grown royal palms. He made the white gravel
paths look almost natural, going nowhere, if fast and in four-leaf
clovers.

Pastors, bleach-blond masseuses, two education-minded Negro
couples, and a bunch of mean little boys gathered, plus me. "Everybody 'bout ready? Come one, come all, then. Price is right, if today
only." Then he performed his entire test spiel. Buck's first jokes did
seem stale, even for 1959 ("Welcome to Florida, Land of Palms . . .
all open!"). But it was like a starter try for us all. If he tended to
ramble, en route Buck charmed, too. He mapped out Amazon
rainy seasons, warned of visa requirements, described his sleeping-
sickness onsets. He showed early claw damage to one forearm. Facing certain snakes, he recounted their especially nasty captures. As
he grew loud, his creatures got stiller and even beadier-eyed, as if

out of guilt. He draped any creature not gator-weighty around his neck. Like leis that flexed, they seemed to like it.

When Buck laughed, he gave off a smell like flint, ham, and 3-In-1 motor oil. Active as he was, one of his fingernails was always black-blue, coming and going. He lived in his great-whiter-hunter gear, jagged khaki collar, epaulets. Pall Malls got buttoned into a customized slot, the Zippo slid snug into its own next door. This man had a brown face like a very good Italian valise left out in a forest during World War Two and just refound. Weathered, but you could still see how fine its starter materials had been.

Oh, he had some pips in there.

Alligators, about forty, and three were the stars — huge, I mean as big as ever I saw in Mother's precious back numbers of the *Geographic*. As with cows, they had whole *sides* to them. They loved their new lake; they showered in its hourly fountain. Huge amounts of lettuce were eaten. (Buck had already payolaed the produce clerks from Piggly Wiggly and Winn-Dixie to bring their castoffs here instead of leaving them lonely in trash vats back of stores. He also fed his reptiles frozen chickens — claimed the birds' iciness made a crunch the beasts considered their own achievement.)

I soon noticed grocery trucks over there at all hours, as much for curiosity as delivery. TV stations covered his Grand Opening. By now, the show was charging full admission and Buck let each visiting child feed one gator apiece. The kid would inch out on a diving board wearing rubber gloves to keep from getting lettuce drool on his little paws. Parents took snapshots. I feared a lethal topple. I briefly wondered about the Reptile Farm's insurance picture; then, suspecting no coverage whatever, thought of something else. Smelling chow, gators hissed like gas leaks. Large white mouths opened, a fleet of Studebaker hoods. Seemed it was always time to feed the gators. Loose luncheon meats, crates of limes, you name it — they ate everything.

Before Buck and his wives appeared, my afternoons had been somewhat less eventful: the local library (open 3–5 Tuesday afternoons)

featured only past-due best-sellers stinking of Coppertone. Come
1 P.M., I had been mostly monogamous with my favorite soap,
"The Secret Storm." Sure, Fridays I might go wild, pop popcorn.
But, finally, in the Parnassus Convent vs. Reptile Coliseum bat-
tle? No contest. By then Buck had made me a charter member of
the Snake Farm Family Board, meaning I got in free.

His one request: "How's about you arrive five minutes prior to
showtime wearing a flowered hat and carrying a purse, Esther? Just
to keep up our sense of how my place is classy, scientific, er, whatever. Pretending to listen like you do gives my talks real tone, your
being the retired educator. Eyeglasses would be good, even your
reading specs. Hell, hon, with intellect and class like yours on view,
I can charge a dollar more per customer."

Oh, he was sly, that Buck. He wore a cap pistol rammed into his
holster, had on thigh-high treated boots, double-thick to keep the
rattlers from snagging clear through. He would be wading into
their humid glass booth, where thirty rattlesnakes curled clicking
like seedpods on a binge.

Nobody hates snakes more than snakes do. That's part of why
we fear them. We recognize our own self-loathing, but slung even
lower, so its armless-legless with self-pity. And yet, even during a
heat wave, snakes piled one atop the other like trying to form some
sloppy basket. I did not get why. Myself being a single person, myself with typing margins set Maximum Wide, with me needing
13,500 sq. ft. just to feel sufficiently dressed, simply watching such
constant summer skin contact made me feel half ill.

Sometimes if I saw a crowd of cars I might wander over. First I
limited myself to Mondays and Wednesdays — plus, of course,
weekends. (Mother had always rationed my attending other children's birthday parties: "You come home a sticky blue from their
cheap store-bought sheet cakes. You forgive their whispering jokes
about your . . . features. Listen to you, still wheezing from having run around screaming till you sound asthmatic, Esther. — No,
we're alike. Too sensitive for groups. You are one overstimulated
young lady. So let's just sit here a few hours and collect ourselves,
shall we, Little Miss?")

Buck's wives swore that if I stayed away too long certain snakes sulked. How could the ladies tell? You mostly recognized different reptiles by their size and how much of that the others had chewed off. I got to know on sight Buck's largest rattlers: Mingo, Kong, and Lothar. Stumpy was the hungriest gator and often got in the way of others' frozen chickens. Stumps never learned. And he paid dearly with his limbs, his tail mass, and, finally, his life. God bless his stubborn appetite.

After hours, hanging out with wives in the Reptile Postcard Shop & Snack Canteen, Buck claimed he had once bought Hemingway a rum drink in Key West and got invited home to "Papa's" hacienda for an all-night poker game. I usually asked him what Hemingway was really like. Buck would shake his head sideways: "Good talker. Sore loser."

During tours, I don't think Buck's grasp of Latin was all it might have been. More than once I heard some pushy customer loiter before a ragged cage, jab his camera toward Exhibit A, and demand, "Hey, what kind of snake is this 'un here?" "That one? That's a big mean red one is what that is. Sooner bite you than look at you. Now, ahead on our left . . ." People would laugh, not knowing if he was joking or mule-headed. But, with this level of poison around, considering his German Luger and hooked stick, no one ever did ask Buck for refunds, repetitions, or corrections.

After one show, I quizzed him: "I guess it's that people love to be scared?"

"No, dear Esther. It's: people love to be scared by something *new*."

I looked at him, I sipped straight bourbon.

Buck had been married four times, and three-quarters of his troubles were still with him. "Buck's harem," locals soon called it. Each gal kept her sleek identical trailer parked behind the backmost palms. I heard tell Buck visited a different lady every night. I'd never stayed up late enough to see. Some part of me did wish he would come nap anytime in any of Parnassus's comfy settings. I kept the central fans of all twelve suites going, just in case. He plainly had no sleeping place not already warmed by a previous nesting wife. "Feeding them's cheaper 'n alimony," one local boy claimed Buck said. But that sounds like any of the hundred rumors that made his stint here on our highway so lively during those glory years of latest Ike-Mamie, earliest Jack-Jackie.

Buck's wives seemed another sort of specimen collection. They wore stage makeup, as if competing with each other during those long hot afternoons spent waiting for Buck's last show to end. Of all ages, his gals were either very young now or had been even better-looking pretty recently. Each still appeared sun-baked with strong ceramic traces of her starter glamour.

Working the concession trailer, they were supposed to sell the tourists food and souvenirs; they mostly drank small Cokes and ate the merchandise. They said funny if cutting things about the paying customers. "With those ears, we should stick ole Clem there out in the monkey cage," or "Some of our exhibits eat their young, ma'am, and if you can't quiet those bawling twins of yours we have the livestock that will." "Now, ladies," Buck came in laughing. "Ladies, m' ladies," shaking his head. He liked them spirited. Of my outfits, he preferred me in the lilac-covered hat and the white patent-leather shoes with matching bag. He wanted his wives to lounge out front in halters, waving at the cars, bringing in considerable business. (Me, I'd drag a kitchen chair into shade off to one side.) Truth is, the girls looked a little better from sixty-five m.p.h. But don't we all?

Come drink time, the former wives changed into beautifully ironed off-the-shoulder Gypsy blouses. They sported pounds of Navajo silver and turquoise squash-blossom necklaces that would bring a fortune today. They were always painting their fingernails and toenails or working on each other's. You felt their tensions crest only at the sound of the final blanks Buck fired to end his show. When at last he stalked in, there'd be this pinball ricochet of love-starved looking: him gaping at the nut-brown breasts of one while another studied Buck's flat backside, as those other two gals kept glowering at each other's fronts. Nervous, I once blurted, "Cold Coke, anybody?" and got one hot glare so unified.

His exes were intelligent girls who had not enjoyed my educational advantages. They'd once felt too attractive ever to need those. Doing crosswords out loud between shows, they'd squeal at how I helped. "Flanders Field!" I found myself yelling as my mother told me not to at parties. "Cordell Hull!" The girls soon treated me like Einstein's sister, and I admit I humored them; I let them.

Christmas and Easter, I had the whole crew over to Los Parnassus Palms for my turkey, dressing, pies. The wives arrived in drop earrings, evening gowns. Slinky and powdered, they unfolded from matching Caddies. Buck would wear a crumpled tux that looked like Errol Flynn at the end.

Beloved fellow snake farmers seemed most impressed by my owning countless solid-silver napkin rings from Mother. (Funds she might've spent on her only child's teeth braces.) "Good weight," Buck said, testing, as all his holiday ladies nodded, giving him hooded looks. His wives had each been in or near the Show Business. Bucks first, Dixie, once worked as a juggler's assistant in Reno; Peggy, numero dos, claimed to have been a buyer (estate jewelry) for Neiman Marcus; Tanya was runner-up to be a studio player at Metro pictures in the class that included Janet Leigh. Over wine, they revealed more of Hollywood's sad secrets. Hearing the crazy vices of the stars, I cried, "No. Not him, too! What leading man'll be *left* for Esther?"

(Later, some local yahoo tried telling me Buck had never married those three girls, said that they were just part of his roadside attraction, that their separate trailers made nightly cash admissions possible. I don't believe it for an instant and I think some people on this road have very dirty minds. They adored him. That was all.)

Not long into Kennedy's Administration, the wives sped off to Bradenton to buy new outfits. That's where the carnies all retire, patronizing a glamour shop the girls'd heard about. I saw their

Cadillac scratch off around three, and at four I notice Buck, waving a big white hanky to make cars stop, looking sick as he comes staggering across four lanes of traffic toward my Parnassus Palms. I can't say I hadn't pictured this house call before. But not in crisis, not owing to illness. When I opened my screen door, he frowned, head wedged against one shoulder, and his face was all but black. He handed me a razor blade. "Esther? Either Kong or Lothar snagged me a good one in the back. Here, cut an X. Then pour ammonia on it. Go in an inch at least. I can't see to reach it and my focus . . . It's already all over, focus sliding, Esther."

He whipped off his shirt. Face down, he fell across my rattan lounger. I now stood behind him. Two fang marks weren't hard to find because of all the purple swelling. "O.K," I said. I dashed to get a towel and the ammonia. I splashed cold water in my face. Bucks upper back was seizing something terrible. And yet its shape was very strong, copper-brown, tapered like a swimmer's. I cut far deeper than I wanted, then blotted at least two pints into a large white beach towel. "Now," Buck said, "I'm going to have to ask you, Esther. And for a friend like you I'd do it in a heartbeat. Feels I . . . feels I'm going into shock here. I'd never ask for any reason shy of Life and Death. —But, honey, would you suck it?"

I might sound funny if I tell you my thin legs nearly buckled. I fought then not to faint. Blame my seeing his dark blood or my viewing his entire back. More than once I had pictured him across the road there being worked on by his full swarm of wives. I'd imagined how Buck might look shirtless, and he looked better, even with blood, which made this more a movie. With Buck in the lounger, I could not bend forward far enough to help. "Here." I lifted him and led him to my davenport. He was only half conscious and the weight of him was wonderful and tested my full sudden Esther strength. I helped him stretch out there, face down. God, how he trusted me!

I settled on the floor beside his ribs. Finally, breathing for two, I rose up on my knees. My teeth are bucked, as you'll have noticed. My own low-cost form of fixing them has always been to make a

joke before others get the chance. "Need a human bottle opener?"
I once heard a handsome young man quip to pals (and me only
seven, trailing embarrassed pretty girlfriends). But now, knowing
I might finally be useful to someone, I managed to say nothing.
No Esther jokes today, Esther!

I tottered on my knees, then pulled the hair back off my forehead. My eyes wet, I drew closer to his snake holes. They were like
twin tears in cloth. At last I pressed my lips down onto those warm
slots black with blood, then, slow, I pulled the poison out of Buck.
Into myself. You might think I'm exaggerating when I say that I
could taste what was poison, what was blood. The poison was bit-
ter with a foamy peroxide kick to it. But blood seemed only salty
and, by contrast to the venom, almost sweet.

"Spit it out, Esther, spit it on the towel. Get all that out of you.
I cannot have you harmed, not for a sec. You're so fine, dear. Bless
your soul for this." I did as he said. I spewed it out then, just as he
told me. I was stooped here over him, him flexed out below me,
star-shaped, Buck. I fought wanting to cry like some little girl
would then. Crying not from horror, not even from gratitude, but
more from simply knowing: *This is my life that I am living.*

"Esther, please hit me with ammonia. Takes acid to counteract
snake acid. There. Yeeks, burns so good. Now I'm going to need
some shut-eye, pet. You sure did it, though. You got it all or most,
and I can tell, dear. But let me sleep, oh, twenty minutes tops. Then
I'll be fine. No more than that or I'll get dopey. I will need to do
something when I come to. Need to have you walk me around.
This has happened maybe ten other times, so I know. But when I
do feel stronger and can roll over, I am going to thank you, Esther.
Living across from us these couple years, you've made our being
here just so much livelier. More civil. And now this. You be thinking if there is anything whatever I can do for you, girl."

Then, at once, he passed out or slept. I eased onto my "Alham-
bra" breezeway. Had myself a cigarette. I'd only ever smoked two
before. But somebody had left half a pack in "Segovia" and I did

enjoy that one slow Lucky, pulling smoke way in, letting it find its own eventual way out. Laissez-faire. Then I realized: here, the only time a man had ever told me in advance I could expect something memorable and I was making my big mouth smell like an ashtray. I had to laugh at myself as I dodged into "Bellagio," 109-A, and swigged down half a bottle of Lavoris. By doing this, I saw I'd made most of a decision.

I only waked him because I felt scared that being out too long might give Buck brain damage or such. I stooped beside my davenport again. "Time," I said. Facing downward, he just yawned, then aimed his elbows out, as if nothing much had happened. So . . . male.

My couch had a new hibiscus print on it, maroon. Whatever blood he shed, it would blend in. But I wished that some might stay there, permanent. So sure, he turned over with a sleepy grin and growled up, "Hiya, lifesaver." First Buck kissed me full on the mouth then more *in* the mouth. It did not prove so repulsive as it always looked when you suspected two movie actors were sneaking doing it.

Then he told me he'd forever been crazy about me after his fashion and right from the start. Said how his liking me so, it had nothing to do with my First Aid just now. Not simple tit for tat. "So to speak," I said, with the valor of an ugly person trying to make light of everything so as to stay hid.

He told me to go pull the blinds shut, and I did. He got himself to sitting, woozy still. Then he patted the cushion right beside him. I, dutiful, feeling frail as if *I* had been snakebitten, settled just where he showed me.

"You won't forever after blame me or be jealous of the others if we do this once, to celebrate my coming back to life with your great help, right?" I shook my head no. He said, "Nothing to panic anybody. No breakage, Esther. Just one thing I want to do. I am too weak for offering up everything right now. I would black out. But this I know I want." And he slid down off the couch and, first, Buck warmed his right hand between my knees. I wore half-stockings and he soon rolled those down with all the care of the earth's best young doctor. Next, he hooked his hands around my drawers' elastic and pulled the pants out from under me, showing me how to lift up so he could do it easy.

He knew I could not have borne to let him see me all undressed. It was just too late for that much. Too late to do everything. But as I kept my hand on his one shoulder not swollen, Buck's white hair, bristly as a pony's, disappeared under my housedress. There was no false start, none of the snaky seeking I had feared. His tongue was there all at once, its own bloodhound locator system, and it could have been a hundred and sixty degrees hot. I had no idea. It, his tongue, soon seemed to be a teacher of infinite patience, then like a sizzling skillet, a little pen flashlight, now featherweight, now flapjack, then just a single birthday candle that—in time, strengthened by doing lap after lap—becomes the forest fire. I had no notion I would ever respond like this, way below where Language ever even gets to start. In brief, certain sounds were made. Snake-farmish sounds, only it was me . . . I. The "I" that soon had her leg crooked around his shoulder, pushing him away, but he leaned into that so it felt like I was playing him in and out of me at exactly my own speed. He was regular as a clock and I was always knowing where he would have been as I allowed myself and just went off again and again and off again, my calves St. Vitus, my feet dancing spasms. The first time was sort of a sea green, the second time more a bronzy blue—there came a red moment but it ended all steamed in hard-baked stone-washed sunflower yellow.

It ended only because I was too proud to let it go on as long as it wanted to. Which would've been as long as both my life and his. Finally, I said, "There, oh my . . ." and started to make one of my jokes, but my dignity stopped me. Funny, I didn't feel ashamed. I felt dignified. I never understood that this was possible. Having another person here, it was less shaming. It was more a way of knowing we are all alike in this. It was beautiful. It was once but it was beautiful.

•••

"Bacon and scrambled eggs and coffee cake," I chanted, gathering myself to stand. I knew I wouldn't risk the ugly comedy of pulling up my stockings or regaining my step-ins. Instead I would eat a meal with a man who had just taken my knickers off and he would know that, while we ate. I'd placed new oilcloth on my little table here in the former Main Office of Los Parnassus and I felt glad the room looked nice. He stayed right on till seven-thirty-six. I asked if he wanted my help to get him back across the highway. "No," he smiled. "Let me picture you right here as you are, girl. You're a saint from Heaven and a wonderful, wonderful woman. You're so strong. I love that in you, Esther."

"Well, thank you," I said, not doing anything funny, not daring to ruin this. I helped refasten Buck into his blood-soaked safari top. We had eaten as he sat there in the half-light with the white hair tangled on his chest and the swelling already going down. He was that healthy, it was cause and effect, once I had hoovered most of the bad stuff out. Fact is, I could still taste him or the poison or probably the mix in my mouth. A blend: walnut, allspice, penny metal, black licorice, lamb medium-well. I watched him go. The traffic parted, like for Moses. "Come one, come all," I whispered through my screen door.

It was Buck's fourth wife took him to the cleaner's. She was not in residence. One July 4th, we heard she'd suddenly demanded half of everything and here he was already sharing with his first three. Her suit tipped him into bankruptcy. I hate that kind of selfishness in women. In anybody. He gave so much. Then she had to claim his car and wallet. The sheriff served a summons mid-show. Flashing lights, sirens, horrible for Buck.

What else shut him down? Not the Health Department, though they could have. Grilled-cheese sandwiches were served to customers off a G.E. appliance meant for home use only and not too often cleaned. Buck's vats, where the gators did their shows (if you could call them shows), those might've used a weekly hosing-down with ammonia, Clorox. I had not volunteered to rush over and help. But *you* try and Ajax around thirty moody rattlers. All I knew, just when our neighborhood's social life had grown so routed through the Reptile Farm Canteen, just as I'd got, first, the taste of poison, then a taste of what other people's physical-type lives must be like and, I guess, daily—here came the state to close him down.

There was a huge new sign: "Snake-Gators-Etc. Going Out of Business. Everything Must Move." Buck soon sold the rattlers to researchers who believed their venom might cure cancer. A nature park outside Orlando sent a huge yellow Allied Van Line for the gators. All thirty-nine (Stumps, deceased, excepted) left here with silver duct tape wrapped clear around their heads, stacked like wriggling cordwood in the back of that dark truck. Oh, it was a black day along this overly bright stretch of U.S. 301, I can tell you. I stood there in Florida's latex glare as the van pulled off with every gator blinkered and discounted, lost to us forever.

In honor of the reptiles' exit, I had worn my lilac hat and all my white patent leather and every Bakelite bangle I could find. We held on to each other, Buck, Dixie, Peggy, and Tanya and me. Plus some young gents and the teenaged boys the girls had flirted with, just to keep them buying Cokes. Buck didn't shed a tear. He was the only one. "Well, I've gotten out of tight corners before, girls. But this is the End of the Age of the Snake Farm, probably. Hell, I'm a realist. All their rocket talk and Russian hatred has nixed many a laugh. Eisenhower and Mamie might've been customers here. But those European-type Kennedys? No roadside attractions for people that French-speaking, clean and stuck-up. Type that changes clothes three times a day without noticing. Thing is, it's nothing personal, way I see it. The Future is here and it gets hosed off way too often. And don't you gals suspect it's all based on damned Bad Science? I think nobody gives good value now, much less a decent doggone show. And where the fuck is the energy and fun in any of it? Excuse me, ladies.'"

"No sweat," I said.

Next morning, hired guys rolled up all Buck's signs. Those now proved no more substantial than window shades, and yet, for three good years, they'd got to feeling pretty monumental. During wind-storms, their canvas snapped like the sails of the Mayflower. That sound and the surf's slamming made this seem the New World after all.

Suddenly, signs gone, the Atlantic's raw horizon showed again. But now it looked like a paper-cut cliff, Niagara. Buck's home-dug lake, gatorless, appeared about as exotic as some miniature-golf-course water trap. Gravel paths bound nowhere now circled back in case they missed it, circled back.

After our group goodbye to the gators, my friends left overnight in the middle of the dark. I later saw that as a kindness, really. The very next noon, a Haitian crew—carrying radios blaring French tunes—showed up like the Keystone Kops. They dug up all Buck's store-bought palm trees. Root balls were still wrapped in burlap from their last sale. Seeing those trees go off lonely and akimbo on one flatbed truck was like witnessing a slave auction of my friends. Unseen, I waved. From the second-story breezeway, I was physically sick. Well, guess who felt bleak to the point of suicide or moving back to Toledo mid-February?

Weeks after, you would see a Piggly Wiggly truck pull up, not having heard or believed, and with enough slimy salad in back to feed all terrariums on earth.

I never doubted Buck's tale about beating Hemingway at poker and what a whiner Papa was over losing sixty bucks. I believed my friend about his being overnight with Ava Gardner. Buck would say no more than that, except, below his dancing eyes, he kissed all his right hand's fingertips. He admitted just "Ava? Ava was a gentleman." And since Buck had once told me I was also somewhat one, that helped.

Buck had been exactly Ava's type: the best gristle-sample of manhood ever to spring up on the wrong side of the snaky tracks. And a man still male enough at sixty-five or nine to keep three exes fighting for some stray lettuce head of his tossed attention. He never bragged, except maybe to tourists he'd never have to see again. You might think Buck had too little to boast of; but there was, in the high times at the Canteen, in our sole evening of sucking the poison out of one another, a kind of grandeur I can only hint at. After his wives, too loyal and numerous, having heard his pistol, powdered their noses and freshened their Liz-Cleopatra eyeliner, all of us knowing our last show was about to end, and after the day's forlorn clump of exiting tourists spent a few last wadded dollars on postcards and plastic shark-tooth key chains, Buck would come chesting in, he would give us all a cobra smile with real white teeth and, including me, including me, say, *"Que pasa,* girls?" He had it. That is all I can say. Buck definitely had it.

Once the Farm closed, if you dared walk over there, considering the sad and sandy blankness and those holes where rental palms had stood, you realized most of the cages had been nothing more than double-thick chicken wire. Made you wonder why the snakes had stayed. Maybe for the reason his ex-wives (and I) did. Because this really had been a working farm. Because everybody did his chores, even the snakes who struck against glass, aiming for the sunburned leg of some passing fat tourist boy, just to make him scream and force his mother, once she found no fang marks, to laugh. "It didn't mean it, Willie. That's just nature being nature, is all. That's what snake farms teach us, son."

Buck's show evaporated overnight, and highway traffic sure moved faster all through here. Especially after a new Japanese-owned driving range removed the Farm's every Day-Glo yellow-and-pink lead-up sign. These had once started promising him twenty miles due north, due south:

> YOU ARE NOT BUT SIXTEEN MILES FROM
> BUCK'S REPTILE FARM: SNAKES AND LIZARDS
> SEEN BY THE CROWD HEADS OF EUROPE!
>
> "EDUKATIONAL" FOR THE KIDDIES, TOO.
> LARGEST GATORS IN CAPTIVITY:
> MONEYBACK GUARANTEE OR A CLOSER LOOK!

That was my Buck all over.

• • •

Even now, one snaggled fact still stands there. Greenish and flaking, it is chipped like a Greek temple salt-preserved in Sicily: yes, his ticket booth's rounded cinder-block steps arranged in a shape as close to scallop shell as blocks that size could possibly become. And up on top there's the little cement platform, five feet above the sand, where people stood to buy admission for their families. Two hurricanes chipped the booth away in two huge molar chunks. But those steps yet survive.

I told myself not to expect to hear from any of the wives or him once they'd slid out of sight. That proved righter than I'd hoped. Still, wherever they washed up next, you wished them well.

(After all, when these showfolk found me here, in '59, my lady library officer's drink of choice—learned at conventions—had been a sticky cherry cordial. And by the time my snake charmers left in the middle of the night in '63, I'd worked my way straight up to straight Jack Daniel's. Who says there is no human progress?)

Those greened steps now stand framed against only browning palmetto scrub. But here's the funny part. Funny in some small, sidelined way. On a cool afternoon, if you park down a ways then tiptoe back, if you take a peek at the little stage that platform makes beside its bog, you'll often catch three to seven dozing there. Real snakes sound asleep, wild ones. They must love the heat a day of sun leaves banked in those old blocks. Maybe snakes enjoy being dry and up out of their usual mud. But, black snakes and cottonmouths, water moccasins and, once, a red-and-yellow coral snake some boy claimed he saw, they all seem to be waiting. Like auditioning, or hoping for a comeback. They seem to still want in, as paying customers, to see other like-minded creatures, but ones grown huge and therefore notable, forty times their weight. It's as if local reptiles can yet remember Buck's whole vivid show. It's like they long, as I once did, to simply hear how he'd describe them!

Soon as the government closed Buck down, things grew silent fast around Los Parnassus Palms. I could not have simply left here overnight when my friends drove off. I owned property. Besides, they never asked.

Still, I knew that, if he ever thought of me, Buck would want his good-sport Esther to be getting on with this, her latest life among the others she'd spent elsewheres on the lam. My heart had lately grown so . . . unsystematic.

When first I bought Parnassus, I'd turned off all its signage. Then bargain-hunting oversexed salesmen kept making me explain myself. Finally, years back, I lit just those two low-watt neon letters. My NO warned cars away. Through monsoons and dry spells, one blue skull and crossbones—my spinster coat of arms—blazed day and night against stucco.

Five months after the Reptile Canteen closed, I spent an evening fearing the latest hurricane with a name like one of Buck's ex-wives'. As I lounged around the Main Office—alone, naturally—I noticed, there beside the table where we'd eaten our aftermath bacon and eggs and his favorite coffee cake, two light switches. Decades back, these'd been marked in some stranger's tiny pencil script N. And, below that, V. I now reached over and, inhaling, with the flair of some magician's assistant, flipped off the N. Then, taking in two lungfuls of sea air, instead I just hit V. For victory? Dream on.

I let it burn there, out in plain and common view. I cannot say it didn't partly shame me. Pink and raw and overly visible, so all by itself (in its upright fifth-grade cursive). I retreated to our crucial maroon davenport. I settled here, now facing our highway's every southbound headlight.

I crossed my arms and felt surprised to find myself this ready: I would wait again. For what? Something. Anything, though not quite anyone. Heck, I'd already had the best. I might need to make a few concessions next time; I knew that.

Buck used to flatter me: "Cozy how my big Show attraction stands right up across the road from your nice Shelter attraction, Esther." "That's easy for *you* to say." I rolled my eyes to make him laugh. He never failed, and in a baritone mahogany.

Now, almost half a year after losing sight of him, I felt represented by that blinking sign out there. He had taught me it pays to advertise. Come one, come all. It's a human right, to name at least what you'd *like* to offer. True, I might not be any motorist's idea of a final destination; but maybe I could pass as just another attraction along a roadside littered with such.—Because, you know what? You never know. And that's a great thing: how they keep us guessing. That comes in second, right after Hope.

Stranger things have happened than life's stopping twice at one convenient off-highway location. Plenty of free parking, God knows. And now, as each headlight played across the slackened front of this, of me—partly ruined yet still far from stupid—I felt I'd outgrown "NO" at last.

Once upon a time in America, a man from nowhere with nothing but shoulders and great teeth, a guy backboned with one idea while enjoying sufficient sharpie patter—he could put up steps to anything that he might make you see as Wonderful. And without bimonthly federal inspections, without any legal charter past a friend or two he called "our Board," that man could shake you down for exactly the number of buckaroos you'd actually part with. And he would send you off glad, with more of your own personal story than you'd had before he took your cash. And all this without exceptional Latin.

Now, through my office plate-glass, I could see the former site of his Attraction. It was lit up tonight, salt-white sand, edges of white breakers endlessly uncoiling. All viewed better thanks to the sudden commercial glare from here, me.

Burning pink, held up against everything, that one word, a full proud three feet high. Too raw a term. Too rude a come-on for a woman alone of my age and homeliness. Wasn't it too hardened an admission, even for Florida, right along U.S. 301, even at 2:18 A.M.?

And yet, leaning back, breathing for one again, my arms folded over a slack chest, I liked going braless beneath a favorite housecoat worn with only "our" bloomers. I would be smoking now, if

I smoked.—Who is this woman hidden back of her neon? Why, it's Esther the Impenitent. Still on the lookout, feeling almost dignified:

VACANCY

Now I knew what it meant.

Allan Gurganus is the author of *Oldest Living Confederate Widow Tells All*, *Plays Well with Others*, *The Practical Heart*, and other works. His books have won the *Los Angeles Times* Book Prize, the Lambda Literary Award, and the Sue Kaufman Prize from the American Academy of Arts and Letters. Gurganus lives in North Carolina. His next collection of short fiction will be *Saint Everybody*. It is to include "My Heart Is a Snake Farm" along with "He's at the Office," a story published in the 2000 volume of *New Stories from the South*.

BECKET LOGAN

Sometimes along a country roadside, you'll see four cross-shaped floral arrangements. These, of course, are loved ones' memorials to traffic fatalities killed just here. My friend, the photographer Burk Uzzle, depicts such byway commemorations. During my one week spent living with these images, I wrote five short stories. None related to a single photo; instead, I would imagine some rustic altar or crumbled thrill-ride, and it would magically trail its own logic, glamour, founders' histories.

So "Snake Farm" began, at its present finale—with that ruined off-ramp staircase leftover, some reptile ranch's optimistic ticket booth now a sun-deck only to wild snakes.

Having invented this image, I needed one teller who might explain it, make it live again. She must surely be a certain age if, as a grown-up, she'd paid full price at such a 1950s tourist trap. She might've once lived right across the highway from this defunct amusement. In such ways, the writer digs a pit meant to trap big game. But once it has sunk to a sufficient depth, once he's covered its top with reeds then lighter palm fronds, he wisely jumps right in himself! Half a page into it, I fell in love with Esther, then her swain.

There is a curious and little-understood by-product of using narrative language. In the way that musical notes written on five-lined paper centuries ago by some composer can be sung aloud today by a very living fifteen-year-old, the love a writer feels for his own characters can prove immediately communicable. It can give his reader-singer a lofting release almost musical. This very hum and lift might offer one childlike way of recognizing Literature.

"Snake Farm" is a resurrection story. I don't feel I actually "invented" these folks. That word's too self-confident. It seems I simply uncovered what appeared, if sand buried, substantially in place before I ever took my broom to it. I feel lucky to have known these folks, and through continued knowing, I am honored to keep loving them.

Gregory Sanders

GOOD WITCH, BAD WITCH

(from *The South Carolina Review*)

In my family, the word "aunt" did not rhyme with either "ant" or "font." Instead it was pronounced "ain't," and while strictly speaking, "ain't" was just a pronunciational variant, it had become a word in its own right. And that is the way I still hear Aunt Aubria's name in my head—Ain't Aubria.

Every Christmas, it was Ain't Aubria who threw the party in Houston, and Grandmother Gertrude who supplied the wet blanket. Christmas morning would begin in Port City with Grandmother Gertrude's querulous plaint at the breakfast table. Didn't my father realize that she had been up all night wrapping presents? Couldn't he see that she still hadn't finished? And until all her presents were wrapped, we couldn't possibly leave for Houston.

Her son considered these objections unworthy of refutation, so every time she raised them, he just pounded his gavel and upheld his previous ruling. "We have to leave here by eight," he would tell her, "because Ain't Aubria expects us at nine." This kowtowing to Ain't Aubria always cut Grandmother Gertrude to the quick. Insensitive to personal insults, she was mortified by social slights. After all, my father was *her* son, not Ain't Aubria's. Her sense of grievance made her all the more determined to drag her feet and if necessary dig in her heels. By the time my father had finally herded her out of the house, he would be worn out from flogging her like Balaam's ass. And always, always we would already be at least a half hour late.

Grandmother Gertrude would hobble along, refusing to be hurried, and although she had the doctors' diagnoses to prove that her arthritis and tendonitis and bursitis and osteoporosis and diverticulitis were real physical maladies, it was hard to believe that the severity of her suffering was not subject to a psychological rheostat. On Christmas morning, when the dial was always spun all the way over to maximum, she could barely maneuver her body onto the front seat, let alone the back. (That was why she always rode in the passenger's seat next to my father, while my mother, who usually sat there, was displaced to the backseat, where she straddled the hump, separating my brother and me.) My father would open the car door for Grandmother Gertrude and she would gingerly lower herself down until at last gravity overcame her and she plopped into place with an oomph. Then, one by one, she would lift her legs in as though they had been paralyzed by polio and were now weighed down with metal braces.

Before pulling out of the garage, my father would remind her to put on her seatbelt. Grandmother Gertrude would protest that it curtailed her freedom of movement, that she could not bear the thought of being strapped in because she might be trapped if the car caught fire. And besides, she could never figure out how the blessed thing worked. When it came to technological innovation, Grandmother Gertrude was *not* an early adapter. After she had made several halfhearted attempts that ended with the belt being retracted instead of fastened, my father would have to reach over and fasten it for her. From the way she squirmed in her seat and noised her discomfort, you might have thought he was catheterizing her.

Once we were underway, she would revisit the ruling that had gone against her that morning. There was no earthly reason why we all had to get up every Christmas at the crack of dawn. Ain't Aubria never had dinner on the table before one o'clock anyway. This was the gist of her brief. Now it would be my mother's turn to remind her that Ain't Aubria would not allow her own grand-children to open any of their gifts until everyone had arrived so we could all have our Christmas tree together. Ain't Aubria saw us as one big extended family, not two separate nuclear ones. And it was just this hegemonic vision that Grandmother Gertrude had so set her face against. She would have much preferred to remain in Port City and have my mother fix us Christmas dinner. As long as we stayed on the family estate, she could at least lord it over her daughter-in-law. In Houston, Ain't Aubria held court, and Grandmother Gertrude was only a dowager empress by marriage. Ain't Aubria had money, and if you had money, things were very different, as Grandmother Gertrude never ceased to remind us. The implication was that if she'd had money herself, she too could have had a big house where everyone foregathered at every holiday. And if *that* were so, everyone would have loved her instead, and deferred to her wishes the way we now deferred to Ain't Aubria's.

Architecturally, Ain't Aubria's house was without distinction. What immediately grabbed your attention was the enormous oak tree smack in the middle of the front lawn, its trunk a good six feet in diameter, as great as Herne's oak in the last act of *Falstaff*. Since it was the only tree on the half-acre lot, its imposing canopy had spread without obstruction. By Christmastime each year, it had buried the grass in brown leaves.

Usually, one of the children would spot the car pulling into the long narrow driveway. Everyone inside would have come out to greet us before we were even out of the car, including Ain't Aubria in her apron (unless she had some sauce on the stove that had just reached critical mass). We would all embrace and say that we were all glad to see each other. Then each of us would individually avow that all the others looked great. While we frantically gibbered and chattered and groomed each other, the two-toed sloth that was Grandmother Gertrude glided stately through our midst. Stretching before her was an arduous trek through the garage and the kitchen, then down an endless corridor that led to the bathroom at the back of the house.

Once she was out of earshot, we would lower our voices like conspirators and someone, often Ain't Aubria's daughter, would ask, "Did Ain't Gertrude give you all a lot of trouble this morning?" This would let loose the floodgates of our disloyalty. Grandmother Gertrude being none of ours, we easily disowned her, and could hardly wait to stab her in the back. This gleeful treason relieved the stress we had always been under of biting our tongues at everything she said, and swallowing our fury every time she enforced some petty tyranny. Only my father declined to swear his fealty to our faction. But if he would not turn his coat outright, neither would he defend his mother. How could he? Instead he remained silent. By the time she returned from the bathroom, we were all in collusion against her.

If Grandmother Gertrude saw the little looks and smiles we exchanged behind her back (and sometimes not even behind her back, but almost to her face), she either refused to take notice, or noticed but failed to interpret these smiles and looks correctly. Like Falstaff, she was oblivious to what we merry wives really thought of her. Hermetically sealed inside her own self-regard, it would have been inconceivable to her (literally unimaginable) that she had become a figure of fun, that we were all sitting around waiting for her to say something self-congratulatory or Pharisaical so we could then repeat what she'd said out loud and laugh about it the next time she went to the bathroom.

Now would have been the time to crowd into the living room and have our tree. My father and Ain't Aubria's son-in-law, who handed out the presents, would read aloud from the tag, who it was for and who it was from. We would all wait until a gift had been found for each of us before we opened our gifts together. Admiration would be expressed and thanks shouted across the room. Then the process would have been repeated with another round of gifts. With so many gifts for so many different people, the gifts always spilled far out into the room as though poured from a horn of plenty. It would be several rounds at least before we reached the ones that were actually under the tree.

We were profligate of wrapping paper, tearing it off in great shards like barbarians sacking a city, but we were thrifty when it came to bows. "Don't throw your bows away," we children would be reminded. "Be sure to save your bows." Even as we were wadding up the discarded wrapping paper and stuffing it into garbage bags, we were sifting through the rubble like archaeologists in search of any bows we might have overlooked earlier. And we would make jokes about how we just exchanged the same bows among us every year.

From her chair in the corner, Grandmother Gertrude would observe us the way a director in an auditorium might observe a rehearsal on a stage. Always when you failed to appreciate the gift she had given you in quite the way she had hoped, she would interrupt your performance to italicize that gift's valuable significance for you.

"Those are *Russell Stovers* candies," she would tell you. "I bought them at *Neiman Marcus*."

Thus enlightened you were expected to improve your line reading. "Oh, really? From Neiman Marcus? Well, I'm sure they'll be real delicious. Thank you so much."

Grandmother Gertrude was one of those people who truly believed it was more blessed to give than to receive. But in her case, you got the feeling this belief had little to do with a spiritual view of material things, and everything to do with putting others in her debt while incurring no corresponding debt of her own.

Could this be why she always received her own gifts so ungraciously? I remember the time Ain't Aubria gave her a bed jacket from Kaplan's Ben-Hur. Grandmother Gertrude held it up and cooed the same admiration as everyone else, "Oh, it's just lovely, Aubria, just beautiful." But then Cinderella's gown became Cinderella's rags as she dropped it back down into the box and added, "Unfortunately, I can't wear it, it's polyester."

Everyone knew that Grandmother Gertrude believed herself allergic to polyester, to rayon, to all synthetic fibers of any kind. Only cotton, silk, linen, and wool could touch her delicate skin.

Otherwise, she would break out in hives. Furthermore, her allergies neither began nor ended with fabrics. Like the Gadarene demoniac, a legion of them bedeviled her. She was allergic to margarine. Her system simply could not tolerate anything but butter. And onions gave her intestinal cramps. Every year she would call upon Ain't Aubria to furnish a verbal guarantee that the cornbread dressing contained no onion. "Oh, honey, you know I wouldn't put onion in your dressing," Ain't Aubria would tell her. On the strength of this assurance, Grandmother Gertrude would then wolf down three servings, apparently with no ill effects even though the dressing actually did have onion in it. Quite a lot of onion, in fact. Hardly a secret, as my mother pointed out. "Why, you could see it with the nekkid eye."

In addition to turkey and dressing, there were mashed potatoes and candied yams, buttered carrots and Kentucky wonder beans, broccoli with cheese sauce and pearl onions, plus olives stuffed with pimento and celery sticks stuffed with pimento cheese, not to mention giblet gravy and cranberry sauce, and dinner rolls that reached the table warm from the oven in two shifts, the first when we sat down to eat, the second halfway through the meal.

Ain't Aubria, and Ain't Aubria alone, had cooked everything spread out before us, since she did not permit either her daughter or my mother to bring a covered dish of any kind, not even so much as a pie. "There's no need," Ain't Aubria insisted. She always had plenty of deserts on hand: pumpkin, pecan, and chocolate pies, plus heavenly salads, such as fruit cocktail with miniature marshmallows folded in whipped cream; also pineapple upside-down cake, and a wide array of cookies and candies.

Especially admired were her kiflins. These little cylinders of sweetened pie crust mixed with nuts and rolled in confectioner sugar could not be duplicated, even using the same recipe, by lesser cooks like my mother.

There was no beer, no wine, no aperitifs, and certainly no brandy or cigars. As good Southern Baptists, we washed our meal down with iced tea and our desserts down with hot coffee. On the whole, we benefited from this arrangement, the conviviality it may have curtailed being more than offset by the aggression it surely forestalled. From all the horror stories I have heard over the years about the alcohol-fueled family feuds that erupted at other people's holiday boards, I have come to see how lucky I am that caffeine was my own family's drug of choice. Passive aggression is so much more peaceful than aggressive aggression, especially if it is the men as well as the women who swallow their rage and suffer in silence. From the way my father, as well as the rest of the family, always placated Grandmother Gertrude, you might have thought she would be disposing of a great fortune upon her death.

She would not of course, but even so, we would all sit there in respectful silence, nobody interrupting, just eating our turkey while she rambled on, some interminable story until at last Ain't Aubria interrupted. "Would anyone like another roll? How about some more iced tea?"

Was there any wound iced tea could not salve, any wrong a hot roll fresh from the oven could not assuage, any grief that could not be comforted by an enormous slice of chocolate pie topped with a half-pint of heavy whipped cream? I always had chocolate pie, instead of pecan or pumpkin, for dessert. Always. When the main meal was over and the women were taking dessert orders, whoever was asking me, would not actually ask but say, "You don't have to tell me, I know what *you* want." Everyone would laugh because it had been a family joke, me and my chocolate pie, for as long as I could remember.

I must have been quite small when the joke got started, no more than three or four, and in those days, it was easier for Ain't Aubria to cater to my finicky tastes since I was her only grandchild. An honorary grandchild to be sure, but even after her real grandchildren came along, the two of us still shared our special memories of the time when Santy Claus came to her house only for me.

At Ain't Aubria's, I had my own room and my parents had theirs, just like at home. I remembered getting up early one morning when the light was still gray and the door to my parents' room still shut. But since the door to Ain't Aubria's room was open, I had wandered in and gotten into bed with her. The two of us lay there and talked for the longest time.

Then we got up and went into the kitchen, where Ain't Aubria made biscuits from scratch. She rolled the wet, tacky dough out and let me help by cutting out big circles with the mouth of an iced tea glass. Ain't Aubria had never judged me for wanting to help her make biscuits or play with the vacuum cleaner or even traipse around the house in a pair of her old high heels.

"If that's what he wants to do, I think that's all right," she would say.

I was also afraid of the dark. And she never judged me for this either. On the contrary, she always made sure there was a nightlight burning in my room, a little Christmas-tree bulb in a blue translucent hood that plugged directly into the wall socket. One night in particular, I can remember her putting me to bed in that dark bedroom, darker than my room at home on account of the dark green walls illuminated only by eerie blue light, and at first I had thought she would tuck me in, but instead she pulled back the sheet and lifted my foot in the air. I was lying on my back, looking up at her with my tiny foot suspended in front of her face and my big toe grasped between her thumb and forefinger as she proceeded to count my toes.

"This little nigger went to market," she said. "This little nigger stayed home, this little nigger had roast beef, this little nigger had none, and this little pickaninny went wee, wee, wee all the way home."

If Ain't Aubria had cut her finger with a kitchen knife and let fly a volley of oaths, I would have been shocked, but I would have been titillated as well, because deep down, I understood that however bad most bad words might be, they were still just words that could not hurt you. But "nigger" was more like a stick or a stone; that was why you never said it, not under any circumstances, because it really could hurt people, and for Ain't Aubria to say it, not just once, but again and again, upended the moral order. I was not only shocked, I was frightened, and with each repetition, I wanted to shout at her to stop, to *please* not say it again. She had already said it four times and was about to say it a fifth when confused, I asked: "What's a pickaninny?"

"What's a pickaninny?" It was as though I had asked her who Jesus was, or whether eggs came from cows.

"Why, a pickaninny's a little nigger child," she told me.

She seemed peeved that she had to explain the punch line to her own joke, but she soon recovered, being a good-natured woman, and having wee wee wee'd my pinky toe to her heart's content, she returned to my big toe and said, "Now you say it."

She had put me on the horns of a dilemma. Ain't Aubria was not allowing me to remain just an observer. She was insisting that I become a participant. I would have much preferred to let the cup pass from me, but she had left me no alternative. "This little nigger went to market," she prompted. And that was when I spoke out.

"You're not s'posed to say that," I told her.

"Say what?" Ain't Aubria seemed genuinely puzzled.

"You're s'posed to say 'Negro,'" I said. "Either 'Negro,' or 'colored.'"

It was as though I had, as a full-grown man, clenched my fist into a tight little ball and slammed it full force into her forehead. That was how shocked she looked, and how hurt. Because she had never judged me, she never dreamed I would ever judge her.

"You told her *what*?" my mother had said, horrified, when I told her the story. With Grandmother Gertrude always scheming against her, my mother needed Ain't Aubria as an ally.

"You should not have said *that* to her," said my mother.

But my father defended me, so she had to back down. "So what *did* you say?" my mother asked.

This was much the same question Ain't Aubria had asked, though with entirely different emphasis. "So what do *you* say?" she had said, her voice clipped, her face frozen. I could tell she was veiling her anger, and not just her anger, her humiliation. I told her that I always said "This little piggy" at home. So she said, "Why don't you just say that?" And I did.

This was in the 1950s. By the 1960s, "nigger" was no longer a socially permissible word, not even in Texas, not even when used by old people who insisted they were just too old to change. But long after others had made the change, Ain't Aubria still resisted. She never got as far as "African-American." She never got as far as "black." She never even got as far as "Negro." The best she could manage was "nigra." She would make some untoward remark about the nigras just as she was disappearing into the kitchen with somebody's empty iced tea glass, and her daughter and my mother would exchange knowing glances, then smile back down at their plates. "Nigra" had become Ain't Aubria's running gag, what chocolate pie was for me.

But why had she been so stubborn about it? Two little vowels and she would have been there. According to my mother, Ain't Aubria was keeping faith with her mother whose real name my mother could no longer remember, everyone had just called her Mammy. My mother did not seem to think this was strange, that a white woman should have been called Mammy, especially a white woman who was a racist.

Well, not a racist exactly. That was too strong a word, my mother insisted. Mammy was never mean to people, she was not hateful, she just had this idea that everyone should keep to their place.

I heard a lot of that in those days, the idea that African-Americans had a right to exist, so long as they knew their place. It made racism sound like a particularly virulent form of snobbery, which it was in a way, and Ain't Aubria's brand of it reminded me of Proust's remark about Charlus: that just because a man was a snob, it did not necessarily have to infect every aspect of his life. I would have liked to think that Ain't Aubria's racism could be compartmentalized, leaving the rest of her untainted, but I was far from sure this was possible. If she had admitted that it was wrong to say "nigger," and wrong to regard segregation as a moral imperative, then she would have been forced to admit that Mammy had been wrong. And this, above all, she could not do. Thus did racism pollute even the best thing about her, her unconditional loyalty to the people she loved, whether they were living or dead.

"Rex, honey, come sit here by me," she had said. (Ain't Aubria had always called everyone honey, and she pronounced my name to rhyme with "rakes.")

She had made this request the last time I saw her, the Christmas before she died, when I was in my late forties. The seating chart at the big table had never been set in stone. Each year, it was renegotiated. But since I was the only left-handed person in the family, I had always been seated at the end, far from Ain't Aubria. Now, if I sat at her left, I would be fencing elbows with the right-handed person to my left. But how could I gainsay her? She was ninety-three and her health was failing.

We all knew that even if Ain't Aubria lived until next Christmas, it was unlikely she would ever again fix us dinner. How had she done it this year? She had started long beforehand, for one thing. The cookies and candy and piecrusts had all been baked or rolled out weeks in advance and then frozen. She was very picky, so her daughter had taken her to the grocery store and pushed her around in the wheelchair so that she could select the celery, the broccoli, the onions, all the produce, herself.

Ain't Aubria was not wheelchair-bound in the sense that her legs were no longer functional. It was just that after two heart attacks she was so weakened, she could only walk a short distance on her own. With a little help from one of her grandsons, she had gotten into a dining room chair, then her daughter had rolled the empty wheelchair into the den and out of sight. It was obviously important to Ain't Aubria how we would all remember her, and she did not want us to remember her sitting in a wheelchair at the table.

"Come closer to me, Rakes honey," she said.

I scooted my chair close to her and she leaned in even closer as though about to show me how big her teeth were, when really, she was just trying to get a good look at my face. Her eyesight failed her at the end, but she was never completely blind. The TV was a blur of color. But she could still read her large-print Bible with a magnifying glass. And she could make eye contact with you if your face was no more than a couple feet away.

"Can you see my tree?" she said.

For a moment, I was not quite sure which tree she meant, the Christmas tree or the great live oak in her front yard, and I realized that when the Christmas tree was not there, you could sit in the living room and look out at the real tree, as perfectly framed by the picture window as the Christmas tree would be when seen from the other side. Since I was always here during the holidays and at no other time, the tree that had been merely decorative, like a flower in a vase, had obscured my consciousness of the tree in the ground that had been Ain't Aubria's proudest possession. This tree was her idea of luxury; it was what made this piece of land so valuable. When she was selling off the property Uncle Otis had left her, she could have sold this lot for a princely sum and then spent it on travel or furs or status-enhancing philanthropy. Instead, she had kept the tree for herself, and built her house in its shadow where she could sit in her living room and look out at it every day for the purely aesthetic pleasure it gave her. She could still see it now in her memory better than I could in real life, my view being obscured by the Christmas tree.

"Yes, I can see your tree," I told her.

"I've always loved that tree," she said.

Her far-off gaze suggested oracular trance, and it struck me that her devotion was more druidic than horticultural.

"This year I hired a nigra man to come rake up my leaves," she told me.

Did I visibly flinch, or did it just feel as though I had? Why did she have to show me this side of her in what might well be our last conversation? It was not as though it turned out to be a great story either. It was just a meandering incident. Her tree had grown so large, it seemed, that for this nigra man to rake up and bag all her leaves took more than one day. On the second day she had noticed that he seemed unhappy ("dragging his feet" was the phrase she used). She had asked what the problem was and he told her that his wife had gone into the hospital that morning. She told him not to worry about the leaves, that he should just go be with his wife, that he could come back and finish raking her leaves after Christmas. And, not only that, she had given him an extra twenty-five dollars.

That was it. That was all there was to the story. And now, she waited for a response. But what could I say? "When a man throws a coin to a beggar, he throbs with contempt"—these were the words that sprang to mind, but of course I did not quote de Sade to her. What I actually said was, "I'm sure he must have really appreciated your doing that."

Clearly, this was not the response she had hoped for. She nodded in disappointment and said, "Yes, I think he did," in a vague distracted way.

I had failed to connect. So I had tried again.

"Do you remember when I was a little boy and spent the night, and we'd get up the next morning and make biscuits?" I said.

Her face lit up. "Do you really remember that?" she said. "I thought you might have forgotten."

We had loved each other then, when I was three or four years old, not that we did not love each other now. But then, we had been Romeo and Juliet of the balcony scene. Now, we were Anthony and Cleopatra with Rome closing in on us, and, if this great tree of hers really was a Herne's oak, this would be the final fugue we sang beneath its naked limbs and danced upon its buried roots. Sitting this close to her, you could not miss the truth. She was so fragile, so frail, and death was so near. The last leaf hung by the merest thread; the slightest breeze would bring it down. It was more than poignant, it was tragic. The terror of death, the pity for her.

It was only after her death a few months later that I finally realized why she had been so eager to tell me that patronizing story about her yardman. She too had never forgotten the time I had rebuked her for counting my toes the way Mammy had always counted hers, and before she died, she had wanted this barrier of my disapproval to be broken down between us.

But how can sins be absolved, unless they are acknowledged as sins? Had she told me some story that illustrated how much she had changed over the years, I could have absolved her easily. But with this story about the yardman, she was saying that she and Mammy never really needed to change, that they had always empathized with, and been generous to their nigras, that in their hearts, they were guiltless. But noblesse oblige is no substitute for justice, and I could not bring myself to pretend that it was, not even for her benefit, not even at the end of her life when she was leaving the world and it no longer mattered how she behaved in it. I do not see this as a particularly admirable stance on my part. When a final choice had to be made, it was real people Ain't Aubria was loyal to, whereas my ultimate loyalty was to abstract ideas. When I was absolutely certain that I was absolutely right, I could be very unforgiving. Judgmental even. Self-righteous. Just like Grandmother Gertrude.

Born in Baytown, Texas, and educated at the University of Texas at Austin, Gregory Sanders now lives in West Hollywood, California, where he works as a film editor. His short fiction has appeared in a number of periodicals, including *RE:AL, River City,* the *Snake Nation Review,* the *Chiron Review,* and the *South Carolina Review,* where "Good Witch, Bad Witch" first appeared. He is currently working on a novel.

*G*ood Witch, Bad Witch" *is a highly fictionalized account of my own relatives. Begun as a humorous anthropology of family rituals, the story took on a darker tone as it approached this question: How should we react when a person we love holds hateful ideas? There is no easy answer, nor does the story provide one. In the end, death resolves the problem, but the emotional ambiguity remains, and the heart is left to search for a truth it never finds.*

Kevin Wilson

THE CHOIR DIRECTOR AFFAIR (THE BABY'S TEETH)

(from *The Carolina Quarterly*)

This is the baby, and yes, those are teeth. They are not important. Don't think about them. Nothing special, this baby with teeth. Usually it is only a snaggletooth, a single, perfectly formed tooth in the tiny mouth, unlike the full set on this baby. Still, it has happened before, is happening now, will happen again, Jesus Christ, get over it. It is nothing to get upset about. They are only teeth, things we all have. So forget we even mentioned it, because it doesn't matter: the baby, the teeth, the unrecognizable pacifiers.

The story isn't about the baby anyway, but the father of the baby. He is having an affair with the choir director of the girls' chorus at the private school where he teaches biology. That is where the story lies. There is guilt and lust and deceit and the things that stories are made of, the condition of our collective lives laid bare. And yet, this baby.

When you are invited to visit the parents just a few weeks after the birth, to see the baby, of course, you walk into the newly decorated, mobiled, yellow-hued room, and you coo and baby talk over this new thing, this well-made and cute thing. And then the baby flashes those teeth, and you . . . well, you scream.

The father, who is sleeping with a beautiful, red-haired woman who sings like a bird, calmly informs you about the teeth, repeating what the doctors said, the pamphlets they had to order from a medical oddities supplier. The wife, who does not know about the affair but knows her husband has things he keeps from her, starts to tear up, watering around the eyes, until she has to excuse herself for a moment. You feel like a real son of a bitch, but why wouldn't someone mention this beforehand. A small warning: this baby will smile and it will startle you. Nothing.

However, the parents are preoccupied. For the father: a woman ten years younger than him, digging her fingernails into his back as he presses her onto a desk in the band room. For the mother: bruises on her nipples from breastfeeding, tiny bite marks that were once made by her husband but no longer. These are not earth-shattering things but they can, if necessary, keep you from examining other aspects of your life.

Later that night, while the mother flosses the baby and prepares it for sleep, you sit in the kitchen and drink beer while the husband tells you about the choir director and how she hits impossibly high notes when she climaxes. He says he is racked with guilt, especially with a new baby to think about, but you can tell he is pleased with himself. A woman sings because of him and no amount of hand-wringing can hide that. He tells you that she has a split uvula and that it drives him crazy just thinking about it when she goes down on him. Now you are a little disgusted, the easy, animal ways that he can get off on the genetic peculiarities of others. With his baby lying in bed upstairs with all those teeth. And there it is again, the baby.

You try to listen to the rest, the times and places and ways. You think you hear the father say that he is falling in love with this woman, but you cannot concentrate. You want to. You know this is the thing that matters, the thing that will affect all their lives in myriad ways, but you cannot do it.

You excuse yourself, blame the beer, and seek the bathroom. Upstairs, down the hall, and into the room, quiet save for the hiss of a humidifier. The baby is still awake, eyes wide open. You smile a little nervously, not wanting to cause alarm. And the baby, god-damn, smiles right back. Big and wide.

If, in less than a year, this baby was to sprout its teeth naturally, that is to say, pushing through the gums until approximating a tooth, you would think nothing of it. In fact, you'd be a little put off, the constant crying, the blue plastic toy pulled from the freezer and jammed into the mouth. Now, however, in the dim light of the baby's room, they are inexhaustibly fascinating. Calcified, enameled, not yet cavied. They really are the color of a pearl. You have heard that cliché of teeth, toothpaste commercials that show the tube, the brush, the tiny sparkle that shines off the front tooth, but now you understand the phrase. You think this baby's teeth could be used as a necklace, something beautiful and perfect that you feel slightly guilty for owning.

Now your hand is moving towards the baby, slowly, index finger extended, as if pointing to a place on a map. You touch the smoothness of one of the teeth, the rounded edge on the bottom. The baby's eyes stay open, calm, but you do not see them, only the teeth. And then the teeth closing around your finger, quickly. Your finger is still there, in the mouth, and now there is skin to be broken, cries to be muffled, shots to be considered.

This was never supposed to happen. You were supposed to stay downstairs with the father and listen to him go on and on about this singing adulteress. Instead, you are wrapping your finger in tissues, bounding quickly down the stairs, wondering aloud where the time went, hugging the father in order to avoid a handshake and reveal the offending finger, and running to your car before you sit there in silence and breathe much too quickly for comfort. You are not listening to the father and his newfound desire to perhaps leave his wife and child and run off to Europe with this choir director to visit old opera houses. You are not there to witness this total lack of judgement and decency and advise yea or nay.

As of this moment, you in the car, staring at those tooth impressions on your finger, you think the father's dalliance will not last much longer and will hopefully cause only a small amount of unhappiness. This is not the truth, of course. Why would we be telling this story if that were the case? But none of this matters to you now as you speed through the night, the radio playing in your car, the windows down, your finger in your own mouth, your tongue finding the impressions left by teeth much smaller than your own.

The gravity of the situation, the mother and father and choir director, becomes abundantly clear to you not long after that night. You are the friend of the father, and so now you have become something more than that: an alibi. You are doing more with the father than you ever have before, though you actually just sit at home in your underwear and read orthodontia journals. Still, in theory, in the mind of the mother, you are hitting balls at the driving range together, going to see the Chattanooga Lookouts play a doubleheader, sitting in on lectures at the Tennessee Aquarium about the eating habits of tree frogs. You are doing so much together, though actually apart, that the mother, who is now beginning to suspect something, begins to believe that perhaps it is you with whom the father is having an affair.

The father will tell you this over coffee one night, the first time you've actually seen him in weeks. He will relate the late-night accusation from the mother, the baby held in her arms like a threat, chewing on a squeaky dog toy in the shape of a fire hydrant. The father will laugh, the same way he is laughing right now as he tells you this, and calm his wife, take the baby out of her arms and bounce it softly against his chest. She will cry, apologize, and they will make love for the first time since the baby was born, soft and cautious at first. Finally, their own fears and questions will come out, and they will bang the bed frame against the wall, the springs squeaking in a rhythm that matches the baby monitor's transmission of the dog toy in the mouth of the baby. And even after they are finished, when they separate and sleep facing opposite directions, there will be the sound of the baby chewing, squeaking, telling them things they either don't want to think about or already know.

You receive a photo Christmas card from the family, and what you should notice is the formal distance between the mother and the father, the grim look of finality on their faces. You don't notice this at all, though, because of that damn baby, wearing a Santa hat and grinning. You can barely make it out, but you get out a magnifying glass, and yes, those are the teeth. You put the photo in a frame, and it sits beside your bed. At nights, after you talk to the husband and agree on his next alibi, you hold the picture close to your face. You squint your eyes and if you try hard enough, you pretend that the parents aren't there at all, their malaise and distrust brushed right off the photo. Instead it is the baby, that hat, those teeth, and of course, you holding the baby, arms outstretched as if to say, "look at this, how perfect, how wonderful." And this, again, tells us just what you are getting out of this story, the wrong things, the things you should not see.

Why do you spend so much of your time in your underwear? We just find it curious. Every time we bring the story to your house . . . never mind, no matter. In any case, you are in your underwear when the father knocks on your door, holding the baby like a salesman about to tell you why you simply must have this baby, cannot say no to this remarkable invention. And you, sans pants, look as if you would pay any amount, if only you could find that wallet, those slacks, somewhere around here.

There has been a complication. The reading by a famous novelist who has written a book about birds and love and architecture which you are going to hear tonight with the father has been compromised. It was already compromised by the fact that the father and the choir director were instead going to a restaurant three towns over and then have sex in a motel and look at a travel book about Austria. And you were going to do . . . whatever it was you were going to do in your own house with no pants. Now though, there are further problems.

The wife is not feeling well. When she asked the father if he could cancel his plans to see the novelist read, he said he really couldn't. You are a lover of the arts, and plans had been made, and you are supposedly very high-strung about keeping one's appointments. So, the wife asked him to bring the baby. Babies are no place for serious readings about birds and love and architecture, but the wife was too busy throwing up to listen to anything else. So, this explains the house call, the baby, the dim shadow of a woman in the car, waiting patiently.

What you should now grasp is that the mother truly knows about the affair. She knows even who the person is, the choir director. This knowledge has made her ill, sick in mysterious ways to the husband, who is so wrapped up in his fantasies about himself and the choir director that he has no idea that he has been discovered. This was bound to happen though, the way in which a marriage so easily becomes something less than that, two people bound by things they can't quite remember. It was always meant to go this way, and this is not really what should be unsettling or cause for alarm. That will come later.

Another thing, perhaps more important, that you should realize from this baby on your doorstep is this: the father cannot be bothered with this child. He is a man concerned only with his new life that he is pretending to make for himself. However, the mother.

The mother does not want this baby either. It makes her sad, makes her think of the disfigured way her marriage began. It seems that you are the baby's biggest fan at this point, the president and sole member of the fan club. The baby has become, for the couple that created it, nothing more than a nuisance, a tactical consideration. It has become less than what it really is, which is what their marriage has become, but you don't realize any of this. You are taking the baby into your arms, carrying it over the threshold into your own home with the baby bag slung over your shoulder, as if the two of you are going on a trip from which you may never want to return.

You sit the baby on the coffee table, and this is the only thing either of you can think to do for some time. You smile, make baby faces. The baby smiles back, politely. You make hand gestures to say, *my house is your house,* and the baby keeps smiling, and you realize this is really all you want. You decide it best to put on pants, wonder if the father even noticed your lack of them.

Inside the plaid baby bag filled with diapers and formula and wipes is the baby's dinner. No strained peas for this baby, no Dutch apples. Two Big Macs. *Cut it into bite-sized pieces.* That is what the father told you, which you thought a strange request at the time. You take one of the Big Macs out of its box, saving the other for yourself, and the baby's wriggling hands reach out towards the hamburger. You tear a piece off and hold it towards the baby, who opens its mouth, revealing the teeth. You drop the food in quickly, now wary of the power and sharpness of those teeth. There is no hesitation for the baby. It has done this before. You work quickly, tearing the hamburger apart, feeding it to those teeth that mash and gnash it into something that resembles normal baby food. You wipe away the special sauce from the baby's mouth. This makes the baby smile, which makes you smile, and with dinner over, there is nothing to do but stare, enjoy each other's company.

You make a little bed out of blankets and pillows, but it seems insubstantial, cheap. Instead, you hold the baby and rock it to sleep, aided by the heaviness of the Big Mac being digested. The baby pulls itself into you, softly kicks its feet out as it drifts away. You begin to think that perhaps you actually love this baby, not just the teeth inside of it. Sitting here in your living room, holding the baby, it seems possible. You decide it is better that way, so you lean back against the sofa and fall asleep. In your arms, the baby silently grinds its soft teeth together, not quite asleep, not quite awake.

Then there is the knock on the door, the transaction of baby between you and the father. It is silent, without thanks or welcome. The father would rather not take it. You would rather keep it. So it goes. There are other things to consider: the mother, laws of nature, financial obligations, keeping up appearances. Nonetheless, this is the long and the short of it, the essential fact. Someone wants something the other does not and unhappiness ensues. It is also the essential fact of the more important thing, the father and the affair and his family. So it goes.

In the coming months, there will be many things. Fights, accu-
sations, declarations of love and hate in ever-changing order. It is
heartbreaking, but you cannot understand. You only want to know
of the baby, where it is, what it is doing, is it smiling. We have
grown tired. The story is hard to tell. The evaporation of love
makes us think of our own lives. We have tried to make you see
this, but always the baby. So here.

Here is the baby in the backyard, near the garden the mother has
long since given up on tending. The parents are inside the house,
and there is arguing going on, but quiet, under the surface. Too
much sugar in one's coffee, newspaper folded and refolded in the
face of questions, mentions of after-school activities. Outside, however, is the baby crawling towards the garden, towards something
moving across the dirt. The baby reaches out with one of its little
hands, picks up the garter snake. It is the length and size of the
baby's shoelace. The baby places the snake in its mouth and bites
down, over and over, simply gnawing through the scales like one
of the chew toys. The snake arches and bends in the mouth, but the
baby's teeth are strong. The parents look out the window and think
the child is being attacked. They run, fear rising up and out of their
mouths. And when they arrive at the edge of the garden, there is
the baby, fingers speckled with tiny drops of blood, lips red and
wet, smiling.

There is the inevitable. The separation, the divorce, the trip to
Vienna. The baby with teeth stays with the mother, who stays in
her house and rarely leaves. The father sends you a postcard of the
Wiener Staatsoper, an opera house so beautiful you begin to think
the father left his old life behind not for the choir director but for
this building. The back of the postcard reads simply: Having a
wonderful time.

The father will soon not be having a wonderful time, we can tell
you that. The choir director will leave him after they return to the
States. His job at the school is rescinded for his indiscretions. His
hair begins to fall out. The mother will not allow him to visit the
baby. He calls you one night and asks if you will check on them,

that he is worried about the mother and the baby. Of course, he is worried, but what he is truly worried about is if they will take him back.

You go, knock, say hello, sit down for coffee. The mother is telling you that she does not blame you for all of this, that she does not think less of you. This should make you happy, but you are not listening. You are watching the baby in its high chair in the kitchen. From the sofa, you can just barely see the baby. It is chewing something, bubble gum you realize. And are those bubbles? You cannot be sure. Perhaps. The mother is still talking. Then she is not. Then she is kissing you. It is time to leave. You call the father and tell him the baby is fine.

Years and years after all of this, when the events have been made less memorable by time, you will see the baby again. Though it is no longer a baby. The father has long since left town, to unknown locations. The mother cannot make eye contact with you, the few times you ever see each other. There is nothing to remind you of any of this except for the baby with teeth that is no longer a baby.

The baby is a teenager now, sullen, acned, unaccustomed to its body. The baby works at the Piggly Wiggly, swiping your items and taking your money. The baby with teeth no longer smiles, no matter how hard you try. And even if the baby were to smile, just a tiny bit, there would be nothing wondrous about it. There would be teeth, the same as anyone else. Perhaps even braces. The things you thought so amazing about this baby are no longer there, if they ever were, and you are embarrassed. The photo in the frame, the teeth marks on your finger, the baby in your arms. There is nothing that you have left for this baby, though the teeth are still there, and this makes you inescapably sad.

And as you look one more time at this baby you once thought the world of, perhaps we have shown you the thing we intended all along. Not in the way we had wanted, through the person we had chosen, but we take some small measure of solace for making you see this. You hand a bag of carrots to the former baby with teeth. Your hands touch briefly. There is nothing, only the transaction of an item. Nothing more. You hand over the rest of the items from your cart and as the old baby reaches over to scan each offering, you begin to understand. Don't you see? The things we once loved do not change, only our belief in them.

Now, right now, you stare at the baby there in the checkout line, and then it is over. You are left with the only things that any of us have in the end. The things we keep inside of ourselves, that grow out of us, that tell us who we are.

———————

Kevin Wilson is a native of Winchester, Tennessee. His fiction has appeared in *Ploughshares, One Story, Carolina Quarterly, Shenandoah,* and elsewhere. A graduate of Vanderbilt University and the MFA program at the University of Florida, and a recipient of a fellowship from the McDowell Colony, he currently lives in Sewanee, Tennessee, where he teaches at the University of the South.

This story was an odd baby from the start. I originally wanted to write a grown-up story, so I thought I'd write about an affair. However, as with all of my stories, I couldn't resist the urge to throw something strange into the mix, so I gave the couple a baby with teeth. As I kept writing, I found myself focusing less and less on the couple and handing over full pages to this baby. Once the story failed, thankfully, I started over and decided to stick with what was working, the baby. Also, while I was writing this story, I was dogsitting for a friend, and I found myself, quickly and without hesitation, falling in love with Rose, the dog. And I was sad at the prospect of her owner coming back and taking her away. That sadness, of loving something that isn't yours, seeped into the story as well. I miss that damn dog, but I am thankful for the story.

Elizabeth Spencer

THE BOY IN THE TREE

(from *The Southern Review*)

On a February afternoon, Wallace Harkins is driving out of town on a five-mile country road to see his mother. He was born and raised in the house where she lives, but the total impracticality of keeping an aging lady out there alone in that large a place is beginning to trouble him.

His mother does not know he is coming. He used to try to telephone, but sometimes she doesn't answer. She will never admit either to not hearing the ring, or to not being in the mood to pick up the receiver, though one or the other must be true.

At the moment Mrs. Harkins is polishing some silver at the kitchen sink. At times she looks out in the yard. In winter the pecan trees are gray and bare—a network of gray branches, the ones near the trunk large as a man's wrist, the smaller ones reaching out, lacing and dividing, all going toward cold outer air. Sometimes Mrs. Harkins sees a boy sitting halfway up a tree, among the branches. Who is he? Why is he there? Sometimes he isn't there.

She often looks out the back rather than the front. For one thing the kitchen is in the back of the house, so it's easy. But for another, there is expectation. Of what? That she doesn't know. Of someone? Of something? Strange mule, strange dog, strange man or woman? So far lately there has only been the boy. When her son Wallace appears out of nowhere (she hasn't heard the car), she tells him about it.

"Sure you're not seeing things?" he teases.

"I do see things," she tells him, "but the things I see are there."

He hopes she'll start seeing things that aren't there so he can talk her into a "retirement community."

"You mean a nursing home," she always says. "Call it what you mean."

"It isn't like that," he would counter.

"There isn't one here," she would object.

"Certainly there is. Just outside town. Two in fact, one out the other way, too."

"If I was there I wouldn't be here."

That was for sure. Once, over another matter, she had chased him out of the house waving the broom at him. She was laughing, to show she didn't really mean it, but when she dropped the broom and threw an old cracked teacup it caught him back of the right ear and bled. "Oh, I'm so sorry, I'm so sorry," she said. And ran right up and kissed where it bled. But she was laughing still, the whole time. How did you know which she meant, the throwing or the kissing?

He dared to mention it to his wife Jenny when he got home. His mother and his wife had been at odds for so many years he believed they never thought of it anymore, but when he said, "Which did she mean?" his wife said immediately, "She doesn't know herself."

"You think she's gone around the bend?" he asked, and thought once again of the retirement home.

"I think she never was anywhere else," Jenny answered, solving nothing. She was cleaning off the cut and dabbing on antiseptic that stung.

His problem was women, he told himself. But going up to his office that morning, he almost had a wreck.

The occasion was the sight of a boy standing on a street corner. It was just past the main business street and just before the block containing the post office and bank. The boy was wearing knee britches, completely out of date now, but just what he himself used to wear to school. They buttoned at the knee; only he had always found the buttons a nuisance, the wool cloth scratchy, and had un-buttoned them as soon as he got out of sight of his mother. As if that was not enough, the boy was eating peanuts! So what? he thought, but he knew the answer very well. He himself had stood right there, many the day, and shelled a handful of peanuts, raw from the country, dirt still sticking to their shells. He always threw the shells out in the street. At that very moment, he saw the boy throw the shells in the same way. Wallace almost ran into an on-coming car.

Once at the office, he was annoyed to find a litter of mail on his desk. Miss Carlton had not opened the envelopes, and he was about to ring for her when she entered on her own, looking fraz-zled. "They all came back last night," she said. "I stayed up till two o'clock getting them something to eat and listening to all the sto-ries. You'd think deer season was the only time worth living for."

"Kill anything?" he asked, more automatically than not. He'd never been the hunting-fishing type.

"Oh, sure. One ten-pointer."

Was that good or bad? He sat slitting envelopes and had no re-action, one way or the other. He had once owned a dog, but ani-mals in general didn't mean a lot to him.

The peanuts had been brought to him from the country almost every day by a little white-headed girl who sat right in front of him in study hall. Once he'd found her after school waiting for a ride (they both had missed the bus), and they went in the empty gym and tried making up how you kissed. Had she missed the bus on purpose, knowing he'd be late from helping the principal clean up the chemistry lab? How did she ever get home? He never found out, for it was not so long after that he had been taken sick.

They took him home from school with high fever. Several peo-ple put him to bed. It lasted a long time. His mother was always there. Whenever he woke up from a feverish sleep, there she'd be, right before him in her little rocking chair, reading or sewing. "Water," he would say and she would give him some. "Orange juice," he said, and there it would be, too.

He told his wife later, "I can't figure how you can be sick and happy, too. But I was. She was great to me."

"You like to be loved," his wife said, and gave him a hug.

"Doesn't everybody?"

"More or less."

When he went back to school the white-headed girl had left. Died or moved away? Now when he thought of her, he couldn't remember.

Wallace Harkins was assured of being a contented man, by and large. When troubles came, even small ones looked bigger than they would to anyone with large ones. Yet he often puzzled over things, and when he puzzled too long he would go out to see his mother and get more puzzled than ever. As for his state of bliss when he was sick as a boy and dependent on her devotion, he would wonder now if happiness always came in packages wrapped up in time. Try to extend the time, and the package got stubborn. Not wanting to be opened, it just sat and remained the same. You couldn't get back in it because time had carried you on elsewhere.

It was the same with everything, wasn't it? There was that honeymoon time (though for several years after they married, it still seemed like honeymoon) when he and Jenny got stranded in Jamaica because of a hurricane, no transport to the airport, no airport open. Great alarm at the resort hotel up the coast from Montego Bay, fears of its being leveled and washed away. They ate by candlelight, and walked clinging to one another by a turbulent sea. "Let's just stay here" was Jenny's plea, and he had shared it. Oh, Lord, he really did. But then it was over. When he thought of it, wind whistled around his ears, and out in the water a stricken boat bobbed desperately. They both had loved it and tried going back, but this time the food was dreary, the rates had gone up, and the sea was full of jellyfish.

"Mother," he asked her, "why do people change?"

She was looking out the back window. "Change from what?"

He'd no answer.

"How is Edith?" she asked. Edith was his daughter.

"Edie is failing Agnes Scott," he said. "She isn't dumb, she just doesn't apply herself."

"Then take her out for a while. Start all over."

I'll do that, he thought. Time marched along. He had gray in his hair.

"Do you remember Amy Louise?" he asked, for the name of the white-haired girl had suddenly returned to him.

"That girl that came here and ate up a lot of candy once? It was when you were sick. I thought she'd never seen candy before. Before she left, she had chocolate running out of her mouth."

"Did she have white hair?"

"No, just brown. You must mean somebody else."

He noted the street corner carefully when he drove home. Nobody was on it.

Wallace had always loved his wife Jenny from afar. When they were in high school together she hadn't the time of day for him, and the biggest of life's surprises came when years later she consented to marry him. "She's just on the rebound," said an unkind friend, for, as they both knew, she had been dating an ex–football player from State College while working in Atlanta. "Just the same," said Wallace, "she said she would."

Jenny liked any number of things—being back in the town, a nice place to live, furniture to her taste, cooking, and going on trips. She was easy to please. She even liked him in bed. Surprise? It was true that his desires were many but realizations few. He had put himself down as a possible failure. With Jenny, all changed. She didn't object when for a warm up he fondled her toes. She said it was better than tickling her. Who had tickled her? He didn't ask.

Jenny was pretty, too. Shiny brown hair and clear smooth skin. He loved the bouncy way she walked and the things she laughed at. He told his mother that. She said that was good. But when he asked if she didn't agree, she didn't answer. But actually anybody in their right mind would have to agree, thought Wallace. He caught himself thinking that. Was his mother not in her right mind? A puzzle.

"She makes you feel guilty," Jenny pointed out. "If I were you, I'd quit going out there so much. She's happy the way she is. If you didn't come, she wouldn't care."

"Really?" said Wallace. The thought pierced him, but he decided to try it.

About this time, Wallace had a strange dream. Like all his dreams, it had a literal source. Out in Galveston, Texas, a man had acquired a tiger cub, a playful little creature. It grew up. One summer day, responding to complaints from the neighbors, the animal control team found a great clumsy orange-colored beast chained in the backyard of an abandoned house. The chain was no more than three or four feet long and was fastened to an iron stake sunken in concrete. In fact, the only surface available to the animal was cement, the yard having been paved for parking. The sun was hot. The tiger at this stage resembled nothing so much as a rug not even the Salvation Army would take.

Reading about it, Jenny was riveted to the paper. "Where's the bastard took that cat in the first place?"

"They'll track him down."

"I hope they shoot him," she said.

"You don't mean the tiger?" Wallace teased her. She said she certainly didn't.

What do you do with a tiger?

The event made headlines locally because a preserve for large cats was located near their town. A popular talk-show host agreed to pay the tiger's expenses for transportation, release, rehabilitation, psychiatric counseling, and nourishment.

"Good God," said Wallace, "they're going to have to slaughter a whole herd of cattle every weekend."

"Maybe it will like soybean hamburgers," said Jenny.

"Wonder if they ever found that guy."

"I've just been wondering if maybe the tiger ate him."

In his dream, some weeks later, Wallace looked out the back door window and saw the tiger, thoroughly cured and healthy, wandering around in the backyard. He went out to speak with it. He thought he was being courageous, as it might attack. At first it glanced up at him and gave a rumble of a growl, and then it wandered away, as though bored. "You bastard," said Wallace. "Don't you appreciate anything?" Then he woke up.

The definitive quarrel between Jenny and Mrs. Harkins had taken place rather soon after Wallace's marriage. They were in the habit of going out to see the lady on Sunday afternoons and staying for what she called "a bite to eat." Sometimes she made up pancakes from Bisquick mix. Jenny was holding an electric hand beater and humming away on the batter when the machine slipped out of her hand and went leaping around first on the table, where it overturned the bowl with batter, then bounced off onto the floor. Jenny shouted, "I can't find the fucking switch!" The beater went bounding around the room. She was trying to catch up with it, but found it hard to grab. Batter, meantime, soared around in splatters. Some of it hit the walls, some the ceiling, and some went in their faces and on their clothes. Mrs. Harkins jerked the plug out of its socket. Everything went still. Jenny licked batter off her mouth and grabbed a paper towel to mop Wallace's shirt. A blob had gone in Mrs. Harkins's hair. Jenny got to laughing and couldn't stop. It seemed a weird accident. "I guess the shit hit the fan," she said.

Mrs. Harkins walked to the center of the room. "Anybody who uses your kind of language has got no right to be here."

"Mother!" said Wallace, turning white.

"Gosh," said Jenny, turning red. She walked out of the kitchen. There fell a silence Wallace thought would never end. He expected Jenny back, but then he heard the car pull out of the drive and speed away.

Mrs. Harkins set about cleaning pancake batter off everything in sight, and scrambled some eggs for their supper.

"I think you both ought to apologize," Wallace ventured, when his mother drove him home.

"You do?" said Mrs. Harkins, rather vaguely, as though unsure of what he was talking about.

"I never heard her say words like that before," Wallace vowed, though in truth Jenny did have a colorful vocabulary, restrained around Edith. In the long run, nobody apologized. But Jenny wouldn't go back with Wallace anymore. What she saw in her mother-in-law's announcement was that she (Jenny) was a lower-class woman, common, practically a redneck. "She didn't mean that," said Wallace. "You can't tell me," said Jenny. Furthermore, she thought the results were exactly what Mrs. Harkins wanted. She didn't want to see Jenny. She had been waiting all along for something to happen.

Within himself, Wallace lamented the rift. But he finally came to consider that Jenny might be right. He took to going alone to see about his mother. Gradually, this change of habit got to be the way things were. In routine lies contentment.

After the tiger dream Wallace went back again. He didn't know why, but felt he had to.

She wasn't there. The house was quiet and empty; she had even remembered to lock the door. The car was gone. He scribbled a note asking her to call him and went away reluctantly. She could be anywhere.

Wallace returned home but heard nothing. He fretted.

"Well," said his mother the next day (she hadn't called). "It was just that boy up in the tree. I finally went out and hollered up to ask him who he was and what he wanted. Then he came down. He just said he liked being around this house, and he wanted me to notice him. He was scared to knock and ask. He rambles. He's one of those rambling kind. Always wandering around in the woods. I drove him home. The family is just ordinary, but he seems a better sort. Smart." She tapped her head significantly.

"I dreamed about a tiger," said Wallace.

"What was it doing?" his mother asked.

"Prowling around in the backyard. It's that one they brought here from Texas."

"Maybe it got out," she suggested.

If only I could stick to business, thought Wallace.

That weekend Edith came home from Agnes Scott. She had flunked her math courses, so could not fulfill her ambition to take a science major, a springboard into many fabulous careers; instead, she had enrolled in communications. She had a boyfriend with her, a nice well-mannered intelligent boy named Phillip Barnes, who within about thirty minutes of his arrival had made up for Edith's inability to pass trigonometry. He knew how to listen to older people in an attentive way. He let it drop that his father ran a well-known horticultural company in Pennsylvania, but his mother, being southern, had wanted him at Emory. He was working on his accent with Edie's help, he claimed, and did imitations to make them laugh, which they gladly did. He was even handsome.

Wallace, feeling proud, suggested they all go out to see Grandmother.

Edith exchanged glances with her mother. "She won't know whether we came or not. Anyway, the house is falling down."

"She remembers what she wants to," said Wallace.

"He's got an Oedipus complex," said Jenny.

They argued for a while about such a visit, but in the end Wallace, Edith, and Phillip drove out on the excuse that the house, at least, was interesting, old as it was.

On their return Edith and Phillip announced that Mrs. Harkins had not said very much; she just sat and looked at them. "Not unusual," said Jenny.

Wallace sighed with relief. For, as a matter of fact, the little his mother had said had been way too much. She appraised the two for some time, sitting with them in the wide hallway, drafty in winter but cool in spring and summer, and remarked that a bird had flown in there this morning and didn't want to leave. "I chased him out with the broom," she said. Wallace well remembered that broom and wondered if she had made it up about the bird. Mrs. Harkins closed her eyes and appeared to be either thinking things over or dozing. Phillip Barnes conversed nicely on with Wallace.

Mrs. Harkins suddenly woke up. "If you two want to get married," she said, "you are welcome to do it here."

They all three burst out laughing, and Edith said, "Really Grandmamma, we haven't got halfway to that yet."

"You might," said Mrs. Harkins, and closed her eyes again.

"It really is a fine old house," said Phillip, who appreciated the upper-class look of old southern homes.

Going out to the car, Wallace whispered to Edith not to mention what his mother had offered. "You know they don't get on," he said.

But Phillip unfortunately had not heard him. Once back home, he laughed about it. "Edie's going to come downstairs in a hoopskirt," he laughed. But seriously, to Wallace, he said: "Gosh, I do like your mother. She pretends not to be listening, but I bet she hears everything. And what a great old house that is. Thanks for taking us."

"What's this about a hoopskirt?" Jenny asked.

"Oh, nothing," said Edie.

But Phillip wouldn't stop. It seemed that he didn't ever stop. "She said Edie could get married out there. Can't you just see her, carrying her little bouquet. Bet the lady's got it all planned."

No sooner were Edie and Phillip on the road to Atlanta than Jenny threw a fit. "What does that old woman mean?" she demanded. "She's doing what she always does. She's taking over what belongs to *me*!"

"But, honey," Wallace said, "we don't even know they're apt to get married."

"They're in love, aren't they? Anything can happen. And don't you honey me."

"But sweetheart, maybe Mother meant well. Maybe she saw an opportunity to get us all back together again."

"With her calling the shots. She's a meddlesome old bitch is what she is."

That was too much. Wallace had looked forward to an evening with Jenny, going over the whole visit a piece at a time, and afterwards having a loving time in bed. He wasn't to have anything of the sort tonight, he realized, and furthermore his mother was not a bitch.

"My mother is not a bitch," he said, and left the house.

How was he to know that Jenny had been mentally planning Edie's wedding herself? She had got as far as the bridesmaids' dresses, and was weighing black-and-white chiffon against a medley of various colors, not having got to what the mother-of-the-bride should appear in.

Wallace wandered. He drove around in the night. He thought of the tiger, but it was too late to look for the animal preserve. He thought of his mother, but he dreaded her seeing what was wrong. He'd no one to admit things to.

He went to a movie and felt sorry for himself. On the way out he saw a head of white-blonde hair going toward the exit. He hastened in that direction but there was only an older woman in those tight slacks Jenny disliked, wearing too much lipstick. He did not ask if her name was Amy Louise.

In spring Wallace threw himself madly into his work. He journeyed to Atlanta to an insurance salesmen's conference; he plied his skills among local homeowners, car owners, small-business owners. He even circulated in a trailer park and came out with a hefty list of new policies. What is it that you can't insure? Practically nothing.

Then, to his surprise, the way opened up for Wallace to make a lot of money. He received a call from some leading businessmen who wanted to talk something over. A small parcel of wooded land his father had left him just beyond the highway turnoff to the town was the object of their inquiry. Why didn't he develop it? Well, Wallace explained, he'd never thought about it. The truth was, in addition, he connected the land with his father, who had died when Wallace was eleven and whom he did not clearly remember. The little seventy-five or so acres was not pretty; it ran to irregular slopes and the scrappy growth of oaks and sycamores could scarcely be walked among for all the undergrowth. Still, Wallace paid the taxes every year, and thought of its very shaggy, natural appearance with a kind of affection, a leftover memory of his father, who had wanted him to have something of his very own. And he did go and walk around there, and though he came out scratched with briars, it made him feel good for some reason.

"Honey, we're going to be rich," Wallace said to Jenny.

"Why else you think I married you?" Jenny asked, perking up.

But what surprised him was his popularity. Prominent men squeezed his hand, they slapped his shoulder, they inquired after his mother, they recalled his father.

"Why do they like me?" he inquired of Jenny.

"Why not?" was Jenny's answer.

He thought it all had to do with business. And he was still puzzling besides over what had happened at the last business meeting. For they had succeeded with him; he was well along the road. Subdivision, surveys, sewage, drainage, electric power . . . But suddenly he had cried out: *"To hell with it! I don't want to!"*

He sat frozen, wondering at himself and looking about at the men in the room. They had kept on talking, never missing a syllable. On leaving, he had asked one of the oldest, "Did I say anything funny?" "Funny? Why, no." "I mean, didn't I yell something out?" "Nothing I heard." So he'd only thought it?

Standing in the kitchen that night, Wallace came across the real question in his life. He scratched his head and thought about it. "You and Edie, do you love me?"

"You like to be loved," Jenny said, and patted his stomach (he was getting fat). She stroked his head (he was getting bald).

She had calmed down since her explosion, but they both still remembered it and did not speak of it.

The trees were in full leaf when he next drove out to see Mrs. Harkins.

The front door was open but no one seemed to be downstairs. He stood in the hallway and wondered whether to call. From above he heard the murmur of voices, and so climbed up to see.

His mother was standing in one of the spare rooms. With her was a boy, maybe about fifteen. A couple of old leather suitcases lay open on the bed, the contents partially pulled out and scattered over the coverlet. She was holding up to the boy a checkered shirt that Wallace remembered well, a high school favorite.

"Isn't it funny I never thought to give away all these clothes?" she said.

The boy was standing obediently before her. When she held up the shirt he drew the sleeve along one arm to check the length. He was a dark boy, nearly grown, with black hair topping a narrow intelligent face set with observant eyes. Truth was he did measure out a bit like Wallace at a young age, though Wallace had had reddish-brown hair and large coppery freckles. They stared at each other and thought of nothing to say.

"This is Martin Grimsley," said Mrs. Harkins. "Martin, this is my son Wallace."

"The boy in the tree?" Wallace asked.

"The same," said Mrs. Harkins, and held up a pair of trousers that buttoned at the knee. "Plus fours," she said. "Too hot for now, but maybe this winter."

For lunch she had made some chicken salad with an aspic, and iced tea and biscuits and banana pudding. Wallace stayed to eat.

"Wallace saw the tiger," said Mrs. Harkins.

The boy brightened. "They keep him out near us with all them others."

"All those others," said Mrs. Harkins.

"I can hear 'em growling and coughing at night."

Wallace asked: "Did you ever stand on a corner uptown eating peanuts?"

"Not that I know of," Martin Grimsley replied.

They lingered there on the porch while the day waned.

Martin Grimsley talked. He talked on and on. He had been up Holders Creek to where it started. He had seen a nest of copperheads. Once he had seen a rattlesnake, but it had spots, so maybe it wasn't. He liked the swamps, but he especially liked the woods, different ones.

Inside the telephone rang. Nobody moved to answer it. They sat there listening to Martin Grimsley, until the lightning bugs began to wink, out beyond the drive.

"Someday we'll go and see," said Mrs. Harkins.

"See what?" said Wallace.

"The tiger," said the boy. "She means the tiger."

"Of course," said Mrs. Harkins.

They kept on talking. Wallace wandered with them, listening. He watched the line of woods where the property ended. The tiger could come out there and the girl with silver hair, walking beside him.

He was happy and he did not see why not.

Elizabeth Spencer was born in Carrollton, Mississippi. She received an MA from Vanderbilt University in 1943. Her first novel was published in 1948; eight other novels followed. Spencer has published stories in the *New Yorker,* the *Atlantic,* and other magazines. She went to Italy in 1953 on a Guggenheim Fellowship. In 1986 she and her husband moved to Chapel Hill, where Spencer taught writing at UNC. Her most recent book is *The Southern Woman: New and Selected*

JOHN ROSENTHAL

Fiction. Her other titles include *The Voice at the Back Door, The Salt Line, The Night Travellers,* and *The Light in the Piazza,* which was made into a movie in 1963 and will premiere as a musical production on Broadway in spring 2005. Spencer has received numerous awards, including the Award of Merit for the Short Story from the American Academy of Arts and Letters. She is a member of the Academy and a charter member of the Fellowship of Southern Writers.

This story developed out of an image I got from something John Cheever wrote about a boy who, in a quarrel with his family, went out to sit up in a bare tree on a cold day. I could not help visualizing the pecan trees in the backyard of the house where I was brought up, in Carrollton, Mississippi, though the story is meant to be set in North Carolina, where I live now. As to who was looking out at the boy (an old lady in an old house) and who would visit her and why and who the boy was—all were questions to be explored. Some years ago, a tiger was found abandoned outside a house in Texas and was rescued and given refuge in a wildlife preserve near Chapel Hill. How the tiger wandered into the story, I don't know, but he seemed to want to come. Who would argue with a tiger?

Janice Daugharty

DUMDUM

(from *The Chattahoochee Review*)

From the store porch, the three men watched the strange car come, out of the south and blue like the tweed highway was blue, but not like the sky was blue, not *that* blue.

The car slowed for the railroad tracks that crossed east to west or west to east, depending on the direction of the trains passing through the dried-up town each morning, evening and night. It was morning now and the tracks ran parallel to the south side of the two-story peeling white building built like a box. A pecan shade tree at the crossing threw still, flocked shadows onto the new blue car roof and slid off the trunk as it bucked and dipped over the shined double rails and didn't pick up speed again, which meant it was going to stop by the store.

The driver had the window up with the air conditioner running—engine hum always gave that away—you could tell it every time. He parked and sat there for a minute, looking to his right and down, maybe taking money from his wallet on the car seat, maybe writing something, maybe listening to the radio or hiding a pistol.

At last, he opened the door and stepped one foot out as if testing the spotty grass and gravel with his polished brown loafer. Then spinning round on the seat and bringing the other foot out and standing, closing the door.

"Hot already, ain't it?" said J.C., raring in the stout chair, right side of the wide doorway. Belly strutted so that the egg stain on his blue shirt stood out and read like a menu. He might have been sixty, might have been seventy; he was so fat you couldn't tell. Smells of cottonseed meal and flypaper or cane syrup spirited out of the dim room and mixed with the heating tar of the highway.

Somewhere, a rooster crowed just to be crowing. A dog barked. A small faraway bell donged, mimicked by a mockingbird in the chinaberry tree across the highway at the start of a dirt road flanked on the right by orange flower bushes. The shady dun road, this side of the hedge, was jamb-up straight as the sun-streaked railroad tracks.

"I guess it is hot," the stranger said, stopping and gazing up at the dome of sky, then all about at the little town set down in the midst of the Southeast Georgia pinewoods. Old but kept frame houses each side of the road, a white voting house the size of a playhouse, north of the store, the two separated by a strip of split-tipped smut grass, knee-high to a man. One house, center-wise on the right, was bigger and of red brick. The same everywhere you went, home of the town's big shot.

The tall stranger stepped up the wide concrete step with smut grass growing through a long, jagged crack like a doormat for cleaning your shoes.

"How y'all boys doing this morning?" he asked, packing his fine white shirt into his charcoal gabardine trousers.

"Can't complain," said Mr. Winston, a thin, decrepit old man with a cane, seated to the left of the doorway.

The younger man next to him had longish curly brown hair and looked soft. "Reckon you'll be wanting a cocoaler?" Cleaning his nails with his pocketknife, he snapped it closed and put it in his pocket and heaved up from his chair with both hands on his knees.

The stranger didn't fool them with that "y'all" talk. He'd likely just passed through so many of these little towns in South Georgia and North Florida that he'd caught on. Funning with 'em maybe.

"Something cold *would* hit the spot," the stranger said, taking his white ironed and folded handkerchief from a hip pocket and mopping his jowly neck. No sweat, and his black beard had been shaved down to a shadow. His jutted square face appeared one step ahead of his trim body, and you could comb your own hair using his glossy black hair for a mirror. He smelled of lemons or oranges—odd smell for a gussied-up man, but not all that bad.

"You just passing through?" J.C. said and walked his chair out from the board wall aways. The chair legs were splayed from the weight of his body. His hair was flossy and white and looked like a wig set atop his head and tugged forward.

The stranger seemed to be wearying of this waste-talk and didn't care much what they thought when he turned from the waist to take in, with a roll of the eyes, this view of their sorry town. Single brick house included. Why would anybody do other than just pass through?

"Guess you heard about our president getting shot?" Mr. Winston said.

The stranger froze, long manicured fingers in the waistband back of his fine creased trousers. "You're kidding me, aren't you?"

Mr. Winston didn't answer. He was not kidding.

"That was six months ago," said the stranger. "But yes—the answer's yes. You'd have to be from another planet not to have heard that."

"Shore bad, wadn't it?" Mr. Winston said.

The small bell they'd been hearing faraway was growing closer, keener, as if somebody was walking, shaking it. Calves bellering and somebody yelling "Whoopie, whoopie, whoopie!" every breath.

"Here he comes with them calves," J.C. said.

The stranger stepped up onto the dusty but swept hardwood floor and into the stale cellar coolness of the store. Shoe heels clicking smartly.

Usually by now, the men would have told a stranger their names, asked his, to be neighborly, and asked what he was selling—shoes probably. But so far he'd proven to be unfriendly, and dense.

Mr. Winston said, "Looks like Cranford'd go on and take that bunch to the cow sale."

"Price is down, he says." J.C. rocked to the floor so he could see beyond the voting booth the skimpy herd of scrawny red calves— could have been donkeys, could have been goats, but it was cows— following the tall tow-headed boy. Middle of the road.

"Good thing ain't much traffic through here this morning," Mr. Winston said.

The stranger was now standing in the doorway, guzzling from a bottle of Pepsi. A Pepsi man. To each his own. They glanced at him then back at the boy and the calves.

One calf loped off to the side yard of the brick house and began snatching clothes from the line with his mouth, wooden clothes-pins snapping free and flying out over the mowed lawn.

"Looks like your wife's washday's bout to start over," Mr. Winston said to J.C.

"Looks like it," said the town big shot.

The boy began alternately chasing the calf and picking up the clothes, hanging them on the line again, eyeing the side screen door and the stout woman standing there shaking her head. You could have guessed that her purpose in life was to feed J.C. and you would have guessed right.

All five calves looked to be about six to eight months old, and all were furry but bony, like wormy dogs with thick dull coats hiding their ribs. The only heifer in the herd had perfectly round white spots, little moons, across the saddle. Another was wearing an old felt hat belonged to the boy's dead granddaddy—as fine a man as ever lived in this county. The calf wearing the tarnished brass bell on a rope around his neck had a bobtail like a bulldog's. All had hay or grass bellies, but one looked like he might burst; his legs were so short his belly almost scrubbed the pavement. The one called Dumdum looked close to normal, if you didn't know better. Problem was, he didn't know his head from his tail.

"Old bull about needs doing away with," J.C. said.

The storekeeper Dean yawned, standing next to the stranger in the doorway. Dean stepped down and moseyed past Mr. Winston to his chair on the end of the porch. "They don't give them old bulls away, you know." He gathered his brown pant legs at the knees and sat. The pants appeared made of some kind of pajama material, not fine but worn and soft as his pale hairless skin, and he had the mildest eyes you could imagine.

"Well, somebody around here oughta up and offer to swap. Alton Fender maybe—he's got a bull been with the same herd going on five year now. They could swap out."

"That's a thought," said Mr. Winston. "Only Cranford and Alton are kind of on the outs."

"How come?"

They hatch up some reason, notion, story, seeming already to have forgotten the stranger, or not to care, except occasionally J.C. would scratch self-consciously at the dried egg dribble on the belly of his shirt. Looking down so that his neck folded to a raw, fleshy cowl.

An old, old black woman came poking with a stripped magnolia stick down the road by the railroad tracks. Her black hatchet face looked almost blue in the hollows of her eyes, the seams of her mighty nose and mouse mouth. She was wearing a long rose print dress and a black shawl with fringe about her stooped shoulders and her hair was knotted back—what was left of it.

"Here comes Miss Glory," Mr. Winston said.

"After her MoonPie and RC," Dean finished for him and laughed.

At the highway she stopped, shaking her head and her stick at the capering calves now scattering out into the yards each side of the road. Them blatting and the boy yelling "Whoopie, whoopie, whoopie!" and chasing after them.

It took her several minutes to labor on across the road, over the shelf of gravel in front of the store. Up the steps, wheezing and covering her mouth with a red rag.

"How you, Miss Glory?" J.C. said loud.

"No good," she said, finally looking up. Spying the stranger in the doorway, her nickel-plated eyes latched onto him.

"After that MoonPie and RC," Dean said. "I declare, if you people ain't crazy bout them RCs."

"You a mess yo'self," she said to Dean. "Ain't he, y'all?"

"A mess," the others agreed. All but the stranger who only nodded, smelling maybe her sharp, musky scent.

"Guess you heard about our president getting shot," said Mr. Winston.

"Hesh yo' mouth!" The woman clamped the red rag tighter over her own mouth.

"Yeah, over there in Dallas, riding in his car."

"They get de shooter?"

"Yes ma'am. They got him."

"Sho nuf." She hummed, shaking her balding head. "A good man, Mr. Eisenhower. Do a world of good for dis country."

Nobody corrected her. The stranger quickly searched their faces: maybe they didn't know either that it was Kennedy who got shot. Dean got up and went into the store and she followed, pecking out a rhythm with her stick on the solid concrete porch floor and then the hollow wood floor of the store. Like doing her part in a rhythm band made up of the cowbell up the road, regular and rapid, meaning the calf wearing it was on the run, and the boy yelling "Whoopie, whoopie, whoopie!" which meant he was trying to get the attention of the brain-dead blatting calves.

J.C. rolled his eyes at the wall behind him. "Miss Glory, you bout to burn up in that 'lil ole shack of mine back there off the railroad?"

Her voice came muffled. "Bout to."

J.C. was speaking so loud the stranger had to step away. "Well you tell them granboys to quit busting out the screens and I'll fix em so you can open up your winders, hear?"

"Yahsuh, I tell em."

"Yeah," J.C. said low to himself, "like last time."

The stranger stepped into the doorway again. "You boys ever

hear of civil rights?" He checked each face to see if they had. Not a flicker.

Miss Glory eased out to the porch, almost stepping on the dipped hem of her rose print skirt, carrying hugged up in one bony, twisted arm a banana MoonPie and her stick, the other knobby hand curled around the neck of an RC bottle. Sipping. The stranger had stepped to one side for her but she didn't even see him now.

Slow across the porch to the doorsteps and down, she said weakly, "Behave yo'self, Mr. J.C. Don't, I take dis stick to you."

J.C. let out a holler, rocked the front legs of the chair to the floor, guffawing and stomping both heavy work boots as if to chase after her. "Old lady, I'll take that stick from you and whip you good, you mess with me."

"I hear you," she said, stopping and repositioning till she had her stick going in her right hand, poking at the grass and gravel, the RC going in her left, and then her feet in walked-down black shoes. At the highway, she looked right and left for traffic, and on the left saw the boy chasing the calves about the yards. Pepped up by her RC, she called back, "I do wish dey get shed of dem no-count cows. Gib me the heebie-jeebies."

"Then don't look, you old hag," shouted J.C.

The men on the porch laughed, all except the stranger.

Drinking the last of his cold drink (hands soft as a lady's), he watched the boy and calves, now frolicking about the mowed and raked-dirt yards, sampling petunias and zinnias and morning glory. The purple-flowering vine was about to be ripped from the lattice trellis at the end of the deep, sloping porch. The woman of the house in a white apron came out on the porch with a raised broom and swung it at the calf as if to strike him. The calf kept on eating at the vine, unraveling it from the lattice to his mouth, while the boy slapped him on the rump, hollering, "Whoopie, whoopie, whoopie!" The calf never looked behind but gradually began to back away, following the boy in reverse out toward the highway and the other four calves who were gazing up and about like the stranger.

"What you think about that?" J.C. asked the stranger, who had finished his Pepsi and was now going inside to place it in the rack.

He came back to the doorway. "Inbred, huh?" He took his white handkerchief and wiped his mouth, then checked it for stains.

"That Pepsi'll leave a stain," Mr. Winston said.

The man glared at him. "You fellows must be Democrats."

"No, Masons," said J.C. and cackled out. "Yaa lordy!"

The boy had the calves grouped and going again now. His cheeky face was red and his blond curls looked darker, damp with sweat. He had on a navy T-shirt, the white letters FFA screen-printed inside a circular logo, and faded blue jeans with split and fraying knees. He was tall for thirteen—grew nearly a foot since last year. His bare feet showed no signs of quitting growing. They looked like sleds.

"Boy, put you some shoes on them feet and they'll quit growing," Dean called out when the boy got within hearing distance.

The boy peered down at his slab feet, bruised and dirty with hoof prints. "Naw," he said, "I'm wanting to see how much they'll grow. Size twelve already and I'm hoping to make it in the *Guinness Book of World Records.*"

"Makes sense to me," J.C. said and laughed. "Yaa lordy!"

"Guess you heard about our president getting shot," Mr. Winston said.

"Daddy said something about it."

The calves were trotting alongside and behind till the boy got to the doorstep and stopped. Then they milled about like fish after bait and began butting at his groin and rump. All tails twitching except the bobtailed one. The boy sat on the right end of the doorstep and the calf named Dumdum sidled up to him, bellering on high-volume.

"Wants a cracker, I guess?" said Dean and got up again and started through the doorway, holding to the stranger's right shoulder for support and squeezing it. "Watch this," Dean said, sniggering and stumping on into the store.

The stranger looked at his shoulder as if to see another stain.

Like the one J.C. was working on, on the catch-all belly of his blue shirt.

They heard the clinking of the glass lid on the cookie jar, then watched as Dean came back and handed the cracker to the boy. He waved it before the calf's walled brown eyes, then under his moist leathery nose, all that had any calf-like gloss to it except for his grass-buffed patent-leather clogs. All that showed the calf might have come from good stock, somewhere along the line, was a slight bow between the eyes to his otherwise flat face.

"Whoopie, whoopie, whoopie!" the boy yelled, almost yodeling.

The calf wheeled, full rotation, presenting his rump as if to take the cracker in through his brown, puckered buttonhole.

The men on the porch whooped and beat their thighs and even the stranger had to smile at that.

The boy patted the calf's left rear haunch proudly—pityingly?— got up with the cracker and walked around to his face and, hand under the calf's chin, began feeding the cracker into his mouth like a baby. Catching the cracker crumbs in his dirty hand for the calf to lick clean with his pumice tongue.

"Boy's heart's as big as all outdoors," said J.C. "Ain't nothing like a big heart, my mama always said."

"Yes sir, boy," said Mr. Winston, "don't think the Lord up above don't see you out there, morning and night, leading them calves out to the pasture, then back to the barn, to make them eat."

"Didn't, they wouldn't come," the boy said. "Besides, Daddy'd take his belt to me." The boy sat again, same spot, elbows ditched on his knees, and pushed at the rump of the calf. "Go on, Dum-dum." The calf's hooves clattered and brattled the gravel as he trotted away.

"That's the truth," they all agreed.

While they swapped boyhood stories about incredible beatings with switches, belts and razor strops, trying to top each other, the stranger wandered out to the edge of the porch and leaned up on one of the rotting square posts above the doorstep, talking to the boy about the calves. Well, sort of—the boy did most of the talking.

An old white and rust pickup slow-motored from the highway crossing north of the store, heading south. It was loaded with girls ranging from what looked like maybe eight to eighteen years of age. None pretty, none ugly, but when the truck drove past the store, J.C. made a big show of yelling, "Hey, Will, you need anymore baccer help, let this boy here know. Danged if you ain't got the prettiest 'lil ole gals in all the county!" The girls, poised on the fenders of the truck bed, giggled and waved, all except the one with the brown ponytail, maybe the age of the boy, who crossed her arms and hung her head. "And the most gals in the county too," Mr. Winston shouted, laughing. Two of the calves gathered at the tailgate when the truck stopped for the railroad crossing, and the girls, minus the puffed up one with the ponytail, hopped up and leaned over patting them on the head. The truck went on and the calves came back, girls forgotten. The boy's ears looked scalded, but not once had he looked up, not once had he quit talking to the stranger.

J.C. sneezed and the stranger butted in on what the boy was saying to say, "Bless you," to J.C., though J.C. doubted the man would spit on him if he was on fire.

The stranger pointed to the calf munching gravel along the edge of the road before the store. The one wearing the hat with ragged holes cut for his ragged ears to poke through, the one wearing the hat like he wouldn't be seen without it. "How do you get him to wear a hat like that?"

"Who? Knob?" The boy laughed and got up and sauntered out to the calf, who looked up but kept wallowing the gravel around in his mouth, against his teeth. No matter that between the north end of the store and the voting house, close to a half-acre of green grass was so rich and sweet you could smell it. The hot sun seemed to draw the smell and the grass teemed with unseen locusts set to buzz on automatic. The purring of a way-off farm tractor competed.

"Bald as a baby's behind." The boy lifted the hat so that the twitchy tips of his ears were all that held it aloft above the calf's head. No hair, not a sprig, just a knob of waxy white flesh like a scraped hog's. "Burn up in this heat without no hat."

The calf named Pusselgut had now ambled up to the doorstep and was lipping the stranger's hand. He crossed his arms. The short-legged calf placed both front hooves on the step, like a goat, and craned his neck trying to reach the man's face for a kiss.

From northwest of the store came a broken rumble, growing solid and loud and mean as thunder.

"Train's coming," said Dean, "better run go get Polkadot and Bobtail off the tracks." He said it slow as if saying it might come up a shower this afternoon. Yawning and tapping his mouth with his hand.

The boy took off running with the other three calves trotting and swinging their anvil heads. In less than a minute, all five were on the tracks and the train was coming on, now a dull trundling braced by a bright whistle and triple toots. The boy was yelling, "Whoopie, whoopie, whoopie." But it was too late—the calves were strung out and excited, blatting and prancing east and west along the tracks with the boy stationed somewhere in between.

"Let's go help him, boys," said Mr. Winston and stood with his cane, poking out.

Spry Dean jumped off the end of the porch nearest the tracks and ran with his elbows pumping, while J.C. rose from his chair and waddled out, holding to the porch post across from the stranger, who only stood cross-armed and grinning, listening to the train charging through the woods like wildfire.

Following three of the calves, the boy and Dean disappeared from view behind the store and along the western section of tracks, head on toward the screeching train, trying to brake. J.C. had the calf called Knob by the tail and was twitching him off the tracks to the dirt road running in front of the store where Miss Glory had earlier dissolved into the privacy of shadows with her RC. Mr. Winston was swinging his cane at the bobtailed calf wearing the brassy bell, chasing it into a patch of tasseling corn—somebody's garden—westside of the road, south of the tracks.

The freight train passed, tooting, whistling, screaling, and the engineer in his square-billed gray-striped cap waved and shouted. Not a friendly wave and you couldn't make out what he said for the racket of the train but didn't have to be real intelligent to figure it was one more warning to keep those dad-blasted calves off the tracks.

The train rumbled out, fading along the sun-streamed tracks east toward Jacksonville, Florida, and the red-faced sweating boy walked around the side of the store nearest the tracks. Dumdum, Pusselgut and Polkadot following close, the latter with a blooming vine of purple verbena caught in the hinging of her mouth.

Mr. Winston hobbled across the track hazing the calf wearing the bell with his cane. J.C. crossed the road to the store, brushing his hands on his khaki pants. The stranger now saw that he was wearing brown suspenders, which he hadn't seen before because they'd been buried in the saddlebags of flesh under J.C.'s arms Knob, whose tail J.C. had been holding to like a rope, was now grazing from the hedge of orange flower bushes at the start of Miss Glory's road.

The sun was almost overhead now and the locusts sounded as if they'd picked up buzzing where the rumbling of the train left off, but you knew they'd been there all along and it was a settling sound following an earthquake.

Dean stepped up suddenly on the south end of the porch, scrubbing the soles of his brown unzipped ankle boots on the floor. "Aye, lordy! If I ain't about wore out running them calves!"

The boy was now standing at the steps again, before the stranger again. He sat at the stranger's feet, wiping his forehead and eyes with the sleeve of his navy-blue FFA shirt and staring down at a line of red ants toting cracker crumbs to their sandy mound. His calves wandered off, two to the north side of the building, grazing the rank grass like normal. Or were they munching locusts?

Everybody else was now seated in their chairs, discussing the close call with the train, which naturally led into other close calls, some closer than others.

"Wadn't that Ralph Harris had a cow hit by the train awhile ago? Sued the railroad?"

"Got two hundred fifty dollars, they say."

"Thy lord in heaven!"

"You know, boy," said J.C., laughing disgustedly, settling into his practiced chair, sweating, "you oughta think about that."

The boy looked around at him. "Naw," he said, switching his eyes to the calf crossing the road. Dumdum, alongside Knob, began grazing sweetly from the orange flower bushes as if he'd just figured out what his mouth was for. "Couldn't do nothing like that." But he looked tempted.

The stranger crossed his slender, polished loafers. They had tassels like the wrecked corn in the patch across the tracks. "What'll you take for them?"

The porch full of men got so still you could hear the drink box humming and rattling inside and even the calm calves slipping the seed heads from the grass stalks north of the store.

Blue eyes blaring in his sun-pinked face, the boy stared up at the stranger. "What? My calves?"

"Yes." The stranger stood straight, pocketing his hands and jangling change and keys—could be bottle caps.

"Hey!" said J.C. "What's a man like you wanting with a bunch of crazy calves?"

"Yeah," said Mr. Winston.

"Sideshow at the fair in Macon," said the stranger, watching Dumdum toddling across the highway to the doorstep and bellering at the boy for a cracker.

"Go on, Dumdum," the boy said and pushed at him, slapping him on the rump as he wheeled, lifting his tail to expose his obscene wrinkled brown rectum. The boy jacked the calf's tail down, covering his shame, till he moved out of reach.

"Here now, what did you have in mind?" said J.C., sitting forward in his chair. "How much?"

"Ten apiece," said the stranger without turning.

"Shoot fire! They'll bring more than that on the sale, low dollar."

"Okay," the stranger addressed the boy. "I'll make it twenty."

"Hey now," said Mr. Winston. "That ain't bad atall, atall."

"Cranford'll be glad of that," said Dean. "And you won't have to nurse them day in and day out, boy."

The boy rubbed his blond curls forward. They sprang back into place. "I don't know. Ain't no tellings what-all they'd do to them in no fair."

"Look at it this way," the man said. "They're not going to mistreat an investment, are they?"

"Yeah," said J.C., "And we ain't gone be running em off the railroad tracks every morning and evening. Eating up gardens and clothes off the line. I'd take it and run, boy."

"Naw." The boy held out both long, corded arms and examined his filthy hands.

"What you mean *naw?*" J.C. spoke up. "You better talk to your pa before you go saying *naw.*"

"Yeah. Listen, boy, you get shed of them calves and that 'lil ole prissy gal of Will's is liable to come around."

"Naw. She ain't studying me."

"Final offer." The stranger stepped down from the porch to the step where the boy was sitting. Dumdum turned and plucked at his pants with his lips. The stranger pushed at his head. He slung it and butted at the stranger's groin. He stepped onto the porch again. Out of reach.

"He's taking a liking to you, mister," said Dean. "Look yonder, boy, Knob's back in Miss Jeanette's corn again."

The boy leaped up and ran and they all watched him walking on the sides of his feet along the hot highway and tip across the tracks to the pecan shade. He took up a brittle stick and hied across the highway into the broken corn and gently tapped the calf. It tiptoed like a woman in high heels back across the tracks. At the corner of the store porch, the boy kept walking around the south side of the building and shortly showed again on the north side with a square-edged shovel and began scooping up piles of manure and bearing them over to the orange flowering bushes along Miss Glory's road. When he could locate no more cow splats, he came back to the doorsteps, leaning the shovel against a post, and sat at the farthest end of the step away from where the stranger was standing so he could look him in the eye.

"Thirty each," he said.

The stranger laughed, started out toward his car with Dumdum and Knob swinging their heads, following. He had to shove them aside to get into the car; they breathed day-moons of vapors on the window glass. The man started the car, air conditioning humming, laboring the engine, lowered the window staring into the walleyes of the two calves with their heads suddenly, magically inside.

"Nice meeting you folks," he said and put the car in gear and motored out slow to keep from running over the two calves now trotting out from the grass patch north of the store.

They all followed, trotting. Brake lights flashed red. The car began to back up slowly with one of the calves backing and the others turning, following the car to its parking spot before the store.

"What you reckon he'll offer now?" Dean said.

"Fifty, seventy-five," said J.C.

"Could be a hundred, man like that."

The stranger hummed down his window. He laughed. "Appears like they're hellbent on following me anyway."

"Do, we'll have to call up the shurf." J.C. laughed but he wasn't joking.

The stranger was staring at his car dash, listening to the radio, turned low.

"Lee Harvey Oswald got shot," he reported.

"Who?"

"Man who killed the president."

"Don't say? Who shot him?"

"Jack Somebody."

"Jack, huh?" said J.C. "All we care, it ain't no Jack from around here." They all laughed.

"Forty apiece," the man said suddenly, speaking to the boy.

"Fifty," said J.C. "You give the boy forty, means they're worth fifty to the fair."

"Good point. Fifty it is—final offer."

"Sixty?" the boy asked. The calves had switched back to their loyal master, gathering. The one wanting a cracker rubbing up to him and bellering.

Much mumbling on the porch. Somebody said, "That's three hundred dollars!"

"Fifty," said the man.

"Still that's two hundred and fifty dollars," said Dean.

"How come that man name of Jack to kill that Oswald? They say?"

"Crazy," said the stranger. "Like everybody else."

"Huh," said Mr. Winston. "Bet he didn't like the notion of somebody shooting our president."

"Sixty," the stranger said, switching off the radio.

"Hey, boy!" J.C. slapped his fat knees. "We got it going now! Somebody go get that calf a cracker, will you?"

"I gotta talk to Daddy first," the boy said. "Leave your telephone number and I'll get back to you."

"On the road. Heading for Macon. Can't do that."

"Boy, take him on up to the house to talk to Cranford right now before he backs out."

Dean handed the boy the cracker and he began waving it before Dumdum's crossing eyes for him to see, under his nose for him to smell, waiting for him to turn and try to take in the treat from his hind-end; instead the calf played out his pink tongue and tasted the cracker, then gobbled it whole from the boy's hand.

"Well, look at that, will you!" J.C. boomed. "Ten minutes ago that calf didn't know his head from his tail, now he's normal as me or you. Tell me old Dumdum here don't learn fast!"

"They don't have no bottom teeth, mister," said the boy. "You know that?"

"Make up your mind," the man said. "I've gotta get on the road."

He looked at the gold watch on his dark-haired left wrist. "Y'all ever wonder why we wear our watches on our left arms, instead of our right?" Nobody answered and he hadn't expected them to.

"Your daddy'll have a fit, you pass up a deal like that," said J.C. "Three hundred dollars'll buy a fine new bull."

"Yeah, and when the fair comes down to Valdosta, in November, you can see them calves all you want."

"Daddy's gone to town." The boy cracked Bobtail on the head for biting his big toe. "How you aim to get em up to Macon?"

"Same way you'd get them to the sale," said Mr. Winston. "Ain't that so?"

"That's so." The man now had his brown leather wallet out, taking out bills. One hundred, twenties, fifties, and fives. Mouthing till the money totaled up to three hundred dollars. He fanned the stack out the window at the boy.

The bobtailed calf walked over and tried to eat the bills. The stranger tapped him on the knob of his head.

From the porch somebody said, "Don't never name a cow, boy. They liable to up and die on you."

The boy crossed over to the car and took the money, holding it high. The stranger opened his hand to shake, and the boy, already heading toward the porch, turned and took it, pumping earnestly.

They all waited while the man, still inside his car, wrote out a bill of sale and a receipt for the money. He passed it to the boy along with a ballpoint pen and the boy placed it on the sun-flashed car hood and leaned over signing carefully while the calves rambled and butted him in the rump and nipped at his faded jeans.

The boy handed the papers back to the man, holding the pen high to keep Dumdum from grabbing it between his lower gums and top teeth.

"I'll be back in a week or so with a truck and trailer," the stranger said.

"They'll be here." J.C. laughed out.

The car pulled away, with the calves trotting behind, and the boy following at some distance, calling "Whoopie, whoopie, whoopie" for them to come.

J.C. said, "That's a sad thing, giving up calves you raised."

Mr. Winston said, "That's a sad thing, our president getting shot."

Janice Daugharty is the author of a collection of short stories and seven novels; her most recent is *Just Doll,* book one of the Staten Bay trilogy. She is writer-in-residence at Valdosta State University near her home in South Georgia. "Dumdum" is her third story to be picked for *New Stories from the South.* Others have appeared in *Story,* the *Georgia Review, Ontario Review,* the *Oxford American, Denver Quarterly,* and other literary journals.

*W*ith *"Dumdum," I decided to write the story like I was hearing it and to hell with the rules of good writing. The first draft about a boy and his inbred calves was already written when I happened upon a letter from Flannery O'Connor to another writer. In the letter, O'Connor scolded this amateur for allowing her third-person narrator to speak in vernacular. Story comes first, I kept reminding myself; voice has to do with mood and place. My narrator was of this place and would naturally speak in the vernacular of my people. I liked the language of the narrator in "Dumdum." I would keep it, for once, just because it felt right.*

APPENDIX

A list of the magazines currently consulted for *New Stories from the South: The Year's Best, 2005,* with addresses, subscription rates, and editors.

The Antioch Review
P.O. Box 148
Yellow Springs, OH 45387-0148
Quarterly, $35
Robert S. Fogarty

Apalachee Review
P.O. Box 10469
Tallahassee, FL 32302
Semiannually, $15
Laura Newton

Appalachian Heritage
CPO 2166
Berea, KY 40404
Quarterly, $18
George Brosi

Arkansas Review
P.O. Box 1890
Arkansas State University
State University, AR 72467
Triannually, $20
Tom Williams

Arts & Letters
Campus Box 89
Georgia College & State University
Milledgeville, GA 31061-0490
Semiannually, $15
Martin Lammon

Atlanta
1330 W. Peachtree St.
Suite 450
Atlanta, GA 30309
Monthly, $14.95
Rebecca Burns

The Atlantic Monthly
77 N. Washington St.
Boston, MA 02114
Monthly, $39.95
C. Michael Curtis

The Baffler
P.O. Box 378293
Chicago, IL 60637
Annually, $24
Solveig Nelson

Bayou
Department of English
University of New Orleans
Lakefront
New Orleans, LA 70148
Semiannually, $10

Bellevue Literary Review
Department of Medicine
New York University School of
   Medicine
550 1st Avenue, OBV-612
New York, NY 10016
Semiannually, $12
Ronna Weinberg

Black Warrior Review
University of Alabama
P.O. Box 862936
Tuscaloosa, AL 35486-0027
Semiannually, $14
Fiction Editor

Boulevard
6614 Clayton Road, PMB 325
Richmond Heights, MO 63117
Triannually, $15
Richard Burgin

The Carolina Quarterly
Greenlaw Hall CB# 3520
University of North Carolina
Chapel Hill, NC 27599-3520
Triannually, $12
Fiction Editor

The Chariton Review
Truman State University
Kirksville, MO 63501
Semiannually, $9
Jim Barnes

The Chattahoochee Review
Georgia Perimeter College
2101 Womack Road
Dunwoody, GA 30338-4497
Quarterly, $16
Lawrence Hetrick

Chicago Quarterly Review
517 Sherman Ave.
Evanston, IL 60202
Quarterly
S. Afzal Haider

Cimarron Review
205 Morrill Hall
Oklahoma State University
Stillwater, OK 74078-0135
Quarterly, $24
E. P. Walkiewicz

The Cincinnati Review
Department of English and
    Comparative Literature
University of Cincinnati
P.O. Box 210069
Cincinnati, OH 45221-0069
Semiannually, $12
Brock Clarke

Columbia
415 Dodge Hall
2960 Broadway
Columbia University
New York, NY 10027-6902
Semiannually, $15
Fiction Editor

Confrontation
English Department
C.W. Post of L.I.U.
Brookville, NY 11548
Semiannually, $10
Martin Tucker

Conjunctions
21 East 10th Street
New York, NY 10003
Semiannually, $18
Bradford Morrow

Crazyhorse
Department of English
College of Charleston
66 George St.
Charleston, SC 29424
Semiannually, $15
Bret Lott

Crucible
Barton College
P.O. Box 5000
Wilson, NC 27893-7000
Annually, $7
Terrence L. Grimes

Denver Quarterly
University of Denver
Denver, CO 80208
Quarterly, $20
Bin Ramke

The Distillery
Motlow State Comm. College
P.O. Box 8500
Lynchburg, TN 37352-8500
Semiannually, $15
Dawn Copeland

Epoch
251 Goldwin Smith Hall
Cornell University
Ithaca, NY 14853-3201
Triannually, $11
Michael Koch

Fiction
c/o English Department
City College of New York
New York, NY 10031
Quarterly, $38
Mark J. Mirsky

Five Points
Georgia State University
MSC 8R0318
33 Gilmer St. SE, Unit 8
Atlanta, GA 30303-3083
Triannually, $20
Megan Sexton

The Florida Review
Department of English
University of Central Florida
Orlando, FL 32816
Semiannually, $10
Pat Rushin

Gargoyle
P.O. Box 6216

Arlington, VA 22206-0216
Annually, $20
Richard Peabody

The Georgia Review
University of Georgia
Athens, GA 30602-9009
Quarterly, $24
T. R. Hummer

The Gettysburg Review
Gettysburg College
Gettysburg, PA 17325-1491
Quarterly, $24
Peter Stitt

Glimmer Train Stories
710 SW Madison St., #504
Portland, OR 97205
Quarterly, $32
Susan Burmeister-Brown
    and Linda B. Swanson-Davies

Granta
1755 Broadway
5th Floor
New York, NY 10019-3780
Quarterly, $37
Ian Jack

The Greensboro Review
English Department
134 McIver Bldg.
University of North Carolina
P.O. Box 26170
Greensboro, NC 27412
Semiannually, $10
Jim Clark

Harper's Magazine
666 Broadway, 11th Floor
New York, NY 10012
Monthly, $21
Ben Metcalf

Harpur Palate
English Department
Binghamton University
P.O. Box 6000
Binghamton, NY 13902
Semiannually, $16
Letitia Moffitt

Hobart
9251 Densmore Ave. N.
Seattle, WA 98103
Biannually, $7
Aaron Burch

The Idaho Review
Boise State University
Department of English
1910 University Drive
Boise, ID 83725
Annually, $9.95
Mitch Wieland

Image
3307 Third Ave., W.
Center for Religious Humanism
Seattle, WA 98119
Quarterly, $36
Gregory Wolfe

Indiana Review
465 Ballantine Ave.
Indiana University
Bloomington, IN 47405
Semiannually, $12
Laura McCoid

The Iowa Review
308 EPB
University of Iowa
Iowa City, IA 52242-1492
Triannually, $20
David Hamilton

The Journal
Ohio State University

Department of English
164 W. 17th Avenue
Columbus, OH 43210
Semiannually, $12
Kathy Fagan and Michelle Herman

Kalliope
Florida Community College–
   Jacksonville
South Campus
11901 Beach Blvd.
Jacksonville, FL 32246
Triannually, $16
Mary Sue Koeppel

The Kenyon Review
Kenyon College
Gambier, OH 43022
Triannually, $25
David H. Lynn

Land-Grant College Review
P.O. Box 1164
New York, NY 10159
Semiannually, $18
David Koch, Josh Melrod

The Literary Review
Fairleigh Dickinson University
285 Madison Avenue
Madison, NJ 07940
Quarterly, $18
René Steinke

Long Story
18 Eaton Street
Lawrence, MA 01843
Annually, $6
R. P. Burnham

Louisiana Literature
SLU-10792
Southeastern Louisiana
   University
Hammond, LA 70402

Semiannually, $12
Jack Bedell

The Louisville Review
Spalding University
851 South 4th Street
Louisville, KY 40203
Semiannually, $14
Sena Jeter Naslund

Lynx Eye
c/o ScribbleFest Literary Group
542 Mitchell Drive
Los Osos, CA 93402
Quarterly, $25
Pam McCully, Kathryn Morrison

Meridian
University of Virginia
P.O. Box 400145
Charlottesville, VA 22904-4145
Semiannually, $10
Jett McAlister

Mid-American Review
Department of English
Bowling Green State University
Bowling Green, OH 43403
Semiannually, $12
Michael Czyzniejewski

Mississippi Review
University of Southern
   Mississippi
Box 5144
Hattiesburg, MS 39406-5144
Semiannually, $15
Frederick Barthelme

The Missouri Review
1507 Hillcrest Hall
University of Missouri
Columbia, MO 65211
Triannually, $22
Speer Morgan

The Nebraska Review
Writers Workshop
Fine Arts Building 212
University of Nebraska at Omaha
Omaha, NE 68182-0324
Semiannually, $15
James Reed

New England Review
Middlebury College
Middlebury, VT 05753
Quarterly, $25
Stephen Donadio

New Letters
University of Missouri at Kansas
   City
5101 Rockhill Road
Kansas City, MO 64110
Quarterly, $17
Robert Stewart

New Millennium Writings
P.O. Box 2463
Knoxville, TN 37901
Annually, $12.95
Don Williams

New Orleans Review
P.O. Box 195
Loyola University
New Orleans, LA 70118
Semiannually, $12
Christopher Chambers, Editor

The New Yorker
4 Times Square
New York, NY 10036
Weekly, $44.95
Deborah Treisman, Fiction
   Editor

Nimrod International Journal
University of Tulsa
600 South College

Tulsa, OK 74104-3189
Semiannually, $17.50
Francine Ringold

The North American Review
University of Northern Iowa
1222 W. 27th Street
Cedar Falls, IA 50614-0516
Six times a year, $22
Grant Tracey

North Carolina Literary Review
English Department
2201 Bate Building
East Carolina University
Greenville, NC 27858-4353
Annually, $10
Margaret Bauer

Northwest Review
369 PLC
University of Oregon
Eugene, OR 97403
Triannually, $22
John Witte

Ontario Review
9 Honey Brook Drive
Princeton, NJ 08540
Semiannually, $16
Raymond J. Smith

Open City
270 Lafayette Street
Suite 1412
New York, NY 10012
Triannually, $30
Thomas Beller

Other Voices
University of Illinois at Chicago
Department of English (M/C 162)
601 S. Morgan Street
Chicago, IL 60607-7120
Semiannually, $12
Lois Hauselman

The Oxford American
201 Donaghey Avenue, Main 107
Conway, AR 72035
Quarterly, $29.95
Marc Smirnoff

The Paris Review
541 E. 72nd Street
New York, NY 10021
Quarterly, $40
Fiction Editor

Parting Gifts
March Street Press
3413 Wilshire Drive
Greensboro, NC 27408
Semiannually, $12
Robert Bixby

Pembroke Magazine
UNC-P, Box 1510
Pembroke, NC 28372-1510
Annually, $8
Shelby Stephenson

PEN America
PEN American Center
568 Broadway, Suite 401
New York, NY 10012
Semiannually, $20
M. Mark

Pindeldeboz
23-55 38th Street
Astoria, NY 11105
Annually, $12
Whitney Pastoree

Ploughshares
Emerson College
120 Boylston St.
Boston, MA 02116-4624
Triannually, $24
Don Lee

PMS
Univ. of Alabama at Birmingham
Department of English
HB 217, 900 S. 13th Street
1530 3rd Ave., S.
Birmingham, AL 35294-1260
Annually, $7
Linda Frost

Post Road Magazine
853 Broadway, Suite 1516
Box 85
New York, NY 10003
Semiannually, $16
Rebecca Boyd

Potomac Review
51 Mannakee Street
Rockville, MD 20850
Semiannually, $18
Eli Flam

Prairie Schooner
201 Andrews Hall
University of Nebraska
Lincoln, NE 68588-0334
Quarterly, $26
Hilda Raz

Puerto del Sol
Box 30001, Department 3E
New Mexico State University
Las Cruces, NM 88003-9984
Semiannually, $10
Kevin McIlvoy

River City
Department of English
University of Memphis
Memphis, TN 38152-6176
Semiannually, $12
Mary Leader

River Styx
634 North Grand Blvd.

12th Floor
St. Louis, MO 63103
Triannually, $20
Richard Newman

Roanoke Review
221 College Lane
Salem, VA 24153
Annually, $8
Melanie Almeder

Rockhurst Review
Department of English
Rockhurst University
1100 Rockhurst Rd.
Kansas City, MO 64110
Annually, $5
Patricia Cleary Miller

Santa Monica Review
Santa Monica College
1900 Pico Boulevard
Santa Monica, CA 90405
Semiannually, $12
Andrew Tonkovich

The Sewanee Review
735 University Avenue
Sewanee, TN 37383-1000
Quarterly, $24
George Core

Shenandoah
Washington and Lee University
Mattingly House
Lexington, VA 24450
Quarterly, $22
R. T. Smith

So to Speak
George Mason University
4400 University Drive, MSN 2D6
Fairfax, VA 22030-4444
Semiannually, $12
Nancy Pearson

The South Carolina Review
Center for Electronic and Digital
    Publishing
Clemson University
Strode Tower, Box 340522
Clemson, SC 29634
Semiannually, $20
Wayne Chapman

South Dakota Review
Box 111
University Exchange
University of South Dakota
Vermillion, SD 57069
Quarterly, $30
John R. Milton

Southern Exposure
P.O. Box 531
Durham, NC 27702
Quarterly, $24
Chris Kromm

Southern Humanities Review
9088 Haley Center
Auburn University
Auburn, AL 36849
Quarterly, $15
Dan R. Latimer and Virginia M.
    Kouidis

The Southern Review
43 Allen Hall
Louisiana State University
Baton Rouge, LA 70803-5005
Quarterly, $25
James Olney

Southwest Review
307 Fondren Library West
Box 750374
Southern Methodist University
Dallas, TX 75275
Quarterly, $24
Willard Spiegelman

Sou'wester
Department of English
Southern Illinois University at
    Edwardsville
Edwardsville, IL 62026-1438
Semiannually, $12
Allison Funk and Geoff Schmidt

StoryQuarterly
online submissions only:
www.storyquarterly.com
Annually, $10
M.M.M. Hayes

Swink
244 5th Avenue, #2722
New York, NY 10001
Semiannually, $16
Leelaila Strogov

Tampa Review
University of Tampa
401 W. Kennedy Boulevard
Tampa, FL 33606-1490
Semiannually, $15
Richard Mathews

Texas Review
English Department Box 2146
Sam Houston State University
Huntsville, TX 77341-2146
Semiannually, $20
Paul Ruffin

The Threepenny Review
P.O. Box 9131
Berkeley, CA 94709
Quarterly, $25
Wendy Lesser

Timber Creek Review
8969 UNC-G Station
Greensboro, NC 27413
Quarterly, $16
John M. Freiermuth

Tin House
P.O. Box 10500
Portland, OR 97296-0500
Quarterly, $29.90
Rob Spillman

TriQuarterly
Northwestern University
629 Noyes St.
Evanston, IL 60208
Triannually, $24
Susan Firestone Hahn

The Virginia Quarterly Review
One West Range
P.O. Box 400223
Charlottesville, VA 22904-4223
Quarterly, $18
Ted Genoways

West Branch
Bucknell Hall
Bucknell University
Lewisburg, PA 17837
Semiannually, $7
Robert Love Taylor

Wind Magazine
P.O. Box 24548
Lexington, KY 40524
Triannually, $15
Chris Green

The Yalobusha Review
Department of English
University of Mississippi
P.O. Box 1848
University, MS 38677
Annually, $10
Joy Wilson

Yemassee
Department of English
University of South Carolina
Columbia, SC 29208
Semiannually, $15
Fiction Editor

Zoetrope: All-Story
The Sentinel Building
916 Kearny Street
San Francisco, CA 94133
Quarterly, $19.95
Tamara Straus

ZYZZYVA
P.O. Box 590069
San Francisco, CA 94159-0069
Triannually, varies
Howard Junker

PREVIOUS VOLUMES

Copies of previous volumes of *New Stories from the South* can be ordered through your local bookstore or by calling the Sales Department at Algonquin Books of Chapel Hill. Multiple copies for classroom adoptions are available at a special discount. For information, please call 919-967-0108.

NEW STORIES FROM THE SOUTH: THE YEAR'S BEST, 1986

Max Apple, BRIDGING

Madison Smartt Bell, TRIPTYCH 2

Mary Ward Brown, TONGUES OF FLAME

Suzanne Brown, COMMUNION

James Lee Burke, THE CONVICT

Ron Carlson, AIR

Doug Crowell, SAYS VELMA

Leon V. Driskell, MARTHA JEAN

Elizabeth Harris, THE WORLD RECORD HOLDER

Mary Hood, SOMETHING GOOD FOR GINNIE

David Huddle, SUMMER OF THE MAGIC SHOW

Gloria Norris, HOLDING ON

Kurt Rheinheimer, UMPIRE

W. A. Smith, DELIVERY

Wallace Whatley, SOMETHING TO LOSE

Luke Whisnant, WALLWORK

Sylvia Wilkinson, CHICKEN SIMON

New Stories from the South: The Year's Best, 1987

James Gordon Bennett, DEPENDENTS

Robert Boswell, EDWARD AND JILL

Rosanne Caggeshall, PETER THE ROCK

John William Corrington, HEROIC MEASURES/VITAL SIGNS

Vicki Covington, MAGNOLIA

Andre Dubus, DRESSED LIKE SUMMER LEAVES

Mary Hood, AFTER MOORE

Trudy Lewis, VINCRISTINE

Lewis Nordan, SUGAR, THE EUNUCHS, AND BIG G. B.

Peggy Payne, THE PURE IN HEART

Bob Shacochis, WHERE PELHAM FELL

Lee Smith, LIFE ON THE MOON

Marly Swick, HEART

Robert Love Taylor, LADY OF SPAIN

Luke Whisnant, ACROSS FROM THE MOTOHEADS

New Stories from the South: The Year's Best, 1988

Ellen Akins, GEORGE BAILEY FISHING

Rick Bass, THE WATCH

Richard Bausch, THE MAN WHO KNEW BELLE STAR

Larry Brown, FACING THE MUSIC

Pam Durban, BELONGING

John Rolfe Gardiner, GAME FARM

Jim Hall, GAS

New Stories from the South: The Year's Best, 1989

New Stories from the South: The Year's Best, 1990

Tom Bailey, CROW MAN

Rick Bass, THE HISTORY OF RODNEY

Richard Bausch, LETTER TO THE LADY OF THE HOUSE

Larry Brown, SLEEP

Moira Crone, JUST OUTSIDE THE B.T.

Clyde Edgerton, CHANGING NAMES

Greg Johnson, THE BOARDER

Nanci Kincaid, SPITTIN' IMAGE OF A BAPTIST BOY

Reginald McKnight, THE KIND OF LIGHT THAT SHINES ON TEXAS

Lewis Nordan, THE CELLAR OF RUNT CONROY

Lance Olsen, FAMILY

Mark Richard, FEAST OF THE EARTH, RANSOM OF THE CLAY

Ron Robinson, WHERE WE LAND

Bob Shacochis, LES FEMMES CREOLES

Molly Best Tinsley, ZOE

Donna Trussell, FISHBONE

New Stories from the South: The Year's Best, 1991

Rick Bass, IN THE LOYAL MOUNTAINS

Thomas Phillips Brewer, BLACK CAT BONE

Larry Brown, BIG BAD LOVE

Robert Olen Butler, RELIC

Barbara Hudson, THE ARABESQUE

Elizabeth Hunnewell, A LIFE OR DEATH MATTER

Hilding Johnson, SOUTH OF KITTATINNY

NEW STORIES FROM THE SOUTH: THE YEAR'S BEST, 1992

Peter Taylor, THE WITCH OF OWL MOUNTAIN SPRINGS

Abraham Verghese, LILACS

NEW STORIES FROM THE SOUTH: THE YEAR'S BEST, 1993

Richard Bausch, EVENING

Pinckney Benedict, BOUNTY

Wendell Berry, A JONQUIL FOR MARY PENN

Robert Olen Butler, PREPARATION

Lee Merrill Byrd, MAJOR SIX POCKETS

Kevin Calder, NAME ME THIS RIVER

Tony Earley, CHARLOTTE

Paula K. Gover, WHITE BOYS AND RIVER GIRLS

David Huddle, TROUBLE AT THE HOME OFFICE

Barbara Hudson, SELLING WHISKERS

Elizabeth Hunnewell, FAMILY PLANNING

Dennis Loy Johnson, RESCUING ED

Edward P. Jones, MARIE

Wayne Karlin, PRISONERS

Dan Leone, SPINACH

Jill McCorkle, MAN WATCHER

Annette Sanford, HELENS AND ROSES

Peter Taylor, THE WAITING ROOM

NEW STORIES FROM THE SOUTH: THE YEAR'S BEST, 1994

Frederick Barthelme, RETREAT

Richard Bausch, AREN'T YOU HAPPY FOR ME?

Ethan Canin, THE PALACE THIEF

NEW STORIES FROM THE SOUTH: THE YEAR'S BEST, 1995

NEW STORIES FROM THE SOUTH: THE YEAR'S BEST, 1996

NEW STORIES FROM THE SOUTH: THE YEAR'S BEST, 1997

NEW STORIES FROM THE SOUTH: THE YEAR'S BEST, 1998

NEW STORIES FROM THE SOUTH: THE YEAR'S BEST, 1999

William Gay, THOSE DEEP ELM BROWN'S FERRY BLUES

Mary Gordon, STORYTELLING

Ingrid Hill, PAGAN BABIES

Michael Knight, BIRDLAND

Kurt Rheinheimer, NEIGHBORHOOD

Richard Schmitt, LEAVING VENICE, FLORIDA

Heather Sellers, FLA. BOYS

George Singleton, CAULK

NEW STORIES FROM THE SOUTH: THE YEAR'S BEST, 2000

PREFACE *by Ellen Douglas*

A. Manette Ansay, BOX

Wendy Brenner, MR. PUNIVERSE

D. Winston Brown, IN THE DOORWAY OF RHEE'S JAZZ JOINT

Robert Olen Butler, HEAVY METAL

Cathy Day, THE CIRCUS HOUSE

R.H.W. Dillard, FORGETTING THE END OF THE WORLD

Tony Earley, JUST MARRIED

Clyde Edgerton, DEBRA'S FLAP AND SNAP

Tim Gautreaux, DANCING WITH THE ONE-ARMED GAL

William Gay, MY HAND IS JUST FINE WHERE IT IS

Allan Gurganus, HE'S AT THE OFFICE

John Holman, WAVE

Romulus Linney, THE WIDOW

Thomas McNeely, SHEEP

Christopher Miner, RHONDA AND HER CHILDREN

Chris Offutt, THE BEST FRIEND

Margo Rabb, HOW TO TELL A STORY

New Stories from the South: The Year's Best, 2002

PREFACE *by Larry Brown*

Dwight Allen, END OF THE STEAM AGE

Russell Banks, THE OUTER BANKS

Brad Barkley, BENEATH THE DEEP, SLOW MOTION

Doris Betts, ABOVEGROUND

William Gay, CHARTING THE TERRITORIES OF THE RED

Aaron Gwyn, OF FALLING

Ingrid Hill, THE MORE THEY STAY THE SAME

David Koon, THE BONE DIVERS

Andrea Lee, ANTHROPOLOGY

Romulus Linney, TENNESSEE

Corey Mesler, THE GROWTH AND DEATH OF BUDDY GARDNER

Lucia Nevai, FAITH HEALER

Julie Orringer, PILGRIMS

Dulane Upshaw Ponder, THE RAT SPOON

Bill Roorbach, BIG BEND

George Singleton, SHOW-AND-TELL

Kate Small, MAXIMUM SUNLIGHT

R. T. Smith, I HAVE LOST MY RIGHT

Max Steele, THE UNRIPE HEART

New Stories from the South: The Year's Best, 2003

PREFACE *by Roy Blount Jr.*

Dorothy Allison, COMPASSION

Steve Almond, THE SOUL MOLECULE

NEW STORIES FROM THE SOUTH: THE YEAR'S BEST, 2004

Tayari Jones, BEST COUSIN

Michael Knight, FEELING LUCKY

K. A. Longstreet, THE JUDGEMENT OF PARIS

Jill McCorkle, INTERVENTION

Elizabeth Seydel Morgan, SATURDAY AFTERNOON IN THE
    HOLOCAUST MUSEUM

Chris Offutt, SECOND HAND

Ann Pancake, DOG SONG

Drew Perry, LOVE IS GNATS TODAY

Annette Sanford, ONE SUMMER

George Singleton, RAISE CHILDREN HERE

R. T. Smith, DOCENT